Semper Fi:
The Education of Caroline

Jane Harvey-Berrick

HARVEY
BERRICK
PUBLISHING

Semper Fi: The Education of Caroline

Copyright © 2015 Jane Harvey-Berrick

Editing by Kirsten Olsen and Alana Albertson
Cover Design by Hang Le

First published in 2015
ISBN 9780992924645

Harvey Berrick Publishing

Cover design by Hang Le / www.byhangle.com
Cover photograph by Michael Anthony Downs
Cover model: Derek Pristou
Formatted by Christine / www.perfectlypublishable.com

Semper Fi:
The Education of Caroline

Jane Harvey-Berrick

DEDICATION

To men and women who served their country, and the families who support them.

* * *

All profits from the e-book go to

Felix Fund
&
EOD Warrior Foundation

Both charities support the brave men and women who work or have worked in bomb disposal, and their families.

ACKNOWLEDGMENTS

To Kirsten Olsen, editor, de-Britisher, best friend, Army wife.

To Alana Albertson, awesome writer and Marine wife.

To fabulous author Tina Gephart for sharing the story about her husband who worked in EOD for the US Air Force—he wore his dog tags around his boots, too (see chapter 15).

To Amélie White Vahlé for the French translation (and apologies for Sebastian's opinions on Geneva!)

To Trina Micotta for her marketing knowledge and expertise, as well as her unfailing study of the hottest models.

To Hang Le for her stunning covers and never-ending creativity.

To Michael Anthony Downs, our lovely cover photographer.

To Audrey Thunder and Dina Eidinger, for loving Sebastian and being his unfailing cheerleaders.

To Sheena Lumsden, for her friendship and all her work behind the scenes.

To Raquel Gamez who sent my books to her husband while he was serving in Afghanistan.

To all the bloggers and readers who have followed Sebastian and Caroline on their long and difficult journey. Thank you for loving them, too.

Thank you Stalking Angels. You know how much you mean to me and you never let me down.

Sheena Lumsden, Audrey Thunder, Tonya Bass Allen, Lisa Sylva, Tera Chastain, Mary Dunne, Nikki Costello, Ashley Jones, Kelly Findlay, Sarah Lintott, Lisa Smith Reid, Lily Maverick Wallis, Andrea Flaks, Kelsey Burns, Celia Ottway, Rhonda Koppenhaver, Caroline Yamashita, Lelyana Taufik, Aime Metzner, Nancy Saunders Meyhoefer, Helen Remy Grey, Heidi Keil, Bruninha Mazzali, Kirsten Papi, Gina Sanders, Gabri Canova, Melissa Parnell, Dina Farndon Eidinger, Evelyn Garcia, Nicola Barton, Jacqueline Showdog, Elle Christopher, Carly Grey, L.E. Chamberlain, Marie Mason, Trina Marie, Kim Howlett, Ellen Totten, Jen Berg, Shirley Wilkinson, Ana Kristina Rabacca, Emma Darch-Harris, Emma Wynne Williams, MJ Fryer, Drizinha Dri, Rose Hogg, Barbara Murray, Beverley Cindy, Megan Davis, Jenny Angell, Mary Rose Bermundo, Clare Norton, Andrea Jackson, Rosarita Reader, Sarah Bookhooked, Fuñny Souisa, Luiza Oioli, Megan Burgad, Lisa G. Murray Ziegler, Krista Webber, Carol Sales, Crysal Ordex-Hernandez, Dana Fiore Stusse, Jade Donaldson, Paola Cortes, Natalie Townson, Hang Le, Erin Spencer, Raquel Gamez, Nycole Griffin, Kandace Milostan, Ana Moraes, Sharen Kallenberger Marzola.

And the Fanfic readers who were there from the start.

Other Titles by Jane Harvey-Berrick

Series
An epic love story spanning the years, through war zones

The Education of Sebastian (Education series #1)
The Education of Caroline (Education series #2)
The Education of Sebastian & Caroline (combined edition, books 1 & 2)
Semper Fi: The Education of Caroline (Education series #3)

All the fun of the fair … and two worlds collide

The Traveling Man (Traveling series #1)
The Traveling Woman (Traveling series #2)
Roustabout (Traveling series #3)
The Traveling Series (Boxed Set)

Blood, sweat, tears and dance

Slave to the Rhythm (Rhythm series #1)
Luka (Rhythm series #2)

Standalone Titles
Dangerous to Know & Love
Lifers
At Your Beck & Call
Dazzled
Summer of Seventeen
The New Samurai
Exposure
The Dark Detective
Playing in the Rain (*novella*)
Behind the Wall (*novella*)

Audio Books
One Careful Owner

www.janeharveyberrick.com

PROLOGUE

January 2012

I was dreaming about her again.

That was nothing new. I dreamed about her most nights. I tried to wash away the memory in whiskey. Sometimes it worked. Sometimes I woke up in bed with a woman I didn't remember meeting, let alone fucking.

Give me a combat situation and I was a good little Devil Dog, but in the underbelly of a soft city, I was a misfit. And I couldn't give a shit.

But when real life decides to smack you between the eyes, you don't have any fucking choice.

CHAPTER 1

You learn a lot in the military. Well, I thought, being an adult, it would be a good career move to have somebody inspect me every day to make sure I put my pants on the right way and had my shoes on the correct feet.

I did get to be a real Marine while I was out in Iraq. I was still with my Unit then, still with my buddies. I spent most of the last two Afghan tours in mud-built villages trying to persuade the tribal elders to side with the allies; maybe it helped make a difference. Now I'm stuck in the armpit of Europe on a chickenshit assignment, supposedly doing MSG guard duty at the Consular Agency in Geneva, all because my last CO in Paris was a dickless dumb-ass.

So I fucked his wife.

Funny enough that's a big no-no in the military—the kind of thing that can get you a court martial followed by a dishonorable discharge. Like I give a shit.

I know how that sounds, because being a Marine is about having to trust your life with the guy who's got your back—so fucking his wife kind of puts a downer on things. And usually I don't go near married women—not anymore. But they both deserved it. Long story short: the no-ball pen-pusher didn't want anyone to know his wife was screwed by a noncom, so he had me reassigned. Mostly I did PR which I hated. I was shit at it, too. Too much time having to smile. But I did work with some journos flying out to Afghanistan, getting them prepped for a war zone.

There are worse places than Geneva. There are worse countries. I've seen a few of them. But there comes a point when you're so fucking bored that you bore yourself thinking about how bored you are. I'd reached that point five months ago.

I'd even thought about getting the hell out of the Marine Corps and doing something else with my life, although I had no clue what. But I'd re-upped, so I had another two years to go. The only glimmer of light was that in Spring 2012 they needed more US-born interpreters in Afghanistan. And for this billet, I'd get a huge bonus. But it was more about getting the fuck out of Cuckoo Clock-land.

I'd put my name out there again, so who knows.

This was my tenth year in the Marines. It had been an interesting life up until Paris two years ago. I'd found that I was good at languages—which was a big fucking shock to actually be good at anything when my parents had only ever told me that I was a fuck up since birth—and I'd been promoted through the ranks. I'd been proud of being a Sergeant and had even thought about trying to get my degree so I could progress further and become an officer. And then Paris had happened. For the last two years I'd been kicking my heels in one miserable office job after another, although I'd made Warrant Officer—just to get me out of their hair, I think. But now I'd got a new CO, so there was a chance I'd get moved on to something useful soon. This guy was in the oxymoron that is Military Intelligence. I'd met him briefly when he was out here for a few days. Nice wife. Blonde. Not my type.

At least I had some leave coming up.

My buddy, Ches, had asked me to come stateside and see his family. I was tempted, but since an incident with his wife's best friend, as well as the friend of her best friend ... I wasn't as welcome as I

3

might have been.

I was toying with the idea of taking off on my motorcycle and seeing some of Italy. I'd never been, although it was somewhere I'd wanted to see ever since. There was a guy I'd met when I was a kid. He was Italian, from Southern Italy, and he'd taught me more about what a father should be than my own asshole dad. Papa Ven was such an amazing guy—and I'd fallen in love with his daughter, as well. But that's another story—no fairytale ending either. So Italy was somewhere that I'd wanted to visit for a while, and now the border was just a few miles away. What the hell. I had nothing better to do.

Well, I did have one offer that I was considering. I'd spent last Christmas in the Swiss ski resort Klosters, with Benita from Düsseldorf. I had an open invitation to visit. I don't normally do reruns, but did I mention I was bored? And I hadn't been laid since Christmas—it was nearly fucking Easter. Well there was that one night with Dorota from Poland who had some business at the UN. She was only in town for one night. Classy chick. Nice ass.

My cell phone rang, interrupting my memories of that one wild night. Polish chicks knew how to have a good time.

I glanced down and was surprised to see that it was my new CO calling.

"Sir?"

"Hunter, quick sit-rep. Something's come up that could be your ticket out of Switzerland. I've got a job for you— shipping out to Afghanistan. Not sure of the date, but could be in about three weeks."

I took a deep breath, feeling a shot of adrenaline wake up nerve endings that hadn't been used for a while.

"Thank you, sir. That sounds interesting."

"It's not a done deal—about 70/30 right now. I see you've got some leave. I suggest you use it up as soon as the

current PR briefing is finished. But don't go too far—no more than a couple of hours from Ramstein. No Stateside trips, Hunter. Understood?"

"Yes, sir."

"Good. I'll be in touch."

The call ended abruptly. I was going back to Afghanistan. I wasn't sure how I felt about that, but it was what I'd been trained for.

I stared over the rooftops of Geneva towards the lake. It was peaceful here—the polar opposite of where I'd being going next.

I sat for some time before I realized that I'd spent 20 minutes just looking out at the water.

I liked my apartment: it was fairly basic but nobody came here except me. It was in an older part of the city where the architecture looked more Italian than Swiss. The cobblestone street was narrow and quiet. I liked the peace. After you've shared a tent in 120°F heat with 19 other sweaty, stinking guys, you'd want peace, too.

It was owned by an old lady named Madame Dubois. She was always trying to introduce me to her granddaughters, but apart from that she didn't bother me.

Today's lesson in sheer fucking tedium was an ear-achingly dull hostile environment briefing—my fifth this month. It was part of my 'rehabilitation' after Paris. I don't know how it was supposed to rehabilitate me. I mean, what part of sending me to Switzerland was supposed to teach me to keep my cock in my pants when it came to the CO's wife? My new boss was 3,000 miles away. With his wife. I'd need fucking super strength sperm to cause any trouble from this distance.

Today I was training journalists—foreign correspondents—to prepare for an assignment in Afghanistan. I was working with a British team: Major Mike Parsons and a Lieutenant Tom waste-of-fucking-air Crawley. I'd learned some new words

5

since I'd met Crawley: 'wanker' was one; 'tosser' was the other. Both worked.

Parsons was okay except for the fact that he hated me. Probably because I always showed up late. I think he knew why I'd gotten this assignment, so he never gave me much shit about it. If he'd been my CO, he'd have handed me my ass, and I wouldn't have blamed him. But we were only allies—civility was an optional extra.

As I pulled on the jacket of my uniform, my attention was caught by the half-empty bottle of Jack Daniel's that was still next to my bed. Yeah, a quick hit of that might actually get my ass moving and make the morning's mind-numbing monotony more bearable.

Might.

I was forty minutes late, which was pretty good for me.

Crawley was droning on about some tedious shit that even had the journos present yawning their heads off.

Parsons didn't look happy when he saw me. Guy had a broomstick up his ass like the rest of the Brits when it came to punctuality. Yeah, well, it was probably an army thing. I was a Marine. Big difference.

"Thank you, Tom. We'll take a short break in a few minutes, ladies and gentleman, and meet back here at 1100 hours. Refreshments will be served in Les Nations lounge. And we're very glad to have our colonial colleague Warrant Officer Hunter join us." He stared at me coldly. "I'm sure his insight will be invaluable."

Wow, wounded by sarcasm at close range. The Brits sure fight dirty. Next it'll be harsh language.

But my timing was pretty good—coffee break already.

I hightailed it out of the hotel, knowing that if I stayed I'd be asked a shitload of dumb questions. I've had some journos come onto me, acting like they're my best friend in the hope that I'll dish the dirt. They must think I'm a fucking moron if they think I'm going to trust them after five minutes. I usually prefer to get kissed before I get screwed.

It was all I could do to drag my weary ass back in that seminar room after the coffee break and hope that my brain didn't completely atrophy before the afternoon pastries. The Swiss French made awesome cakes.

"Just a quick roll-call before we go on," said Major Parsons, "now everyone is here…"

Yeah, yeah I can take a hint. Jeez, he'd be hurting my feelings in a minute.

"Elizabeth Ashton?"

"Present and almost correct."

"Tek Burczyk?"

"Obecny."

"Henri Ducat?"

"Oui."

"Ricardo Esteban?"

"Si."

"Heinrich Keller?"

"Jawohl."

"Marc Lebuin?"

"Je suis présent."

"Lee Venzi?"

A woman at the back raised her hand but didn't speak. I glanced over.

What the fuck? No fucking way!

My heart started pounding and I was having trouble breathing. That woman. *That woman. No fucking way!* The woman who'd torn out my heart and danced all over it. The woman who'd told me she loved me, then disappeared without a backward glance. Ten years ago. *What the fuck was she doing here?* And what was with the new name?

"You're Lee Venzi?"

I must have spoken out loud because everyone

was staring at me. I rearranged my face back to boredom. Inside I was anything but. My heart was shuddering and beating so fucking hard I thought it would break out of my chest.

It took every ounce of self-control that I'd learned over the last ten years to keep standing and not completely lose it and run out of the room. My mouth was dry and I felt a cold sweat break out all over my body. Adrenaline was burning through me and I couldn't tell if it was fight or flight.

I wanted to run.

I wanted to hit something.

I was frozen to the spot.

My hands were shaking so badly, I shoved them in my pockets and tried to concentrate on getting air into my lungs.

How could it be her? After all these years? How could she be here?

I thought I was having an out-of-my-fucking-mind-out-of-body experience. I fought to breathe normally, all the while thinking I was having a fucking heart attack.

My body was shaking so hard I thought it must be obvious. This was worse than a goddamn RPG attack by the fucking Taliban.

What was she doing here? Was it some sort of set up? Did she know I'd be here? No, not possible. She looked so shocked to see me. Shit, she hadn't changed. She looked exactly the same as the day she walked out on me.

Fuck! Fuck! Fuck! Breathe, you dumb grunt, breathe.

I stared out the window, but it wasn't Geneva I was seeing—it was Ocean Beach, Point Loma, San Diego. I was 17, and Caro was 30 and married. She was so fucking beautiful, wearing that yellow bikini, her skin all golden from the sun.

I blinked, trying to clear the image, but it was as if the whole summer we were together was nailed to my brain and playing relentlessly like a horror film where you know someone's going to get the guts ripped out of them. Yeah, that was me. I was the one who got ripped to pieces. And as for her? She got to walk away and start a new life.

Bitch.

Why the hell did she have to come back and haunt me now? *The ghost of fucks past.*

How was I going to get through the next day-and-a-half of this screwed up briefing? I was sweating just thinking about being in the same room as her. I needed to get out. I could leave, say I'm sick. The way my body was responding, nobody would doubt that I was completely fucked.

Crawley continued his mindless lecture. It was an almost pleasantly dull rumble in the background. Mentally, I was ten years and 6,000 miles away.

God, she'd been so beautiful—the most beautiful woman I'd ever seen. If I was honest, no one else had come close since. Well, fuck. She'd fooled me. I thought I was something special. Along with my belief that the world wasn't completely shit, she'd taken my virginity. Or I'd given it. Willingly. I thought we were in love. Really got that fucking wrong. At least I knew that she hadn't gone back to the asshole she'd been married to at the time.

I risked a quick look.

So fucking beautiful. She wasn't looking at me but I had to turn away again—it hurt to see her face, to see her sitting in the same room as me. But I couldn't help noticing she was slumped in her seat and her cheeks were flushed. I'd have given my left nut to know what she was thinking.

Crawley droned on.

"Because most attacks occur upon reaching home, always ensure that you can drive straight into your garage or compound, and secure the door or gate behind you."

I could hear the British woman whispering something that made the other journos laugh.

Crawled-up-his-ass Crawley didn't like that.

"This is serious, madam. What I tell you today may save your life."

The British woman inflated immediately. Fuck, her tits were enormous—and not in a good way.

"Listen, sunshine, you may think you're something special with a weapon of mass destruction dangling between your legs, but let me tell *you* a thing or two: I've been to the frontline of every war since Uganda in 1979, before you were bloody well born." She started ticking them off on her fingers. "Angola, Croatia, Rwanda, Bosnia, Iraq, Kuwait, Afghanistan, and ... bloody hell, places you've never even heard of. And this woman," she pointed her chin at Caro, "has been in more hot spots than you've had hot dates."

Of course. *Lee Venzi*. She'd changed her name, which was why I hadn't recognized it when Parsons gave me the list of journalists attending the course. She'd been Carolina Wilson then, my Caro. I'd never known her maiden name. I'd read some of the articles and assumed this Venzi character was a guy— probably ex-military. But now I knew the truth: it figured. Caro had grown up around military bases and spent her whole married life with Captain Cocksucker. She knew military.

I wasn't happy to hear that she'd reported from dangerous places, but what the fuck was I expecting? This pack of journos was all heading for Afghanistan. I glanced over again, but turned away the minute she looked towards me. I couldn't give her a way in or she'd fuck me over again.

Shit. Was I really that weak?

I tried to keep my eyes off of her, but every time they were magnetically drawn back.

Focus, you pathetic fucker! Translate the National Anthem into Pashto, if you have to! Don't look at her.

By lunchtime, I was so fucked. The second Parsons called a break, I was out of the starting blocks like a goddamn sprinter.

I didn't know what the fuck I was doing: I just knew I couldn't go back to that briefing; I couldn't see her and not touch her. I was a fucking lunatic. I *hated* that woman. She destroyed my life and hadn't even looked back when she walked out on me, leaving me behind with no clue how to find her.

And the worst of it was I'd believed that she loved me. Some fucking fairytale. But I'd believed her, and I'd waited for her. My fucking father had driven her away. Because I was 17 and underage, he'd threatened her with a statutory rape charge—unless she left quietly. But after three years, the Statue of Limitations freed us. I thought she'd find me when I was 21. I'd believed it every day for three long years. But she never came. I never heard from her again. And she was a journalist—how fucking hard would it have been for her to reach out to me?

I stormed down the street, ignoring pedestrians who jumped out of my way for fear of being mowed down.

And then I found myself heading for my favorite bar. Appropriately enough it was named L'Antidote. I really fucking hoped it would live up to its name tonight.

The room was long and thin, with almost no daylight. It was as close as the Swiss came to a dive—damn near perfect.

I headed inside and saw Jean-Paul the bartender. He nodded at me and poured a whiskey without me even having to ask. I tipped it straight down.

"Laissez la bouteille."

He raised his eyebrows but pushed the nearly bottle towards me and left it, as I'd requested.

After my third shot, I started to pull myself together, disgusted by being such a pussy and running out.

Fuck, I used to be *good* at my job. You know, actually *cared* about it. Paris changed all that. My CO had hated me from day one. He tried to bully me and constantly belittled me. I found out he was a buddy of my old man. Figured. Then the asswipe CO got my promotion to Warrant Officer blocked. Bastard. I'd fucking *earned* that promotion, and what he'd done to me could be a career-ender. So I decided if my CO wanted to screw around with me, I'd screw around with him—or rather, his wife. That was easy. Getting caught was harder because he was so fucking unobservant. She was definitely the brains in that marriage.

He got the message eventually. Found his wife with her mouth wrapped around my dick. That was a good day. By that point I didn't give a shit what happened to my career.

I guess someone higher up the chain of command smelled a rat, because out of the blue I got my promotion and was sent to Geneva.

To Caro.

No. Not to her. This was my chance to make her pay, to take what had been mine, and leave her wanting. Yeah, the chance to leave her in the dust—that's what I wanted; that's what I needed.

I took another shot, just me and a close relative of my good friend Jack Daniel's for company.

By 6PM, I was well on my way to being completely wasted. I only knew it was later when the bar started filling up with office workers. They must have sensed I wasn't in a friendly mood because they all gave me a wide berth.

I wondered what *she* was doing. She'd looked pretty cozy with that French journalist, Lebuin, sitting next to her. Fucker was practically drooling over her, all smiles and Gallic fucking charm. It made me want to punch his guts out through his backbone.

I tried to think of something else, but every time I came back to the look of shock on Caro's face when she saw me. Not pleasure—shock.

I emptied another shot down my throat,

enjoying the increasing numbness that it gave me.

"May I sit?"

I looked up slowly. For a second I thought it was *her*—the long, chestnut hair was so familiar. I remembered that hair sweeping over my chest as we made love in the sand dunes. *Not love—sex. Get the fucking facts straight.* But this woman's eyes were blue.

I shook my head to clear it, then waved at the seat.

"Merci."

I grasped the bottle of whiskey as if I was afraid she'd steal it.

"You like to drink alone, perhaps?"

I shrugged, and she turned to Jean-Paul to order herself a glass of white wine.

Yeah, buy your own drinks, lady. I'm not interested.

I looked at her again. She was attractive, dressed in a skirt suit, high heels, with long, tan legs. For a moment I could imagine those legs wrapped around my waist.

She saw the direction of my gaze and smiled.

"Or perhaps you prefer some company? I'm Gabri."

She held out her hand and after a second's hesitation, I shook it.

"Sebastian."

"American?"

"Yes, ma'am."

"No, no. That makes me feel old. Please, you must call me Gabri." She paused. "So, why is a handsome young soldier drinking alone? It is either money or a woman. I do not think it is money."

Her tone annoyed me, and I turned to glare at her.

"And why is an attractive woman talking to strange men in bars? It's either business or pleasure. I don't think it's business."

"Touché!" she said laughing lightly, then ran her hand over my thigh. "I am French, not Swiss. It is

13

always pleasure with us—even in Geneva."

She leaned forward and I caught the smell of her perfume. It was strong and musky—nothing like Caro. My stomach churned and I stood up suddenly, taking her by surprise.

"You're right, mademoiselle. It is a woman. It's always a woman—the same fucking woman."

She rested her hand lightly on my arm. "Perhaps I can make you forget her?"

I laughed harshly. "Yeah, good luck with that. I've been trying for ten fucking years."

I pushed past her, amused by the look of disappointment painted on her face.

When I hit the fresh air outside, I nearly staggered. Fuck, I was trashed.

I could have hailed a cab, but I didn't live far, so I wandered home, occasionally cannoning off lampposts that seemed to leap into my path. Goddamn if I wasn't seeing double.

I don't remember getting up the stairs or falling asleep fully dressed.

The alarm scared the crap out of me when it went off at 5:30AM. I ended up diving onto the hard floorboards, thinking it was a fucking mortar attack.

I sat up slowly, rubbing my hip where I'd hit the deck. I always set the alarm early so I could go for a run before whatever drudgery the US Marine Corps was doling out. But this morning there was no chance of that. I just about made it to the bathroom before I threw up.

I splashed some water on my face, which made absolutely no fucking difference, and then drank straight from the faucet.

I crawled back into bed for another two hours.

When I woke up for the second time, there'd been no miraculous cure—I was still hung-over as fuck, and the room stank of whiskey.

Revolted, I pulled off my rank uniform and

stood under the tepid shower for as long as I could stand it.

After I'd shaved, and managed not to cut my throat, I glared at my Charlies—the formal Dress Blue uniform. They looked like I'd slept in them. I had a clean shirt, but there was no way I'd have time to get the pants and jacket dry-cleaned.

Sighing, I pulled on a pair of jeans and a t-shirt and went to ask Madame Dubois for use of her ironing board and iron: desperate times called for desperate measures.

She took one look at my pathetic condition and took pity on me.

"Les hommes ne savent pas repasser!" she insisted, wagging her finger at me and pulling my uniform out of my hands.

I wasn't going to argue if she was going to offer to iron for me. When she finished I smiled and thanked her.

"Vous êtes un jeune homme espiègle!"

She waved me off with a smile. If I'd kissed her on the cheek, she'd have taken out her teeth and whistled.

Yep, I still had it; gran-mère was hot for me.

Clean in body if not much else, I headed to the hotel for the second day of the briefing. It began much like the first—I was late, and Parsons was pissed. I'd eaten a roll of mints before I walked in, but I was pretty certain he could smell whiskey on my breath. Hell, if the room didn't have air conditioning I'd be sweating whiskey.

I tried to keep my eyes off of *her*, but it was an impossible task. After the first hour, I wanted to tear out my eyeballs and use them in a pinball machine.

When it was time for my language session, I knew I had an hour with Caro. I didn't know why I didn't combust on the spot. Except she seemed uninterested in looking at me. How fucking ironic.

I went through my usual spiel for the Afghan

Jane Harvey-Berrick

tour: how to introduce yourself (differently for men and women), how to give your job title, the agency you worked for, and nationality, in Pashto and Dari. And I always threw in a useful passage from the Qu'ran for emergencies.

This shit could save lives, so it really pissed me off that Caro wasn't paying attention. Shit, she could end up smeared all over a Kabul street if she didn't take it in.

"Perhaps Ms. Venzi can answer that question," I said, nearly choking on my tongue as it wrapped itself around her name.

"Excuse me? Um, what was the question?" she stammered.

Fuck, I couldn't look at her—it was too much. I was only human.

Shit! Shit! Shit! What could I tell her that she might actually remember; that might be useful?

Inspiration struck.

"A typical reply to a question an Afghan can't answer would be for him to say, 'because the sky is blue and the sea is green'," I said by rote, risking another glance at her.

She looked annoyed and my heart punched against my ribs.

I had to get out. I *needed* to get out.

I don't remember anything about the last 45 minutes of the seminar. As soon as Parsons cleared his throat, signaling the end, I was on my feet.

But before I managed to leave the room, Caro spoke to me.

"May I have a word, please?"

I almost skidded to a halt, afraid to turn and look at her, afraid of how I'd feel to look in her eyes again. All my plans for ignoring her were shot through and shredded; and all it took was one glance from her.

"I'm rather busy, Ms. Venzi," I coughed out.

"Too busy to say 'hello'?" she snapped.

God, she was so beautiful.

And then I realized I hadn't answered her.

"Yes, I'm too busy for that," and I ran.

Fucking pussy! Candy-ass chickenshit fucking pussy!

I couldn't go back, but I couldn't kid myself anymore either. I wanted her. Badly. And maybe, if I had her one more time, I could stop thinking about her. Maybe if I fucked her hard, I could exorcise her ghost once and for all. Maybe revenge was what I needed.

Maybe.

On impulse I stopped and bought some condoms from a small pharmacy. I got a semi just thinking about using them with her. I knew I wasn't making any sense—I hated her and she hated me—but I couldn't help myself.

Jesus, just seeing her, and I was suddenly 17 again.

How the hell was I going to make that fucking fantasy happen? I'd barely spoken to her for the last two days.

I needed to talk to her, but I needed to get her alone.

I wandered through Geneva, trying to work out what I was going to say to her, how I'd get to fuck her. We used to have this amazing chemistry. We'd just look at each other and get turned on. I wondered if it was still there.

My steps slowed as my thoughts grew heavier, remembering everything that had passed between us, the plans we'd made. Fuck, we'd talked about it all: living together, marriage, kids. I'd wanted it all with her—and I thought she'd wanted it with me.

I realized I'd stopped walking and was standing outside a jewelers. One of those small, unassuming, family-run places that you could still find in the old part of Geneva.

My eyes were drawn to a display and I found myself staring at rings. One of them caught my attention—a smallish but pretty single diamond mounted on a gold band. The breath left my body as I imagined how that would look on her small hand, with those delicate fingers that used to touch…

This was seriously fucked up. I needed to walk away, fast. But I couldn't. Instead, I went inside and was soon talking to the sales assistant, an elderly man who looked like a gnome. He was showing me the ring and placing it in a dark blue satin ring box, and I was handing over my credit card for €2700.

Back in the fresh air, I knew I'd lost my goddamn mind, but somehow I didn't care. I imagined saying the words, asking her to … yeah, right. As if.

Eventually I went home and took another shower, then changed into civvies. I was going to go straight to her hotel; I'd talk to her, seduce her, take her to bed and fuck her brains out.

I pussied out.

Instead, I went back to L'Antidote and started drinking.

There were so many things I wanted to say to her—and I had no fucking clue how to start. I had another drink, trying to calm the fuck down. Then another. And another.

When I'd finally gotten up the courage, I headed towards Caro's hotel near the Place des Nations. For some reason, my body seemed disconnected from my feet. It took for-fucking-ever to get my ass going in the right direction. Weird.

All of a sudden I was standing in front of her hotel room, with no recollection of how I had even gotten there. I knew where she was staying from the security briefing info in her file. And now, she was just a few feet away from me.

I knocked three times.

There was a pause followed by a scuffling sound, then her voice.

"Who is it?"

"Let me in, Caro."

There was another pause—longer this time.

"What do you want, Sebastian?" she called through the door.

Fuck. This wasn't going how I'd planned. She needed to open the door for me to speak to her properly.

"Let me in. I need to talk to you."

I banged on the door again.

"Caro!"

Slowly, the door opened. All she was wearing was a thin, silky robe.

My cock leapt to attention as my eyes drank her in.

"Caro."

Christ it felt good to say her name.

"What do you want, Sebastian?"

No, not like this. I needed to be in the same room as her. I pushed my way past her. *Fuck, she smelled good.* I was inside the room, but I wanted to be inside *her.*

"What are you doing?" she asked sharply.

She was so feisty. God, I loved that about her.

"Catching up with old friends," I said, smiling at her.

"How did you find me?"

Seriously? Didn't she know what I did?

"Military intelligence," I grinned, tapping the side of my head.

I thought that was as funny as fuck. It occurred to me that I might be a little drunk.

While she closed the door, I took off my jacket and threw it onto the chair. Then I sat on the bed and hoped she'd take the hint.

"Come and sit with me, Caro."

But she stayed standing, her arms folded across her chest.

Beautiful.

"Why are you here, Sebastian? You had your chance to talk to me earlier today, but you preferred to ignore me."

Did I?

"You still have a great ass, Caro."

Tight and round and perfect in my hands when we…

"Okay, I think you'd better go now," she said. "Whatever you have to say to me can wait until you're sober."

She had a great everything.

She walked towards me and my heart started pounding in my chest again. *Christ, it hurt so fucking much. How could it hurt so much if I wasn't dying?* Or maybe I was. I didn't know anymore. Because when she came towards me, it was just her and me again. Just us. No one else. She wove her magic and the world went away.

I pulled the robe open and buried my head in her body, kissing her, relishing the feel of her flesh against my lips. It had been so long. *So long.*

I tried to tell her that I loved her, that I'd always loved her. I don't know if she could understand what I was saying. I just knew that her arms were around me and we were together again.

I don't remember much about what happened then, but I fell asleep with her at my side.

The next morning I woke to the sound of an alarm ringing in my ear—it was fucking annoying. Then I realized I wasn't in my apartment—and I wasn't alone.

I peeled my eyelids and looked up. Warm brown eyes the color of melted chocolate gazed down at me.

"Caro?"

I wasn't sure if I was still dreaming.

"You're awake then," she said pointedly.

Oh. Awake. Right.

And yet again: *what the fuck?*

I vaguely remembered coming to her hotel and wanting to fuck her. Did we do it? I had no memory. What a fucking irony: I'd planned to get rid of that ghost once and for all—and I couldn't even remember doing it.

"Did we…?"

"No, we most definitely did not," she hissed, her eyes shooting bullets at me. "You woke me up in the middle of the night by banging on my door, and then passed out on my bed."

Shit. She sounded pissed.

"Oh, right."

I leaned up on one arm and looked down at the clothes I was still wearing. Huh, maybe we hadn't then. I really fucking wanted to.

"Sorry about that. We can make up for it now if you like?"

Yeah, that could have come out better. Fucking word vomit.

"Astonishing as this may seem, Sebastian," she said in a voice that could have frozen helium, "your charming offer doesn't thrill me."

Shit. Fucking bitch was always on my case. Hell, *she'd* invited *me* into her room. I think.

"Whatever."

I started to get up, but realized I only had socks on my feet.

"Where are my boots?"

"Under the chair," she said, pointing. "Along with your jacket."

Ah hell, morning wood, just to add to the overall sense of joy. I don't suppose she'd let me … nah, no point thinking about it.

Then she said, "Why did you come here last night, Sebastian?"

The look on her face was so sad, my heart crashed. Her eyes were hurt and confused, and all the words I wanted to say to her just dried on my tongue.

Christ, just let me get the fuck out of here. If she says one more word, just one, I'll be down on my fucking knees begging her to take me back. I wouldn't survive her leaving me twice.

I shrugged, pretending indifference.

"I don't remember."

I turned around and looked at her—confusion and anger were all etched into her expression.

"See you around, Caro," I said.

When I closed her door behind me, shutting out her image, I couldn't lie to myself anymore. I still needed her.

And she hated my fucking guts.

CHAPTER 2

I stood outside her hotel taking deep breaths, trying to slow the pounding in my heart, wincing at the pounding in my head. The artificial smile I'd given her had long since slipped from my face.

I was tempted to find a bar and get shit-faced, but goddamn it, no! I was a fucking US Marine—first into battle, last out, and I was *not* giving up. I needed a plan.

I also needed some sleep that wasn't alcohol induced. And I smelled like shit.

Walking slowly, thinking hard, I made my way back to my apartment. I had to convince Caro to give me another chance. And I might not have much time: she could be shipping out any day now that her course was finished. The first thing I had to do was fuck with her travel docs. If I could stop her from leaving Geneva for a week, I'd have time to work on her.

All that took was a single phone call—there were times when having connections with Military Intelligence was useful.

Now I needed to get her to meet with me. I could be fucking charming when I wanted to. Although I wasn't sure that was going to work with Caro—she knew me too well. Or she used to. Shit, I wasn't even sure I was the same person anymore. In fact I was pretty certain that I wasn't.

I wasn't vain, even though I was an arrogant son-of-a-bitch, and I knew that women liked the packaging. Six-two, sun blond hair, weird blue-green eyes that chicks seemed to dig. That was only skin deep—I didn't know if they liked what was on the inside, not that I ever showed that. Except with Caro—maybe.

But like all grunts, I kept myself in shape: every morning I did 20 pull-ups from the full hang position, 100 crunches in two minutes, and a three-mile run in less than 18 minutes. Some guys let themselves go a little in a non-combat zone, but being a terp, I never knew when I'd be sent out on a mission. My CO said that they needed US interpreters who spoke the Afghan lingo. There weren't enough US born terps. Recently, there had been an increase of green-on-blue attacks. These were sudden and often fatal attacks on US soldiers by either the Afghan National Police or Afghan National Army. Most of them were good guys, but they'd also been infiltrated by Taliban. So for a top secret mission, they needed someone like me. The fact that I'd been kept non-combatant for so long was down to my asswipe former CO. The new guy said there was nothing definite, but in three weeks or less, I could be sent to the front line, even if it was in the armpit of the world. I'd make sure I was ready ... but now there was Caro...

My apartment was what you'd call minimalist. I didn't really care what it looked like—it was just a place to sleep. If I wanted to get laid, I went to the woman's hotel.

The narrow single bed and lack of heating didn't bother me. It had an awesome view of Lake Geneva, and since I'd grown up next to the ocean, I missed the peace that comes from being beside the water.

I didn't miss home, fuck no. My old man was a drunken bastard who used to whale on me all the time. Not that he'd be able to now; I'd kill him if he tried.

But after tours in Iraq and Afghanistan, where all I saw was yellow dust and endless lunar landscape, I wanted to be close to the ocean. A lake was the best I could get in Switzerland.

Caro. My memories betrayed me.

That woman had shred my cold heart. I'd known her my whole life—well, since I was eight years old and she was 21, and I'd been in love with her forever.

When I was a kid and had already learned that my parents hated me, Caro was the one good thing in my life. I'd go to her house after school every day and we'd bake cookies and read stories, and she'd talk to me endlessly, never treating me like I was dumb kid.

And then her fuckwit of a husband had been redeployed and she'd left.

Life had been pretty shitty until I was 14, when my buddy Ches and his family had moved to the military base in San Diego. If it hadn't been for him and his parents, I'd have gone crazy.

I dated some in high school, but nothing serious. I'd rather go surfing than on a date. Maybe it was because I was waiting for her—for Caro.

When I was 17, her husband was moved back to So Cal. She was 30 then, and just as beautiful as I'd remembered. I was in love with her all over again. And she made me feel like a man, not a boy.

I could see the unhappiness inside her, and it made me furious that her asshole husband didn't treat her like a fucking queen. If anything, he treated her more like a servant. Her beautiful brown eyes were sad even when she smiled. I would have done anything for her, anything. It blew my mind when she let me touch her that night.

God, the memories. Her skin was so soft, her hair brushing over my chest, her fingers on my body. The humiliation of that first time when I lost my load the moment she touched my dick. The words that healed me, putting me back together one piece at a time. Being inside her. Laughing, loving, planning for our future.

My dad found out about us and made sure she couldn't be with me. I was a few short weeks from my 18th birthday, but he made it sound like she was some dirty pedophile. I hated him for that, even more that I already did. My mom was too drunk to care one way or another.

I shook my head, trying to shake away the pain. It didn't work; it never had. What a joke. She left and didn't look back. Not even once.

But now I'd been given another chance. I was on a mission to win Caro again, and I didn't care how I did it.

A few hours sleep and I was good to go. So, shit, shower and a shave, and then head back to Caro's hotel room.

But when I got there, I was gutted because the receptionist told me she'd gone out for the day. And totally fucking furious when she said Caro had left with that French cunt Lebuin. He'd be learning what my extreme fucking irritation looked like. But I smiled at the receptionist and watched her cheeks color with a mixture of lust and embarrassment. *Why the hell couldn't I have that effect on Caro?*

And then I hit the motherlode of intel: Lebuin had asked Mademoiselle Receptionist to recommend a restaurant. She'd suggested a family run Italian place not far from here.

"C'est très romantique, m'sieur," she giggled, fluttering her eyelashes.

I wanted to smash her computer through the desk when she said that—the thought of Lebuin taking *my* Caro somewhere romantic. *No fucking way!*

I was about to crash their date.

When I arrived, they looked *very* fucking cozy, and were finishing a carafe of red wine. All my plans to be smooth and charming went out the window.

Mine.

I stormed inside, and it took everything I had not to punch that fucker in his smug face. Then my eyes zeroed in on Caro.

"We need to talk," I seethed from between gritted teeth, and I grabbed her arm to pull her up.

Lebuin stood immediately.

"Let go of her, m'sieur, or you and I will have a problem."

I scowled at him, and it really pissed me off that he was right. What the fuck was I thinking treating Caro like this?

Caro stood up quietly.

"It's okay, Marc," she said, her voice soft and soothing.

He raised his eyebrows, staring at me, then back to her, choosing to take her at her word. *Really fucking smart.*

"Very well, but I will be phoning your mobile in 15 minutes to check on you, chérie."

She smiled at the bastard then blew him a kiss.

Were they together?

"Who the fuck does he think he is?" I snarled as we left the bistro.

Caro stared at me in amazement. "A friend! What's it to you?"

Good question: what was it to me? Answer: everything.

We walked down the street in silence, but in my head a thousand furious questions were drowning out rational thought.

I ducked into a small bierkeller that I knew and ordered us drinks.

"Deux whiskies."

Caro's eyes snapped to mine, fury making them blaze, a look that always made my cock hard.

"No merci," she said, her voice heated with anger. "Je préfère le vin rouge, monsieur."

Shit! Could I do anything right? I took a deep breath and downed my whiskey in one gulp as a glass of red wine was placed in front of her.

"What are you doing here, Caro?" I asked, needing to know what Lebuin was to her, and why she was risking her life going to a warzone.

"That's a good question, Sebastian," she replied icily. "Right now, I'm wondering why the hell I'm listening to you order me around."

"Oh, for fuck's sake!" *That isn't what I meant!*

"Seriously, what is it to you?" she asked.

I ran my hands over my hair in frustration.

"It's dangerous out there, Caro," I replied tightly, pointing out the insanely clear fact. "In Afghanistan, I mean. I know that's where you're going—obviously."

She took a deep breath, and I got the impression that

she was forcing herself to stay calm. I was glad one of us was, but it probably wasn't a good sign.

"Sebastian, apart from the fact that I've already had assignments reporting from Iraq and Darfur—which weren't exactly summer camps—it's none of your business."

Was she fucking joking?

"It *is* my business!"

"Based on what?" she snapped back.

Ten years! Ten fucking years, and I can't get you out of my head. But I couldn't say that.

"You know, Sebastian," she said, her voice rising as her own anger started winning out, "I spent 11 years being told what to do by my ex-husband—I don't need *you* to do it as well. You of all people should understand that."

Is that what she thought? She was comparing me to *him*?

"Caro, that's not it, I…"

But she wouldn't even let me finish my sentence and stood up to leave.

"Caro! Don't … don't go."

Her expression softened as she met my eyes.

"Why did you bring me here, Sebastian? And I'd *really* like to know why you assaulted me last night."

What?

"Assaulted? I didn't! I'd never…"

How could she say that to me? I'd never, *never* hurt her. So why did she look so angry?

"Actually you did," she stated, her voice trembling with barely suppressed emotion. "You were just too drunk to remember it. You're damn lucky I didn't report you. Although I'm fairly sure you can work out the reason why I didn't—why I couldn't. Good night, Sebastian."

I was trying to take in what she was saying, why there was so much venom in her voice. But the hits just kept on coming.

"I hope you have a nice life, I really do. And while you're at it—quit your drinking before you really do something stupid. More stupid."

And then she turned on her heel and left.

I was too stunned to follow her. I sat at the bar with my

head in my hands, trying to process everything she'd said.

Jesus, she'd accused me of *assaulting* her! I knew that wasn't possible—I *couldn't* hurt Caro. But an ugly voice inside my head was sneering at me. *Yeah, you think, you fucking asshole? So you can remember every detail about last night? Huh, didn't think so. Had another blackout, didn't ya? Who knows what you did while you were shitfaced and filled with poison and anger?*

I felt sick. I ordered another whiskey to help keep the nausea at bay, trying to decide what to do.

She didn't report me because she was afraid the past was about to get dug up; she was afraid that the label of sexual predator would come back to haunt her because of what happened when I was 17. What a twisted joke: if anyone treated sex like hunting for prey, it had been me, for the last seven years.

No, I had to talk to her. I couldn't let another night go by without speaking to her or explaining or something.

Twenty minutes later, I was standing outside her hotel room again, sweating with nerves. I was calmer under enemy fire—but one look from this woman eviscerated me.

I raised my hand and knocked. There was a brief pause, then I heard her voice through the door.

"Yes?"

"Caro, it's me. Can we talk?"

Another pause.

"I think we've said everything, Sebastian."

Shit. "Can I come in? Just to talk."

"Is that a joke?" her voice was disbelieving. "No, you can't!"

I leaned my head against the door and tried one more time.

"Caro, please. I won't … try anything. I just want to talk to you. Please."

I held my breath as she finally replied.

"Okay," she sighed. "Listen, I'll meet you in the lobby in five minutes. That's my best offer."

"You … you don't trust me?" My voice was strangled as I forced the words out, but she didn't reply. "Okay," I said, at last, "I'll be waiting."

My hands were shaking as I walked away.

What the hell had I done last night that had scared her so much that she was afraid to be alone in a room with me?

I waited in the lobby, sitting on a long, low sofa, my head in my hands, wondering if she'd even turn up.

But then the elevator doors opened with a soft hiss, and she was there, walking towards me. I stood up, wanting to touch her, but scorched by the wary expression on her face.

She sat across from me, on the edge of the sofa, her body rigid with tension, and waited for me to speak.

"You came," I said quietly.

"Evidently. What do you want now, Sebastian?"

Her voice was cool and distant, and some of the hope that had risen when I saw her walking toward me slipped away.

"Would you like a drink?"

She raised her eyebrows. "Is that supposed to be funny?"

"No ... I..."

I would have given a lot to have a drink right then, but she was still waiting for me to speak.

She crossed her arms and stared at me coolly.

"What you said earlier..." I took a deep breath. "I didn't really assault you, did I?" *Please say no.* "You were just saying that to get back at me."

If it was possible, her expression turned even colder.

"No, Sebastian, you really did," she bit out. "You were drunk ... I couldn't ... couldn't stop you."

She closed her eyes, and shivered at the memory. I thought I was going to vomit.

"If you hadn't passed out when you did ... you scared me," she said, looking me in the eyes, the sadness in her face spearing shrapnel into my heart. "It reminded me of your..."

No! No! Please don't say I made you think of him. But I could see the truth in her face.

"I reminded you of ... of my father?"

She nodded, the wary look back on her eyes.

"You were really afraid to let me in your room just now? I scared you that much?"

She didn't reply, leaving my appalled question hanging in the air. I dropped my eyes, filled with shame and revulsion.

"Oh God! Caro … I never … I couldn't…"

I looked up. She was staring at me, her eyes filled with doubt.

"Fuck, Caro! I'm so sorry."

We sat in painful silence until her cell phone rang. My nerves were so shot, I flinched at the sound.

Caro snatched it out of her purse, listening intently.

"Oh, shit! Sorry, Marc. Yes, I'm fine. Really. You don't need to worry."

That bastard. Always in the fucking way.

"We're just sitting in the lobby at my hotel," she said, her eyes shooting to me. "I'm good, really." She paused, listening. "I won't, but thanks, Marc. Have a safe flight and look after yourself—I wouldn't want anything to happen to you. Ciao."

I frowned, unable to stop the stupid words pouring out of my mouth. "Was that your *friend?*"

Caro rolled her eyes.

I took a deep breath and asked the next question that I needed to know, dreading the answer.

"Is he your boyfriend?"

She laughed out loud, but she didn't look as if she found the question amusing.

"Marc is a good friend," she said, at last. "He was just … being concerned."

"Yeah, right." *Concerned, my ass!*

"Actually, I think you're more his type."

Huh? Oh. He was gay? I hadn't picked up that vibe. Normally I could tell if a guy was into dudes. And suddenly I was feeling very relieved.

But then again, if he was concerned for her, it implied that she'd told him *something* that he might be concerned about.

"Did you tell him about me?"

"Which bit?" sighed Caro. "It doesn't matter: the answer is no—it's not anyone's business but mine."

Then she looked pointedly at her watch.

"Sebastian, it's late and I'm tired. If you've got anything else to say to me, say it quickly. Otherwise I'm going to bed."

I stared at my hands, trying to find the words. Begging her to stay without being able to say it.

"I'm sorry I've been such a jerk," I said quietly. "It was just … a shock … seeing you again."

"For me, too," she said, her voice soft.

For the first time it sounded like she felt something other than irritation or disgust for me. It made me hopeful.

"Let me make it up to you, Caro," I pleaded, desperation seeping into my voice. "Let me take you out tomorrow. I could show you the city. I've been here for months—I know my way around pretty well."

"I don't think so…"

She shook her head, and my desperation began to crescendo.

"Caro, come on. I'll be on my best behavior, I promise—I know your travel permit hasn't come through."

She narrowed her eyes. "How do you know that?"

"Well…" *Oh shit.* "That was just the impression I got. You'd have been packing otherwise. Please, Caro, I know some great Italian restaurants. It'll be like…"

I hesitated, but then she finished the sentence for me, "…old times?"

I smiled with relief. "Do you have anything better to do?"

She sighed, and I knew she was giving in. "No, I don't. Fine. But one false move, Hunter, and you'll regret it."

I couldn't help grinning at her, relief flowing through me like cool water in the desert. "Yes, ma'am!"

She smiled back and then her gaze dipped over toward the bar. "I think I will have that drink now."

Before she could stand, I was on my feet.

"I'll get it. A red wine?"

"Yes, thank you."

I remembered that Barolo had been her favorite. It was the first wine I'd ever drunk—and she'd given it to me. Although I was more of a whiskey kind of guy these days.

She looked surprised when I handed it to her, but I

wasn't sure why.

"I got you a Barolo."

"Mmm, my favorite."

"I know. I remembered you liked it."

She stared at me in amazement.

I remember every second we were together, I wanted to say. Jeez, my inner 17-year-old was a real pussy.

"Oh, well … thank you."

The tension began building between us again, and automatically my cock hardened. Things had always been intense between us: ten years hadn't changed that.

"How was it … after I left?" she asked.

I leaned back on the sofa, my eyes closed. I usually tried not to think about that time—those had been dark days.

"Bad," I admitted at last.

I wasn't sure how much I should tell her—definitely not about the time my dad hit me so hard I lost a tooth; or the time he trashed my room, smashing my computer and cell phone; and definitely not the time that mom called Caro a whore, and said I was too stupid to live.

I was almost ready to agree with her. Thank God Mitch and Shirley knew what my parents were like.

"Mom and Dad were … in the end Mitch went to see them—I didn't know what he said at the time but he and Shirley took me to live with them. Later, I found out that Mitch had threatened to go to my dad's CO and tell him that he'd been … beating up on me."

She looked so shocked, I knew I could never tell her the whole truth. I took a deep breath.

"On my eighteenth birthday I enlisted in the Marines." *Except that Dad blackmailed me to join, saying he'd have Caro arrested for statutory rape if I didn't do what he said.* "That's pretty much it."

She chewed on her lip, her beautiful eyes downcast. This conversation really wasn't going the way I'd hoped. But at least we were talking.

"And Mitch and Shirley?" she asked. "Ches?"

Mitch was a Staff Sergeant in the First of the First, and the reason I decided to join the Marines instead of the Navy like my old man wanted.

Mitch and Shirley were good people. If it hadn't been for them, I wouldn't have known what a real family was like. They'd done more for me when I was growing up than my own sorry excuse for parents. Ches was more a brother than a friend.

"Mitch and Shirley were stationed in Germany soon after I enlisted. Ches was studying at UCSD, so when I had leave I used to hang with him and his college buddies. He's married with two kids now."

I smiled at the thought, as crazy as it was true. Caro seemed to agree with me.

"You're kidding me? Really? Did he enlist, too?"

"He was going to, but then he met Amy at college and she talked him out of it. He's the manager at La Jolla Country Club now."

My mind immediately drifted back to that summer and the few weeks when I'd worked at the country club, and one extremely hot encounter with Caro in a changing room storage closet. Just thinking of that dark space, our bodies covered in a layer of sweat as I fucked her against a wall, it had the blood in my body heading south.

I shifted uncomfortably as my dick tried to climb through the zipper of my jeans. Discreetly, I shrugged out of my jacket and laid it across my lap.

A faint blush colored Caro's face, and I wondered if she was remembering the same thing. She cleared her throat.

"Are Shirley and Mitch still out in Germany?"

"No. Mitch got sent to Parris Island as an instructor. But last time I saw them, they were hoping to go back to San Diego. I guess they want to be near their grandkids."

"Where did Donna and Johan go?"

Hearing those names was weird. Captain Vorstadt— Admiral Vorstadt as he'd later become—they had lived on the Base near us. I remember that Mrs. Vorstadt was friendly with Caro. She'd been there when we'd been ripped apart and Caro was sent away. They'd been stationed at NAS Key West after that. But that wasn't what caught my attention.

"How did you know they went away?"

Caro hesitated before she replied.

"I wrote to them," she said at last.

I leaned forward, staring at her, trying to ease the truth out of her.

"When?" I croaked.

"Around the time of your 21st birthday, Sebastian. And I wrote to Shirley and Mitch. My letters were returned to sender, unopened. I assumed they'd either gone away or…"

I swallowed several times.

"So, you did try to contact me?"

I couldn't believe what she was telling me. Did that mean…?

"Yes and no," Caro said carefully. "I wanted to believe that you'd gone on with your life and I didn't want to disrupt anything. That's why I tried to contact Shirley and Mitch. I wanted to find out if my approach would be a positive thing—or not. When my letter was returned…"

She'd tried to find me? It smelled like bullshit. Two fucking letters in three years. She'd *promised* me that we'd be together forever and...

She was a journalist, for fuck's sake—she could have found me … if she wanted to.

"Everyone said I should just forget about you." I laughed without humor. "As if that was even possible. I tried to find you, Caro, but I didn't know your surname—your unmarried name—and the only person who knew was…" *your ex-husband.* "I left messages everywhere I could think of. I asked the new tenants at your house, at Shirley and Mitch's, and Donna's—I asked them to forward any mail to me … I guess that didn't happen. Fuck, Caro, we would have been…"

All these years wasted. IF she was telling the truth.

I took a long drink of wine, hoping that she hadn't noticed my hands were shaking.

"You thought I didn't care."

Her voice was soft and filled with sadness. I didn't dare believe it.

"I didn't know what to think at first. Later … yeah, I guess I thought you'd … moved on."

She sighed, dropping her gaze. "I did move on,

Sebastian: I had to. When those letters came back ... and even before I sent them, I thought you'd be better off without me. I suppose I hoped that your life would be different. More like Ches's. I guess that explains why you were so unpleasant these last few days."

She was right—I'd been a prick.

"Shit, I'm really sorry about that. It was just such a fucking shock. I didn't know what to think. It sent me into a real tailspin."

"It was a shock for me, too, Sebastian," she said firmly, "but I didn't behave like a dick."

She was feisty these days. I couldn't help smiling.

"Not your style, Caro."

God she was beautiful. She wasn't wearing a ring, but there was no way she could be single after all this time, even if she wasn't dating the French asshole.

She stared at me then leaned back in her chair.

"Just ask me, Sebastian."

She'd always been able to read me.

"You're so fearless, Caro, I love that about you. I was wondering ... if you were seeing anyone."

I held my breath until she answered.

"No, I'm not."

Thank fuck. "But you were? I mean ... since..."

She shook her head, but I wasn't sure what that meant.

"I dated a couple of times," she explained slowly, "but no, there was nothing serious. Besides, I travel too much to sustain a relationship. And I definitely don't want to get tied down again."

Was that her way of telling me she wasn't interested in me?

"What about you?" she asked. "Any significant other?"

I snorted and rolled my eyes. "Fuck, no!"

She gave me a challenging look and raised her eyebrows. "That's not what I heard."

"What? What did you hear?" I demanded.

She blinked a couple of times.

"About your CO's wife—in Paris? Maybe it was just gossip."

I couldn't help grinning. "Oh, that. Guy was a first class

bastard—he deserved it."

Caro shook her head disapprovingly. "And did she 'deserve' it? His wife?"

My smile vanished. Celia, my CO's wife, was a vain cunt who had screwed her way through half the staff before me.

"Yes, she did." *Stupid bitch.*

"And the possibility of getting court-martialed and thrown out of the Corps ... that didn't matter to you either?"

I shrugged. "I don't give a shit." It was the truth.

Suddenly, Caro pushed her glass away.

"Well, I think I'll call it a night now, Sebastian."

Wait, what?

"Don't go, Caro! We've only just started talking again. You haven't finished your wine, you..."

"No, I'm tired," she insisted.

She started to stand but I reached out, resting my hand on her leg.

"Caro, I really want you."

Her face darkened, and I realized my words had come out really fucking wrong.

"For God's sake, Sebastian!" she hissed, her voice quietly furious. "We have one civilized drink together and you think I'm just going to fall into bed with you?"

"You used to."

"How dare you!"

Oh shit. "I didn't mean it like that," I said.

But she stood up to leave so I grabbed hold of her hand, desperate to stop her.

"Caro, wait! Shit! I'm sorry."

She shook me off.

"Sebastian, we can't just roll back the last ten years and pretend it never happened. Too much has happened—too much time has passed."

"Come on, Caro, don't say that."

"Good night, Sebastian."

And she walked away. Again. I couldn't believe it. How had I managed to fuck things up so sensationally for the umpteenth time?

I sat there, hoping she'd come back, even though I knew

she wouldn't. I toyed with the idea of knocking on her door again, but I didn't think that would help. She was tired and pissed.

I'd had the target in my sights, but I'd missed.

I needed a new strategy.

Hours later, I sat in my apartment with the window open, staring out across the lake. The pool of darkness surrounded by the lights of the city mirrored how I felt.

I'd been here for months, but this wasn't home. I wasn't sure where that was anymore. I missed my Unit. I'd had friends then—guys I'd give my life for and who'd give their life for me. Finding out I had skills with languages had been a double-edged sword, because it left me isolated within the Corps. But I hadn't felt this lonely since Caro first left.

I hated her—what she'd done to me, the person I'd become without her in my life. But I hated more the thought of losing her again.

I'd have to mount a charm offensive, hoping for more charm and less offense this time.

I eyed the half-full bottle of whiskey waiting by my bed and seriously thought about diving into it. But I also knew that turning up hung-over and stinking of bourbon was not going to win me any votes with Caro. Instead, I changed into my sweats and took off for a run, pushing my body to the limit, trying to drive out the demons.

Sometimes it worked.

The next morning I woke early. It was something of a novelty to wake up sober; I might even start to like it again. But my nerves were kicking in, demanding a whiskey Band-aid before I headed out. This wasn't just some woman: this was Caro. And so far I'd fucked up every encounter we'd had.

I picked up the bottle and unscrewed the lid, but Caro's words came back to me: *quit your drinking before you really do something stupid.*

I screwed the lid back on and left the apartment before the urge to self-medicate became too strong. And I needed to get to Caro's hotel fast.

My bike was a Honda ST1100; a serious machine that

had the comfort of a tourer and the fun of a sportsbike. I'd bought it in Paris while I was stationed there, and ridden it to Geneva. Riding a motorcycle gave the illusion of freedom—a loose term when you've signed your life away to the military.

The roads were still fairly empty of traffic at this time in the morning. Unlike Paris, where you could find a party or a card game day or night, Geneva was sober and studious, but with drink and drugs and high-class hookers in hotel rooms if you knew where to look. And I did. But the Swiss liked to hide any sign that showed they were as corrupt as everyone else, like the Nazi gold that still lay hidden inside Zurich's bank vaults.

I broke a few speed limits getting to Caro's hotel, just because it felt good—reminded me I was alive. As if I needed reminding this morning. My nerve endings were firing like the business end of a M16.

I by-passed reception and took the stairs to Caro's room two at a time. I knocked quickly and took a deep breath waiting for her voice, waiting for the door to open.

But there was nothing.

I knocked again, leaning my head against the door as if trying to get closer to her.

"Caro, it's me. Look, about last night—I'm … can you open the door for a minute?"

But she refused to answer.

Goddamn it! The silent treatment was driving me crazy. Couldn't we talk like adults? I know I hadn't done a great job of that so far, but…

I pounded on the door again.

"For fuck's sake, Caro! Can we please just talk?" *Still no answer.* I ran my fingers over my hair, frustration snapping at my nerves. "This is fucking crazy," I muttered to myself.

"That's one of the words," said a quiet voice behind me.

Caro.

I flinched, wondering how much she'd heard. But then my eyes started wandering up her bare legs to the hotel robe wrapped tightly around her, covering her breasts. Her hair was wet and I could smell chlorine.

"I thought you weren't talking to me," I admitted.

"That certainly would have been one of my better ideas," she replied coldly, and I couldn't help wincing at her tone even though she *was* talking to me.

I sighed, rubbing a hand over the scruff on my face.

"Don't be like that, Caro. Look, I'm sorry. I mean it. Around you, I just seem to open my mouth to change feet."

"You can say that again."

"I will if you let me buy you breakfast," I offered, giving her my best smile, the one that usually worked on women. But not today.

"Are you stalking me, Sebastian?" she said bitterly. "I thought we said everything we had to say to each other last night."

Ah shit.

"I just want … can't we be friends?"

I didn't really want to be friends, but I'd take what I could get.

"Friends? I was under the impression you wanted to fuck me out of some sense of revenge."

What the…? No. Maybe … choose the right answer, Hunter!

"No!"

"Are you sure about that?" she bit out. "Because last night you told me that's exactly what you did to your CO's wife. Why should I be any different?"

I stared at her in disbelief. *That was what she really thought of me?* I was still gaping at her when she spoke again.

"Just go," she said wearily, fingering the keycard in her hand.

Fuck, no!

I took a deep breath, trying to push the desperation away.

"I know I'm saying everything wrong but … we used to have fun, didn't we?" I pleaded. "Let's just spend some time together—get to know each other again. You're right: we can't pretend the last ten years never happened. Just … give me a chance. I'm not the heartless bastard you seem to think I am. I'm still me, Caro."

She hesitated and I could see the indecision on her face, sensing that she was weakening.

"We could start with breakfast," I suggested hopefully.

"Who knows, I might be able to get through a whole meal without making you mad at me."

A reluctant smile crept across her face.

"It seems unlikely," she said, her words failing to match her expression.

I smiled with relief.

"You gonna wear that robe? Not that I give a shit—you could go naked for all I care. In fact…"

She groaned. "I'm going to take a shower. I'll see you in ten minutes."

"Want me to scrub your back?" I suggested, only half joking.

I knew I was pushing her, but I couldn't help it.

"Sebastian, I thought you were going to try and make it through breakfast before making me mad at you—right now your adolescent flirting is just annoying."

I held up my hands in a gesture of defeat, but the smile on my face wasn't going anywhere soon.

"Okay, I get the message. I'll see you downstairs."

I turned away quickly before she changed her mind, still grinning, then started whistling to myself.

Fucking whistling! What a pussy.

I didn't like to admit that it was the song that always reminded me of her when I was 17: Van Morrison's *Crazy Love*.

At the hotel's restaurant, I let the waitress lead me to a table by the window. I wasn't hungry, so I ordered a black coffee and sat waiting, memories spooling out relentlessly.

I wasn't even sure what I wanted anymore—definitely more than just a quick fuck. But if friendship was all that was on offer, I'd take it—even if it killed me.

When I saw Caro walking across the restaurant toward me, that unfaithful friend named hope made a swift reappearance. My heart stuttered, then restarted at a quick march.

She was simply dressed in old jeans and a pale yellow t-shirt. She'd always looked good in yellow. Her dark hair curled over her shoulders and down her back, thick and glossy. I remembered tangling my hands in that hair, lost in

41

the curves of her amazing body.

But all I could manage to say was, "You look great."

She snorted in disbelief, and I didn't know how I'd managed to piss her off. I only knew that I had. Maybe she thought I was giving her a line. I wasn't.

"Did you order yet?" she asked

"No, just the coffee: I was waiting for you."

"I usually have the continental breakfast."

I waved to the waitress, and she walked over briskly to take Caro's order. From the way she swung her hips as she walked, I got the impression that she'd have given me more than the full continental. *Yeah, not interested.*

I tried to think of something to say that would ease things between *us*—because right now the tension was making me crazy.

"Was there anything in particular you wanted to see in Geneva?" I asked, trying for casual, the kind of trite shit that other people seemed to manage with a fucking problem.

"You have to make it through breakfast without being irritating first," she reminded me, but the smile on her face told the truth.

"Yeah, well, I like a challenge," I grinned. "Seriously: anything you want to see?"

"Not especially: I saw quite a lot wandering around yesterday. The Russian Church, maybe? I hear that's pretty amazing."

I folded and unfolded my napkin several times before I made my suggestion.

"I had an idea of something we could do—if you like."

"Which is?"

"How about a trip to Chamonix? It's only an hour away—or just a bit longer if we take the scenic route through Lausanne. It'll be a really great trip through the Alps." *Please say yes.* "I'll have you back before bedtime."

She eyed me warily, but I could tell she was wavering. I bit back the smile that was threatening to break out.

"And you absolutely *promise* you'll bring me back here by evening? No accidentally running out of gas or getting lost?"

"I wouldn't dream of it," I said, lying through my teeth.

I'd already thought of several scenarios that ended with us having to share a hotel room.

"Okay," she said, shaking her head as if she couldn't believe what she was agreeing to. "But I'm serious about getting back: I'm waiting for my travel permits and I can't afford to miss them."

My conscience pricked at me, making me shift uncomfortably in my seat.

"Caro, I'll get you back here tonight, I promise."

I wasn't hungry when the food arrived, but I'd gotten used to eating whatever was put in front of me *whenever* it was put in front of me. I'd lost too many meals to sudden RPG attacks in hostile environments. Bastards liked to hit at chow time.

"Tell me about Ches's kids," Caro said suddenly.

I couldn't help smiling, just thinking about them.

"They're great. They call me 'Uncle Seb' ... well, Simone, the youngest one, she calls me 'Zed' because she still gets her words mixed up sometimes. She's nearly three. Ben is four and he's a little surf-rat already. I see them as often as I can, but every time they seem so much more grown up. Jeez, they grow fast."

"What's Amy like?"

"Yeah, she's okay."

Caro looked amused at my lukewarm response.

"Let me guess—she doesn't approve of you?"

Well, no...

"What made you say that?"

Caro smiled.

"Firstly, because you're single, and married women get nervous that their husband's single friends will lead them astray; secondly, because, from the sound of it, you've had more women than most men have hot dinners, and *that* will make her nervous because she won't want you reminding Ches of what he's missing out on; and..."

She stopped mid-sentence. I guessed that whatever she was leaving unsaid was even worse.

"And what?"

"Well, the drinking, Sebastian. She wouldn't want that

around her husband and kids."

Her words hit a nerve.

"Yeah, I guess that about sums it up."

"When did you start drinking?" she asked gently.

My temper fired quickly. "What do you mean? I don't drink that much, not like that bitch mother of mine."

Caro's gaze didn't waver. "Well, twice in as many days you've been so drunk you've either passed out or made inappropriate comments to me."

Shit. She was right.

"I think my question stands," she said.

I didn't want to go there, but I guess she deserved the truth.

"When I was 21," I said at last. "That's when I started drinking."

It was true: apart from the odd beer, the occasional shot, I hadn't drunk that much—a lot less than most of the guys in my Unit, that was for sure. But when I realized Caro wasn't coming back for me, my world had fallen apart. I anesthetized myself with women and booze. I'd done that for the last seven years. Maybe now it was time to feel everything again—even the pain.

Caro looked horrified.

"Sebastian, I'm so sorry. I had no idea."

I shrugged and looked away. "Old news, Caro, don't worry about it."

She looked like she was struggling to speak, but when she did, she'd reverted to small talk. I guess it was more comfortable for both of us.

"Do you like living in Geneva?"

"It's okay, but I miss the ocean."

"Ah, no famous Swiss surfing beaches."

Her words made me smile.

"I haven't found any yet."

She smiled back, and it felt good to be at ease with her. But now I was eager to start our day trip—apart from anything else, the thought of having her body pressed against mine on the back of my bike made me impatient.

"Are you done eating?" I asked. "Should we go?"

"I just need to go back to my room and pick up a jacket and, I presume, my passport, but otherwise, yes, I'm good to go."

I frowned. "You're a journalist: you should always have your passport with you. Hell, it was in the fucking tedious lecture that Parsons gave the day before yesterday."

"So you were listening," she swatted back.

I shook my head and smiled.

"Yeah, yeah, just grab a sweater, too: it's going to get cold."

She rolled her eyes, muttering something under her breath about me being bossy as she walked away.

Give me the chance and I'll show you how 'bossy' I can be.

I went to pay the check, but the waitress said she'd put it on Caro's room tab as instructed. I wasn't very happy about that, and I was even less happy when she passed me her phone number. But I guess old habits die hard, because I slipped it in my pocket and winked at her as I left the room.

I took the elevator to the basement and brought the Honda to the hotel's entrance.

Caro's mouth dropped open when she saw me.

CHAPTER 3

"Are you kidding me, Hunter? You expect me to get on that thing?"

Caro gestured at the bike, looking shocked. Guess I'd forgotten to tell her we'd be traveling on two wheels.

"Sure! It'll be fun," I said encouragingly.

"Do you know how to drive it?"

Her voice was laced with suspicion.

"Caro, I rode it from Paris—I think I can manage 88 kilometers to Chamonix," I grinned at her.

"I don't know," she muttered, shifting from foot to foot. "I've never been on the back of a motorcycle before."

I was surprised. "Really? Because we used to talk about doing that and riding from…" I stopped abruptly.

Was it ever going to get easier to talk about the past? She met my eyes, the shadows of our shared lives never far away.

"Oh, what the hell," she said, shaking her head and walking towards me.

"Such faith in my abilities, Ms. Venzi."

"If I get killed on this thing, I'm going to come back and haunt you!"

"Promise?"

"Oh, you'd better believe it, Hunter!"

I loved seeing this side of Caro. With each sentence it was more like how it used to be … and I fucking loved that.

I pulled my spare leather jacket out of the saddlebag and helped her put it on. It was old and battered, but it would give her some protection from the cold, or an accident—which *wasn't* going to happen on my watch.

She was so tiny compared to me that her hands

disappeared inside the long sleeves, and I had to fold back the cuffs so she could free her hands. I pulled up the zipper, my fingers dangerously close to her lush tits.

"Suits you," I said, raising an eyebrow and ignoring her frown.

I passed her a spare helmet, waited until she'd fastened it, then swung a leg over the bike and held out my hand to help her mount behind me.

The seat slanted her forward so her thighs automatically gripped mine. I liked that *a lot.*

"Hold on tight," I said, pleasure coursing through me from the sheer fucking joy of this moment—a moment I thought would never happen.

She wrapped her arms around me; I never wanted her to stop.

The engine started with a gravelly roar that crescendoed as I revved the accelerator. I took it slow to start with, letting her get used to being on the bike. I waited until we were at the lakeside road heading north-east to Lausanne before I really opened the throttle.

This moment. This woman.

She gripped me tighter as the bike flew around the curves of Lake Geneva, the air cool as the miles rushed past. When we reached Montreux, I slowed the bike, giving her time to appreciate the chocolate-box old town with chalets and Disneyland castle. I preferred being surrounded by open space and empty roads, but I thought Caro might like it.

"Do you want to get a coffee?" I called over my shoulder.

She nodded enthusiastically, bumping her helmet on the back of mine as she gave me a thumbs up.

I pulled up outside a small café that looked over the lake, then kicked down the stand and cut the engine. The sudden silence seemed to reignite the fire between us. I was sure I wasn't the only one who was feeling it, but I forced myself to keep it casual.

I pulled off my helmet and grinned at her.

"How was that?"

She struggled out of her own helmet and ran her hands

through her long hair tangled by the wind.

"That was … surprisingly okay."

I laughed, but my eyes dropped to her full lips and I knew she saw in my eyes what I was thinking, because she scrambled off the bike hastily then rubbed her hands together, although whether it was from nerves, I couldn't tell.

"Are you cold?"

"A little: just my hands."

Without saying a word, I took her hands in mine and lifted them to my lips, warming them with my breath and rubbing them gently.

After a moment, she pulled free, her cheeks tinged with pink. Although that could have been from the cold.

"That's fine, thank you."

I wanted to kiss her. I wanted to pull her into my arms and tell her that she'd never stopped being important to me. But then she looked away, her expression conflicted.

"This café looks good," she said quickly.

She strode into the café and found a table by the window.

I followed more slowly, sliding into the chair opposite her. The waiter ambled over and I ordered coffees for both of us.

"Un espresso et un caffé americano, s'il vous plâit."

"Do you speak French, as well?" she asked curiously.

I shrugged. "I lived in Paris for two years so more than enough to get by. I never studied it."

"And the Dari? The Arabic? How did that come about?"

"My first tour in Iraq. I was playing soccer with some of the local kids who used to hang around the Base. They taught me a few words and I just started picking up some phrases. My sergeant heard me talking to the kids and sent me on a couple of training courses. When we started pulling out of Iraq, they figured I should learn Pashto and Dari so I could be useful in Afghanistan. I found I could just *hear* it, all the different cadences." I laughed coldly. "Finally found something I was good at. Who knew."

She seemed surprised by my scathing tone.

"You were always good at lots of things, Sebastian."

My Caro—still trying to make me feel good.

"And you picked up Italian really quickly," she said insistently.

"That's because I had an Italian girlfriend," I pointed out.

"Really? When was that?"

She was seriously asking me that? I rolled my eyes—I'd learned Italian from her ... in between fucking each other's brains out.

"Oh, right," she muttered, embarrassed. "And you taught me to surf, don't forget."

I couldn't help grinning. *Damn, that brought back some good memories.*

"Yeah, that was fun. Did you ever keep it up?"

"I go quite often in the summer," she said, her face lighting with a bright smile. "I bought a place in Long Beach and..."

Her words ground to a halt as she saw the expression on my face. That had been *our* dream: together, not...

"Sorry," I said, as she continued to bite her lip. "It's just ... well, we used to talk about going to Long Beach and checking out the surf spots."

"I didn't have any other plan," she said quietly. "When I left you ... when I left San Diego, I drove for eight days until I got to New York. That old Pinto I had, died just as I reached the city. I got an apartment in Little Italy because I didn't know anywhere else, and you mentioned it once. I lived there for eight years. You were right: I did like it."

I closed my eyes, letting my head drop to my hands. We'd been so close to having that together. So fucking close.

"God, Caro, when I think about how things could have been ... it makes me a little crazy."

"I know what you mean," she said softly. "But there's no point thinking like that."

The waitress returned with our coffees, breaking the mood, but I could see the shadow of sadness in Caro's eyes.

"I'm glad you went there," I said, only half lying. "I'm glad you did the things we said we'd do."

"Not all of them," she amended.

"Fuck, if only…"

"Stop, Sebastian," she said forcefully. "No 'what ifs': what if we'd never gone to that Sicilian restaurant that night; what if Brenda hadn't seen us; what if she hadn't told your parents … there's no point thinking like that. Like you said, it'll just make us crazy."

"I know you're right," I murmured, "it's just that…"

I couldn't get the words out, instead running my hand over my head in frustration. *That should have been us: together.*

"Hey, stop," she said, grabbing my fingers. "It is what it is. We can't change anything."

I held on tightly, letting her anchor me to the here and now.

"Mind you," she said, "if I ran into Brenda again, I might have to give her a quick slap."

I couldn't help smiling: there was a time when I'd felt the same. My ex-girlfriend was the one who'd lit the match that exploded our world.

"Yeah, I'd like to see that," I admitted. "Although she felt really bad about what happened."

Caro looked surprised and leaned back in her chair, releasing my hand.

"You spoke to her about it—what she did?"

Her voice told me she was pissed, so I decided to tread carefully. Although now I thought about it, maybe she sounded … jealous? I really liked that idea.

"Well, yeah. She kept bugging Ches until I agreed to see her. By then it was kind of obvious why she'd done it."

"Obvious how?" Caro huffed out.

"She was pregnant—got knocked up by that bastard Jack Sullivan. You remember that older guy who used to hang out at the beach? Yeah, well, when she found out she was pregnant, she freaked. Got this crazy idea in her head that if she could get back with me, she'd get me to sleep with her and pretend the baby was mine."

I shook my head, still amazed at the fucked up behavior of a scared 18 year-old girl and the trail of destruction that she'd set in motion.

"She thought if she got you out of the way, we'd get

back together," I explained. "She had no idea what she'd done. Until after—and it was too late."

"And did you? Sleep with her?"

Jesus, what?

"For fuck's sake," I snapped. "I told you. I didn't even touch another woman for three years."

She took a deep breath.

"Sorry."

"Yeah, well," I said, letting my sudden anger drain away, "she had to face her parents eventually. Jack wouldn't have anything to do with her, and she wouldn't say who the father was. Everyone assumed it was me anyway."

That just gave my old man another reason to bitch at me, saying I was refusing to face up to responsibilities or some shit. Yep, he made a personal visit to my training base—he really wanted to put the boot in once he couldn't beat the shit out of me anymore. The fact that he wet his dick in half the nursing staff at the Base hospital was irrelevant, I guess.

I continued with the story. "But when Kimberley was born, she had all this dark brown hair and dark eyes; it was kind of obvious I wasn't the father."

"Kimberley?"

"She's a great kid. I see them sometimes when I'm on the West Coast. Brenda married a car salesman a couple of years back. He's a pretty nice guy and good with Kimberley."

Caro nodded slowly.

"Well, I'm glad it worked out for her—in the end." She paused. "You didn't tell me what happened to Donna and Johan. They were always kind to me."

The walk down memory lane was painful, but I guess after all this time we needed it … needed to say things.

"Shirley stayed in touch with them. I saw them a few times after … Johan retired a couple of years back, and they moved to Phoenix. I heard he was pretty sick—leukemia, I think."

Her face fell and she looked down.

"I'm sorry to hear that—they were a nice couple."

I nodded but didn't reply.

"What about that funny little friend of yours—Fido? What was his real name ... um ... Alfred? Albert? Arnold! What happened to him?"

God, these memories didn't get any easier. Catching up really sucked.

"He enlisted just before me: the Rakkasans, 187th Infantry. He died eight years ago in Iraq—IED. Poor bastard never stood a chance. He didn't even make it to twenty."

Caro's hands flew to her mouth and she looked distressed.

"Oh no, I'm so sorry!"

We finished our coffees in silence, each of us lost in the past. I really needed to get out of here; if I kept moving, maybe the memories couldn't catch me. *Yeah, right.*

"Ready to head for Chamonix?" I asked, pretty fucking anxious to get going.

Caro smiled, her eyes softening, making me feel things I wasn't ready to feel. I had to look away.

"Yes, ready as I'll ever be. Actually though, it's more comfortable riding on that machine than I thought it would be. I just wish I'd worn something warmer."

"Put your hands in my pockets this time," I suggested. "That will help. And there's a shop in Chamonix where we can get you some good gloves."

"That's not necessary."

"I can buy you some fucking gloves, Caro!" I said, my voice unnecessarily gruff.

"Fine!" she said briskly. "Although I have no idea what 'fucking gloves' are: made of latex, I suppose!"

I couldn't help laughing loudly. "God, I love you, Caro!"

Oh fuck!

Did I really say that?

The startled look on her face told me that I did.

"Slip of the tongue," I mumbled.

We crossed into France at Saint Gingolph. The border guard was an asshole and held us up longer than necessary when he realized we were American. I don't think it helped that the occupation on my passport said 'US Marine'. He wanted to show that he was one tough mofo by making us wait. I ran into his kind all the time—guys who thought they'd look like a big man if they took on a Marine. Let's just say I'd be the one who was still standing at the end.

Eventually the dickwad let us through, and soon we were passing winding roads that threaded their way up into the Alps.

"This road leads to Italy," I yelled over my shoulder. "How about a quick trip across the border?"

"Two countries in one day is enough!" Caro shouted back.

I hadn't been serious, but now the thought had snuck into my brain, I really liked that idea. *Caro, me, my bike, and the open road to Italy.* Yeah, I really liked that idea.

Chamonix soon appeared out of the low mist that had settled in the valley. If I'd been in Afghanistan, I would be reaching for my weapon, on the lookout for an ambush, but all I could see here were picture-postcard chalets and fat, placid cows grazing on the lush grass.

To my left was the looming presence of Mont Blanc, thick snow capping the summit. Great snowboarding country.

But the town was almost deserted at this time of year: the winter skiers and snow-bunnies long gone, the summer tourists not yet arrived. That was fine by me.

I pulled up outside a shop that sold ski equipment. It wouldn't be as good as a bike shop, but at least Caro wouldn't be cold on the ride back.

"We'll get you some ski gloves to wear," I said, as I climbed off the bike. "Best I can do for now."

The sales assistant stayed close as she followed us around the shop. It was slightly unnerving and I wondered if I'd ever fucked her. But she was smiling at me, so either I'd played nice in the morning—which seemed unlikely—or she was looking for a hookup.

Caro was quiet and I wondered what she was thinking. I picked up the first pair of gloves that I guessed were about the right size.

"How about these?"

"Ninety Euros!" she gasped. "Are you kidding me? That's $115! For a pair of gloves!"

"Just try the damn things on, Caro," I growled, irritated that she wouldn't let me buy her something. When I was 17, I'd have given her the stars if I could, but I'd had no money. I had plenty now. All I'd ever spent my pay on was booze and bikes.

"No. That's ridiculous," she insisted, folding her arms across her chest, not realizing that pushed her tits together in a way that had my dick sitting up and paying attention. "There must be something cheaper."

"If you don't try them on, I'll just buy them anyway," I threatened.

"No! It's a waste of money."

I turned to the sales assistant and handed them over. "D'accord. Je les prends."

"Wait! Attendez!" Caro yelped.

She snatched them back and pulled them on over her hands. They fit perfectly. The look of annoyance on her face had me grinning.

"You argue too much, Caro."

"I can't imagine why," she said dryly, a smile creeping onto her lips, even as she tried to hide it.

"Should we find somewhere to have lunch?" I suggested.

Her eyes snapped to mine.

"What, you're actually asking me, Hunter? As in, seeking my opinion?"

I winked at her. "Sure!"

"In that case, yes; but only if I treat you—non-negotiable."

"I love it when you tell me what to do, Caro," I teased her. "Brings back memories."

She blushed. It was a good look on her. And she knew *exactly* what I was talking about. Other than Italian, the one thing she'd taught me was how to give her great orgasms. I'd paid attention.

I couldn't help smiling at the chagrined expression on her face. Yep, her mind had gone straight to the gutter—just like mine.

I wrapped my arm around her shoulders, automatically pulling her into a hug. I couldn't help dropping a soft kiss onto her hair, as well.

"Just teasing you, Caro."

She shuffled away from me, and I let her go reluctantly. Damn, she was cute when she was embarrassed.

"Do you want to try fondue?" I asked, still trying not to laugh.

"Fine," she muttered.

Fucking adorable.

At a small bistro, we both ordered the cheese fondue and were given a basket full of different rolls: focaccia, olive breads, breadsticks; and a fondue made up of mozzarella, dolcelatte and parmesan. It was the perfect lunchtime fuel, especially on a cold day in the spring.

"Mmm, this is good," Caro mumbled over a mouthful of olive bread. "Have you been here before?"

"A couple of times."

"Ever bring your women here?"

I didn't want to answer that. "You make it sound like I had a fucking parade of them," I complained, hoping to avoid the issue.

"Didn't you?"

My temper, always so near the surface when she was around, broke through.

"What do you want me to say, Caro? I fucked everything I could get my hands on when I realized you weren't coming back. It was years before I trusted a woman enough to be able to make love to her, and even then..."

I stopped, not wanting to see that look of hurt on her face again.

"I'm sorry," she murmured, her eyes downcast. "I didn't mean ... it's none of my business, Sebastian. I apologize."

I took a deep breath, tamping down the anger and resentment, afraid of what I'd say if I didn't keep a hold of it.

"I'm sorry, too. I didn't mean to yell at you."

We ate in silence for several minutes, although my appetite was officially shot.

"How long have you had the motorcycle?" she asked,

obviously trying for neutral territory.

I blew out a breath, relieving some of the tension, and leaned back in my chair.

"This one, about two years. But I've had one on and off since I was 19. Bought my first bike as a birthday present to myself. It's still in Ches's garage."

"Really? Well, there's another reason for his wife to think you're leading Ches astray. Or is he the responsible father-type now?"

I smiled.

"He's a great dad—really patient. He fucking loves those kids of his. But we still take the boards out and catch some waves when I'm there."

"Uh-huh, and how many meals have you made him late for, just catching 'one more wave'?"

Yeah, she knew me well.

"Too many for Amy's taste!" I admitted. "But he goes out when Mitch visits, too, so she can't blame me for that."

"Oh, I don't know—it sounds as if she'd think of a way. I'd like her: a woman immune to the Hunter charm."

I had to laugh at that.

"She's immune alright. But yeah, she'd like you. I'll introduce you when we're stateside."

Wow, I really said that. I was already thinking of a future when we were still together. Caro looked as surprised as I felt.

"In case you'd forgotten," she reminded me, oozing sarcasm, "I live about 3,000 miles and ten states from San Diego."

"Yeah, well, in case *you'd* forgotten, they've invented airplanes."

"Touché."

I raised my glass of water in a toast.

"What happened to that friend of Mitch's—Bill—the one who was at the wretched military 'fun' day that Donna dragged me to?"

That fucker—always sniffing around Caro.

"Why are you asking about him?" I growled out.

"Just wondering. He was in your surfing crowd, wasn't he?"

"Oh, right. He got married again a few years back, I think. He was sent to Quantico. Mitch keeps up with him—Christmas cards—something like that." *Who fucking cares?*

I turned the conversation back to us—my new favorite topic. Besides, I wanted to suggest my Italian plan to her.

"It felt good having you on the bike with me today, Caro."

"Hmm," she said, the sound filled with skepticism.

"Well, I've had an idea about that..."

"Oh, another of your ideas?" she said, a smile hiding behind the snippy words. "That sounds dangerous."

I grinned at her.

"You know how we always talked about traveling through Italy? I just thought, while we're both here, why don't we?"

She frowned as if she didn't understand what I was suggesting.

"Why don't we what?"

"See Italy. We could take the motorcycle and go see all those places we talked about: Milano, Verona, Capezzano Inferiore—see if your dad's relatives still live there."

That was the ace in my hand: I knew Caro's dad was from southern Italy and we'd talked about going there one day. From the look of longing on her face, I could tell she still wanted to.

"Don't you have work to do?" she answered evasively. "How come you've got all this time off?"

"I'm on leave," I said. "I'll be shipping back out to Afghanistan—in about three weeks."

"Oh," she said, her voice soft. "I didn't realize ... I thought you were stationed in Geneva."

"I was, but they need interpreters and they're getting antsy about using locals. Too many green-on-blue attacks. So, what do you think about Italy?"

She shook her head.

"I can't, you know I can't. My papers could come through any moment and I'll be on my way out there myself." *Oh, I don't think so.* "Besides, three weeks with you—that's definitely a dangerous mission."

I suppressed a smile at her choice of words.

"Don't you trust me?" I asked, pretending to be hurt.

"No, not particularly."

I grinned at her. *Yep, she had my number.* "Oh, don't say that. I'll be good. Scout's honor."

"You were never a boy scout."

"True," I agreed, more serious now. "What if I promise I'll behave myself: separate bedrooms and everything?"

"No way, Hunter. I've heard about your *reputation*, remember? Besides, I don't know how soon I'll get a flight to Leatherneck. I don't want to risk losing my slot."

"It won't happen for at least two weeks."

She narrowed her eyes, and I knew I'd said too much. *Shit.*

"You sound very sure of that. What did you do, Hunter?"

I had two choices: lie my ass off, or tell the truth. Neither particularly appealed, but I decided to go with truth.

"Let's just say I know people in the right places," I admitted.

Her voice started rising, and I could tell she was genuinely pissed.

"Are you telling me you've blocked my application?"

"It's not blocked, Caro, not entirely. I ... just threw a few well-aimed monkey wrenches in the works. It'll take at least a week to sort out—probably two."

Oh shit, this was not going well. The fury on her face was clear and her small hands clenched into fists.

"This is my *work*, Sebastian," she hissed. "This is how I get *paid*. How dare you interfere like this! You're unbelievable. You can't butt into my life like this!"

By now she was yelling, and people were turning to stare.

"I'm not the insipid little woman I was ten years ago!"

I blinked in surprise.

What the fuck was she talking about?

"You were never that," I insisted.

The air started heating between us, and I knew she felt it as well, even if she was too stubborn to admit it.

"You'd better damn well get that monkey wrench out, Hunter! I mean it."

Time to admit the truth, the whole truth and nothing but the truth.

"I can't, Caro, it's out of my hands now. But I promise it's temporary. I just ... after all this time ... I wanted us to be able to spend more than a few hours together. I don't know when I'll see you again," I said quietly. "I've already waited ten years."

She was silent, and when I looked up, the anger had vanished from her eyes, leaving them tinged with sadness.

"Will you at least think about Italy?" I begged.

She nodded jerkily, but looked away from me.

We finished our meal in silence and then spent the afternoon wandering through the town, stopping to look in shops and patisserie windows.

"I wouldn't mind coming back here in the winter," I said, gazing up at the stormy face of Mont Blanc, "try out the snowboarding."

"That's something else I've never done," Caro murmured, staring up at the mountain apprehensively.

"I'll teach you," I offered.

"Oh, something you can teach me, Hunter?" she shot back, showing that her irritation with me hadn't entirely dissipated. Then she glanced at her watch. "I think we should be heading back now. I can't get a signal on my phone here. My editor might have been trying to contact me."

I knew that was extremely unlikely, but I didn't want to get into another argument with her. Instead, we headed to the bike and mounted up. Even if she was still pissed with me, she had no choice but to wrap her body around mine again. Definitely a bonus.

I took the AutoRoute back to Geneva, arriving in slightly under an hour. I felt the loss instantly when she climbed off the bike and handed the spare helmet and jacket to me. I stowed it in one of the empty saddlebags, giving myself time, trying to think of something to say. But it was Caro who found the words.

"I really enjoyed today, Sebastian. Most of it, anyway. Thank you."

"You're welcome, Caro."

We stood gazing at each other. Without knowing why, I felt awkward, the tension stretching tightly between us.

"Okay, well, thanks again," she murmured, turning to go.

"Can I see you tomorrow, Caro?" I asked, my voice desperate even to my own ears. "Will you think about the Italy idea?"

She hesitated and licked her lips. Automatically, my eyes dropped to her mouth, and I let myself admit how I was feeling—something I hadn't done for a long time. *Too long.*

"I want to kiss you, Caro. Very badly."

Her eyes glowed, and I held my breath as she slowly raised her hand to my cheek. I leaned into her warmth, my eyes closing as her fingers brushed down my neck, heat and desire rising everywhere she touched me.

I took a step closer, resting my hands on her small waist. Then she pulled my head toward her and I felt her lips on mine at last. So soft, so sensuous. I could feel her breath stroke my face, her lips parted and my tongue swept into her mouth.

And then the emotions, the memories that burned through me—every pain, every regret scorched in the heat of her touch. I remembered: her body arching as mine moved above her, inside her, the intensity of every moment seared through me.

I pressed my hips into her, my erection painfully obvious as her mouth devoured every breath.

"God, I want you, Caro. I want to make love to you," I whispered against her lips.

"Yes," she said. "I want that, too."

CHAPTER 4

I could have taken her there and then. My body was crying out for her.

Instead I had to go park my bike in the hotel's secure underground garage and hope to hell that Caro didn't change her mind by the time I came back. I thought she might. She could come to her senses at any moment and think of all the reasons why this was a bad idea, why I wasn't good enough for a successful career woman who could have her pick of guys. It was hard to believe she was forty. She was still smokin' hot.

The truth was I'd never be good enough for her, but that didn't stop me wanting her. And if she had low standards, who the hell was I to complain?

She was waiting for me in the lobby, sitting on the same sofa where I'd sat last night during our excruciating heart-to-heart. She looked anxious, a frown creasing her forehead. I was sure she could read me, tension and expectation in every molecule of my body. Ten years. Ten long years I'd waited for this moment. And I was a man now, not a boy, and I knew I could make this good for her. If she let me.

I wondered if we'd still have that amazing chemistry. It felt like we would, if the way my body was reacting to hers was anything to go by.

I crossed the lobby to stand in front of her, my eyes searching her face, for any part of her that didn't want this. I held out my hand and she took it without hesitation. If it was a mistake, then it was one we both made willingly.

A relieved smile flickered across my face as I pulled Caro to her feet, braiding my fingers through hers as we headed toward the bank of gleaming elevators.

All were busy, crammed with tourists returning from day trips, politicians and businessmen heading to their rooms. The bastards were eyeing Caro with approval, so I pulled her to the side and shot them some serious fuck-off glares, before wrapping my arms around her waist and pulling her back into my chest, and allowing myself to rain soft kisses onto her hair.

The doors opened again with a soft hiss and several other people got off at the same floor, following us along the corridor, chatting noisily. Caro and I were silent.

She pulled the keycard out of her wallet, and I could see the tremor in her hands as she pushed the door open and walked inside.

I stood watching her as she moved around the room, turning on the side lights, pulling the curtains, shifting her laptop from the duvet. She still hadn't looked at me, so I walked in slowly and sat on the edge of the bed. I caught her hand as she hurried past on another pointless circuit.

"Hey, it's okay. I'm nervous, too."

She stared at me in amazement.

"*You're* nervous ... why?"

"Because it's you," I said simply.

And it wasn't a line. Just because I'd fucked my way around every city I'd ever lived in, it didn't mean shit. *This*, here and now, *this* was what mattered. With her. I'd been numb for so long and now I wanted to feel again—it scared the fuck out of me.

I raised her hand to my lips and kissed it gently, hoping to reassure her. I didn't want my so-called reputation getting in the way.

"Only if you want to, Caro."

And I meant it: she had to want me, too.

"I do," she stuttered. "I just feel, I don't know, embarrassed. It's so stupid."

I couldn't find the words to reassure her, so I decided to show her what she meant to me. I lay back on the bed and gently pulled her down next to me, then began kissing her throat, my hands moving up from her waist. The soft warmth of her body heated mine, and I couldn't help pressing myself over her, wanting to feel her everywhere.

But then she froze underneath me and spoke the words I'd been dreading since the moment I told her that I wanted her.

"No, Sebastian," she gasped, pushing me away.

I stopped immediately, my heart shuddering as my stupid body fought to continue what we'd started. I took a deep breath and rolled away from her, forcing a smile to my face. I wasn't sure if she meant not now, or not ever, or no fucking way. But she wasn't making me leave, so I kept the smile glued to my face, even though she looked like she was about to bolt.

And then I had an idea that might help her to relax.

"Let's just make out," I suggested.

She seemed stunned, as if she'd expected me to get up and leave.

"Make out? As in…"

"Lie on the bed, watch trashy TV in French or German—your choice—and make out," I clarified.

I raised my eyebrows challengingly, then sat up and shrugged out of my jacket, dropping it on the floor, before unbuckling by boots and tossing them into the corner with my socks.

Caro used to tell me that she thought my feet were sexy. I remember thinking, *What the fuck?* But I'd use everything I had—whatever that was.

I grabbed a couple of pillows, piled them against the headboard and launched myself backward.

"Where's the remote?"

She pointed silently to the cabinet on her side of the bed and I leaned across her to retrieve it. She didn't flinch as I rubbed up against her, so I took that as another good sign.

She watched as I surfed through a few channels before I found some badly-dubbed TV show, then grinned up at her, patting the space on the bed beside me.

She blinked and seemed undecided. I held my breath while she unlaced her boots and dropped them next to mine. But then she crawled up on the bed next to me, and I pulled her into my arms so she was resting against my chest. *God, the memories this brought back. The many times we'd made love—but never enough.* I kissed her forehead, and settled back on the pillows with a sigh when she snuggled into me.

"This feels good," I said, a deep contentment flowing through my body. "Should we order room service?"

"I'm not hungry."

"Would you mind if I ordered myself a beer?"

She shook her head. "No, I don't mind."

I pulled the hotel telephone toward me to order a beer and a sandwich, then relaxed with my arm around her, enjoying the scent of her hair, her body soft against mine. I wanted more, but I could wait.

The Swiss were efficient, I'll give them that. The beer arrived within five minutes, and the 'sandwich'—an enormous French baguette—was stuffed with cold cuts, lettuce and tomato.

Result!

I grabbed the bread and started inhaling it as quickly as I could. A broad grin spread across Caro's face.

"Food instead of sex?" she asked, a smile tugging at one corner of her mouth.

I nearly choked, but managed to swallow in time. *Hmm, swallowing.* Yeah, food versus sex—it was a running joke we'd once shared. I was stupidly happy that she'd remembered.

"For now," I teased her. "I'm still kind of hoping the sex comes later."

"How's that going for you?"

"Not sure: she's playing hard to get. I was going to ply her with alcohol and have my wicked way with her, but I guess she's wise to my game."

"Women!" she laughed, rolling her eyes.

I finished the sandwich and brushed crumbs from my t-shirt, then lay back with the bottle of beer and wrapped my free arm around her again.

"I could get used to this," I admitted, nuzzling her hair.

"What, badly dubbed reruns of 'Frasier' and TV dinners?" she snarked back at me.

"You know exactly what I mean, woman."

"Oh, 'woman', is it?" she said, thumping me on the chest.

Something snapped inside me, and I couldn't pretend any longer.

"Yes, a beautiful, amazing, talented, gorgeous woman."

Caro's brown eyes stared up at me and I saw the uncertainty and lack of belief in herself that had always plagued her. Maybe she hadn't changed as much as I'd thought.

I placed my beer on the bedside table, then pulled her gently into my chest, caressing her ear, gently sweeping her hair aside. I studied her face carefully before leaning in to kiss her, a soft reassuring kiss—nothing that would scare her away again.

My mouth drifted across her face, tasting, teasing, hovering over her eyelids, brushing over her chin, then returning to rest on her full lips.

Her hand crept up my stomach then inched across my chest, pausing for a moment just over my heart. I was sure she'd feel how fast it was beating, then my cool, calm cover would be blown.

She lifted her hand to cup my cheek, and I turned my face to kiss her palm.

I pulled her in more tightly, so she was half-lying across me, and I ran my hands up her spine while I kissed her neck. I was so turned on I was finding it hard to keep control as I ran my tongue over her throat, then tugged on her lower lip, begging to be inside her one way or another … and then I was, and my heart swooped and spun, like an airplane about to crash and burn.

She moaned against my lips, a long, drawn-out sigh of need and pleasure as she hooked her leg over my thigh, pulling our bodies closer together. My balls were aching and my dick was granite, trying to climb out of my jeans to get to her.

The kiss deepened, but whether it was her or me, I couldn't tell. My hands dropped to the waistband of her jeans and I pulled her t-shirt free, at last reaching bare skin, before I played with the elastic of her bra. *Too soon, moron!* My brain screamed at my dick, so I dropped my hands down to cup her ass.

She trembled, and I froze. *Was I pushing her too fast? Was this going to blow up in my face again?*

She pushed away from me and my heart jolted, but then she reached up to touch me.

"Are you sure, Caro?" I asked quietly.

"I'm sure," she said.

Then she sat up and pulled off her t-shirt. I nearly swallowed my tongue.

Her breasts were every bit as good as the warm flesh that had haunted me in too many dreams for too many years. I yanked my own t-shirt over my head, ignoring the ripping sound as they tangled with my dog tags. I was desperate to feel her skin against mine.

I reached for her again, but then paused, watching her eyes roam over my body. Most women liked what they saw—I hoped it still worked for her. Her fingers hovered over the top of my left arm.

"You got a tattoo?"

Yeah, women always liked that.

"Standard Marine issue," I joked.

I'd got the ink back in San Diego just after I'd graduated from boot camp. Most of my graduating class had done the same thing.

I let her fingers trace the shape while I slowly stroked the silky skin of her back.

"The Marine insignia, right?" she said. "What does it stand for?"

I smiled—I had no doubt she knew exactly what it stood for, but if she needed to take a moment, that was fine by me.

"The eagle represents the nation, well, protecting the nation—see the way its wings are spread out? The globe is our worldwide presence, and the anchor is because of our naval heritage."

Then she squinted her eyes to read the words written on the ribbon in the eagle's beak.

"*Semper fidelis*—always faithful," she whispered, her eyes serious.

I nodded. I wanted to tell her that I'd never stopped loving her, although I wasn't sure that was entirely true. She'd haunted me for so long, there were times when it had felt more like hate than love. I was one fucked up mofo.

She pressed her lips over my tattoo and then lay back on the bed, pulling me toward her. This time there was no uncertainty in her eyes, and I pressed her down into the mattress, kissing her hard. I let myself reach up to touch her beautiful breasts, my fingers roaming over the firm flesh, gliding my fingers under her bra and teasing the nipples until they were rigid.

I snapped her bra open easily and pushed the shoulder straps over her arms, tossing the lacey scrap of material onto the floor.

I tasted her, grazing my teeth over those tight little buds, hearing her biting out a moan of pleasure as she arched her back. I hooked my hand underneath, half lifting her off the bed.

She responded by dragging her nails down my spine, making me hiss with an edge of pain. My hips ground against her and I sucked the skin on her shoulder, biting hard enough so she could feel my teeth.

Her hands were all over me, and I was lost in the sensations of everything she was doing, but then she slid her hand inside the front of my jeans, and squeezed hard enough to make me see stars.

"Fuck, Caro!" I groaned.

Taking her lead, I pushed my hands underneath her waistband, stroking her ass, then moving to the front of her jeans and running my fingers under her panties, pulling gently on the soft curls, massaging her in slow circles, letting my index finger drift lower.

A woman didn't have to go bare to turn me on. Maybe because Caro had been my first, I'd always had a thing for manicured pussy. I'm not saying I liked an 80s bush, but completely bare was always something of an anti-climax. Just sayin'.

When I realized how wet she was, I nearly lost it; instead I forced myself to have some fucking control, and moved my fingers in and out slowly, building her up until she was crying out and moaning.

That just about finished me. I sat up quickly and unzipped her jeans, hauling them roughly down her legs, before catching my fingers through the fragile fabric of her panties and tossing them to the floor.

Now I had her naked, I touched her everywhere without apology: her chest, down her stomach, across her hips and along her thighs. Then I went for her sweet spot with my index finger, pressing hard, back and forth. *Target identified, take aim…*

She groaned, and pushed my hand away.

"No. You. I want you," she gasped.

Oh fucking yeah!

I unzipped my pants and stood to let them drop to the floor, but before I could lie down again, she knelt up on the edge of the bed, pushing her breasts into my chest, and grabbed a handful of my ass. Then she tugged my briefs down my hips and finally my dick was locked and loaded and ready for her.

She licked her lips in a way that had me breaking out in a sweat, and I bit back a groan as she ran one hand down my shaft and squeezed my balls with the other.

"Fuck, Caro!"

She rubbed the thumb over the sensitive head of my cock, and I couldn't help the shudder of pleasure that flooded through me.

I was one second from throwing her down and plowing into her, but then I remembered something pretty fucking important.

"Are you on the pill?"

She shook her head, a disappointed expression on her face. "I don't usually have a need for it. Please tell me you have condoms, otherwise 'making out' is all we're going to be doing."

Did she really think I was unprepared? I bent down and pulled a pack of condoms from the pocket of my leather jacket. *Oo-rah!*

"Just wondering," she said, glancing up at me, a small

smile threatening to break into a full-on grin, "but when did you buy them, or are they old stock?"

"Nope, new packet," I said, and tossed her the small box. "Check it out."

She toyed with the packet for a moment before looking up at me.

"So, no need to practice putting one on then?"

No way, baby. I knew she was teasing me, reminding me that as a horny 17-year-old, I'd admitted to her that I'd practiced putting on a condom so I'd be good to go if and when we ever got it together. Even then I'd been the poster boy for latex. I guess you could say I'd been wrapped and ready ever since.

"Well, I haven't practiced *that* recently," I said, challenging her with a look, "but I think I can remember what to do."

"You're avoiding the question," she said, her own challenge evident in her voice. "When did you buy these?"

"Second day of the hostile environment training."

Her mouth dropped open with surprise.

"But you were still mad at me then!"

"Didn't stop me wanting you," I replied truthfully.

She shook her head even as she smiled.

"Hmm, well. Let me see if *I* can remember what to do."

My smile was pretty damn big by now, and I stood in front of her with my hands on my hips, my dick making his own feelings pretty damn clear.

She tore open the box and pulled out a foil packet, running it down my length, and smacked it against the tip, making me jerk back.

"Whoa, careful!"

"Wimp!" she laughed "I thought you were a Marine not a mouse."

"Just be careful with my weapon," I shot back.

"Close your eyes and relax," she said, her voice suspiciously soothing.

"Why, what are you going to do?" I asked warily.

"Don't you trust me?" she smiled.

"Not with that look on your face," I muttered, but

closed my eyes anyway.

I heard the foil being ripped and I was expecting to feel her hands on my dick, but it was her warm, wet mouth that surrounded me, making my eyes fly open in surprise.

"Fuck!" I hissed, as she stroked me up and down, sucking gently.

I rested my hands on her shoulders, hoping my knees didn't give way, and couldn't help flexing deeper into her throat. She pulled back slightly, unwrapping her lips from her teeth, and making every part of me tremble. She sucked harder, and I was close to losing it.

"No, baby," I hissed, clenching my jaw. "I want to be inside you."

She didn't respond right away, and I faced the unappealing idea of pulling out when her teeth were still exposed. But then she gave another not-so-gentle tug and released me.

I shook my head, letting her know with my eyes that she wasn't going to go unpunished for that.

Caro just smiled up at me and ran her hands over my ass.

I nodded at the condom. "Just put that fucking thing on, Caro. You're killing me here."

"Oh, don't be such a baby, Sebastian," she scoffed. "We've waited ten years; you're not going to expire in the next 30 seconds."

"I wouldn't be too sure about that," I muttered.

She rolled the condom on so fucking slowly, I knew she was still teasing me. *So not happening.* I brushed her hands away as soon as she was finished.

"My turn," I said, and it wasn't a suggestion.

She lay back on the bed and raised her arms to pull me down.

No, baby. I'm in charge.

"Oh, I don't think so," I said. "My turn, remember? Pull your knees up."

"Yes, sir!" she barked, and threw a salute.

God, I loved the way her tits bounced when she did that.

"Are you mocking the US Marine Corps, lady?" I

70

pretended to snarl.

"Why? What are you going to do about it?" she asked, a challenge in her voice.

You'll see. Fuck, yeah!

She slid her feet up the bed, her knees wide apart. Her vulnerability made her apprehensive—and I was going to give her the tongue-lashing of her life; I'd make her pay for all that teasing. I gave her one more heated look and then my head was between her legs, my hands resting on the soft skin of her inner thighs.

I gave one long lick upwards and she moaned as her body convulsed. It was such a strong reaction even though I'd hardly started. I looked up, met her astonished gaze, and grinned back at her.

I circled my tongue around the nub, then penetrated her as deep as I could go, tasting her, touching her, arousing her until everything she felt ended in primal cries and groans, growing louder.

Needing to get still closer, I hooked my shoulders under her knees and lifted her lower body off the bed so her weight rested on her upper back.

Her orgasm was fast and powerful, but I didn't stop until her whole body was heated and limp, her face, chest and clit glowing.

I'd done a lot of shit with a lot of women, but seeing my Caro laid out before me like that, I was so fucking turned on that I knew I was a heartbeat away from shooting my bolt. And I couldn't wait.

I let her hips drop to the bed, then positioned myself over her.

"I've waited a very long time for this," I said. *Ten fucking years.*

I pushed inside her, increasing the pleasure, entering into her soft, wet pussy, inch by slow inch.

"Fuck, you feel so good, Caro. I can feel you all around me. *So fucking tight!*"

God, this was really familiar. How could it have been 10 years and still feel like it all happened yesterday? My body *knew* this, here, with her. It was fucking confusing.

She ran her nails lightly down my back again, pressing the tips of her fingers into my muscles.

I was trying to take it slowly, to make it last after all this time, but I couldn't. My body disengaged from my brain and I started thrusting faster. Caro's breath was burning across my chest, and I could feel her body trembling again. I looked down, even more aroused to see my dog tags dragging between her breasts, and below, my cock sliding in and out of her. That's when I lost it. I fucked her hard. I fucked her until there was nothing but sensation joining us.

I stared down into her beautiful brown eyes, eyes that scorched me with their trust, then I kissed her hard. But when she moaned out my name and tilted her hips up to meet me, my body and head exploded at the same time.

She wrapped her legs around me, locking her ankles behind my waist and her pussy clenched, milking every last bit.

My arms give way and I buried my face in her shoulder until my breathing began to return to normal.

After a moment's silence, I pressed my lips lightly against her neck, then pulled out slowly, holding onto the condom.

Fucking things. They did the job, but it was never as good as going bareback—something I'd only ever done with Caro, and then only a few times.

I rolled onto my back, peeling off the rubber and tossing it into the garbage can.

She still hadn't spoken and her silence was beginning to unnerve me. So I leaned up on one elbow to look at her, resting my free hand on my stomach and stroking her gently.

"Are you okay?" I asked, planting a quick kiss on the tip of her nose.

She avoided my eyes when she replied.

"Yes, I think so," she said carefully.

Then she pushed my hand away and sat up.

What the fuck?

"Where are you going?"

"Just to get some water," she said, still refusing to look at me.

She walked into the bathroom, pushing the door closed.
What the hell had just happened?

A few seconds later, I heard her running water into the sink and I waited for her to come out again, but she didn't. I rolled out of bed, hesitated for a second then pushed the bathroom door fully open.

She was standing in front of the mirror, a hairbrush held loosely in her hands.

"Caro, what's wrong?"

"Nothing," she said, a weird fake smile on her face. "I'm fine."

She didn't look fine. She looked totally freaked out—and her frozen expression was giving me chills.

I took the brush from her hands and carefully brushed out the tangles from her glossy brown hair. It was soft and silky and so familiar—it had haunted my dreams for long enough.

"You have beautiful hair, Caro. I'm glad you kept it long."

She shrugged, as if my words meant nothing.

"Every now and then I decide to get it cut off, especially after I've been somewhere I haven't been able to shower for a couple of weeks."

I couldn't believe she'd even consider it.

"That would be a crime," I said quietly.

"You can talk!" she snorted, pointing her chin at my buzz cut.

"Believe me, babe, I'd grow it if I could. Maybe I should go to my CO and tell him my girlfriend wants me to…"

Ah shit. So shouldn't have said that. She wasn't my girlfriend—I wasn't anything to her.

She sighed, our attempt at levity gone again, killed by a severe case of foot-in-mouth. I suspected it was terminal.

"It's okay," she said. "I keep forgetting which decade I'm in, too. It's so strange."

I nodded, relieved that she understood.

"Yeah, this is so weird, I feel the same. It's as if nothing's changed but everything's changed. It's like being in some crazy time machine. I keep expecting your husband to be banging down the door."

She winced, and I wanted to kick my own ass.

"Fuck, sorry. I'm doing it again."

She smiled painfully.

"Oh well, I imagine you've had some experience with husbands banging on the door."

No, I wasn't taking that hit.

"Don't, Caro."

Our eyes met in the mirror, then she pushed past me, back into the bedroom.

Fuck! Fuck! Fuck! Why did I keep on saying the wrong thing? I took a deep breath, then remembered that she'd come in here to get some water. I took the glass from beside the sink and filled it from the faucet.

When I walked back into the bedroom, she was sitting on the bed, her back toward me. I walked around and handed it to her. She took a small sip before placing it on the cabinet.

"Thank you."

I sat back on the bed, covering my lower half with the sheet. I tried to think of how to explain the confusion I felt—the confusion that she must feel, too. Our relationship, if you could call it that, had fallen apart 10 years ago, and now we were trying to fix it based on an hour of sex? Even I knew it would take more than that.

"Caro, I know this is fucking weird but it's good, too, isn't it? I mean, not everyone gets a second chance."

"Is that what this is, a second chance?" she snapped. "But a second chance at what? A second chance to rip ourselves apart again?"

She sounded pissed and made an obvious effort to calm herself.

"Today was fun," she said carefully, "and tonight was … good…"

Just good? I came so hard I saw stars.

"But the reality is this: I'm based in New York and spend between three and six months of the year away from home. You're a Marine and go wherever they send you. Presumably this next tour of Afghanistan will be six months or maybe longer? And then where, because let's face it,

Sebastian, the chances of you getting posted to the Corps' Division of Public Affairs in New York is slim to none—especially with your record. So I'm not sure what sort of 'second chance' you have in mind."

No way! No fucking way was she going to fuck us up again with this dumb crap!

I leapt off the bed, glaring down at her, fists clenched and trying not to yell.

"Christ, it's like listening to an old record, Caro! You *always* try to think of reasons why we can't be together!"

Her expression was confused.

"What do you mean 'always'? I haven't seen you for ten years."

"That's the whole fucking point!" I yelled, my determination to keep calm crumbling. "You used to say this shit to me when I was 17, and you're still doing it now. We wasted *10 years* and you're worried about a few thousand miles? Hell, we've got airplanes, we've got email, they've invented fucking cell phones. I could even take the shitty option of a billet on recruiting duty anywhere in the US. Jesus, if it comes down to it, I'll even write you a fucking letter!"

Her mouth dropped open then twisted as if she wasn't sure if she should laugh or cry.

"You write letters?" she asked.

My shoulders relaxed slightly, but I was still angry and determined to force the point.

"I'll write you on both sides of the fucking paper, Caro."

A smile quivered at the corners of her mouth.

"How can I refuse such an astonishing offer?"

"Are you laughing at me?" I snapped.

"Are you shouting at me?" she shot back.

"Yes!"

"Then, 'yes' to you, too." She sighed again. "Look, today, tonight—it's been fun. But like I said to you before, I'm really not looking to get tied down again. I work *a lot* and I love what I do. I'm still mad at you for screwing up my travel papers. I won't get paid until I've filed a story, and I won't be able to do *that* until I get to Leatherneck. All this time, I'm not earning—and I have a *very* expensive mortgage to finance."

I let my hands rest on my hips, not caring that I was utterly naked, and I looked her in the eye.

"I'm sorry about the money, Caro, and I'm sorry that I made you mad at me again, but I'm not sorry about what I did. I hoped I'd get a chance to spend some time with you, but I would have done it just to keep you safe."

She shook her head. "This is getting us nowhere."

Defeated, I sat down on the edge of the bed with my back to her, letting my head hang down.

Nothing I said seemed to change her mind. I took my final shot.

"Caro, I've got 17 days before I ship out. I'd like to spend them with you. That's all. If you don't want to see me after that … well, I guess that's it."

I turned to look at her over my shoulder.

"What do you say?"

CHAPTER 5

She didn't reply. I stood up, preparing to dress and leave before she broke me completely.

But then she spoke.

"I'm going to need a cushion to sit on if you expect me to ride on that motorcycle of yours all the way to Salerno."

She was saying yes?

"Really? You're sure?"

"Well, to paraphrase you, what the hell." She paused. "But I reserve the right to fly back if you're being too much of an ass."

I couldn't help the smile that spread across my face.

"Huh, well, you'd better give me a sliding scale of assaholic behavior, just so I know."

She raised an eyebrow. "That could be quite a long list."

"Try me."

"Okay," she said, sitting up straight and diving right in. "First, no getting drunk and passing out in my bed; second, no more interference in my career *of any kind*—that's a deal breaker; third, no territorial displays of adolescent jealousy; fourth…"

Wow, that list was getting long already.

I jumped on her, pinning her to the mattress, my kisses hard and determined. They weren't the only things that were hard—just being near her was enough to get the juices flowing, and my dick was fighting its way through her bathrobe. But then she pushed me off.

"What was that all about?" she asked breathlessly.

I shrugged.

"It sounded like a very long list, I thought I'd try to

distract you."

"Diversionary tactics?"

"Yeah, we're schooled on that in the Marines," I agreed, my lips twitching with a smile.

"I bet you are! And by the way," she said, pointing at my dick, "you can put that away—I'm exhausted. Somebody dragged me all over Switzerland and half of France today."

"Sure I can't persuade you?" I asked, leaning down to bite her thigh.

She jumped and pulled her robe together tightly.

"Quite sure, thank you. This forty-year-old woman needs her beauty sleep."

God, that made me furious. She was beautiful—anyone could see it. Anyone but her, apparently. It irritated the fuck out of me that she was still playing the same riff from ten years ago.

"I wish you wouldn't do that, Caro."

"Do what?" she asked, blinking in surprise.

"Keep going on about your age. You're older than me— I get it. And guess what? I don't give a shit. I never did. I just wish you weren't so hung up about it. It's kind of annoying."

Her mouth dropped open in shock.

"Feel free to say what you really mean, Hunter!"

I grinned at her. "Okay."

She shook her head and folded her arms across her chest, but I could tell that she wasn't really angry.

"So, we can go tomorrow?" I asked. "Start our road trip?"

"Well, I suppose so. But I don't know how we'll get my suitcase on the back of your motorcycle."

"Don't worry about that. We'll just take what you need and leave it at my place till we get back." *So far, so good. Time to take another step.* "So, can I stay the night, or are you going to kick me out into the cold, dark world, all alone in a strange city, where foreign women might try and have their evil way with me?"

Her eyebrow lifted as she stared back at me.

"That's a sob story, if ever I heard one, although I strongly suspect it's a highly edited one."

"Is that a yes?" I asked hopefully.

"It's a yes, providing sleep is what you had in mind."

Nope. "Mostly. Good enough?"

She shook her head, capitulating immediately. She really hadn't put up much of a fight.

"Fine. You want to use the bathroom first?"

"No, go ahead."

I lay back on the bed, grinning up at the ceiling. Twenty-four hours ago it had seemed impossible that I'd ever be here again. Then I frowned, wondering what the reality was of making this work. I was a Marine: I went where they sent me. But then I figured other guys had wives and families—why couldn't I? Sure, there'd be compromises, problems, but we'd deal.

I took my turn in the bathroom and let her enjoy the floor show as I strolled around naked. If using my body was going to get her to give me a chance, that worked just fine for me. So, wearing my dog tags and a big smile, I sat down next to her then crawled across her body, dipping down to take a nipple in my mouth.

"Sebastian, what are you doing?" she gasped.

"Taking a shortcut," I said, then stole another kiss.

She reached up and pulled me deeper into the kiss before pushing lightly on my chest.

"Sleep! Now!"

"Sure I can't change your mind?" I asked, eyeing the boner that was beginning to make its presence felt.

"Oh, put it away!" she gulped, unable to take her eyes off my dick. "I'm tired."

There was always tomorrow. And I was a big fan of morning sex.

So I let her win that one, sliding under the duvet on the other side of the bed.

She turned off the light, and in the darkness of the room I sighed in contentment as my hand drifted over her waist. I kissed the back of her neck softly.

"Night, baby."

As I fell into a deep sleep, I wondered if this time life would bring us back together or push us further apart.

It was barely light when I woke abruptly. Caro was thrashing around in the bed, fighting the duvet, her eyes screwed shut and a terrified wail surging from her throat. Whatever she was dreaming about, it was some scary shit.

I shook her awake and her panicked eyes blinked up at me.

"Caro, are you okay?"

She didn't reply immediately, rubbing her hands over her face as awareness leaked back into her eyes.

"Oh, sorry, did I wake you up?" her voice trembled. "I was dreaming."

"It sounded more like a nightmare."

"Sorry. Yes, I'm okay."

It hurt that she wouldn't tell me what had upset her. It made me realize there was a lot we didn't know about each other. And a hell of a lot I had to hide.

She shivered and sat up, the duvet slipping down to her waist. I lost my train of thought as I stared hungrily at her breasts.

"Your eyes are going to fall out, Hunter," she muttered.

"Just looking, boss," I grinned.

She stood up, stretching stiffly, then picked up her bathrobe and shuffled into the bathroom.

I lay back on the pillows with my hands behind my head, planning out the route and how long it would take to get to Genoa. I'd planned on driving further than that, but Caro had made it clear that riding pillion wasn't her most favorite thing.

But when she reappeared from bathroom, her whole face was lit with a sexy smile. Damn, that was a turn on.

"Hi," I said, wondering what she was thinking.

"Hi yourself."

"You seem better."

"Why, Warrant Officer Hunter," she smirked at me, "what masterful skills of observation you have."

"Yeah, much better."

"Well, now that you mention it, I am in a much better mood, although I'm rather hungry."

"Do you want to go down for breakfast or should I call room service?"

"Let me think about that for a minute."

I was already reaching for the phone when she untied her robe and pulled the belt out of the loops, winding it through her fingers. I froze, watching the robe slide to the floor, leaving a very naked Caro standing there. *Fuck. Me.*

"I was thinking about eating *you*," she purred, "but as you're such a stubborn, annoying man, who makes me pissed with every other sentence he utters from between his beautiful, badly-behaved lips, I thought I'd better tie you up first. What do you say?"

My mouth dropped open.

"I'd say, where is Carolina Venzi and what have you done with her?" I managed to croak out.

Her grin grew wider. "I'm just taking your advice, Hunter."

I shook my head, confused, but liking where this conversation was going.

"I don't know what advice I gave you, but it must have been damn good."

"Let's find out, should we? Put your hands on the headboard."

"Yes, ma'am."

I wrapped my hands through the metal framework as Caro crawled up the bed, her thighs straddling my body. Then she threaded the belt through the headboard and tied both wrists tightly.

"Have you done this before?" I breathed out.

"Only in my dreams, Hunter. Now, be quiet, or I might have to gag you, too."

My mouth went dry. "Fuck!"

"Maybe later," she replied, her voice low and teasing.

Then she whipped the duvet off the bed and stared down at my erection.

"Now that's a sight for sore eyes, Sebastian. Maybe I should just leave you here: the hotel maids might appreciate that. Or, better still, maybe I'll take a photograph of you on my phone. Don't worry, I won't post it on the internet, it'll just be my screensaver."

What the fuck? Was she serious? Was this some sort of payback?

The look in her eye was making me nervous.

"Caro!" I said, a serious warning in my voice.

"Spoilsport," she said, pretending to pout at me. "No sense of adventure."

I was relieved this was part of the game, but I felt vulnerable, too. I'd never let a woman tie me up before. I mean yeah, I was all for bedroom games, but I preferred to be the one in control. Everything was different with Caro.

I tested the strength of her knots—they were pretty tight. I could probably get out of them, but only by destroying the headboard. That was plan B—I hoped plan A involved more sex and less damage to property.

She leaned forward and placed a kiss on each of my biceps before sliding back down my body.

I licked my lips as she knelt across my shins and then ran her tongue from my balls to my tip. *Holy fuck! That was…*

But then she climbed off the bed and disappeared into the bathroom.

"Where are you going?"

"Back in a minute," she called.

Shit. What was she doing? I rattled the headboard and yelled out.

"Caro! What the fuck?"

"Are you getting impatient, Sebastian?" she called back.

"Fuck, Caro!"

But then she strolled back into the bedroom, pulling her hair into a ponytail. "Couldn't see what I was doing," she explained, her impassive face hiding a grin.

"There's going to be payback for this, Venzi," I warned her.

"Bring it on, Marine."

She knelt back on the bed and ran her hands over my chest and stomach, then took my dog tags in her mouth and sucked hard.

Damn, she looked sexy doing that. I closed my eyes, breathing in deeply.

My whole body was on fire as she kissed, nipped, bit, licked and sucked her way downwards. When she found a sensitive spot, I couldn't help bucking my hips, cursing wildly, losing my final shred of control.

"Sebastian, your language!" she teased.

When she ran her tongue down my dick and held my precious man-jewels in her teeth, I stopped breathing altogether. If she didn't stop soon, this was going to get very ugly.

I may have sent up a prayer of thanks when she released me without injury or maiming, but I wouldn't say I relaxed because she kissed the tip of my dick and then took all of me in her mouth. It was the mother, father and holy spirit of all blow jobs, and I think she took me from heaven to hell and back again.

She started increasing the speed at the same time she increased the pressure, and I knew I was close. I tried to warn her, but it was too late. I thought I was going to pass out as I shot my wad into her mouth and she swallowed around me. I saw stars, galaxies, whole fucking universes as my heart pounded hard enough to break through my chest.

When I felt strong enough to push against the ton weights that were resting on my eyelids, she was snuggled up on the bed next to me. I swallowed several times before I could speak.

"Jeez, Caro! That was ... that was ... wow!" I tried to pull her into my arms but realized I was still tied to the headboard. "Are you going to untie me now?"

She shook her head sleepily. "Don't think so. I like having you as my beck-and-call boy."

I laughed quietly, then rattled the headboard again. "Seriously, I want to hold you."

Grumbling to herself, she untied my wrists. I flexed my hands as the blood began to flow again, a tingling sensation shooting up each arm.

"Where did you teach yourself to do that?" I asked teasingly, as she settled back onto my chest.

"Night school," she said with a yawn.

I laughed and kissed her shoulder. "Is it my turn now?"

"I thought you wanted to take me on a road trip," she said sleepily

"Yeah, but I could be quick..."

She was definitely considering it and my dick twitched back into life. Bastard never knew when he was beaten.

"I'll take a rain check," she said at last.

Wrong answer.

"Okay. In that case, I guess we should get going."

I started stroking her ass with one hand, and teasing her nipple with the other.

"What are you doing?" she asked, her eyes still closed.

"Nothing," I whispered, as my hands drifted down and I slipped a finger inside her.

She gasped and her eyes flew open.

"Sebastian!"

My name came out in a long moan.

"Shh, baby," I said, reaching for another condom.

She wouldn't let me shower with her afterward, on the grounds that we wanted to leave the hotel before nightfall. She was packing up her suitcase when I finished my shower, although that didn't stop her checking me out, and yeah, I may have posed for her, enjoying the feel of her eyes on my body again after all these years.

I dressed quickly and watched as she pushed her camera into her bag. That and the laptop she used looked expensive. I guess they were the tools of her trade, but it also showed that she was a serious and successful journalist. I was proud of her for achieving her goals, but it made me wonder what she was doing with me. God, I hoped this wasn't just a pity fuck.

"Do you want to get breakfast here?" I asked, going for a casual tone. "You didn't eat anything after lunch yesterday."

She shook her head.

"No, it'll take too long. You must know some little café we could stop at? Maybe on the lake?"

"Yeah, okay. But I need to swing by my place first and pick up a few things."

We headed down to the lobby, and while she went to settle her bill, I collected my bike from the hotel's underground garage.

Then I drove to the front entrance and lifted the visor as

I reached for her suitcase.

"Where are you going to put it?" she asked, her voice bemused.

It was a good thing she traveled light, because I was going to have wedge the suitcase between me and the handlebars. I nodded at her to get on behind me.

It wasn't exactly legal to travel like that, but we weren't going far.

When I cut the engine outside my apartment, Caro pulled off her helmet and almost fell sideways off of the bike. I couldn't help smiling at the chagrined look on her face.

"Nothing to laugh at, Hunter. Just because you're about a foot taller than me," she huffed.

"Shrimp," I said, then had to dodge out of the way as she tried to swat my backside.

"You're feisty this morning," I grinned at her. "I think I like it."

She muttered something I couldn't hear—probably just as well.

I grabbed her suitcase and opened the door into the hallway.

"Sorry," I told her, "no lights."

My apartment was at the top of three flights and I'd chosen it for the view. I didn't need much, but it occurred to me that it might look a bit bare to her.

"This is it."

She stepped into the room and gazed around, an oddly blank look on her face. I frowned, trying to see the place through her eyes. The walls were painted white, and my single bed was covered with a USMC-issue blanket and pushed against one wall. Some old paperbacks were resting on the bookshelf and my dress uniform was hanging from a hook on the wall, still inside a drycleaner's bag.

I had a wooden chair by the window and a chest of drawers next to the door with my iPod and laptop.

I pointed toward the window.

"It's got a great view."

Caro walked over to stare out across the tiled rooftops toward the lake.

"Yes," she agreed softly, "very pretty."

I shrugged. "It's all I need."

She turned away, taking a moment to flick through my books.

I resisted shoving my hands into my pockets. Shit like that got drilled out of you in the Marines, but I felt exposed having her here in my room.

"Still the Conrad fan," she said, her voice sounding tight, like she was in the grip of some strong emotion.

Because I read Conrad? I know 'Heart of Darkness' isn't exactly a chuckle a page, but it's a classic, right?

"You should get yourself an e-reader," she said, trying to find a normal tone of voice. "The whole of Conrad's oeuvre for two bucks."

I was reaching under the bed for my overnight bag, so my voice came out muffled.

"Yeah, I guess I should—if I knew there'd always be somewhere to charge it up when I'm in some shithole Stone Age village."

I was being polite, but an e-reader would have been fucking useless for me when I was in Iraq or Afghanistan. With the kind of jobs I was given, I didn't get to go back to the main camp at night; I'd be in some godforsaken village, eating air-dried goat, and trying to persuade some village elders to work with us. I could be gone for weeks at a time. And even some of the guys who got stationed in the ass-end of nowhere like Helmand Province where I was going next, they could be there for months. No laptops or skype chats, just 20 minutes of sat-phone home a week, if you were lucky. Not that I'd ever had anyone to call. Most of the time I gave up my minutes to one of the married guys. It was hard enough to keep a relationship going when you were overseas.

I tossed my bag on the bed, then pulled a bunch of my t-shirts out of the drawers, along with skivvies and a couple of pairs of socks.

"What happened to all the colors?" Caro blurted out suddenly.

Puzzled, I turned to look at her. For some reason she looked upset.

"Sebastian, the most colorful thing in this room are your Dress Blues," she cried. "The first time I saw you again, you were wearing those ridiculously bright red boardshorts."

I looked down at the pile of white t-shirts, gray briefs and black socks. I kind of saw what she meant. And I remembered those boardshorts.

"Oh yeah. I've still got those somewhere. In a box in Ches's garage, I think."

"It sounds like Ches has all your worldly possessions."

I could hear something that sounded like sadness in her voice, although I didn't understand why.

"Pretty much. I didn't take a lot when I left my parents' place. But what the hell—it's easy to pack up and move on when you're not laden down."

She looked so sad and I hated to think that look was for me. I didn't need her pity. I changed the subject.

"Caro, how much of this stuff do you need?" I asked, pointing at her suitcase. No way we could take that into Italy.

"I definitely need my laptop and notebooks…"

"I mean clothes, Caro. I wouldn't dare suggest to a reporter that she goes anywhere without the tools of her trade."

"That's right," she said sharply. "You'd just stop her going where she needed to go in the first place."

Were we back to that? I wasn't going to apologize again for wanting to spend time with her. I decided that ignoring her comment would be best for both of us. Maybe she thought the same thing, because she started digging through her suitcase and putting clothes into my overnight bag.

"See," she said, pointing. "Pink, green, blue, yellow and orange t-shirts. These are called 'colors'. They're what you get when you're not wearing black, white or gray."

"My jeans are blue," I smirked at her.

She rolled her eyes. "So they are, Sebastian. Way to go."

"I could maybe get into colors," I commented, holding up a really fucking sexy lace bra in dark pink.

"I don't think it would suit you," she smiled.

"No," I said evenly, "but I'm really looking forward to taking it off you."

"That's assuming you get lucky, Hunter," she shot back. "You promised me separate rooms, remember?"

Ah shit, I did say that, didn't I?

"You're not going to hold me to that, are you, Caro?"

Her bright smile was teasing.

"I don't know—depends how irritating you are."

"What if I promise to be on my best behavior, ma'am?"

"Mmm, maybe. I was impressed how well you took orders earlier today."

Oh fucking yeah!

"And there'll be payback for that, Ms. Venzi," I said challengingly.

She tried to step away as I paced toward her, but I caught her in my arms, brushing against her cheek and kissing her throat.

"And I'm looking forward to collecting. Maybe we should christen this bed," I said, tugging her toward it.

"Christen it?" she said, sounding surprised. "I would have thought it had seen plenty of action."

I paused, looking up at her. *She still didn't get it.*

"No, you're the first woman I've brought here. It's … private."

Her eyes widened, then she wrapped her arms around my neck, pulling my head down, meeting my lips with a kiss that had me hardening against her thigh.

"We'll christen it when we get back," she whispered.

"Something to look forward to."

She pulled away and continued with her packing. It didn't take long. Not like some women who take an hour just to re-touch their lipstick and put on a sweater. I guessed that being a journalist she was used to packing fast.

"Okay, I'm done," she said, zipping up the bag. "By the way, where exactly are we going? It's a pretty long way to Salerno, so I presume we're going to stop somewhere en route."

"Yeah, it's just over 1100 kilometers, so…"

"Give me that in good, old-fashioned US miles."

I laughed.

"Seven hundred miles. I thought we'd stop at Genoa

tonight—that's just under 200 miles—take us about four hours."

Or less, if she let me drive the speed I liked to go.

"How come you know all these distances off the top of your head?" she asked, as I stuffed a map of Italy into my jacket pocket.

"I've been planning to do this road trip for a while." She seemed surprised. "You and I talked about it once, you remember? All the things we were going to do, all the places we were going to see? I just figured that as I was here, I'd go anyway. And … I remembered that you said your dad came from that village near Salerno. I thought I might find … I don't know what I thought. I just wanted to see it."

Shit, I was telling her too much too soon. I didn't want to come over like I'd done nothing but obsess over her for the last ten years, even though that was pretty close to the truth.

She shook her head in disbelief, but at least she was smiling.

Outside, I loaded up the bike, packing everything away into the saddlebags.

"We could go straight to Genoa, using the Mont Blanc tunnel," I suggested, "but I really like the idea of going up through the high pass. There'll still be quite a bit of snow around—you up for that?"

I didn't want to stress her out by saying that the mountain route was 100 percent hairpin turns.

She weighed the options, then said, "I vote for the route over the Alps."

I picked her up, swinging her around, then kissed her firmly.

"God, you're amazing, woman!"

"Wait, I should write that down," she laughed, pretending to make a grab for her notebook.

"No way! You might use that against me in court. Do I have the right to an attorney?"

"Get on the damn bike, Sebastian, before I change my mind."

I could definitely get used to the feel of her thighs against mine as she sat pillion on the bike.

Before we left Geneva, we had a quick breakfast of sweet rolls and coffee in a café overlooking the lake, then headed up into the mountains. Soon we were seeing heaps of snow at the sides of the road. Some were as high as six or seven feet: they'd been piled up by snowplows clearing the road. I was glad I'd insisted that Caro got some quality ski gloves to keep her hands warm. The woman argued too much.

A couple of miles later we really began to climb; the asphalt disappeared and we were riding on compressed snow. I dropped the speed as the hairpin turns began to take us up the mountain.

Caro lost her relaxed posture and tried to sit up straight when I leaned into the bends. She was throwing off the balance and making the bike wobble. I pulled to the side of the road and flipped up my visor.

"Baby, you're going to tip us over if you do that, and I don't know about you, but it looks like a helluva long way down to me."

"What … what did I do?" she asked, nervously staring at the vertical drop.

"You're trying to sit upright on the bike: don't. You've got to lean into it or the balance goes for shit. Don't try and do anything, just sit real tight and hang onto me."

She swallowed several times as her eyes tracked down the sheer mountainside.

"Okay, good safety tip. Glad you mentioned it."

Her hands gripped my waist even more tightly as I drove off slowly, keeping the speed low, the bike zigzagging up the mountain. The views were stunning and I decided to stop at the highest pass, allowing Caro to enjoy the scenery.

I cut the engine and turned around to smile at her.

"It's really something, isn't it?"

She clambered from the bike awkwardly and tugged off her helmet, shaking her hair free.

"Wow," she breathed.

I couldn't agree more—but I wasn't looking at the view.

While she was staring down to Geneva spread out below us, the lake mirror-like in the sun, the valley of Z-bends that we'd just driven up, the sky too blue to be real, I was looking at her. I felt grateful to be here: this woman, this time, this place. Second chances didn't come any better.

"Thank you for this, Sebastian," she breathed. "Thank you for bringing me."

Thank you for giving me another chance, Caro.

She leaned into my body and I wrapped my arms around her, taking the time to appreciate her soft lips. She deepened our kiss immediately, her tongue moving possessively into my mouth—and I loved it.

Oo-rah.

When she pulled away, her face was flushed, and I was wondering if it was too cold for outdoor sex at the top of a mountain pass in the snow.

She must have guessed what I was thinking, because she said, "Save it, Marine. We've got a long way to go yet."

I stood back while she snapped some photographs, then helped her climb onto the Honda. Moving slowly until the roads cleared, we started the steep descent down through the Alps to Italy. It was strange that I felt such a connection to a country I'd never been to before. Caro's father was born near Salerno and I wanted to see his village. He'd been the only real parental figure I'd ever met until I was 14 and Ches's family moved to San Diego. He'd been the one to start teaching me Italian, and it was from him I'd learned what a father should be. Taking this journey with Caro was the past crashing into the present. I wasn't used to feeling so much.

A short while later, I pointed at a sign that read 'Italia', and then we were showing our passports to a border guard who was eyeing Caro with appreciation. Not that she noticed—she never did.

We were 20 Km from Genoa when the ocean came into view. It was a deep dark blue, calm with no waves, and white colonial-style villas followed the tree-line upward.

I took the shore road, passing dozens of concrete docks filled with yachts and expensive motor-cruisers as well as huge cargo vessels. Nothing military that I could see.

We drove through the city center, cruising past buildings that were hundreds of years old and what looked like a real castle on the top of the hill.

I stopped briefly to check the map. "Not far now," I told Caro.

She gave me a quick thumbs up, and I headed up the mountain. Our route took us off the main drag, and we bumped up a steep and stony road. A sign next to a small, whitewashed villa welcomed us to 'Casa Giovina'.

I pulled up, but let the engine idle.

"This is it. It only has one guest room, but it's out of season ... want to try it?"

When I'd planned this trip, I hadn't expected to have company. The places I'd chosen to stay might be a bit basic for Caro's taste. She was used to upscale hotels on her newspaper's budget; she might not like my choices. I didn't need the reminder that I didn't know her so well anymore.

But then she smiled and I felt the tension ease from my shoulders.

"It looks charming. Let's go see, but if the owners have a pretty daughter, we're out of here."

Was that a joke?

An old woman dressed in black opened the door.

"Posso aiutarvi?"

"I hope you can help us," Caro replied, in Italian. "We were wondering if you had a room for the night?"

It was a good thing that I'd let Caro do the talking, because the old lady was eyeing me like she was afraid I was going to burglarize the place. I was pretty certain she wouldn't have let me across the threshold if I'd been by myself.

"Are you married?" the old woman asked, folding her arms across a pair of enormous tits. I was afraid to look at them—I couldn't help thinking that if they weren't covered up, they'd be hanging by her ankles. I shuddered at the thought.

Caro was stuttering out a surprised answer when a man in his fifties hurried down the corridor.

"Mama! You can't ask people questions like that! I apologize—my mother is very old-fashioned. Are you French?"

"No, American."

"But you speak Italiano! Americans never speak our language."

I decided he might respond better to a man, so I rolled out the Italian I knew, although it wasn't as fluent as Caro's.

"We mean no disrespect to your mother—this beautiful woman is my fiancée," I lied, "but if your mother would feel more comfortable, I will happily sleep in a separate room."

I already knew that they only had one guest room—as did Caro. I kept my expression neutral, waiting for his answer.

"No, no, that won't be necessary," said the owner, as his mother rolled her eyes to heaven and crossed herself twice. "Besides, we have only one room. Please, come in."

The room was sparse, filled by a large old-fashioned bed, but the views out toward the ocean sold me on the room. Caro was smiling, which I guess meant she approved, too.

"The bathroom is across the hall, signore; it is to share."

The owner shrugged in apology, but it didn't bother me and Caro didn't look fazed either.

"Breakfast is at 8AM, signore, signorina. There is a ristorante just two kilometers up the road. It is very good—run by my brother."

"That sounds great."

We hadn't stopped after our quick breakfast, and my stomach was growling.

"Ah, signore, one more thing: if you would refrain from riding your motorcycle after dark. My mother doesn't sleep well, you understand, and she has the room next to yours."

"That won't be a problem," Caro muttered, once he left. "I'm not getting on that thing again tonight if you pay me."

"Feeling a little tender, Ms. Venzi," I asked, pulling her toward me and rubbing my hands over her ass.

"Not really. It's more the feeling that I'm still in motion."

"I know something that will cure that," I offered suggestively.

"Would that have anything to do with taking off our clothes and making mad, passionate love on that bed?" she asked, frowning at me.

Busted.

"It might have," I admitted, eyeing her warily.

"Oh, alright then. I'll try anything once."

"Is that a yes?" I asked, hoping I hadn't misheard.

"Yes, that's a yes," she stated, her eyes glittering. "But you'll have to hurry—the ristorante probably closes before midnight."

I glanced at my wristwatch, completely confused. "It's only five o'clock?"

"Like I said—you'll have to hurry."

Okay, now I was on the same page. Damn! I liked the way she thought.

"Well, in that case, woman, you're wearing too many clothes."

"By the way," she said, taking a step away from me, "your *fiancée?*"

"Seemed like a good idea at the time."

"Hmm, well, I like *my* idea better—the one where we commit as many sins as possible in the shortest amount of time."

And, to make her point, she unzipped my jacket and ran her hands down my chest, before tracing a finger around the waistband of my jeans.

I was there. I was *so* there, and then some bastard knocked at the door. I yanked it open, ready to take the fucker's head off, a murderous look on my face. It had the villa's owner taking a couple of steps back.

"Ah, mi scusi, signore, signorina," he stuttered, throwing nervous glances in my direction. "I have just telephoned my brother: he is closing at 7:30PM tonight. If you wish to eat there, it would be best if you leave now."

"Thanks," I said, in a tone that telegraphed my extreme fucking displeasure.

Caro was trying to hide her wide smile—it wasn't working. "Rain check?"

"Looks like," I grumbled, adjusting the un-fucking-comfortable boner in my jeans.

"Never mind," she smiled. "Come on, let's get you fed

and then I can have my wicked way with you."

That got my attention, but did nothing to ease the tension in my pants.

"How wicked?"

"Not that wicked, so stop drooling. Just moderately naughty—it's been a long day."

I was pretty sure I could change her mind.

CHAPTER 6

We climbed the steep road to the ristorante, and I kept her hand in mine the entire way. I wasn't usually the kind of pussy-whipped guy who held hands, and believe me it's not something you do a lot of in the Marines, unless you're talking hand-to-hand combat. I wouldn't mind doing some of that with Caro—I was looking forward to seeing her capitulate, naked, coming apart under me.

I was so preoccupied with my plans for later on in the evening that we arrived at the ristorante before I realized it. So much for my skills of observation—if I didn't get it together before the flight to Afghanistan, I'd be a fucking health hazard.

I was surprised to see that this out-of-the-way place was almost full and a load of kids were running around. Happy families—not something I knew much about.

The noise tailed off when they saw us. I heard the word 'Americani' whispered several times before the owner came over.

I guess his brother hadn't given him the heads-up, because he seemed stunned when we spoke Italian and that we were happy to eat whatever was available. I don't know where he got his opinions of Americans, but after years of eating MREs, he could have served me road kill, and if it had good gravy, I'd eat it.

There was no chance of having a table to ourselves, so I resigned myself to having to share Caro for a few hours. The unfamiliar feeling of jealousy seemed to be hovering near the surface ever since she'd been parachuted back into my life. It was a fucking uncomfortable feeling and it was making me act like a possessive asshole—something that definitely wasn't going to impress her. I needed to regroup, so maybe it was just as well that we were seated at the corner end of one of the long tables, wedged in next to a family of seven.

They were wary of us at first, but when I shrugged out of my leather jacket, a little girl of about five or six noticed my tattoo and asked her mom about the 'picture'.

Her mother tried to hush her up, but I smiled and used my limited Italian to explain that the tattoo was because Marines were warriors of the sea and the 'picture' reminded me of my work.

"Is that because you forgot?" she asked, running her hands over the globe and anchor.

The whole room burst into laughter as I smiled wryly.

After that I guess I was her new best friend, because she kept up a stream of questions that meant I hardly got a chance to eat my meal, although I managed to chug down some of the local wine. Then she reached up to run her hands over my regulation buzz cut, but it was the look of longing and sadness in Caro's eyes that caught my attention.

Ten years ago she'd wanted children, but somehow it had never happened for her. I had no idea why, because she was fucking beautiful. I'd be lying if I said it didn't get me thinking.

The meal finished with small bowls of honey ice cream, although Caro was such a lightweight, I finished most of hers, too.

"Having fun, baby?"

She smiled back at me.

"Do you realize this is our first dinner-date?"

No way. "What about back in San Diego—that Sicilian place?"

"That doesn't count," she laughed. "You wouldn't let me finish because you wanted to drag me back to the hotel."

"Oh yeah, I definitely remember that!" I grinned, eyeing her speculatively.

"Besides, your *friend*, Brenda, was spying on us. I'm half expecting to see her now, tossing her hair over her shoulder and thrusting her boobs in your face like she used to."

I was amused by the jealousy I heard in *her* voice. If this was a two-way thing, I guess I didn't have to feel so bad.

"She thrust her boobs in my face?"

"Don't pretend like you didn't notice," she accused. "Anyway, if any boobs are to be thrust in your face, they'll be mine. Right, Hunter?"

Yeah, she was definitely tanked.

"Anything you say, boss. Looking forward to it."

"But then I was thinking," she went on, "if this is our first date, I probably shouldn't sleep with you. I don't want you thinking I'm easy."

Seriously? She thought she could win this game with me? Trained in strategy and tactics, baby. I pulled out my phone and started scrolling through the numbers.

"Who are you calling?" she asked, sounding pissed that I wasn't following her script.

"Well, my date just told me she wouldn't sleep with me, so I thought I'd see if I had Brenda's number on speed dial."

Caro winced, then sat back in her chair, her arms folded across her chest. Yep, I loved it when she did that—it pushed up her tits like she was serving them on a plate … or maybe an all-you-can-eat buffet.

"Fine, fine. I'll sleep with you," she pretended to huff. "But if my reputation is in ruins, it's all your fault."

I winked at her, then stood up to pay the bill.

As we left the ristorante, a chorus of good wishes followed us and the little girl blew me kisses, deciding that she was naming me 'Angelo'—because I was blond, I guess.

I wasn't feeling angelic—although I had something in mind that would have Caro calling me 'God'. I pushed her up against the wall and kissed her hard, thrusting my tongue into her mouth, slow and possessive, gripping her waist with one hand, pressing the other over her mound.

I knew she could feel my rock hard dick against her hip, and I was seriously considering taking her there and then, but the ristorante started emptying and suddenly we had an audience.

Trying to catch my breath, I let Caro push gently on my shoulders.

"Should we try and make it back to our room this time?" she asked, her voice husky.

"Good idea," I muttered. "I don't think I could take a third interruption in one evening."

The moon lit our path as we headed back down the hill. Caro didn't seem to be in much of a hurry, but energy and desire was making me want to grab her caveman-style and run the rest of the way so I could fuck her senseless. The Marines teach you to target your objective and put a plan together that will achieve it with the least amount of effort or risk. Just sayin'.

When we got back to Casa Giovina, the villa was in near darkness. A small lamp glowed in the hallway, and Caro crept up the stairs as if she was afraid of being caught. It was pretty damn funny.

She grabbed her toiletry bag and ran into the bathroom, so I stripped off my shirt and kicked off the boots and socks. When she hurried back in, I have to admit I enjoyed the open look of desire on her face.

"Seems like *your* eyeballs are the ones in danger of falling out, Ms. Venzi," I couldn't help teasing her.

"That is true, so hurry up and get your ass back in my bed."

Fuckin' A!

"Yes, boss!"

I almost sprinted into the bathroom, tried my best to piss through a semi, forcing myself to concentrate so I didn't spray the floor. Then I brushed my teeth and strode back into the bedroom, a man on a mission.

Caro was sitting in the bed, the sheet pulled up tightly across her chest, an odd expression on her face. Women usually liked the jeans and bare chest look, so I was kind of irritated that she seemed as though she was trying not to laugh.

"What?" I snapped.

"Nothing," she said, snorting back a giggle.

"What's so funny?"

She shook her head, holding a hand over her mouth, but her laughter had left my dick as soft as Jello.

Jee-zus, what did a guy have to do to get laid?

I stripped out of the rest of my clothes, yanked the sheets back and started to slide over to her, but the bed creaked so loudly, it sounded like a round from an M-16 cracking over my head. I couldn't help flinching and Caro laughed out loud.

"Sorry! I think we got the you're-not-married-so-you-damn-well-won't-be-getting-any bed. It's got a built-in anti-screwing alarm."

Okay, so it was pretty funny, but I had the target in my sights, and it would take a tank running over the villa to divert my attention right now.

"You think a noisy bed is going to stop me?"

Caro looked taken aback.

"The old lady is right next door! She doesn't sleep well—remember?"

"I can't help that. Besides, it'll bring back happy memories for her."

She raised an eyebrow.

"Huh, you think you're that good?"

Wrong question.

I gave her a smile full of promise, then ducked down under the sheets. As I ran my workout-roughened fingers across the soft skin of her inner thighs, her body tensed up. But when I licked up the length of her slit, a ragged groan spilled out of her.

"Oh, God!" she sighed, her voice muffled by the pillow she'd pulled over her head to stifle her moans.

"Yes, baby?" I laughed at her.

I gave her a few more licks and sucks, nipping at her clit in a way that had her almost levitating off of the bed, then replaced my tongue with my fingers. The mattress creaked and groaned loudly, protesting as I slinked over her, resting my weight on my forearms, my dick pressing into the soft flesh of her stomach.

Soon she was writhing under me and when I sucked her left nipple into my mouth, she fell apart, calling my name loudly.

Her body trembled and a deep, pink flush spread across

her whole body, leaving her looking heated and satisfied.

So far, so good.

"Still embarrassed by the bed?" I teased.

She didn't reply, her chest rising and falling rapidly as she gasped in oxygen.

The mattress creaked again as I slid off to dig out a condom from my toiletry bag.

"You want to do this, baby?" I suggested, holding it out to her.

She blinked up at me, still spiraling down from her orgasm. I waited, but she didn't seem capable of speech, so I took that as a no. I tugged my dick a couple of times, *lock and load*, kind of like priming a rifle, sending a bullet into the chamber, then rolled the rubber down, making sure it was in place.

"Roll over, baby, I want you from behind."

When she still didn't move, I leaned down and sucked her swollen nipple until she woke up enough to respond.

"Give me a minute," she grumbled.

Nope. Done waiting.

I picked her up and tossed her face down on the bed, positioning her peachy ass so the target was in the cross-hairs and I was rimming her tight little butthole. She wiggled beneath me, but didn't tell me to stop. Definitely something I'd be taking further at some point in the future.

I lined up and pushed into her pussy slowly, the warm, soft heat, taking my breath away.

"Fuck, Caro!"

And then I lost it. Not lost a little, not just slightly out of control, but pounding into her like a fucking maniac, ruthlessly chasing my own release. The bed creaked and groaned, the headboard slamming against the wall, the antique springs my very own cheer team urging me on.

A second orgasm shot through her, making her pussy clamp around me so tightly I had no choice but to finish with her.

"Oh fuck!"

I stuttered, pulling out of her quickly, gripping hold of the rim of the condom, wondering whether I should tell her that it had split—I didn't want her freaking the fuck out.

And then, through the thin wall that separated us from the owner's mother, I heard the sound of someone clapping, and her thin voice called out, "Bravo! Bravo!"

"What the fuck?" I gasped.

Caro started to laugh. "I think ... I think we just got a round of applause!"

"You're fucking kidding me!"

She shook her head weakly. "That's what it sounded like. I guess she was impressed by your performance."

Oh yeah! I am the man! I sat up and called out loudly, "Grazie, signora!"

"Prego!" she replied through the wall.

I lay back on the bed, my hands behind my head, and a huge-ass grin on my face. Caro rolled onto her side to gaze up at me.

"Something making you smile, Hunter?"

"Yeah! I never got a round of applause before." *Although there was that one time the women's lacrosse team at UCSD gave me a platinum star rating on their facebook page.*

"Maybe she was applauding me," Caro suggested, her eyebrows raised cockily.

"Nah, she thinks I'm a stud, I can tell."

I peeled off the used condom, hiding the split.

"Well, it's a good thing you don't have performance anxiety; that can put a man off his stride, so they say."

Her words evoked a powerful memory, and despite my decision to leave the past in the past, the screwed up 17 year-old that I'd once been, resurfaced.

"Do you ever think about the first time we were together? You know, when..."

She interrupted me, saying my name softly, like a prayer or a promise.

"Sebastian, you don't have to remind me—it's not something I'm likely to forget."

"Sorry. It's just ... I thought about it a lot at the time and seeing you again this past week ... it's brought it all back."

"For me, too."

Lost in the memories, I leaned over to run a finger across the satiny skin of her cheek, before laying back again.

"Do you know how amazing you were that night? You took care of me after my dad had beaten the shit out of me." I closed my eyes, pushing away the darkness of that memory. "I thought my heart was going to fucking stop when you undressed me and you took your clothes off. And then you touched me and my cock just exploded. I thought you'd laugh at me or something. It was so fucking humiliating."

I paused, emotions too strong to control forcing the words out.

"But you didn't. You made me feel like a man. I remember every word that you said. You told me it was going to be okay, and I didn't know how it could be, but somehow you made the world go away, like it was just you and me."

She was silent, drifting in her own thoughts.

"That's how you make me feel, Caro, like the world just goes away and it's just you and me. I ... I didn't think I'd ever feel like that again. All those other women, I know it bothers you, but it was just sex. It wasn't ... this."

Her voice was soft when she replied.

"So, there was never anyone special, where it was more than just sex?"

I needed to be honest with her—no more secrets, no more lies, no more hiding what I felt about her. I was tired of the fear I felt when I was with her—fear that she'd leave me and I'd be alone again.

"There was one girl, Stacey, that I sort of dated for a while. She was ... okay, but I wasn't interested in anything long-term."

"What happened?" Caro asked quietly.

I shrugged and looked away. She hadn't meant anything.

"I heard her telling a girlfriend that she'd got me 'tamed'." *Stupid bitch—just because I'd been playing nice with her— and only then because she was a friend of Ches's wife.*

"Oh, I can guess how much you enjoyed hearing that," Caro said, shaking her head. "What did you do?"

"I slept with her best friend."

The breath caught in her throat and a look of deep

disapproval spread across Caro's face which I didn't really understand.

"I see," she said sharply.

I shrugged and stared up at the ceiling.

"You asked me why Ches's wife didn't approve of me, and that's the reason. Stacey was a friend of hers. And before you ask, no, I didn't sleep with Amy—it was another girl. I would never do that to Ches."

Caro took a deep breath.

"Well, I'm not surprised Amy doesn't like you after you did that to her friend … and it's not very reassuring to hear that you've shown your dick to half the female population of California—and Paris, or so I've heard—but that's your business. But surely you see that you made things difficult for Ches."

What the fuck? How did we go from Stacey to this?

"How's that?" I asked, not hiding the irritation in my voice.

"You put him in the middle, making him choose between his best friend and his wife."

"What? How was I making him 'choose'?"

"Well, I bet you anything Amy would have said she didn't want you in the house if you were going to treat her friends like that, and Ches would have had to find some way of defending what was, frankly, indefensible behavior."

She was accusing *me* of indefensible behavior? What about the way she'd shrugged me off like a cheap suit ten years ago? What about the way she'd left me to deal with my parents and all the shit that went down? I was 17. *Seventeen.*

"You get on your fucking high horse damn quickly, Caro," I snapped.

"I'm just saying…" she began.

"What? What the fuck are you 'just saying'?" I grit out, unable to stop my voice growing louder with each syllable. "You were a fucking journalist, Caro! You could have found me any time if you'd wanted to. It would have been so easy for you. So easy! I didn't even know your last name. I was so desperate to find you that I even tried to see that prick of a husband of yours, but he slammed the door in my face and called my CO. I was on fucking punishment duties for weeks after that. But you didn't give a shit, did you? It's just lies. You just tell me what you think I want to hear. How can I ever trust you?"

"Sebastian, I…"

"I really want to hear this, Caro!" I yelled, my heart pounding and adrenaline shooting through my body as fight or flight warred inside me. "I really want to hear how hard you tried to find me. You knew my fucking father was forcing me to enlist *because of you*, but you didn't even bother to make a few fucking phone calls. *Three years* I waited for you, Caro. *Three fucking years*, while you were off building your career and having a great life traveling all over the world. So yeah, I fucked some women who deserved it, because I'd already been fucked over once and I wasn't going to let it happen again."

She looked sick, gripping the sheet to her chest like she was afraid of me. *Christ! As if I could ever hurt her … the way she'd hurt me.*

"It wasn't like that, Sebastian. Just listen to me for a moment! Let me explain, I…"

"Go tell it to the Marines, Caro," I shouted, fury and ten years of resentment overtaking me, "because I'm not listening."

She sat up and reached for her t-shirt. *Shit! She was leaving. Again. I fucking knew it! I knew she was lying! She'd lied about it all.*

"Where are you going?" I snarled at her. "Running away again? Yeah, well, it's what you do best, isn't it? Run away. Fuck that! I'll save you the trouble."

I leapt out of bed, pulled on my jeans, thrust my bare feet into motorcycle boots, then scooped up my t-shirt and jacket.

I was shaking with anger, unable to believe that it was happening again. Again!

I had no idea where I was going when I stormed out of there—just away—before my still-beating heart got ripped out of my chest and tossed into the dirt.

As I kick-started the bike's engine, the loud roar echoed

the way I wanted to yell, pouring out my fury, refusing to admit that the pain was crushing.

I tore down the stony track to the highway, too fast for the skittering headlight, bumping and swerving over the rutted tracks, covering my boots and jeans with a layer of thick dust. When I hit the highway, I opened the throttle and let her go, taking the bends too fast, not caring if I was still alive on the other side. Ten miles down the road, the engine began to sputter and I realized the reserve tank was running on fumes. I slowed down when I saw the lights of small town, pulling into the first place I saw that had a parking lot.

Well, color me fucking ecstatic—the neon sign welcomed me in. I went to stand at the bar, not even looking at the *al banco* price list, instead just waving to the elderly bartender with the cartoon villain mustache to bring me a bottle of grappa when he admitted that there was no whiskey. Not that I cared—I just wanted to get shitfaced and numb as fast as possible.

I threw some Euros at him, then dragged the shitty grappa towards me, downing three shots one after the other. The bartender muttered something under his breath, shrugged and walked away.

Anger and hatred burned inside, and it took all my training not to go find someone to beat the shit out of. To err is human, to forgive divine—and neither of those was Marine Corps policy. *Ooh-rah.*

So I drank, hoping numbness would follow. But instead the memories poured through me: the first time I saw her, the first time she smiled at me, the first time I made her laugh, the first time we made love. The way she listened to me like my words had value, the way she smelled after her shower— the scent of her skin after sex. The way she touched me, the words she'd said as the left: *Ti amo tanto, sempre e per sempre.* The lies.

Other memories began to swirl through my foggy brain: the day I walked into the recruiter's office; the first day of boot camp when every other guy there was wondering what the fuck they'd done, and I was relieved to get away from my parents for good; the day of my graduation as a United States

Marine when my fucking father had showed up and I'd had to salute the bastard—the look on his face before he walked away; first day in Iraq; the first IED I heard exploding; the first dead body I saw—a child; the first time I shot my rifle for real, 18 years old and piss scared—and the pride when I held it together and fought with my brothers; the day I won my first stripe, Private First Class.

And it had been good, being part of something again, something that mattered. The Marine Corps was the family I'd never had. And for three years it was home, even though I traveled all over the world. And then I was sure, so sure that Caro would find me. Because after three years, my fucking parents couldn't touch us—and her 'crime' of sleeping with me when I underage was beyond the Statute of Limitations. But she never came. And I hated her. I thought I hated her—I tried.

I was still trying to hate her but my cock had other ideas, hardening to titanium the first moment I saw her again in that boring-as-fuck hostile environment briefing, and every moment since. I tried to forget how she looked when she saw me, or the way she felt when she came apart under me. So I drank.

When the bar began to empty at 3AM, the bottle of grappa was less than a quarter full. The bartender approached me slowly, and I gazed at him with bleary eyes while he explained that they were closing.

His expression changed from wariness to understanding as he watched me stagger towards the exit, pawing at the door to pull it open. When it refused to budge, he gently turned the handle to push it open. Then he patted me on the shoulder and said, "Chè per vendetta mai non sanò piaga."

My alcohol soaked brain took a moment to translate: *Revenge never healed a wound.* If I'd translated more quickly, I'd have told him to fuck off.

I fumbled for my bike keys, trying to figure out why there were two Honda ST1100s in the parking lot. I tried to swing a leg over the saddle but somehow ended up lying on my back, staring up at the stars. It occurred to me that there was a possibility I was drunk. I had a feeling I was supposed to do something, but I didn't know what it was. In the distance I could hear the sound of waves rolling up the narrow beach, so I decided to go for a walk with my new best friend who answered to the name of *Grappa*.

The two of us made our way down to the beach and sank down onto the sand. I couldn't understand why the bottle was empty—I thought *Grappa* was my friend. Guess I was wrong about that bastard, too. I decided to lay down for a short nap—maybe then I'd remember what the fuck I was supposed to be doing.

When I woke up, some asswipe was shining a light into my face that made my eyes water, and some other shitbag was pounding on my head with a cement block. I sat up cautiously, blinking in the light of a brilliant spring morning. Fuck, I felt rougher than a docker's armpit. At the sight of the empty bottle of *Grappa*, I heaved up my guts, coughing and retching until there was nothing left.

I felt too ill to care who'd seen me, but kicked some sand over the mess all the same. I wondered what time it was. From the position of the sun, probably between 10:00 and 11:00. I wondered where Caro was—and then the memories of the night before came crashing back. A sick feeling that had nothing to do with the amount of alcohol I'd drunk made my stomach lurch. Fuck me, had I really said all that poisonous shit to her?

I squinted up and down the beach, trying to get my bearings as my pounding head tried to make sense of everything that had happened.

Then my bladder began to complain, urging me to drain the mainframe before I did anything else. I lurched to my feet and took a long and satisfying piss against the wall of an old fisherman's hut, watched by a one-eyed dog.

"Don't look at me, buddy," I croaked. "I'm in worse shape than you are."

I ran my hands across my scruff and took a tentative sniff at an armpit. Not too rank. Well, that was something.

I found my bike still intact in the bar's parking lot then remembered that the tank was nearly empty. Luckily a local gas station had opened, selling fuel at the extortionate sum of

€1.73 a liter, or about nine bucks a gallon in good ole US dollars.

I headed back toward Casa Giovina, wondering what to say to Caro, wondering what she'd say to me. But just before I reached the turnoff, I saw her walking along the highway, my overnight bag slung across one shoulder. *Shit! She was already leaving!*

I pulled over, but when she recognized the bike, she put her head down and started walking faster. Annoyed, I jogged up behind her, cursing the movement that made my stomach and head protest in stereo.

"Caro, wait!"

But she didn't, so I grabbed the handles of the bag, forcing her to stop.

"Caro, I'm sorry." *No response.* "Okay?" *Still no response.* Pissed, I tugged on the handles of the bag again until she had to let go. "Are you going to talk to me?"

"I think you've said enough—for both of us," she snapped.

"Fuck, Caro! It was the alcohol talking, that's all…" I protested.

"It was more than that and you know it, Sebastian."

Her dark eyes flashed with a fury that matched my own.

"Can't you take a fucking apology?" I barked.

"I don't know," she hissed. "Can you make one?"

We stood staring at each other; both hurt, both angry.

I ran my hand over my hair and frowned at her. "Can we just go somewhere and talk? Or are you going to walk back to Geneva?"

She folded her arms across her chest, glaring back at me. "Yes, frankly. I was going to get a cab to drive me to the airport. I'm sure I'd have no trouble getting a flight."

I tried to make my voice softer because I could see that being pissed was getting me exactly nowhere.

"Don't leave like this, Caro," I reasoned. "Let's just talk and if we can't … fix this, I'll take you to the airport myself."

Even as I said the words I knew with certainty that I didn't want her to go. I had to man the fuck up and make this right.

She hesitated for five long seconds, then nodded coldly. I stowed the bag and silently passed her a helmet.

When I climbed back on the bike, she refused to take my hand, preferring to scramble on awkwardly by herself. I heaved out a sigh when she held onto the small grab-bar at the rear of her seat instead of linking her arms around my waist as she'd always done before.

I swung the bike around in a slow U-turn and headed southeast, away from the airport, following the coast road. After a few miles, I pulled up by a beach café in the small town of Bogliasco.

"Do you want a coffee?" I suggested.

"An espresso and a glass of water, please," she replied stiffly.

The waiter was talking to a group of old guys and seemed surprised to have customers so early in the morning.

I thought I might feel better if I ate something, even though my stomach rebelled at the idea.

I leaned back in my chair, staring across at Caro, not flinching from her gaze as she stared back. I had no idea how to start this conversation, especially as she didn't look like she wanted to talk to me.

Our coffees arrived along with a basket of rolls, and I wondered who was going to break the silence first.

I pushed the basket toward her but she shook her head.

"No, thank you. I've already eaten."

"Did you check out of that place?"

"Yes," she clipped out.

"Did you pack up my stuff?"

She seemed surprised by my question. "Of course!"

Yeah? Well, I'd expected her to have tossed my stuff or left it behind.

"Okay, thanks," I said quietly. "What do I owe you for the room?"

"Nothing. Forget it."

"Just tell me what I owe you, Caro."

"Seeing as you didn't stay in it, I don't see why you should pay."

I took a deep breath, trying to calm my irritation.

"Is this how you're going to be?"

"How would you like me to be, Sebastian?" she asked coldly. "Because, honestly, I just don't know."

Fuck fuck fuck.

I grabbed a roll as a distraction, needing to do something with my hands so I could think, and started tearing it into pieces.

"Look, maybe we should just cut our losses," she said, her voice empty and tired. "I'll get a cab to the airport and you can … do whatever you want, Sebastian."

God, no! Was that what she wanted? I stared at the crumbs on my plate.

"I don't want you to go," I admitted, the tug of desperation making my gut churn again.

She waited for me to say something else—but I had no clue what she needed to hear. What the fuck did I know about relationships? I'd gone out with Brenda when I was 16, then met Caro, and had boned so many women since her that it was lucky my dick hadn't died from over-use.

"Sebastian," she said, with the tone an adult uses when a kid is pissing them off but they're trying not to lose it, "you're going to have to tell me why on earth you'd want me to stay. Last night you said some pretty unpleasant things: and I'm not going to accept your explanation about having drunk too much. It's clear that you've been hanging on to a lot of anger toward me. And I don't know what I can do about that."

She was right. Christ, I hated that. I needed to give her something; explain the flashpoints that kept setting off my explosive temper.

"Caro, did you really try and find me when I turned 21?"

She sighed, looking disappointed.

"I'll tell you exactly what I told you before: I wrote to Shirley, and I wrote to Donna. But no, I didn't try and find you directly, because I simply wanted to know that you were okay. When both letters were returned unopened, I suppose I took it as an omen that it wasn't to be. I didn't feel I had the right to interrupt your life and risk doing further damage. I felt a great deal of guilt at the devastation I left behind me: I didn't want to remind you of all that, or make you feel any obligation toward me. It never occurred to me that you … that you'd be waiting for me."

Was she for real? I leaned forward, my tone angry. "But I *said* I'd wait for you. I promised I'd wait. Hell, Caro, it was the last thing I got to say to you. And you … you said…" I stopped, wondering if she even remembered what she'd said to me.

Her gaze softened and her eyes creased with emotion.

"Oh, Sebastian … I'm so very sorry."

I swallowed hard, hearing the regret in her voice. "Did you mean it, Caro? Did you mean it when you said you loved me?"

"Yes, tesoro," she whispered.

Her admission stunned me, that and hearing the nickname that she'd had for me all those years ago … but was it all in the past tense?

"I loved you very much," she continued, but then her back straightened, and some of the softness hardened again. "But you're not the person I knew ten years ago. The Sebastian I knew was sweet and gentle and loving, but you … you can be like that, but your anger scares me. The hatred I saw in your face and heard in your words—that was hard for me. I can see that you think I let you down badly ten years ago, or when you were 21 … and I can't tell you how sorry I am for that, but I can't fix it either—I can't change the past."

It was so hard to hear what she thought of me now, so I turned away, staring out at the waves.

"I'm confused about what you want from me, Sebastian," she went on, her voice serious and determined. "One minute you say we've been given a second chance and that we should try again, and the next minute you're blaming me for every bad decision you've taken in the last ten years. If you hate me that much, if you resent me that much, why am I here?"

"I don't hate you, Caro," I said quickly.

"Sebastian, you called me a liar; you said you could never trust me."

I winced, hating to have my words thrown back at me.

"You asked me to come with you on this trip," she said

crisply, "and then the first time something goes wrong, you fling the past in my face. If you really believe I did what I did because I didn't care, then I don't see how we're going to get past that."

My hope, which had never been great to begin with, drained away.

"Look," she sighed when I didn't speak, "I wouldn't be who I am now if I hadn't met you—that's the truth. I'd probably still be locked in a loveless marriage. But that's only half the story."

That made me look up.

"It was really tough for me when I got to New York. I had almost no money, no contacts, nowhere to live, no job. Do you want to know how I survived? I cleaned people's houses; I scrubbed their toilets. For three years. Until eventually I earned enough from my writing."

"I didn't know," I said, sad beyond words that she'd had to struggle so hard.

"No, because you didn't give me the chance to answer you last night."

I decided that I needed to know more about the missing ten years, but there was only one important question left for me to ask.

"You said you dated a couple of times."

"Excuse me?"

She sounded surprised. Well, she knew my dating history—I needed to know hers.

"The first night we talked. I asked you if you were seeing anyone, and you said you'd dated a couple of times."

"Yes, so?"

"When?"

"What, you want dates?"

"Yes."

She sighed and shook her head, but she wasn't saying no.

"I met Bob on my 35th birthday when I was having drinks with friends. We dated for three months and then he was transferred to an office in Cincinnati. Eric was a couple of years later: we dated for about six weeks before he dumped me for a younger woman."

I waited for more but she just stared at me.

"That's it?" I questioned.

I was stunned. She'd waited *five years* before she'd dated anyone after she left me? Seriously?

"I had a one night stand with a reporter when I was on assignment in Mexico," she said defiantly, her head held high. "That's it. Now you know my entire sexual history. Although I very much doubt you could be as succinct about yours."

I had to concede a wry smile. "I deserve that," I admitted.

She closed her eyes and leaned back.

"Are you okay?" I asked.

She shook her head slowly and her lips turned down. "Not really."

I was tired of trying to think of the right thing to say, so I just told the truth.

"I am sorry, Caro. I just get fucked up in the head sometimes."

Her eyes were still tinged with hurt and anger.

"You can't deal with it by lashing out at me," she sighed. "And *I* can't deal with it if you keep blaming me for something I can't change."

We'd come so far and waited so long, and if last night had taught me anything, I wanted this second chance. Badly. And I was fucking it up. Again. My head sank into my hands as I mumbled a reply.

"Don't give up on me, Caro."

"Last night I thought *you'd* given up on *me*," she said firmly.

I really wanted to kick my own ass.

"Can we start again, Caro?" I asked, no longer too proud to beg. "I promise I'll try not to fuck up again."

She took a deep breath.

"Sebastian, it's not a case of starting again; it's about working things through when we have a problem. Funny enough, it was you who taught me that, ten years ago: you made me face up to things. You can't promise me you won't fuck up, because you will. And I can't promise you that I won't fuck up, because I will. We can deal, and we can move on. Or, we can say it's been an interesting few days, and go our separate ways."

I reached over and took her hand carefully, examining her narrow wrist and slender fingers.

"I want to go on," I admitted to her, to myself. "With you."

She stared at me for several long seconds, and I had the weirdest sensation that she was trying to read my mind.

"Okay, then," she breathed out slowly. "Let's try."

"And I promise not to sleep with your best friend, especially if it's that scary British woman I saw you with in Geneva."

I hoped my lame joke would lighten the moment, but her expression told me it was too soon for that.

"Sorry," I said quietly. "Another foot-in-mouth moment."

She pulled her hand free and sat back to pick up the cup of lukewarm espresso in front of her. Absentmindedly, I watched her lips as she sipped her coffee, forcing some pieces of bread into my mouth, hoping it would help settle my stomach.

"Did they say anything about last night?" I asked suddenly, realizing that I'd left Caro with a fucked up situation to deal with. "The people at the villa?"

"Not really," she said mildly. "They were mostly embarrassed. I think we've managed to ruin it for any other Americans who might want to stay there. But the old lady told me that you'd be back."

That surprised me.

"Really?"

"Yes," she said with a half smile, "and I'm pretty certain it was me not you she was applauding last night. She probably thought I should get a medal for putting up with you."

"Yeah," I agreed, "a Purple Heart."

"Wounded in action?" she asked seriously.

My smile slipped away. "I'm really sorry about what I said."

She shook her head slowly. "We're moving on,

remember? But, for the record, apology accepted."

I looked down and ate some of the pieces of bread roll, more for a distraction than anything else.

"I got drunk and fell asleep on the beach," I admitted. "In case you were wondering."

I didn't want Caro to think I'd spent the night with another woman.

She looked away and frowned.

"Well, thank you for telling me."

"I panicked when I woke up: I thought you might have gone. And then I saw you walking along the road. At first I was relieved but then … I just thought you'd walked out on me. That's why I was…"

"…such an ass?"

I managed a rueful smile at her sharp comeback.

"Yeah, that about sums it up."

"Well, like I said, thank you for telling me." She took a deep breath and tried to smile. "Now, what's the big plan for today?"

She was letting me off the hook. Thank fuck for that.

"I thought we could go to Pisa—take a look at that big, old leaning tower. It's about two hours away."

"Sure, that sounds fun."

Her smile wasn't 100% natural, but she was trying. I guess we both were.

I swallowed a few more pieces of roll, hoping it would soak up the remainder of the alcohol in my system, then threw some Euros on the table and stood up to go. Without thinking, I held out my hand to Caro. Her reaction was a little strained, but she took my hand and I wrapped my fingers around hers, squeezing gently.

We walked to the bike and I pulled on my leather jacket as she stowed her luggage in the saddlebags, refusing to meet my gaze.

"I really want to kiss you," I said, hoping that she'd truly forgiven me.

She hesitated, and my stomach dropped to my boots before she looked up and nodded once.

"Okay."

Relieved that she was going to let me touch her, I rested my hands on her waist and brushed my lips to hers. She pulled back quickly.

"Caro…"

"Just hold me, Sebastian. Just hold me."

She laid both her hands on my chest and leaned her cheek against my shoulder. I wrapped my arms around her, hugging tightly.

"I'm sorry," I said for the millionth time. "I'm so sorry," and I pressed a small kiss into her hair.

When I could bear to let her go, she looked up and gave me a quick smile. A real one.

"We'll get there," she said.

CHAPTER 7

Pisa was slammed, getting high on festival fever. Music blared from every café and ristorante, competing with the street entertainers and musicians, and the streets were filled with people partying. If I'd been here a week ago, still resolutely single, I'd have joined them, drinking and flirting, until I found a piece of pussy to hook up with for the night. But not now: the only girl I wanted was riding behind me on my bike.

I found a parking lot filled with battered Fiats and old Renaults. It wasn't the most secure place in the world, but it would have to do.

"Are you taking your camera?" I suggested to Caro.

"Might as well," she said, flinging it loosely over one, slim shoulder. "Who knows, maybe I'll be able to sell a travelogue of biking through Italy."

I was definitely on board with that idea. I'd much prefer Caro wrote articles from places that weren't in a warzone. "It's got to beat reporting from shitty military camps in fucked up countries."

She shrugged, and I could tell that if I pushed her on the subject of her work, we'd be fighting again. But I really didn't get it. I'd met foreign correspondents in Iraq and Afghanistan: they were a bunch of hard-drinking adrenaline junkies. I also knew guys who made a nice pile of extra cash by passing low-value info to journos who were hoping to get the next scoop. Yeah, I was glad that they reported to the people back home, because the sooner this fucked up war came to an end and we pulled out, the better. But the reporters I'd met—much like that scary British woman back

118

in Geneva—they weren't happy unless they were in the heat of the front line: total fucking bullet magnets. Caro wasn't like that.

Holding in a sigh and biting back further comments, we walked into the city to explore.

Leaning tower. *Check.*

Bunch of old buildings. *Check.*

More old buildings. *Check. Yawn.*

Even more old buildings. *Fuck me.*

After what felt like half a lifetime, I was seriously done with seeing anymore old ruins or piles of rubble. I didn't care if they were built by the Romans, the Italians or the fucking Egyptians. And I was so hungry, I was ready to chew my arm off.

Caro had been mostly silent, but taking photo after photo of everything we saw. Well, I guess she saw more in it than I did: still a bunch of fucking bricks.

"A penny for your thoughts," I asked.

"I was just thinking about Papa—wondering if he ever came here."

It explained why she'd been so quiet. At least she wasn't still pissed at me. Well, not as much.

"I really loved your dad, Caro," I admitted, thinking back to the guy with a crazy mustache who played with me and talked to me, and taught me more about the world than my asswipe of a father. "I was kinda jealous of you when I was a kid—I wanted so badly to have a dad like him, not the sack of shit I was saddled with."

"Do you … keep up with your parents at all?"

That's a hell no!

"Last time I saw the old bastard was at my graduation from boot camp."

"Oh," she said, sounding surprised, "that was … nice of him."

I stared at her incredulously. I thought she knew what a mean shit my dad was.

"Are you fucking kidding me? He only did it because he knew it would piss me off to have to salute him."

"Oh, right," she said, frowning. What about Estelle?"

I shrugged. "She's still in San Diego. Ches sees her around now and again. He banned her from the country club—drinking. They got divorced a few years back. Dad shacked up with some stripper. I don't really know. What about your mom? Do you see her?"

She shook her head. "No, we're not in touch. I know she's living in a retirement village in Florida, but that's all."

I didn't know anything about Caro's mom—she'd never visited when her dad came to San Diego, so I hadn't met her.

"Why aren't you in touch? She couldn't have been as bad as my mom."

"Don't be too sure about that," Caro grimaced.

"What did she do?"

"She didn't do anything, Sebastian. That's the point. When I … when I left David, she told me I'd made my bed so now I could lie in it. She didn't want anything to do with me. Wouldn't lend me a red cent to help out when I went to New York. She wouldn't even send me any photographs of Papa. I only have a couple of old pictures of him…"

Her words trailed off, and I automatically went to pull her in for a hug, but she resisted me without even being aware of it. I shoved my hands in my pockets so I wouldn't be tempted to touch her again. It was fucking choking me

"Do you see anything of him … David?" I grit out the name of her ex-husband, managing not to spit on the street as I said it.

"No. We had to correspond over the divorce papers, but that's all. I believe he stayed in the Navy. You said you tried to see him … when was that?"

Really didn't want to talk about it. I sighed, looking up at her expectant face.

"About four months after you left. It was killing me not knowing how you were, or where you were, or how to get in touch with you. Dad had already trashed my computer and deleted all my email accounts before I went to live with Mitch and Shirley. I didn't even think the bastard knew how to do that stuff. Took my cell off me and smashed that, as well. Anyway, I was getting pretty desperate, so I went to your old house—but it was a waste of time. The asshole yelled at me that I'd ruined his marriage; I told him he didn't deserve you and was a bastard for the way he'd treated you. He threatened to call the police. That was it."

She looked so sad, that my ever-present anger began to boil over.

"You don't feel sorry for him do you, Caro?" I snapped.

"A little. He just married the wrong woman, but he wasn't a bad man."

The hell he wasn't!

"But you didn't ruin my marriage: David and I managed to do that all by ourselves. You ... freed me."

It took a second for her words to sink in. She thought I'd freed her? *Thank God.*

"Please let me hold you, Caro," I begged. "It's driving me crazy that you won't let me touch you."

I reached out again, but she stepped away from me. Again.

"Just ... just give me some time, Sebastian. I don't deal with rejection well."

Her words stunned me. "Is that how you see it? That I rejected you."

She stared at me disbelievingly. "Of course. There's no other way to see it."

I ran my hands over my hair in frustration. Why couldn't she see how wrong she was? That my anger came from fear—fear that she'd realize I wasn't worth the effort, and leave me for a second time, a final time.

"Fuck, Caro! Last night was about my shit, not about you. Don't you see that?"

"No, I don't." she said, shaking her head. "Not really. But I don't want to go over that again. I'm trying to put it behind us ... I just need time."

"Okay," I sighed. But it wasn't okay. It really wasn't.

"Do you want to go find somewhere to eat?" she asked, making an effort to lighten the mood, I guess.

"Yeah, I was hoping you'd say that. Do you feel like Italian?"

She raised her eyebrows, a small smile hovering on her lips.

"Oh, very funny. You should be on 'Saturday Night Live'."

We wandered through the crowded streets, checking out some of the cafés and ristorantes.

"What about that place over there because…?" she started to ask.

Suddenly, she lost her balance and I had to catch her arm.

"My camera!" she screamed, pointing at the thief who'd grabbed her and pushed her over.

Not on my fucking watch!

I sprinted after the douchebag asshole, tackling him to the ground and landing several good punches, one of which broke his nose with a satisfying snap. Blood leaked onto his t-shirt, and I was just about to express more of my extreme fucking displeasure, when Caro ran up behind me.

"Sebastian, no!" she gasped.

I uncurled my fists, shaking them out, then stood up, handing the camera back to her. I realized that a crowd was beginning to form, pointing and yelling. I really didn't want a run in with the local Polizia.

"We'd better get out of here."

"What about the police?" Caro whispered, her eyes glued to the thief and the blood pooling on his chest.

"Fuck them!"

I grabbed her hand, dragging her through the ring of onlookers who were watching the show. There were a few angry voices aimed at our backs, but no one tried to stop us.

Caro was pale and shaky. I would have thought a foreign correspondent wouldn't get faint at the sight of blood. Maybe she was just hungry? Or maybe she was pissed that I'd made a mess of that fucker's face? I never knew what she was thinking anymore. The thought made my gut clench.

I dragged her down a side-alley, and a moment later, we emerged into a wide piazza.

"Are you okay, Caro?"

"I'm fine," she said weakly, looking away from me.

"Come on," I ordered. "You should eat something."

She nodded, and didn't argue when I led us into a small

restaurant pulling out a stool at the bar for her.

"Thank you for saving my camera," she said quietly.

I was relieved—understatement. "I was waiting for you to chew me out for hitting that guy."

"Well, I'm glad you stopped punching him when you did, obviously, but I'm very fond of my camera. I worked hard to afford to buy it. Thank you, Sebastian."

I smiled, shaking my head in amusement. "You never cease to amaze me, Caro."

Then she reached over and took my hand. "How are your knuckles?"

I chuckled quietly. "Much better now," I said, running my thumb over the back of her hand.

The waitress sauntered over to take our order and was pretty damn obvious about checking me out while she did it. Better still, it was making Caro pissed, so at least I knew she still wanted me.

"Not my type," I whispered, jerking my chin in the waitress' direction.

"I'm glad to hear it," Caro whispered back. "She's not mine, either."

I nearly fell off my stool, my imagination going straight to the gutter.

"Not interested in three-ways?" I croaked.

"I don't know," she replied, casually. "Do you have friends in the Marines who are as cute as you?"

No fucking way!

"No. I don't."

She laughed, and I'd have done anything to see that happiness on her face again. Although there was no way I'd let her near any of the grunts I used to hang with.

"Tell me about being a Marine," she said. "What do you like about it? What don't you like about it?"

"Are you interviewing me, Caro, or is this off the record?" I smirked at her.

"Off the record—for now," she said.

I decided to answer her question seriously. I hadn't had a choice about joining the Marines, but I'd been so desperate to leave home, I didn't care either.

"I get to be part of a family," I said, shrugging lightly. "The guys I work with, they're my brothers, like we share DNA. We fight and piss each other off, but I get them and they get me. We've all gone through the same things so I guess it bonds us together or something." I looked at her, "And I didn't have much of a family growing up."

She smiled sadly. "No, you didn't."

"A lot of guys thought that boot camp was the worst thing ever, but I loved it. Yeah, it was physically tough— swimming, running, going through exercise courses, and learning how to shoot and take apart guns—but it took my mind off … stuff. For others, the toughest thing was being away from their families, but for me that was the best part."

"And the downside?"

"Dickhead officers…"

"And their wives?" Caro laughed.

"Well, yeah!"

"Would you say you love it?" she asked, cocking her head questioningly.

"I used to. I was good at something for the first time in my life. Being part of my Unit—those guys were solid. Being a terp, yeah, I like that okay when I'm on deployment, but being stuck in a fucking office all day…" I shook my head. "I'm a good Marine but a lousy desk POG."

"POG?"

"Person Other than Grunt."

Caro smiled. "Yes, you always preferred action to words, I seem to remember."

I waggled my eyebrows at her suggestively, "If you're offering, ma'am!"

Her mood shifted immediately, and I cursed myself for being so dumb. I wanted a Caro who was happy to hang out with me, not one who was uncomfortable when I flirted with her. Dumb fucking bootneck! I changed the subject quickly.

"How did you meet your friend Liz?"

She smiled at the memory. "We were the only women on a press tour of refugee camps in Darfur. We just bonded. She's totally committed to what she does and is a complete professional. She'll go anywhere, talk to anyone, and she's never afraid to ignore the line we're being sold by politicians and top brass military. She has an amazing nose for a story." Caro smiled. "And she parties harder than you do. She's a wonderful reporter, but she's no respecter of authority."

"Yeah, she's pretty scary. I thought Crawley was going to piss his pants when she targeted in on him."

"Aw, feeling a little threatened, were you?"

"Hell yeah! My balls were just about ready to curl up and hide."

Caro shot me an amused look, but then stifled a yawn.

"Are you tired?"

"Yes, definitely ready to head for bed, Sebastian. To sleep."

Her comment was pointed, but I wasn't going to let it faze me.

"Okay, let's see what we can find. There were a couple of streets I saw online that are mostly pensiones. Should we try one of those?"

When I'd planned the trip, I'd worked out that these small, family run hotels were cheap accommodation in the cities—I just hadn't counted on it being festival time..

"Sounds good," she said, yawning again.

I paid the bill and we headed out. I was reaching for her hand again when she stopped me, a serious look on her face.

"Sebastian, don't get mad at me, and don't read too much into this … but I'd really like to have separate rooms tonight. Just…"

That definitely wasn't what I wanted to hear. How were we going to work through this if she wouldn't let me close to her? But she'd asked, and I couldn't say no.

"Whatever you need, Caro," I said quietly.

She relaxed immediately, a relieved look on her face.

"Thank you."

I was so frustrated, thinking of a million things I wanted to say, that I hadn't realized we'd walked nearly half a mile toward the pensiones in complete silence.

"This is the street," I muttered, pointing toward a long line of narrow townhouses.

The first two we tried were fully booked and the third

could only offer a single room. If worst came to worst, Caro could take that room and I'd find an all-night bar to hang out in—or maybe she'd let me sleep on her floor?

"We could try going more upscale," I suggested tiredly.

"Well, we have to walk along this street to get back to the main hotel area, so we may as well try a few more on the way," Caro offered.

"Yeah, okay."

At the fifth pensione, we struck gold. Sort of.

"I'm sorry, signora," the owner said to Caro. "I have one room with two single beds, but that's all. It's the Festival, you see," she said, gesturing helplessly. "You're lucky—I had a cancellation."

I was willing Caro to take it, but she turned to look at me doubtfully.

"Pajama party," I mouthed.

She rolled her eyes and smiled. "Si, we'll take the room. Grazie."

Oo-rah!

Our room looked like it was last refurbished in the 1970s, but it was clean and had two beds pushed together, and that was all I cared about.

I threw myself down on the bed nearest to the window, smiling as it creaked slightly.

"Not as noisy as last night," I said, raising one eyebrow.

"I don't think that's even possible," Caro agreed mildly, ignoring my flirting.

I was honestly trying not to, but with her it just wasn't possible. I counted to ten, then turned to our overnight bag and tossed her toiletry bag onto the other bed.

"Thanks for packing up my stuff," I said, looking across at her. "I thought I'd probably seen the last of these shirts."

"What a tragedy," she said snidely. "You might have had to do something shocking, like buy t-shirts in different colors."

I smiled, but didn't reply. She was just pissed that she hadn't gotten rid of me for the night. I was fucking ecstatic. All I needed was time, I was sure of it. Almost sure.

I pushed open the window and gazed down into the

street, watching people enjoying the festival. I'd like to have been down there and take Caro dancing.

"Listen to that," I teased her. "Sounds like being in Italy."

She stood and listened for a moment, a small smile softening her expression of irritation. "Yes, it sounds ... happy."

Her words surprised me and I turned to look at her. "Are you happy, Caro?"

She nodded slowly. "Getting there."

"Good."

We stared at each other until she looked away, then left the room to take a shower.

I gazed out into the night, imagining a future where Caro and me were together. It was possible, wasn't it? I'd re-upped two years ago, but other guys in the Marines made it work. I'd be in Afghanistan for the rest of the year anyway, maybe more. But we'd survive—we had to.

When Caro arrived back in the room, her hair was damp and she was wearing an oversize t-shirt and a pair of tiny shorts. Both the sight and scent of her fresh from the shower made my mouth water, but I didn't want to scare her off.

"Back in a minute, baby," I said, winking at her.

The shower was cold, which was probably a good thing, helping to deflate my eager dick. Bastard was like a guided missile the way it aimed at Caro 24/7. I can't say the aching cock and blue balls were doing me any favors.

I tried to ignore everything below my waist.

"You doing your writing?" I asked, as I walked back into the room.

She was sitting on her bed Indian style and typing on her laptop.

"No, just catching up with my girlfriends."

She'd told me a little about her New York friends while we were at dinner.

"Did you tell them about me?"

"I told them I was traveling through Italy with an old friend."

Not what I was hoping to hear. Was I still her dirty little

127

secret? The thought pissed me the hell off.

"So, what do you want to do tomorrow?" I asked, trying to find something to talk about that wouldn't irritate either of us. "Look at more old buildings?" *Or I could just slit my throat now and save dying of boredom.*

Caro smiled, her expression amused. "Whatever. This is all a bonus anyway. Where would you like to go?"

"There're a couple of surf spots I'd like to check out, if you don't mind," I suggested hopefully.

"I don't mind, Sebastian. I could use some beach time—sleeping in the sun sounds perfect about now."

Relief.

"Okay, cool! The surf isn't great in the Med, but there are a few breaks that look like they might be rideable."

I undressed quickly down to my skivvies, then jumped onto my bed, laying back with my arms behind my head, smiling across at her.

"Are you going to tuck me in?" I asked.

Caro shook her head and laughed. "I think you're old enough and ugly enough to do that yourself."

"Ugly?"

"Hideous. I can hardly bear to look at you."

"You could close your eyes," I offered.

"I could, Sebastian, but I might get the urge to peek.

Damn, she was turning me on. In fact the way she looked in her sleep shirt was making me hard. Again.

"Well, can I get a goodnight kiss?"

"Sure. I'll ask Signora Battelli if she's available."

Fuck no! The pensione's owner was at least seventy and must weigh 300 pounds. "I've never kissed a woman with a mustache."

"First time for everything, Sebastian," she laughed.

"Please, Caro," I begged. "I'll be good. Promise."

"Hmm, I've heard your promises before."

I gave her my best puppy dog eyes. They always used to work on her.

"Okay, one kiss. But that's all!"

Fuck, yeah!

She stowed her laptop back in its bag and sat on my bed,

allowing me to pull her down into a hug. She laid her head on my chest while my hands stroked up and down her back.

"We're okay, aren't we, Caro?" I asked quietly, seriously.

"Getting there," she said softly.

Then she wriggled free and planted a quick kiss on my lips.

"Good night, Marine," she said as she turned off her bedside light.

"Night, boss."

I listened to her even breathing telling me that she was asleep. I rolled onto my stomach and pushed my hands under the pillow. It was like a dream for me to be with her again. I'd really fucked things up last night, letting a decade of bitterness and resentment ruin our time together. I saw a future with her, and I hoped that she did, too. I had 11 days of leave left to prove I was worth it.

But she was a successful journalist, and I'd be some unemployed grunt with a few language skills that weren't going to be of much fucking use back in the US. I wouldn't be able to get a job as a translator because I was shit at reading Arabic, let alone the Pashto alphabet. I was a good terp, but that wasn't going to get me far. Maybe I could be a personal trainer—it wouldn't take much to get those qualifications, and I thought the GI Bill would be good for that. I wondered if…

Suddenly, Caro cried out, scaring the shit out of me as she thrashed around, tangling the sheets around her.

I bolted out of bed, grabbing her shoulders and shaking her gently.

"Caro, wake up!"

She sat up quickly, wide-eyed and trembling.

"Fuck, Caro! Another nightmare?"

She nodded silently, tremors running through her whole body.

"Come here, baby."

My heart hurt seeing her so scared when she was usually so strong. I wrapped my arms around her, pulling her in tightly so she was resting against my chest.

"What was it about, baby?" I asked quietly.

She shook her head. "Just a nightmare."

"You can tell me anything, Caro."

There was no reply, and much as it killed me not to know what was upsetting her, I couldn't force her either. I held her in my arms, protecting her with my body, hoping that she knew I'd always keep her safe.

After a few minutes, her heart rate returned to normal.

"Scoot over," I whispered. "I'll just stay till you go back to sleep."

She didn't fight me this time, instead rolling over so there was room for me.

"Thank you," she murmured.

I slid down next to her, my chest to her back, and pulled her in close. And then we slept.

I woke up to Caro lightly stroking my arms where they were still wrapped around her.

I stretched out slowly, enjoying the feel of her body next to mine. I rubbed my eyes and smiled at her, happy to have her next to me, although I'd rather have had her under me.

"Wow, I've got this beautiful woman in my bed. I really like this dream."

"Actually, Sebastian," she sniffed, trying to hide her amusement, "you're in *my* bed."

"Oh, yeah. You must be one of those fast women I heard about at boot camp."

"Hmm, well, I think that lecture was supposed to warn you off them."

"Oh, I guess I didn't hear it right. Explains why I didn't get into Officer Candidate School."

She looked at me closely.

"Did you try?"

"Nah, not really. Not my thing. I took some college classes for a while, but then…" *I knew you weren't coming back, so I gave up caring.* "I was already fucking around. Guess I pissed off the wrong people."

"You'd make a good officer, Sebastian," she said seriously. "Maybe you should think about it."

Did that mean she wanted me to stay in the Marines? I

shrugged. "I'm a Warrant Officer—highest ranking for noncoms." Then I grinned at her sheepishly. "Yeah, you know that stuff. Sorry. I did get asked to join the Navy SEALs, though."

"Really?" she said, her face lighting up. "That's great! I mean, that's a real honor, isn't it? You'd like that—all that super-macho stuff."

I smiled at her description and ran a finger along her arm. "I turned them down."

Her jaw dropped open and she looked amazed. "Why?"

"Caro, there's no way I'd join the same service that my father is in. Fuck that! Can you imagine if we ended up at the same Base?" My voice started getting louder as the old anger surged through me. "I'd end up killing the bastard."

"Shh," she said, resting a finger on my lips. "We're in Italy; it's a beautiful day, and we're going to go and find some waves for you to surf."

I took a deep breath and calmed the fuck down.

"Okay," I said, letting my hand drift down her thigh, until I was tugging at the material of her panties. "You know what would make this day even better?" I asked.

"Oh no, Sebastian," she said, shoving my hand away. "I'm not falling for that. I'm going to take a shower, and you'd better have some damn clothes on by the time I get back."

She jumped out of bed, then stomped around the room picking out a clean shirt to wear. She was so cute when she was mad.

"Are you sure?" I asked, letting my hand disappear under the sheets as my cock started to throb.

She muttered something under her breath, threw me a look that should have scorched my eyeballs, and slammed the door as she left the room. I lay there, lazily stroking myself, imagining it was her hands on my dick, her fingers working the sensitive head. Desire and need spiked along my shaft almost immediately, and I groaned as a long stream of cum landed on my stomach. It was her fault I was so damn horny.

On deployment, most of us lived like monks. Unless you got lucky with one of the women working in the Motor T—

the vehicle shop. I preferred not to hit on female Marines. Apart from anything else, I didn't shit on my own doorstep.

I cleaned off as best I could, then pulled on a pair of jeans, waiting for my turn in the shower.

Caro's temper didn't seem to have improved as she stormed back into the room.

"You shouldn't wander around like that," she chided, trying not to look at my bare chest. "You'll give Signora Battelli a coronary."

She wasn't fooling me. Looked like my tactics were working. I gave her a grin then headed out for my shower. I planned on having Caro back in my bed tonight.

When I strolled back, she was looking at a blog on surfing in Italy. Even though she was still punishing me by not fucking, she hadn't stopped caring about me or what I might like to do on vacation. *God, I loved this woman.*

"Whatcha find?" I asked, standing behind her as she studied the screen on her laptop.

"We seem to be in between surf spots here, but about 30 miles away, there's a place that looks like it might be okay. There's a big campsite there and it says they rent out boards, so it seems like a good bet. Want to try it?"

"I'll try anything with you, baby."

"Sebastian, focus," she huffed out, pointing at the map then folding her arms.

"Sure, baby," I said, winking at her. "I just need to fill up the gas tank, but otherwise we're good to go."

I wrapped my hands over her shoulders and planted a quick kiss in her hair.

"Come on then, Hunter," she snorted, reaching into our bag and throwing me a t-shirt. "Let's go see what Signora Battelli has got us for breakfast."

When we walked into the dining area and saw the table covered with mouth-watering food, my eyes widened, and I had a hard time not drooling: fresh fruit, warm bread, sweet rolls, cereal, yogurts, Italian cheese, salamis and cold meat. Fuckin' A!

Signora Battelli probably hadn't counted on having a Devil Dog at her table, and I made three trips to the buffet before I finally called quits.

It hadn't escaped my attention that a couple of American girls were sitting at the table next to us. They'd been eye-fucking me every time I'd gone to get more food. Once I might have been interested, but why go out for burgers when you've got steak at home?

One of the girls was asking Signora Battelli questions about cooking pasta.

"But how much should I give guests at a meal?" she asked. "How will I know how much to buy back home?"

"Young woman," said Signora Battelli, resting her pudgy hands on her enormous stomach. "You buy a half pound of fresh pasta per person … except for my son: he eats one pound of pasta!"

I wondered if the son was another fat fucker who ate all the pies. I could eat anything I wanted and I was in the best shape of my life. Going into a warzone was very fucking incentivizing.

But then the girls started flirting with me in front of Caro. I would have told them off, but I knew Caro wouldn't like it. So I answered politely, tolerating but not encouraging them.

"I've never ridden a motor-sickle," said the one called Lydia.

"Well, I'm sure you'll enjoy it when you get the chance," I replied then stood up, having reached my limit of tolerance for their amateurish flirting. I held out my hand to Caro impatiently.

"Come on, baby."

She took my hand, a huge smile on her face, and I couldn't resist bringing her fingers to my lips and kissing the inside of her narrow wrist.

Her smile got even wider, and there was something in her eyes that I hadn't seen before.

"What?" I asked, curious about what she was thinking.

"Sometimes you can be very sweet."

Her words were like a punch in the gut and I couldn't look away from her. Ask any of the guys that I'd trained with or fought with and 'sweet' is not a word they'd use to describe me. But to hear it from her for the first time in ten years, all the walls I'd built around me crumbled.

"Tesoro, what did I say?" she whispered, her forehead creasing with concern as I continued to stare at her.

I looked into her eyes, so she could see the truth of my words.

"I love you, Caro, so much. I haven't changed how I feel. I still love you—I've always loved you. It's only ever been you."

I stopped breathing as she gazed back at me, her lips moving wordlessly. And then she spoke.

"I love you, too, Sebastian. More than you'll ever know."

That was all I needed to hear.

I leaned down and trapped her lips with mine, kissing her softly and sweetly because I wanted so badly to mash my mouth against hers, bruising her lips, showing the world that she was mine. Maybe that would come later, but now I needed to be the man she thought I was—the man I could be, for her.

I felt everything. I felt the moment when she let herself believe in me, in our fierce love that a decade apart hadn't been able to kill; the moment she believed in herself, and everything that I knew she felt, too; and the moment that my heart knew I'd spend the rest of my life with this woman … this amazing, brave, fearless, loving woman.

"You mean everything to me, Caro," I whispered, my voice raw with emotion.

I knew she could feel the weight of my words.

"You're so brave, tesoro," she said simply. "You've never been afraid to love."

I smiled because she was so wrong. I was fucking terrified of loving her again—but I was past caring.

"That's because I learned from you, Caro."

She shook her head in denial.

"It's true," I said gently.

She sighed and pulled me a little tighter against her, and that was just fine with me.

We stood there until I became aware that we were the center of attention, the other diners staring at us, as well as

Signora Battelli.

I rubbed Caro's arm and stood up straight.

"I guess we'd better get going before the signora starts vacuuming around us," I murmured, my lips still against the smooth skin of her neck.

She smiled up at me, her eyes so full of love that she cracked me wide open.

"Okay," she said.

We walked back to our room in a silence that was full of meaning as I squeezed her soft hand, needing that small physical connection.

"I can't stop smiling," she confessed. "I think I've pulled a muscle in my mouth."

"I know what you mean," I laughed. "Although I've got some ideas about how you could do that for real later."

She slapped my arm.

"You don't change, do you, Hunter!"

I threw myself back on the bed and grinned up at her.

"Do you want me to change?" I asked, wondering for real what her answer would be.

Women always tried to change you, even when they said they wouldn't. But Caro just laughed.

"Oh, you could do with a bit of polish here and there, but otherwise, no, you'll do."

"I'd like you to polish me right now," I said, arching my hips off of the bed suggestively.

"Well, I'd love to oblige," she smirked, "but Signora Battelli is going to be knocking on our door in about two minutes."

"We could make it quick."

"Oh no, I want to take my time."

"How much time?" I asked as my dick hardened in my pants for the third time this morning.

Her dark eyes sparkled with humor and something else … desire?

"Hours, possibly days … whole months even," she murmured, her eyes locked on mine.

I groaned and closed my eyes, images of her naked in my bed, eating meals off of her perfect, olive skin. "Months?"

"Years," she said softly. "A lifetime."

My eyes snapped open and I sat up quickly, my heart beating too fast. "Do you mean it, Caro, a lifetime?"

Her eyes were serious as she replied.

"Yes."

I closed my eyes again, breathing in deeply. When I looked up, a huge smile stretched across my face.

"Okay," I said, because the words I wanted to say were too big.

CHAPTER 8

We packed up quickly, moving around the room with an easy familiarity that was new, touching each other as we passed, an outward expression of how we were feeling inside. I was glad that it wasn't just me feeling so much anymore—or maybe that Caro felt confident enough to show how she felt now. Whatever—it was fucking wonderful.

I was definitely on a roll, so when I paid Signora Battelli, I may have gone a little overboard, saying it was the best place I'd ever stayed, and ended up kissing her hand.

Caro poked me in the ribs as we left.

"You are so smooth, Hunter!" she teased.

"I was just telling her the truth," I grinned at her. "I think we should come back here, and book the same room every year—then spend the night fucking."

"You're such a romantic," she scoffed, trying to hide her smile.

"Yeah, I know, baby."

We headed out of town and southeast along the coastal road, burning out of Pisa and racing south. I felt good—more than good; I'd been given a fresh chance and I was going to make the most of it.

With Caro's arms wrapped me, I felt like I could conquer the world. And if things went the way they could in Afghanistan, I might have to. I pushed the thought to the back of my mind. I still had 10 days of leave left—I was going to make the most of it.

The campsite Caro had found was just an hour from Pisa, outside the village of Polveroni, and right by the ocean. And there were waves. Holy hell, the Mediterranean had surf—three to four feet of clean lines rolling up onto a beach break. I'd have gone body surfing and been stoked, but that bitch lady luck was with me today—and I saw a shop with boards to rent.

"Game on!"

Caro laughed as I almost sprinted inside, for once leaving her to stow the helmets by herself.

The owner looked up as I came in.

"Buon giorno! Can I rent a longboard for the day?"

"Si, signore! I got seven footers and eight footers—what do you need?"

Usually, I'd have taken the seven footer, but I suddenly had the urge to get Caro on a board with me. Ten years ago we'd caught some waves together—I wanted to do it again, this time knowing that she was mine and nothing could take her away from me.

I bought a huge beach towel and a pair of boardshorts, wincing at the bright Hawaiian pattern. I knew Caro would bust my balls about that.

"We don't have a tent; do you rent rooms, too?" I asked.

I really liked the idea of spending the day surfing, the evening fucking, and the night listening to the waves break on the beach.

The owner grinned at me. "Sure, I have one cabin I rent out. It's my brother's, but he's away. It's small, but it has a bathroom. The bed is large," he said, and winked at me. "You can use it. Thirty Euros?"

As soon as Caro saw me, she honed in on the boardshorts, a vomit-inducing red, orange, yellow and lime green.

"Hey, Marine! You're in danger of doing color!" she laughed

I grinned back at her.

"Yeah, well, it was all they had. Either that or I'd have to do it in the nude. What do you think, Caro, naked surfing?"

"It could catch on, or you could get arrested. But I'm telling you, Sebastian, if you do get arrested and I don't get laid tonight, I'm going to be mighty pissed at you."

I grinned at her stern expression.

"Now you're talking. By the way, the guy in the shop said that he rents out rooms. He said it's pretty basic—just a big, old bed and a small bathroom. But I thought it would be kind of cool to be able to hear the waves tonight. Is that okay?"

"Very okay," she smiled.

The day was going great, but then I saw the ugly as fuck swimsuit that Caro was holding. *Seriously? My girl was gonna wear a granny suit in dark blue?*

"Wait, *that's* what you're going to wear?" *No fucking way!*

"Yes," she said, puzzled. "Why?"

"Stay here," I commanded.

I headed back to the beach shop and the owner looked surprised to see me back so soon.

"Hey, I need a bikini for my girlfriend."

"Sure, we have several," and he pointed at a rack in the corner.

I picked out something that I knew she would look hot in—and something I was looking forward to taking off of her later.

I jogged back outside, pleased with the fifty Euros I'd just spent.

"Here. Wear this."

Caro's mouth dropped open, a look of horror on her face as I passed her the bikini. Admittedly there wasn't a lot of it…

"I can't wear that, Sebastian," she gasped. "There's nothing to it! I'm forty, not twenty!"

I wanted to roll my eyes at that comment—I didn't.

"You'll look amazing, Caro. I want every guy on the beach to know how hot my woman is."

"I may as well go topless!"

"Yeah, baby."

She shook her head, but her eyes were saying yes. "You're crazy."

"Crazy in love," I agreed, scooping her into a kiss that rapidly became heated.

"Fine, I'll wear it," she said breathlessly when I put her down.

Damn straight!

I held up the beach towel while she changed, taking a few sneaky glances. She was so preoccupied with not being seen by anyone else on the beach that she didn't even notice. She tugged at it a few times, trying to cover up a little more, but there was a reason I'd picked out that swimsuit.

"I can't wait to take that off you," I whispered into her ear.

She gave me a half smile.

"Sex or surfing, Sebastian?"

"Sex," I said at once. *No brainer.*

Her cheeks pinked up, but then she laughed and shook her head.

"Well, you'll have to take a rain check—we haven't booked that room for the night yet. And I've warned you what will happen if you get arrested."

"You owe me a lot of rain checks, Caro. I'm going to enjoy cashing them in."

Giving her a look that told her I always collected a debt, I yanked off my t-shirt, enjoying the way her eyes tracked across my chest and stomach, then I dropped my jeans and briefs, standing buck naked in the sunshine.

"Sebastian!" she hissed, glancing around to see if anyone was watching—but not before she'd taken a long look herself. *Oh yeah, my woman loved to look.*

But I'd already pulled on my boardshorts by the time her eyes flicked back to me. I laughed at her surprised expression.

"Years of practice changing out of my wetsuit in windswept parking lots along Sunset Cliffs, Caro," I explained. "I'll show you how quick I can get out of my clothes now if you like?"

I wasn't joking and she knew it.

"Go. Surf," she commanded.

I pulled off my dog tags and placed them around her neck, and fuck me if it wasn't the biggest turn on, the way they nestled between her breasts.

"Here—look after these for me." I took a deep breath and dragged my eyes up to meet hers. "Those look hot on you, Caro. Really fucking hot."

She fingered the small pieces of metal, a smile lifting the corner of her mouth. That finished me, so I pulled her into my arms, kissing her thoroughly, dipping her so low her hair brushed across the sand. Then I stood her back on her feet, holding on until she stopped swaying. She shook her head in amusement, but I didn't miss her slight breathlessness or the heat in her eyes.

I winked at her, scooped up the rented board and jogged down to the water's edge.

The ocean had always been my safe place—away from my parents, away from school, or work, or whatever was weighing on my mind. When I was 17 and Caro came back into my life, the beach became our place, away from prying eyes and the judgment of the world. And when she left me, the ocean was the place I came to remember and to forget. Catching waves, being one with the water, whatever bullshit reason you wanted to make up, the ocean gave me peace, because when you're catching a wave, you don't have the time or space to think of anything else. In that sense, it's a bit like sex. Fuck knows what Freud would have said if he met me.

When Fido was killed by an IED, I'd been in the south of Iraq and couldn't get home for his repatriation and funeral. So on my next leave, I'd organized a paddle-out with a few of my buddies and the guys who'd known him. He'd have liked that.

Today was the first chance I'd had to surf in over a year. I'd missed it. Being in a dump like Afghanistan, surrounded by nothing but deserts and death, Stone Age villages, and women hidden away, the ocean seemed like a dream from another world.

I surfed for an hour, reveling in the freedom, the salt spray in my face and the sun on my body. Every now and then I'd look back at the beach, checking on my girl, watching her relax in the sunshine.

But the next time I glanced over, some fucker was hitting on her. I caught the first wave back to the beach and jogged across the hot sand.

By then, the asswipe had disappeared in the other direction, so I assumed Caro had given him his marching orders. The amused expression on her face told me the rest.

"What did he want?" I asked, trying and failing to keep my voice neutral.

"Don't blame me, Hunter," she said, raising one eyebrow, "You're the one who bought this itsy bitsy teeny weeny bikini for me. Anyway, I told him my boyfriend was surfing, so you don't need to worry."

Not fucking acceptable. Fucker should have stuck around to get his face rearranged.

"Did you have fun?" she asked, and I knew she was trying to distract me from homicidal thoughts of any other guy touching my woman.

"Yeah, not bad. Got some good rides."

"I know, I was watching," she said, pointing to the camera, "I got some great shots, too."

"Really? I've never seen any pictures of me surfing."

I sat down on the towel next to her and scrolled through the photos she'd taken. I was impressed, both by the way she'd framed the shots and the quality of the images. I knew her camera was expensive, but these photos were good enough to make it into *Surfer* magazine.

"Wow! You're a really great photographer, Caro."

"I have excellent subject material," she smiled, then snapped a close-up of me.

"What's that for?"

"Just so I know you're real. I think you're a figment of my overwrought imagination, and you might disappear when I wake up. But now," she said, waving the camera at me, "I have proof."

I grinned, loving the current easiness between us.

I pressed her back into the beach towel with my body, kissing her the way I wanted to with no apology. She ran her fingers over my damp hair and smiled up at me.

"You're cute when you're wet," she smiled.

"So are you," I teased.

We ate our lunch on the beach, some bread and fruit sold by a kid under a sunshade. I felt deeply relaxed. Even the shadow of imminent deployment couldn't dampen my good mood. I even fell asleep in the sun, something I never normally did.

When I woke up, I wanted to head out for a final surf. The guy in the rental shop said that the air pressure was rising and that tomorrow the sea would be flat. And there was something else I wanted to do; I wanted Caro to ride the board with me—tandem surfing—something I hadn't done since the last time we'd been together.

"Come on, Caro, I've wanted to try this for a long time. Let's take the board out and catch a wave together. I'll do the paddling and I can stare at your gorgeous ass while I'm doing it."

I pulled her to her feet and she tried to adjust her bikini top so her beautiful tits didn't spill out. God, I loved that bikini.

Once in the water, Caro lay on the board first, and I jumped on behind her. I couldn't resist giving her ass a quick bite.

She squeaked and tried to slap my arm. *Too fucking cute.*

We paddled out to just behind where the waves were breaking, then as the water started to rise, I turned the board around and we began to speed down the front of the wave.

"Get ready to pop up!" I yelled. "Go!"

She scrambled to her feet and the board wobbled slightly so I had to make some minor balance adjustments before I popped up, one hand steadying her hip as we raced down the face of the wave.

It was the best feeling—pure joy with no bullshit, no one else but us.

When we caught the last wave back in, Caro's skin was cool to the touch and she was shivering slightly.

"Your nipples are hard," I remarked, studying them carefully.

"Well, what a shocker," she snarked. "I've never seen them like that before."

"Is that right?" I said, raising my eyebrow. "I'll see what I can do about it later."

"Promises, promises," she sighed.

What the fuck? I didn't care if it was a joke—that was what I'd call a challenge.

"Bed, woman. Now."

Caro's eyes grew really big and she bit her lip.

"Don't you want to find somewhere to have dinner first?"

Hell, no. I shook my head, my eyes raking up and down her body, hypnotized by the way droplets of seawater rolled into the amazing valley between her tits.

I tugged her along the beach to the shop, only slightly repentant that she was having to jog to keep up, but she didn't complain. We got the key to our room quickly, but when the owner wanted to talk surfing and whether San Diego or Monterey had the better break, I was grinding my teeth with frustration. I wanted to tell him to take a hike, but seeing as he'd cut us as a deal on the room, I didn't want to piss him off.

Caro winked at me and walked down the beach to our cabin. My eyes followed the movement of her ass the whole way.

"You have a very beautiful girlfriend, signore," said the owner, his smile too fucking appreciative by a long way.

I cleared my throat and his eyes snapped back to mine.

"Yeah, I know. And I'm taking her for dinner tonight— can you recommend anywhere?"

"Ah, si! I know just the place. L'Acquapazza in Marina di Cecina. Just five kilometers. Is very good food, very good views. My cousin, Lazzero, is the owner. Tell him Salvi sent you."

I nodded my thanks and headed to the cabin. By the time I got there, I was revved up and ready to go. So I was somewhat fucking disappointed that Caro wasn't naked in bed, but shutting down her laptop. I guessed she'd been catching up on her messages.

"What's so funny?"

She looked up, a huge smile on her face.

"Oh, I just had an email from my friend Nicole in NYC. She wants me to have mindless sex with an Italian stallion."

Was that supposed to be funny? "Why is she saying stuff like that to you?" I bit out.

Caro rolled her eyes.

"Oh, don't be such a prude, Sebastian! It's just a joke. She's always nagging me to find a man."

"What about me?" I growled, my tone angrier than I'd intended.

Caro huffed quietly. "I haven't told anyone about you. I like having you to myself. But I will, if you want me to."

Was she ashamed of me? Was this just a summer fling to her after all?

The old fears rushed back—I was a secret, her dirty little secret. Again.

"I want to know your friends, Caro," I tried to explain, before my anger and fear bubbled through. "Although I'll fucking tell 'Nicole' that she can keep her comments about 'Italian stallions' to herself."

Suddenly her phone rang and she stared at it in surprise. It was the first time I'd heard it ring since we'd been traveling.

She picked it up, her eyes widening as she read the caller's ID.

"Nicole, hi! Wow, it's great to hear from you. How are you?"

I wandered around the room, moving her shit off of the bed, listening to one half of the conversation.

Then she said, "Nicole, I sent you a picture of him. His name is Sebastian."

So she had mentioned me? I couldn't help looking across and smiling at her.

"No, seriously, Nicole. That's a photo of my friend. I promise you."

Caro was smiling and shaking her head.

"I'll tell you some other time ... I can't. Later ... because he's standing right here, Nicole ... it's true."

She raised her eyebrows at whatever was being said. "What?" She shook her head again then she handed me her cell. "She wants to talk to you."

Surprised, I took the phone. "Hi, Nicole. This is Sebastian."

"Wow! So you really do exist!" said a female voice with the clipped voice of a native New Yorker. *"Well, listen up. Lee is my best friend and one of the nicest, most honest people I've ever meet, so if*

*you're planning on using her, don't even think about it. If you do
anything to upset her, I will hunt you down to the ends of the earth and
rip your balls off with a blunt spoon. Capiche?"*

I understood that she was looking out for her friend, but
yeah, I didn't appreciate the way she said it.

"You don't want me to use her?" I confirmed, glancing
at Caro. "Well, Nicole, I was planning on taking her to bed
and using her in ways that aren't even mentioned in the Kama
Sutra, but now you've told me that, I think I should go take a
cold shower instead."

Caro glared at me and snatched the phone back as I
grinned at her.

"Sorry about that, Nic!" she huffed out. "Nic?" Then
she started smiling at whatever the über-bitch was saying to
her. "I'll get back to you on that, Nic."

As far as I was concerned, the conversation had gone on
long enough, so I started untying the straps of Caro's bikini
and kissing down the back of her neck. She gasped when I
tossed her bikini top to the floor, massaging her nipples into
tight little peaks.

"I'll have to call you back, Nic," she said breathlessly,
then ended the call and threw herself at me, knocking both of
us onto the bed.

She straddled me and I let her push my hands above my
head as her mouth met mine and her breasts were crushed
against my chest.

Our tongues were twisting together, our teeth clashing,
and I was achingly hard.

I sat up suddenly, cradling my arms around her waist as
she squeaked in surprise. I kissed her neck, running my
tongue over her throat.

"You taste like the sea," I rumbled against her, "and
your skin smells like sunshine."

She moaned happily, and I ran my fingers up her back,
letting them tangle in her hair, then pulling her face back
down to mine.

"I want to be inside you, Caro."

I could hear the need and desperation in my voice. But
she smiled against my lips, then rolled off me, scooting down

to the bottom of the bed.

"Raise that glorious ass," she said, tugging on the hem of my boardshorts.

I grinned at the way her eagerness matched mine, lifting my hips from the bed. She pulled off the shorts, threw them behind her, then sat back on her heels staring down at me.

As her eyes wandered along my body, I propped myself up on my elbows, wondering what differences she saw between now and the boy of 17 that she'd known. There was a small white scar across my left hip where a piece of shrapnel from an RPG attack had nicked me. I had another puckered scar across my right shoulder from parachute training where the webbing had gotten twisted and left a mark almost like a burn. That had been fucking painful, but the mark was faint now.

And of course there was the *Semper Fi* tat, but I got the impression she liked that.

"You're beautiful, Sebastian," she whispered, her voice soft and so fucking sweet. "I love to look at you. I love to see you like this, when it's just the two of us. Why does it feel so right?"

I shook my head slowly, a little stunned by the depth of sincerity I saw in her eyes.

"Maybe it was just meant to be. I mean, shit, could we have had any more challenges thrown at us?"

"We've certainly had our share," she sighed.

I sat up and held her cheek with my hand.

"Don't be sad, Caro. We've got our second chance … or maybe we're on our third … I kinda lost count already."

"That is very true," she laughed, lightly. "Now you seem to have a very desirable hard-on there, so what say we have some fun with that?"

I smirked at her as she licked her lips.

"I'm all yours."

She grinned and jumped off the bed. "Are the condoms in your toiletry bag?"

"Yeah, baby."

I watched as she rooted through the overnight bag until she found what she was looking for. But when she looked up,

147

her expression was irritated.

"Sebastian, there's only one condom left in here," she said, shaking the box at me.

"Shit! You're kidding! Fuck, how did I … ah, crap. Give me that fucker—I'm going to make the most of it."

I reached for the condom, but she backed away from me, smiling

"Oh no, Hunter," she said, waving the foil packet at me, "this one is all mine."

I swear my cock swelled some more and twitched, just from the way she was looking at me. She'd always turned me on more than any woman I'd ever met.

"Feeling a little needy, baby?" she chuckled, as she walked around the bed.

"Fuck, Caro!" *This woman was gonna kill me.*

I tried to catch her hand, but she danced away.

"Dear me, someone is impatient," she laughed, determined to torture me.

"Yeah, very!" I agreed quickly.

She stood at the end of the bed, looking down at me, her expression heated and amused.

"Would you like me to take these off?" she asked in a sing-song voice, tugging gently on the delicate laces of her bikini bottoms.

Fuck, yeah! I nodded silently.

"Or maybe you'd like to take them off me?"

She climbed up from the foot of the bed and crawled all the way up until she was poised above me, the foil packet held in her teeth. I reached up to untie first one, then the second ribbon, and the small strip of material fell away.

I let my hand drift up the inside of her thighs and then gently slid my index finger inside, massaging her slowly. Her eyes were locked on mine: watching me, watching her, watching me. Her gaze was scorching and my body overheated quickly.

I pushed another finger inside her, moving faster, and her breath began to come in short gasps.

"Come on, baby," I encouraged, my voice strained.

She clenched around my fingers and then tried to push

my hand away.

"No, baby," I crooned to her, "you can take more."

"I can't! I can't!" she gasped, her eyes begging, but I wouldn't stop, and another orgasm ripped through her, arching her spine as her body shuddered and trembled.

Then she collapsed onto my chest, and I stroked her back, running my hands down her spine, feeling soft tremors still running through her.

Gently, I rolled so she was on her back, then kissed her neck and chest, sucking and tugging on her nipples with my teeth until they were tight little fists. Her body was limp and pliant, so when I pushed her knees apart, there was no resistance as I slid inside her.

Only then her body tensed up and she gripped onto my shoulders.

"Sebastian, no! Don't!"

I was too lost in sensation, my mind fogged by heat and lust.

"Come on, baby, you feel so good."

I rolled my hips, and she trembled around me. But then she shoved hard against my chest and I pulled out, confused and more than a little pissed.

"No!" she yelled, her eyes hard and accusing. "What are you doing, Sebastian?"

"I just want to make love to you, Caro."

"I know ... but, you're not wearing a condom."

She opened her hand, showing me the foil packet that she was still holding, unopened.

"We don't need that, Caro."

I didn't want anything between us ever again.

"What?" she yelped. "Are you crazy, Sebastian? I could get pregnant!"

"Would that be so bad?"

I wanted it all with her—why didn't she understand that?

"You *want* me to get pregnant?" she stammered.

I sighed and closed my eyes, rolling onto my side.

"I want to have a life with you, Caro, for the rest of my life. Look—kids—whatever. If it happens, then great; if it doesn't, that's fine, too. Just as long as we're together. This

149

time, forever."

She pushed away from me and flung her arm over her eyes. But I reached up and pulled her arm away, forcing her to look at me.

"Caro?"

I needed to know what she was thinking.

"Sebastian…" she stuttered, trying to pull herself together. "We were apart for ten years. I saw you again less than a week ago, we had sex, a couple of dates, more sex, we fought, we broke up … and now you're saying you want to have children with me?"

Now she was getting it. "Yeah."

"Do you know how crazy that sounds?" she gasped, her mouth hanging open.

"That's our story, Caro. Crazy in love."

She stared at me like I'd just grown two dicks.

"I … I don't know what to say."

I shrugged, a little amused and a lot puzzled by her freak-out.

"You don't have to say anything, Caro. You don't have to *do* anything. Like I said: if it happens or not … whatever … we'll deal."

"And what … you'll give up being a Marine to look after the kids?"

My jaw dropped and then I grinned at her. "Kids? As in, plural? Sure, why not?"

"You … you'd do that?"

I could tell that this wasn't the reaction she'd been expecting.

"Caro, I'll do whatever it takes to be with you," I explained slowly, so there was no misunderstanding this time. "I've been in the Marines for nearly ten years and I've had tours in Iraq and Afghanistan, been stationed in Germany, Paris and Geneva. I didn't care because I didn't have anywhere to go home to. But with you, we'll have a home, and I won't want to be away from you."

I had no fucking clue what I'd do if I left the Corps, but I'd worry about that later.

She struggled to sit up, still obviously thrown by the

conversation.

"I … I…"

I grinned at her. "I thought you were supposed to be the one who was good with words, Caro."

"Usually," she choked out.

I leaned over to stroke her flat stomach, my hand drifting suggestively lower, hoping she'd take the hint and do something about my raging hard-on that was still standing up straighter than a Drill Sergeant.

"So, what do you think?" I suggested. "Should we just keep going?"

She shook her head quickly.

"I … no … look, just give me some time to think about this. We've got this lonely, little condom, so let's use it and talk again later. Okay?"

Well, she wasn't saying no to sex, but I had to admit that I was disappointed. My dick agreed with me, not wanting to be wrapped after he'd known the insane fucking pleasure of being inside her bare, and started to wilt.

"Feeling a little flat here, baby. You wanna pump me up?" I asked hopefully.

She shook her head again, but I could tell she meant the opposite. Fuck, women were confusing. They should come with a manual.

"Yes, I think I can do something about that," she smiled. "Lay back."

I grinned up at her. "What are you going to do?"

"Absolutely nothing."

Huh?

HUH?

"What?"

"I'm not going to touch you, Sebastian," she purred, "and you're not going to touch me. Yet. I'm going to show you how good I am with words."

"I have no idea what you're talking about baby, but it's making me feel horny."

She smiled. "That's the point, Sebastian. I'm going to make you so hard, I'm going to get you so wound up, I'm going to turn you on so much, that all I'll have to do is touch you with one finger to make you come."

"Fuck!"

Was that even possible? I had no idea what she was going to do that, but fuck me, it sounded hot!

She laid down next to me so we were close, but not touching.

"Close your eyes," she breathed.

I gave her one hot lingering look, then did as she asked.

"I want you to see it all in your mind, Sebastian. Imagine everything I'm saying: see it, hear it, taste it, feel it, breathe it in. Understand?"

I swallowed and nodded, feeling my dick hardening again with every word she said.

"You're lying on the bed and it's very quiet. It's night time, but there's a full moon, and the shadows on the floor are almost blue. You hear the door open, but your eyes stay closed. You hear my footsteps across the wooden floor; you know it's me because you recognize the soft sound of my footfalls. I'm standing right next to you, looking down at your naked body. You can hear the rustle of my clothes as I slowly start to take them off. You can hear the zipper of my dress. I must be wearing silk, because the material whispers as it falls from my body. Then you feel the mattress moving under you and my weight presses down on your body. My naked breasts are brushing against your skin; it's cool and my nipples are hard when you take them in your mouth."

I groaned, seeing it all in my mind, almost *feeling* what she was saying to me.

"I move up your body, hovering over you. I moan slightly and you know it's because I'm touching myself, turning myself on for you. My fingers are inside me, circling slowly, and when I pull them out, I place them on your lips and you suck them hard. You can taste me and you can smell the muskiness of my scent. You long to touch me, but then I take your fingers in my mouth, sucking them one by one. You imagine what my mouth would feel like around your cock: my lips, my teeth, my tongue swirling around. You can imagine what it would feel like when you move into my mouth and your tip touches the back of my throat."

Fuck! Could this get any hotter? I was so close to coming and she hadn't even touched me.

"My hair brushes the skin on your chest as I arch away from you, and your skin is so sensitized you can feel every strand, every wave, every individual hair. I take your hand and move your fingers against my clitoris. I'm wet, very wet, and you know it won't be long before your hot, hard cock is stroking inside me. I run my fingers around you, gripping you, squeezing you, and you know that I want you—every inch of you—inside me. You're at the entrance of my sex, and you sink into me: slowly at first, then getting faster and harder, going deeper and deeper. Your control is unraveling because you can feel that hot, soft, sweet flesh all around you. My body starts to buck under yours and you know that I'm close. You can feel ripples of pleasure pulsing through me and you're wondering how long you can hold on before you come. You're trying so hard to hold it back but then I clench around you, squeezing you, milking everything you have. And I'm begging you to give it to me again. I'm begging you to take me from behind, so you pull out, even though you're aching to come, your balls hot and heavy, and then you're looking at my ass, knowing that I want you so badly, waiting just for you."

Her words were driving me insane, and my breathing was becoming rapid. I needed her hands on me or my own—some fucker needed to relive the pressure building in my balls.

"You plunge into me and it feels so deep this way; it's never felt this good before. You're so hard, your cock is aching for release..." *Fuckin' tell me about it!* "...but you want to enjoy every moment of it, so you hold back, hold back, hold back. But it's hard, so hard, because I'm coming again and you desperately want to come with me, but you want me to have every second, every ounce of pleasure, so you hold back, hold back. And then I'm coming hard, like you've never felt before; and it's so hot and wet and sweet—you spill into me, on and on and on."

And then she grabbed my cock, hard, and I spilled into her fist, the cum overflowing onto my stomach as she continued to stroke me.

My breath was roaring and my blood was pounding so loudly in my head I thought I was going to pass out. *Holy fuck! What just happened? She barely touched me!*

I was vaguely aware that Caro was cuddling against me, her warm breath fanning out across my shoulder.

Eventually I managed to peel open one eye and looked down at myself in amazement. Nope, I hadn't dreamed it— thick loops of cum were cooling on my stomach and I was a mess.

"Fuck, Caro!" I rasped out. "How … how…"

"So, you're the one who's speechless now?" she said, more than a little smug.

I couldn't speak coherently, so I just watched as she reached into her toiletry bag, pulled out a bunch of tissues and began to clean me up.

"Enjoy my bedtime story?" she asked, her eyes glittering wickedly.

"Fuck, yes!" I huffed out. "I still can't believe you did that to me, Caro."

I was trying to process exactly what had happened, but so far I was coming up blank. I did know that my brain had disconnected from the parts that moved, and all thought processes had ground to a halt. I'd just had one of the most intense orgasms of my life, certainly in the last 10 years, and my body needed to reboot. Or something—shit, I was flying so high, I was somewhere near Venus.

"Well, Sebastian," she said, leaning in close and whispering into my ear, "now you have something to think about when we're apart, or when you're doing a tour. Now you can imagine me talking to you."

I groaned as her words made my limp dick twitch again.

"Are you fucking kidding me? With twenty other horny Marines sharing the same grot?" I winced. "Aw, hell! I won't be able to get rid of that image now."

She laughed, deep and throaty and totally fucking sexy. "That's kind of the point, Sebastian."

I shook my head, slowly. "Fuck, Caro! You are so fucking amazing. Did I ever tell you that?"

I felt the mattress move as she sat up and smiled at me.

"You may have mentioned it once or twice, but feel free to repeat yourself."

Then she slapped my chest. "Come on, let's go shower. I'm hungry. For food." And she jumped off the bed and headed for the shower. I closed my eyes, drifting quietly, about a foot above where my body was laying on the bed.

I don't know how long I lay there, but I was aware that the bathroom door had opened, with warm, damp air and the scent of citrus gusting across the room.

Caro leaned down and kissed me firmly, and even though my eyes were still closed, I could feel the smile on her lips.

"Are you going to be moving anytime soon, Sebastian?"

"Nope."

"Come on! You need feeding!"

"Just gonna lie here and die a happy man," I muttered.

"Sebastian! Get up! I'm hungry!" she laughed, poking me in the ribs in the one fucking place that was ticklish.

I rolled away from her so she leaned down and bit my ass.

"Hey, no fair!" I groaned.

"I thought Marines were supposed to have stamina," she grumbled, nipping me again.

"Okay, okay, I'm going," I complained. "No need to be so rough, jeez."

I struggled to my feet, my legs shaky, feeling like I'd just finished a twenty mile hike carrying 80 pounds of equipment. I mean, it was kind of embarrassing. On some missions, I deployed with 100 pounds of equipment if I was away for a few nights, and I was in better shape at the end of each day than I was right now. It was a mind-fuck that she could affect me like this. *Shit. I was is in so much trouble.*

CHAPTER 9

The shower revived me enough to jumpstart my brain, but I still was a little out of it. Well, a lot out of it.

"You okay?" Caro asked. "You seem a little discombobulated."

"Fuck, yes," I said, nodding my head, "and I don't even know what that means. Fuck, Caro, I can't get over that. I mean, you barely touched me. It was just ... hot."

She smiled, her eyes warm and wicked. "Ah, the power of words."

"There's going to be payback," I muttered.

"Sebastian, if I wasn't so damn hungry, I'd be dragging you back to the bedroom now and tying you down until you made a dishonest woman of me."

Wow, who was this woman?

"Jeez, you've gotten so bossy. I like it."

She laughed happily. "You've been taking orders from the wrong people, Marine—but I'm going to help you with that."

"Can't wait," I admitted, shaking my head in disbelief.

I pulled her into a hug, burying my face in the sweet-smelling hair at the side of her neck, still damp from the shower. It was one of my favorite places.

"I have missed you so much," I said, fucking terrified by the power this woman held over me.

"I've missed you, too, tesoro."

We stood there quietly, our arms around each other, neither of us willing to break the spell.

Eventually, I heard her stomach rumble and I stepped back smiling down at her. "Let's go eat."

L'Acquapazza was on the waterfront. And Salvi was right about the views, but I couldn't help thinking that he meant his cousin would enjoy the views of Caro, so I made sure we were given a seat in the corner.

But she stopped by the entrance, her gaze drawn toward a dozen well-thumbed newspapers that stood in a rack by the door. She pulled one out and carried it to our table as we sat down, turning to the middle pages and scanning for international news, specifically about Afghanistan.

"Always the journalist, Caro."

Her eyes snapped up to meet mine. "I bet you can tell me how many people there are in the restaurant without looking," she challenged.

I was surprised that she'd noticed me checking out the place; I thought she'd been concentrating on the newspaper.

"Six couples, a table of three men, two male waiters, and a kid filling the water glasses who had better take his eyes off of your tits if he wants to live."

Caro laughed. "See! You're always working, too. Did you think I hadn't noticed that each time you sit with your back to the wall so you can see who's coming in?"

I smiled but didn't answer. She was right, but the other reason I kept my back to the wall was so that I knew an attack couldn't come from behind.

One of the waiters handed us each a menu.

"What the hell is that?" I asked, pointing at one of the items. "Cipolline agrodolci alla Cinque Terre. Is that onions?"

"Yes, sweet and sour onions: it's a local delicacy. You want to try them?"

"Normally I'd say yes, but I'm really craving … steak," I grinned at her.

She rolled her eyes. "You're so American! You want fries with that?"

"Yeah, now you mention it. Anyway, I've got to keep my strength up. This woman I've met is milking me dry. She can't keep her hands off me."

"What a slut."

I winked at her. "Well, she hasn't been that slutty, but I'd really like to see her in slutty stockings and garter straps—

no panties." *Oh freakin' yeah!*

"Hmm, well I'm sure we can arrange it at some point, but I have to admit, Sebastian, I don't actually own anything like that."

"Not at all? I thought all women…"

I stopped when I saw the expression on her face. I was kind of a novice at relationships, but even a dumb grunt like me knew that you don't talk about past women with your present woman. *Major fail.*

"Maybe all your previous women, Sebastian," she said snippily, "but no, not me, I don't."

I winced and kept my eyes on the menu.

"Sebastian," she said, slightly more calmly, "apart from you, I last had a date nearly three years ago. And there's not a lot of need for slinky underwear on assignment to military bases—well, not for me, anyway. Maybe you know differently?" she raised her eyebrows, making a joke of the situation, but I was caught up by something else she said.

"Why don't you date, Caro? I mean, you're fucking gorgeous, anyone can see that, and you're clever and funny. Any man would have to be blind not to want you."

Her expression softened and she glanced away briefly before looking back at me and meeting my gaze.

"I've just … not been that interested. No one's really caught my eye."

I still found it crazy that she'd been single for so long. Fuckin' happy about it, though.

"Oh, wait, Major Parsons asked me out," she smiled. "Mike—from the hostile environment training. He was pretty cute."

"That bastard!"

She looked a little surprised at my reaction. Really? She wanted to tell me that Limey guy had hit on *my* woman and didn't think I'd be pissed as all hell?

"Sebastian, I said no," she said hurriedly. "And actually, he was really sweet about it. He wasn't pushy or anything." Then a puzzled look crossed her face. "What were you thinking, that first day, when we saw each other at the press training? You looked really mad."

Wow, was that only a week ago?

"Just so fucking shocked," I admitted. "I saw the name 'Lee Venzi' on the training list. I recognized it because I'd read some of your articles…"

"Really?"

"Yeah, sure. I check out all the journos who go on these gigs. I want to know what kind of shit … sorry, what kind of writing they do. I thought yours was good."

She shot me a look.

"No, really. I'm not just saying that. I kind of assumed you were ex-Forces because of the way you understood the military. And we were all expecting you'd be a guy. Obviously somebody screwed up on the background checks…" *Dickwad Crawley was supposed to be taking care of that.* "But as far as your online presence, you're definitely a man."

She smiled happily. "That's the general idea. I've had quite a few assignments given to me because people assume I'm a man; jobs they wouldn't give to a woman."

"Yeah, but there could be a good reason for it, too. I mean, some of the places you go are dangerous and…"

But she stopped the rest of my rant by pressing her fingers over my lips.

"Shh, tesoro. They're a lot less dangerous than where you go, and we're not having this conversation."

"The fuck we aren't!"

"No, I mean it. This is my work. Please drop it."

I could tell by the look on her face that she meant it. I wasn't happy, but a smart Devil Dog knew when to withdraw and regroup.

"You were going to tell me what you thought when you first saw me," she repeated.

"Shock. At first I thought you'd done it deliberately somehow. And then I saw the look on your face, like you didn't know what to say to me either, and I realized it was just as weird for you as it was for me."

"And then?"

"I just kept thinking how mad I was at you; blaming you for all the shit. I kept trying to hold on to all that anger, but you just looked so … you looked just the same. And I kept thinking, maybe I got it wrong. And then I remembered that you hadn't come looking for me and ... it was so fucking confusing, Caro."

I stared out at the surf washing across the beach, smaller now as the high pressure continued to push in from the west.

"And then you tried to talk to me and I just freaked. I couldn't ... not in front of all those people, not with all the things I wanted to ... I found a bar and just started drinking... getting up the courage to go see you. I really screwed that up, didn't I?"

"Completely," she said, her voice sad.

I dropped my eyes and stared at my hands. They were still callused from all the training I did, despite the fact that I'd had a desk job for most of the last three years. I wondered again what she was doing with a guy like me who'd never even gotten a college degree. If I left the Marines I'd be nothing, no one. What then?

"It doesn't matter now, Sebastian," she said quietly.

I shook my head, trying to fight off the darkness that was threatening to pull me down again.

"What did you think, when you saw me?" I asked.

"You mean after the oh-my-God moment? I thought you looked bitter: your eyes looked so cold and hard. Gorgeous, of course, but you looked like you'd really changed. I was ... intimidated. And then Liz told me you had gotten this reputation ... as something of a lady-killer..."

Fuckin' bitch.

"Well, you did ask," she said, reaching out to take my hand.

"Yeah, well ... what else did you think?"

"She said you were brilliant, too, if that makes you feel any better."

"Not much."

She sighed. "I just thought I'd try and talk to you by yourself, but you kept avoiding me. So, I assumed you didn't want anything to do with me. I was ... hurt, but I guess I accepted it. Can we talk about something else? This is making me feel blue."

"Sure, baby," I said, kicking myself because my

depression was bringing her down, too. "How about we plan the rest of the trip?"

"Yes, please," she responded quickly.

I reached into my jacket pocket and pulled out the map.

"Well, it's up to you, Caro. We could keep going down the coast road to Salerno, look up your dad's old village. Or take it slower, go see some of Tuscany. Siena is supposed to be amazing and there's this old hilltop town, Montepulciano that looks really cool. Or go right down to the bottom—check out Sicily."

She studied the map for a moment, her eyes tracing the route south.

"What do you want to do, Sebastian? I don't mind having another day on the beach if you want to do some more surfing—it's your vacation, too."

"Nah, that's okay—it's going to be flat tomorrow—I already checked."

She smiled and shook her head. "Of course. Silly me."

"It's about 250 miles to your dad's village. We could be there this time tomorrow. If you want."

I thought she'd go for that, but I could see unease on her face, as well. Maybe she was afraid of building it up too much. Neither of us had been given a great hand when it came to family, but her dad was different. I could tell she was afraid of hoping too hard that there'd be some trace of him. Realistically, that wasn't likely. He'd left Italy more than 40 years ago and Caro didn't know if he'd left any family behind.

"No, let's take it easy," she said at last. "I'd like to see some more of Tuscany. I've heard of Montepulciano: they have good wine. And honey."

She always made me smile. "How come you know all this food stuff?"

She stared back as if I was missing an obvious point. "I'm Italian, Sebastian."

I laughed out loud, making the waiter at the next table spill the wine he was pouring. But I was too busy sweeping Caro's hand into mine and kissing her fingers. A sultry look crossed her face, and I could feel myself getting hard *again*. Fuck me, I hadn't had this much sex since I was 17 and with

Caro for the first time—although there was that one weekend I went to Tijuana for Ches's bachelor party. That had been memorable, too. But I didn't want to think about what I'd done with other women—not anymore.

The waiter arrived with our order and smiled apologetically as I was forced to let go of Caro's hand.

The food was good and I chowed down hungrily. I hadn't been joking when I said I needed to consume some calories after breaking a fucking record for fucking; my stomach thought that someone had cut my damn throat. So we were quiet for several minutes as we ate.

But I could tell that Caro was distracted. I gave her a few minutes to ask whatever was bugging her, but she sat in silence, pushing the remainder of her food around her plate.

"What is it?" I asked at last, laying down my knife and fork.

"What do you mean?"

"You have that look on your face—like you want to ask me something. You can ask me anything, Caro."

She looked surprised that I'd noticed.

"Well, there was something … did you mean what you said about quitting the Marines?"

My stomach clenched, but I kept a smile on my face.

"Sure. I mean, I re-upped two years ago, so I'd have to do another two before I punch out…"

She sucked her lower lip and looked down.

"Do you think you'd have to do another tour in Afghanistan?"

I wasn't sure how much truth she wanted. The answer was 'yes', but I could tell she didn't want to hear that.

"I don't know, Caro. Most guys wouldn't be sent out again that quickly, but … well, they're short of interpreters, especially non-locals, and military intelligence..."

Fuck! I wasn't supposed to tell her that I was working for Chair Force Spooks.

She saw my hesitation and leaned forward so our conversation was more private.

"Sebastian, whatever you tell me, that's between us. I would *never* use it in my work."

"I know that, baby, but there are some things I can't tell you … and some things that it's better you don't know."

She smiled sadly.

"They're not going to be pleased that you're dating a journalist."

"Nope. Don't think so," I agreed, "although they couldn't stop me…"

"So … I guess it would be better to keep this between us, just for now?"

I nodded, then leaned back in my chair.

"Would *you* give it up, Caro? Working in war zones, traveling all over the world?"

She didn't seem surprised by the question—perhaps she'd been expecting it ever since our truncated discussion about having some rug rats of our own.

"I wouldn't want to give it up completely, Sebastian, that's the truth. But I could agree to a maximum amount of time I spent away in a year, maybe."

A better answer than the one I'd expected. "Okay, I guess."

I stood up and stretched, gazing around the restaurant for the bathrooms. I wanted to take a leak, but I was on a mission, too.

"Where are you going?"

"Restroom. I'm hoping they have vending machines that sell rubbers."

She smiled. "We still have one left."

Just one. Fuck that!

"Yeah, but that's not nearly enough for what I have in mind … unless you want to do what we talked about earlier?"

She shook her head determinedly.

"That's another discussion for another time, Sebastian. When you've finished this next tour: we'll talk about it then, I promise."

I guess that was the best offer I was going to get—for now.

The waiter pointed me in the direction of the bathrooms, but it was a BS mission.

"Fucking useless!" I fumed as I walked back to our table. "They didn't have any in the restrooms and I checked with the waiter—all the nearby supermarkets and pharmacies are closed on Sunday evenings."

"Oh, dear," she said, although not sounding concerned. "Well, never mind. We'll just have to get creative."

"Yeah, okay," I sighed. *Why did women always want 'creative'? I didn't have a problem with it, but what was wrong with good, hard fucking and watching a woman come apart under me … watching Caro come apart under me?*

She raised an eyebrow. "I hope you're not getting bored with me already!"

I had to laugh at that. "You're like a freakin' drug to me, Caro. I can't get enough of you. And I really like wake-up sex."

She smiled, her quiet laugh heating my blood unintentionally. "We'll figure something out. Don't sweat it, Hunter."

Nope. Wasn't working. Still want to fuck hard.

But then again, we still had that one condom left—and I was intending to make the most of it as soon as possible.

The second Caro put her fork down and pushed her plate away, I was on my feet and hunting down the waiter to pay for our food. Then we were out in the parking lot and on the bike.

I accelerated hard, racing back to our cabin. I could feel Caro gripping me tightly, which turned me on even more.

I was so intent on getting back and getting naked, that my reactions were fucked. I groaned when I saw two Italian Polizia waving me down. Fuck, I thought I could get away with it on this road. Guess they were bored and trying to fill their quotas.

I pulled over to the side of the road and dismounted, pulling off my helmet and walking toward them.

"Sei Francese?" asked the first policeman, looking at the bike's license plates.

"Americano."

The policemen looked surprised.

"È questa la tua moto?"

"Si."

"You have papers for this motorcycle?"

"Yes, in my wallet."

I started to reach into my jacket when the younger officer immediately went for his gun.

"What the fuck?"

I raised my hands quickly, and the dumb fucker pushed me down to my knees, reaching for his handcuffs.

Caroline ran towards us with her hands out.

"No, per favore! He was just trying to show you his papers."

"Signora, he was driving at 120km an hour; the speed limit here is 90km an hour," said the older guy.

"Please, let him show you," she said, her voice polite but firm. "I'll get his wallet!"

She moved slowly so they could see exactly what she was doing. That was my girl—always cool in an emergency. She reached into my inside pocket and carefully lifted out my wallet.

"What am I looking for?" she whispered, urgently.

"The *Certificat* d'immatriculation—the papers in gray. Caro, I…"

"Just don't speak, Sebastian," she hissed. "Let me handle this."

Probably a good idea.

She handed over the document that proved I was the bike's owner, watching as the two officers looked at the papers even though it was obvious neither of them could read French.

"Are you authorized to ride this motorcycle, signora?" asked the older guy.

"No, but…"

"Then we'll arrange to have it removed," he said.

Shit! My CO was not going to be happy about having to bail me out of jail a couple of weeks before we deployed. But I hadn't figured on Caro, either.

"Please don't arrest him!" she begged. "He's only on leave for two more weeks, then he's going back to Afghanistan."

The two men looked at each other and I kept my mouth clamped shut. There was a chance that the military/police solidarity that existed back home also held true in Europe. It hadn't so far, in my experience, but Caro was my lucky mascot. When she showed them my military ID, the older officer looked more sympathetic.

"My son-in-law is serving out there," he said, shaking his head. "Very well, we will let you go, but this one time only. Obey the speed limits."

He signaled for me to stand up, and the younger officer put his gun away. *Thank fuck for that!*

"Thank you so much," Caro said quickly, throwing me an angry look that I didn't understand.

"Make him obey the speed limits, signora," said the older officer, wagging his finger at her.

"I will. Thank you!" she gasped out.

"I will pray for you both," he said.

We watched as they wandered back to their car, relaxed and at ease.

"You were great, Caro," I grinned at her.

She slapped my arm hard. "No more speeding!"

"I don't know … I've got my own Caro-shaped 'get out of jail free' card."

"Yes, well, do that again, and you might be finding out what Italian jails are like," she snapped.

"You wouldn't let that happen to me, baby."

"Don't bet on it, Marine! I've got enough gray hairs without you giving me anymore."

I pulled her in for a hug.

"Nope, can't see any," I said, kissing her hair.

She pushed me away—I guess I wasn't entirely forgiven yet.

"Another two weeks with you and I'll have to color my grays," she snorted.

I laughed, which was probably another mistake.

"It's not funny!"

"God, you're beautiful, Caro!"

She climbed onto the bike, and I drove back to the campsite like a Sunday-afternoon granny-driver—nothing she could complain about there.

While I locked up our helmets, Caro stomped off to the

cabin. I was confident that she'd chill out, or hopefully want to work off the calories we'd just eaten. But when I walked into the room, she looked like she was ransacking the place, every drawer hanging open. Yeah, that didn't look too good.

If I knew my girl—which I did—she was building up a good head of steam. I suspected that when I was in firing range she'd launch her attack. I stood back and watched her for a moment.

"I can't open the fucking wine!" she snarled, her eyes shooting darts at me.

Wow, she really was pissed.

"What's the matter, Caro?" I asked warily.

"I just told you!" she yelled. "I can't open the wine!"

I used my Swiss Army knife to pry out the cork, frowning at the furious energy that was radiating from Caro.

"I think some of the cork fell in," I said mildly, placing the wine on the table.

"Thank you," she muttered.

"Caro…"

"What, Sebastian?" she grit out. "You could have got arrested back there? That was so stupid and reckless!"

Is that this was all about? "Nothing happened…" I started to point out.

"It could have!" she yelled. "And if you take chances like that out in…"

Finally, I understood what was upsetting her. That little speeding stunt had made her think that I was reckless. It was only partly true.

"Hey, come here," I said softly. "It's okay."

I pulled her into a hug, but her body was still unresponsive and stiff as a plank of wood.

"Caro, tonight was just dumb, I admit that, okay. I'm just enjoying being … free, here and now, with you. Don't cry."

"I'm not crying!" she yelled. "I'm mad at you!"

"Yeah, got that message, baby."

She pushed me away and grabbed the wine bottle, taking another long slug. Then she threw herself on the bed, piled the pillows behind her and tipped another large quantity of

167

wine into her mouth, scrubbing the back of her hand across her face to catch the drips.

"Are you going to share that?" I asked carefully.

"No. You drink too much."

"You're just going to sit there and finish the whole bottle by yourself?"

"Yes."

"You don't like drinking," I pointed out reasonably.

"I do tonight."

"It'll make you sick."

"I'm being reckless. You do it all the time."

Ah, shit.

"Caro," I said, rubbing my forehead, "come on, that's enough."

I hated seeing her like this. I knew it was hypocritical, but her getting wasted wasn't going to solve our problems. I pulled the bottle out of her hands and put it on the other side of the bed.

"Give me my goddamn wine, Sebastian," she snapped.

"No," I said, sitting next to her.

She tried to reach over me to get it, but I blocked her.

"Fine!"

She leapt off the bed and stormed out of the room. I hoped she'd come to her senses and turn around, but she didn't. This relationship crap was hard.

Sighing, I picked up the bottle of wine and followed her.

I could see her silhouette on the beach, her arms pulled around her knees, shivering slightly, but too stubborn to go inside. I saw her tense when she heard my footsteps, but she didn't pull away as I wrapped my jacket around her shoulders. She didn't look at me either.

"Want some wine?" I asked. "It tastes great straight from the bottle."

I was trying for a smile, but instead she sighed and leaned against my shoulder.

"Sebastian, promise me you won't be reckless. I couldn't stand it if anything happened to you now."

"Caro, I'm never reckless when I'm working," I said seriously. "Well, maybe some of the off duty stuff, but not when I'm working, I promise. I'd never have gotten promoted if I was a complete fuck-up. Don't worry about me. Besides, I've got a reason to come home now, okay?"

"I will worry," she whispered.

"And I'll worry about you, too. You've still got a chance to go home where I know you'll be safe, Caro. Please?"

She sat up stiffly.

"Don't even think about screwing up my papers again, Hunter!"

"Whoa! Slow down!" I wrapped my arms around her, trying to calm her with my body. "I promised I wouldn't, Caro, even though I really fucking want to." I felt her relax slightly. "So, have you finished stomping all over me with your boots?"

"For now, unless you ask me to, nicely," she grumbled, making me laugh.

"I'll bear that in mind. Can I kiss you, or am I risking serious injury?"

She didn't reply, instead pushing me flat onto the sand and situating herself across my chest. I shivered when she ran the tip of her finger along my cheeks and nose and chin, then leaned down to kiss me softly.

"This brings back memories," she said, her voice calm.

I smiled up at her. "Yeah! Sex on the beach was one of those things that everyone at school used to brag about, and then I got to do it with you. That first time, that was one of the best nights of my life."

"The first time we ever spent a whole night together."

"You want to relive good times, Caro?" I suggested, shifting my hips into her.

"Can't."

"Why not?"

"I left our one and only condom in the room."

Crap.

"Besides," she continued, "I've kind of got a thing for beds these days. Call me old-fashioned."

"Yeah, I guess." Couldn't argue with comfort when you were fucking your woman, although... "I really liked having sex in your car. That was hot."

169

"Oh my God, yes!" she laughed, her eyes widening. "But I'd have to say that sex in that closet at the country club was pretty amazing, too. No, wait, the hotel in Little Italy. That room looked like a wild animal had rampaged through it by the time you'd finished!"

"Wild animal, huh?" I commented, raising an eyebrow. "Yeah, well, I think I can improve on that now, baby."

"Oh, you do, do you?" she replied, her voice sarcastic. "Because I've got to tell you, Sebastian, you never ran out of condoms when you were 17."

"Ouch! Low blow, Ms. Venzi."

She laughed. "True, though."

"Yeah, well, I'll fix that tomorrow and then you won't be getting *any* sleep, woman."

"Heard it all before, Marine, but it ain't happened yet."

She lay back down, her fingers roaming across my chest, an innocent action that was turning me on.

"So, who was your first woman, after me, I mean?"

Fuck, what?

"Why do you want to know that?" I asked cagily.

"Just curious."

"I don't really want to go there, Caro. It was … a bad time for me."

She paused, her fingers continuing their soft stroking.

"Okay, I'm sorry. You don't have to."

We lay there in silence for several minutes before either of us spoke.

"Will you tell Ches that we're … back together?" she asked softly.

"Of course I will, Caro. Ches is my brother."

"He'll be surprised."

"Fuck, yes!"

"Do you think he'll be okay about it? I mean, I'm sure my name would have been dirt with him."

I could hear the anxiety in her voice. I hadn't realized how much she cared what Ches would think—and I wasn't sure why.

"Ches isn't like that. He was pretty shocked by everything that went down that day at your place, but he knew that what we had was real. He's my buddy: he'll be pleased."

"When are you going to tell him?"

"I hadn't really thought about it. When are you going to tell your friends about me?"

"Are you kidding?" she laughed. "After your little stunt with Nicole it'll be hot news in NYC by now. Your photograph will be on screensavers everywhere."

I couldn't deny it—hearing that her friends would be talking about me was reassuring.

"Yeah?"

"Oh, don't be all coy with me, Hunter. You know you're cute."

I grinned up at her. "Just as long as you think so."

"I think you're devilishly handsome, with the emphasis on 'devil'."

"Yeah, well as it happens, Ms. Venzi, I think you've got some devil inside you, too."

"Oh, I'd really like to have some devil inside me right now, Sebastian."

She was killing me! I sat quickly, pulling her up with me.

"Let's go."

She stood and brushed some of the sand from my clothes while I picked up my jacket and the bottle of wine, discreetly rearranging my junk at the same time.

We strolled back to our room, and every now and then I couldn't resist kissing her hand gently.

But once I'd closed the door to the cabin, I didn't hold back. Pushing her against the wall, I kissed her hard, one hand roaming across her full, heavy tits, the other working down into her jeans.

"Where's that fucking condom?" I muttered, my lips against her throat.

"Bedside table," she gasped.

I strode over and snatched it up, ripping off the foil and unzipping my pants. I'd been hard for the last half an hour and it was getting fucking painful.

"Sebastian, the bed?" she hinted.

"No, here."

My dick was begging to join the party, weeping with relief when I shoved my jeans over the curve of my ass and rolled the rubber on, wincing when I snapped the latex at the end.

Caro's zipper went the same way and I lifted her up, my cock rubbing against her.

"Wrap your legs around me, baby," I said tightly.

"How?" she gasped, pointing at her jeans trapped around her knees.

"Ah, fuck it!"

I tugged hard but they were caught on her boots. I wasn't going to wait for her to stop and unlace them, so I stepped over the denim, ignoring the trailing material and rammed into her so hard she cried out. I needed her now, and I knew the way her body was responding she felt the same. My breath was becoming labored as I thrust faster and faster, her fingers gripping into my shoulders, and I was about four seconds from coming so hard that...

And then my goddamn phone rang.

"Oh, fuck!"

"What?" she gasped. "Don't stop, Sebastian!"

I had no intention of stopping, but I had to take the call whether I wanted to or not.

I carried her to the bed, taking care not to trip over her trailing jeans while we were still joined together, then I pulled my phone out of my jacket pocket.

"Sebastian," she whimpered.

"Just a minute, baby, I've got to take this call. It's my CO's ringtone." I pressed 'accept' while she glared at me. "Hunter, sir."

She huffed quietly against my chest and wriggled on my cock, sending tremors through my body. I gave her a warning stare. I wasn't going to be able to concentrate if she did that again, but to keep her quiet, I started to move slowly, sliding my dick in and out of her in a way that I knew she loved.

"At last!" my CO snapped. *"Are you still in Europe, Hunter?"*

"Yes, sir."

"Geneva?"

"No, Italy, sir."

I must have thrust too hard, because Caro moaned loudly.

"What's that noise, Hunter?"

"Um … I've just been out for a run."

"Hmm, keeping in shape then?"

"Yes, sir."

"Good man. So it's like this: the word's come down that they want to move up the mission. Operation Moshtorak has just gone to status critical. There's friction between Quetta and Peshawar and that appears to have reduced the Taliban's ability to maintain a strong presence in Helmand. We need to capitalize on that. Our contact is Gal Agha. Your job is to find him and bring him in. We have to move fast because now intel says that the local Taliban are making noises and stopping anyone who's thinking about collaborating with us. It's imperative we get to Gal Agha first. It'll be a political coup, but more importantly, it'll keep the boots on the ground safer if we can make Southern Helmand a no-go area for Taliban recruitment for at least six months. We can't trust the ANA interpreters, so we need one of our own. Understand?"

"Yes, sir."

"I'm sorry, Hunter, but all leave is being cancelled and key personnel are being flown out via Ramstein at oh-nine-hundred hours on Thursday. Once you're in Kabul, you'll meet up with Captain Ryan Grant of MEU who's the mission leader, and he'll give you your orders. This is important, Hunter, so don't fuck up. I had a helluva job persuading the powers-that-be that you were the man for this job and to overlook what happened in Paris. Don't make me out to be a liar. I know it doesn't give you much time to pack up your place in Geneva, but that's the way it is. I'll send a staff car to pick you up at oh-six-hundred."

"I'll be there."

He disconnected the call and I threw the phone in the corner. I'd worry about the implications of that conversation later. Right now, I had a mission of my own to think about.

I dropped Caro onto the bed, raising her hips and grinding into her in a way that made her gasp. She threw back her head and I sank my teeth into her nipple, feeling it harden even through her bra and t-shirt.

She screamed my name so loudly, I thought I'd lose

hearing in my left ear. Not that I gave a fuck. It was worth it just to hear her coming apart like that. As she clenched around me, I lost it too, my cock swelling as I pumped into her, then collapsed on top of her, my weight pressing her into the mattress.

We lay there, trying to catch our breath.

"Sebastian?" she gasped, her voice shaky and astonished.

I pulled out carefully and looked down at her, my smile wide and relaxed. "Did you get what you wanted, baby?"

"Excuse me?" she huffed.

"You said you wanted some devil inside you. I aim to please."

She scowled and slapped my arm, trying to squirm away from me, but my body was still pinning her down.

"Sebastian, you just fucked me while you were talking to your CO!" she hiccupped, sounding breathless and a little pissed.

"What, you think men can't multitask?"

She stared at me in disbelief.

"I can't believe you did that!"

I couldn't help laughing at the outraged expression on her face. She didn't fool me—she'd needed to come as badly as I had.

"Felt good! Don't tell me you didn't enjoy that because either it was you moaning, baby, or my CO had a stomach ache."

"I ... you ... that ... unbelievable!"

I rolled off of her and lay down, pulling her firmly into my chest.

"I haven't even taken my boots off," she muttered.

"Me neither," I reminded her.

Reluctantly, I sat up and peeled off the condom, tossing it in the garbage. Then I stood and yanked up my pants, before heading to the bathroom for a much needed piss.

She was still lying on the bed when I came back, not even caring that she was naked from the waist down, her panties and jeans caught around her ankles. I picked up her foot and started to undo the laces, tossing the boot over my shoulder where it landed with a thud. When I tugged off her sock, I couldn't help wanting to kiss and suck her perfect little toes.

"Sebastian," she whimpered, "you're supposed to do foreplay *before* sex."

I smiled down at her but didn't reply, just copying my movements with her right foot. Finally I was able to free her legs from her clothing.

"Very nice," I said, planting a soft kiss on her belly button.

Then I lifted her limp body so I could take off her t-shirt and reached around to unhook her bra.

Just a quick taste.

"Mmm," I said, taking a bite of each nipple.

She pushed me away.

"Don't start what you can't finish, Sebastian," she snapped, obviously still a little annoyed with me although I wasn't sure why.

"Who says I can't finish? You were the one who said we should be creative. I'm just doing as I'm told, ma'am."

I turned to unbuckle my motorcycle boots, kicked them into the corner, and dropped the rest of my clothes onto the floor in one quick movement.

Then I scooped her up and carried her into the shower, enjoying the feel of the hot water as I soaped her carefully and kissed every inch of soft, warm skin.

"You want some more, Caro," I offered, as I massaged between her thighs.

"I'd love to say yes," she said, yawning, "but really I just want to go and sleep. Rough sex during phone calls always does that to me."

"Always?" I questioned.

"Always," she stated with a subtle smile.

"Hmm." *I wasn't sure I liked that answer. Who else had taken the idea of phone sex to a whole new level with her?*

"By the way," she asked, "why was your CO calling? What did he want at this time of night?"

Damn. I was hoping she wouldn't ask about that until morning.

"He wanted to know where I was."

"I gathered that. Because?"

"I'm sorry, Caro; I'm going to have to be back in Geneva in four days … and then back to Afghanistan."

"Four days?" Her voice shook as she spoke.

"I'm so sorry, baby."

"Well," she said, trying to smile even as her lips quivered, "we'll just have to make the most of the four days then."

"I'll make it up to you," I said quietly. "I promise, Caro."

"Sebastian, don't worry," she said, putting some grit in her voice—for my benefit, I guessed. "Every day with you is a bonus. And we've got the rest of our lives to see Italy."

Hearing her words was the best fucking thing ever.

"Promise?"

"I promise."

And there was no doubt in her voice as she said the words. Then she pulled me into her arms and we stood together, letting the hot water flow over us, trying to reassure each other that it would be okay.

When the water began to cool, she turned off the faucet.

"Come here, let me dry you, tesoro."

God, this woman. It had been years since anyone had tried to take care of me. Even as a kid, I'd had to look after myself.

I held out my arms while she stroked the towel across my body: my back and shoulders, chest, stomach, arms and legs; slowly, carefully, methodically, soaking up each droplet of moisture.

"There you are—all done."

A weird, achy feeling settled in my gut. I didn't know what to call it, but it felt like caring; it felt like love.

Watching her closely, drinking in every feature of her face soft and pink from the shower, I handed her a fresh towel, then carefully rubbed her hair with a small hand towel.

"You shouldn't sleep with damp hair," I said.

I don't know why I said that, because I did it all the time, but it felt like something a guy should say to the woman he loved. And for some reason my words made her smile.

"Sebastian, I've done a lot of foolish things—reckless, you might say—since I met you: sleeping with damp hair doesn't figure particularly high on that list."

I frowned. I didn't like her describing being with me as 'reckless'.

But then she dropped a soft kiss onto the tip of my nose.

"Race you to the bedroom!"

She ran from the bathroom and launched herself onto the bed.

"You're so slow, Hunter," she laughed at me. "You're really out of shape. Maybe you should go for a run, like you told your CO."

I gave her a wry grin as I walked naked from the bathroom.

"Tomorrow, Caro, I'm getting a fucking shit-load of condoms, and I'm going to make you regret every word you've just said."

She lay there smiling up at me, looking like sin and sex all rolled into one fucking amazing package.

"Like I said, Sebastian, promises, promises. I keep hearing about these fuckathons, but nothing ever happens."

Damn woman! I was going to make her regret challenging me like that. I just needed to find a fucking farmacia and then I'd buy me enough preservativi to wipe that smug look off of her face. Period.

But then she yawned loudly, and I couldn't help smiling down at her as she snuggled under the sheet. I slid in beside her and pulled her against my body, breathing in the amazing scent of her damp skin.

With her in my arms, all the bullshit fell away. The years of wanting her and missing her and trying to hate her; surviving boot camp; the hell that was Iraq. Ten, long, lonely years of wanting what I couldn't have, of seeing Ches fall in love, marry, have children—all the things I thought I'd have with her. And in four days I'd be gone again, knowing what I'd be missing, daring to hope that she'd wait for me this time.

"God, Caro. You make it all worthwhile. Thank God for you."

"I love you, tesoro," she whispered.

CHAPTER 10

Waking up in the morning, the first thing I saw was Caro's beautiful face. She was still sleeping, her breathing slow and steady.

I watched her for the longest time, scared by the depth of emotion I felt for her, that I'd always felt for her. I knew she thought that a 17 year-old boy couldn't understand adult love, but she'd been wrong about that: nothing had changed for me. She was still the only woman who'd ever owned my heart.

I wondered what sort of man I'd be when I came back from my next deployment in Afghanistan. Each tour changed you, hardened you, closed off a part that you could never talk about. And I couldn't tell her that this was one of the most dangerous missions I'd ever go on. We'd have to travel deep into the mountains in a region where the Taliban were actively recruiting. It was impossible to tell who was friend and who was enemy. And the whole point of the mission was to make friends with powerful people in hard to reach places.

The guy leading the mission was from the Marine Expeditionary Unit. MEU is a quick reaction force, deployed and ready for immediate response to any crisis. Normally, this was 2,000 plus men, with air and ground combat elements and logistics under one commander. They were a tough crew, and I knew that they'd have picked a competent guy to lead our significantly smaller team of a dozen men. But if anything went wrong, air support was more than 30 minutes away. You could do a lot of dying in 30 minutes.

Caro shifted against me and her eyes fluttered open.

"Hey."

"Ciao, bello!" she said, her voice husky with sleep. "How long have you been awake?"

"Not long. Just enough time to remind me that I'm a lucky bastard."

She smiled sleepily and stretched, her warm body pressing against mine.

"I could get used to this, Sebastian, waking up next to you."

But then her smile turned sad, and I knew that she was thinking about the time expiration on that.

"So, what's the new plan?" she asked, forcing herself to be cheerful. "Do you want to see some more of Tuscany, or should we go further north?"

I was confused. Since when was that the plan? "What about Salerno?"

"It's too much driving, Sebastian," she said, shaking her head. "We don't have a lot of time and you…"

"Hell, no! I want to see where your dad came from as much as you do. Fuck the driving, Caro! We're going to Salerno. If you get your beautiful ass out of bed, we can be there in maybe five hours."

I could see that she wanted to give in, but was worried about the miles we'd be clocking up if we carried on heading south.

"Anyway," I said, "we're out of condoms, and much as I'm enjoying being creative, I really just want to fuck you into next week."

She rolled her eyes but couldn't hide the huge smile on her face.

"Such sweet words, Sebastian. How did you get to be such a smooth talker?"

"I don't know, baby," I grinned, "but it works every time."

"Every time, huh? But you know, I have to say, last night wasn't particularly creative—we weren't even naked."

I laughed loudly.

"Not creative? Hell, Caro, I managed to keep a conversation going with Cardozo; I thought that was pretty fucking creative."

"Is that the name of your CO?"

"Yeah, he's an okay guy."

"He must have his hands full dealing with you." She paused, giving me the stink-eye. "What's his wife like?"

I grinned back at her. "Blonde, attractive ... about forty. Why, are you jealous?"

"Of course," she said, without missing a beat.

I shook my head and kissed her gently. "You've got nothing to worry about, baby."

I'd meant to reassure her, but as soon as our lips touched she moaned low in her throat, pushing her body against mine, her tongue plunging into my mouth. It was so fucking hot, my body ignited.

"Caro," I groaned, as she ran her hands over my thighs.

"Shh, tesoro."

She kissed down my chest and stomach, then took my dick in her mouth, which shut off every lucid thought I had. The feel of her warm, wet tongue working over the head of my cock—you could have shot off my kneecaps and I'd still be a happy man.

I was just about coherent enough to slide my fingers towards her pussy, working her clit so she got hers, too.

Ten minutes later, we were both flat on our backs, panting. I had the biggest fucking smile on my face.

"You ready to get up, baby?" I asked, stroking her perfect ass.

"Mmm, if I have to," she mumbled. "But to tell you the truth, I'd be quite happy staying here all day, if someone brought us food. And condoms."

Her comment was very fucking motivating, so I kissed her tits quickly, just to be polite, then kicked the sheets back, making her flinch.

"Hey!" she complained.

"Up," I ordered, standing over her, waiting for her to move.

When she pouted and glared up at me, I leaned down and fastened my teeth over her left nipple, tugging gently.

"You cheat," she grumbled, finally rolling out of bed and staggering the short distance to the shower.

I swatted her ass, just to help her along.

The water wasn't hot, so we showered quickly, avoiding touching too much so we didn't get turned on. It wasn't working. I mean, come on! Hot woman naked in my shower—it was asking too much. I tried to ignore my ever-ready dick and stuffed it inside a pair of jeans, then watched as Caro ran a comb through her wet hair and tied it back.

"It doesn't take you long to get ready, does it, Caro? You never even bother to put on makeup.

"I do sometimes," she huffed, sounding a little defensive, although I wasn't sure of the reason. "If I'm going out somewhere dressy. But not usually, no. Why?"

I shrugged. "Nothing. Just saying. It drives me crazy when women spend hours getting ready to go out."

Not that I had to suffer that too often—I was more a hit it and quit it kind of guy; I didn't stick around for dates so much. Until now. But my words had dug up another memory.

"You remember that time we went clothes shopping in San Diego? You had to buy a new dress?"

"Oh, sure, I remember that! The sales assistant was flirting with you?"

Huh, didn't remember that.

"She was?"

I wondered if she'd been hot. Whatever.

Caro looked equal parts annoyed and amused. "Don't you remember, she was asking you if you were a pilot from Miramar?"

Nope, definitely didn't remember that.

"Well, I'm not surprised," she said, smiling to herself, "in those days you never used to notice other women flirting with you. You were such an innocent. Not like now."

"Hell, you should complain, Caro! You were the one I lost my innocence to—a hot, older woman."

"You know what I mean," she laughed slapping my arm away as I reached for her.

Damn, I'd really thought I was the shit back then, catching the eye of a seriously hot woman—not a girl—even though she was married. And hell, I couldn't deny it was a turn on ... fucking her behind her husband's back, in his bed even. Not that it was the reason I'd fallen for Caro—she'd always been special to me. But yeah, I felt like The Man when she let me into her bed and into her body. No woman had meant a thing to me since then, except to scratch an itch. I knew I'd behaved like a bastard, but I was finding it hard to care. There was only one woman whose feelings mattered to me.

I caught her hand, pulling her down, until she was sitting in my lap.

"Caro," I said seriously, "you're all I want. You don't have to worry about other women. Yeah, so I fucked around a lot, but you know what? It was just a game—I was using them, they were using me. It gets pretty old after a while." I paused, tucking her hair behind her ear and kissing her throat. "But I might have to hunt down those old boyfriends of yours and beat them to a pulp."

She laughed, which was the reaction I'd hoped for. "Double standards, Sebastian?"

"Nope, just two sets of rules ... but I was thinking about the black dress you bought back in San Diego. You looked so fucking hot in that."

"I've still got it somewhere," she said, frowning, "although I haven't worn it in years."

Her words gave me an idea.

"We should do that, Caro; go out somewhere you can dress up."

She sighed softly. "I used to fantasize about seeing you in a tux."

"Really?"

"Sebastian, I spent far too many hours fantasizing about you in a variety of, um, situations. And just recently, it's become my new hobby."

I laughed, making a mental note to find out more about these fantasies at some point in the near future. But for now, I let her off the hook.

"I've never worn a tux," I said off-handedly.

"Never?" She sounded surprised. "Not even at your high school prom?"

I shook my head. "I didn't go. I hadn't met you again, and I'd split up with Brenda. Ches didn't have a date either— he swiped some of Mitch's beer, I scored some weed—and we got trashed on the beach instead. It was a pretty good night—I think. I don't remember that much about it. We didn't need any women to have a good time … but that was before I met you again."

"Hmm, very virtuous of you," she smiled. "But didn't you wear a tux for Ches and Amy's wedding?"

"Nah, Amy kind of got off on the whole military thing, even though she didn't want Ches enlisting, so she asked me and Mitch to come in our Dress Blues. I don't know, I think she thought it would look cool in the wedding pictures."

I rolled my eyes, remembering the psycho that was pre-wedding Amy.

"She turned into a complete nightmare-bitch-from-hell over the whole wedding thing. Ches was freaking out, thinking he was about to marry some crazy person. She even tried to ban him from having a bachelor party." *And she failed, because Ches's bachelor party was epic—a whole weekend of drinking, dancing and dicking around in Tijuana.*

"Gee, I wonder why," Caro said, oozing sarcasm. "Maybe she didn't trust *you*."

I grinned at her.

"Yeah, well, she was probably right about that…"

"I don't want to know, Sebastian!" Caro said quickly.

Instead, I kissed her, changing the subject back.

"So what do you think?"

"About what?"

"Going somewhere upscale, really dressing up? I'd love to see you like that again."

"Well, okay," she said thoughtfully. "Let's do that when you get back from this tour. Then we can really celebrate."

"Let's do it *now*," I said.

If there's one thing that being a Marine teaches you, it's to take an opportunity when it arises—we don't stand around with our thumbs up our asses waiting for someone else to tell us what to do.

"There must be some place in Salerno you can get

women's stuff," I encouraged her.

"Stuff?!"

"Yeah, silky dress, stockings, high heels … stuff. And then I could undress you—slowly."

I really liked the idea of that. There's nothing like the feel of a woman's silk panties as she straddles your body, hot and ready to make the beast with two backs.

"Okay," she smiled. "I'll do it if you do—dress up."

I wasn't really interested in fancy clothes for myself, but if it was what Caro wanted, why the hell not?

"Sure, if I can find somewhere that will rent me a tux, why not? It'll make a change from being in uniform."

Then I kissed her quickly, scooping her off of my lap and setting her back on the floor.

"We'd better get going. Got me a date planned with a really hot woman."

Instead of traveling along the coast road, we headed inland for the Autostrada del Sole, the highway that runs from Milan to Naples. I could tell the heavy traffic made Caro nervous, but it was the fastest route to Salerno.

We stopped briefly just outside Rome to give Caro a chance to work some of the stiffness out of her body, and then we pushed on south, past Naples until we ran out of road.

Salerno was just how she'd described it to me all those years ago, terracotta roofs, whitewashed square buildings built into the cliff, the Mediterranean Sea deep blue in the evening sun.

I pulled off my helmet, stretching out my back muscles, before climbing off and holding my hand out to Caro.

"You alright, baby?"

"I'm fine," she said, hiding a wince as she massaged her ass, a job I'd happily have done for her. "How are you?"

"Yeah, good. Look, I think it might be easier to find a pensione or hotel in Salerno than in your dad's village. We're only a couple of miles away so we could easily shoot on over there in the morning. What do you think?"

She nodded readily, stretching her arms above her head,

and unconsciously pushing her tits out in a way that would be rude to ignore.

"Anything that doesn't involve getting back on your bike sounds good, Sebastian," she said with a grimace. "My ass is numb already."

I pulled her into a hug, willingly laying hands on that peachy ass, and rubbing gently.

"Better, baby?"

"Mmm, much," she sighed, resting her head on my chest.

I kissed her lightly, loving the soft smile that made her eyes glow. I swallowed, fighting to control the feelings that threatened to overwhelm me. *Goddamn it! I was a US Marine, not some lovesick teenager.* Pity my body couldn't tell the difference.

"Come on then," I said quickly, "let's walk for a while. We'll find a room—and a pharmacy."

"Good to see you've got your priorities in order, Sebastian," she laughed.

"Trained by the Marines, baby. What can I say?"

We walked lazily through the warm streets, as crazy drivers in cars and scooters raced past us. A few of the men were giving Caro sleazy stares, so I slung my arm around her and glared at the ones who were the most obvious. I felt her hand slide around my waist as she smiled up at me.

When I saw a small sidewalk café I realized how thirsty I was.

"I could really use a beer," I suggested.

But Caro shook her head.

"This is the home of limoncello, Sebastian, the real thing—made with Sorrento lemons. I think we should try some."

"Yeah! You used to make those amazing ones when I was a kid."

She shrugged, wincing slightly as we both remembered that I'd first met her when I was eight years old and she was a newly married woman. Other than my fucking parents, Ches and his family were the only people who knew that. No one else would ever understand what we'd been to each other then. She'd been the only person in the world who cared for me then, and even as a little kid, I knew that I wanted to save her. It was fairytale stuff, and it wasn't until we met again when I was 17 that I recognized what a douche her husband was. Those memories were private.

"Sure, but these are alcoholic," she said, glancing up at me with a smile. "We could order them with a pitcher of water, too."

"Sounds good," I said, knowing that it was her way of challenging me not to get wasted. Whatever, but it wasn't like the military made many teetotalers.

The waiter was a kid who needed a fucking lesson in manners. He cheered up when Caro spoke to him in Italian, but I stared him down when I caught his eyes on her tits.

"And would you know of anywhere we could rent a room for a couple of nights?" Caro asked him. "Nothing too expensive?"

"My Uncle Aberto might," said the kid, smiling at her, caught in her spell like so many other guys. "I'll go and ask him."

"You didn't have to flirt with him, Caro," I said, at the same time kicking myself for sounding like the jealous asshole she'd been married to.

She stared at me, completely confused.

"Excuse me? Flirt with him? I was being friendly, that's all."

"Well, it didn't look like that from here," I snapped, trying to rein in my temper—and failing.

She shook her head and held up a finger. "Rule number three, Sebastian, of my conditions for coming on this road trip with you: no displays of adolescent jealousy. Remember?"

I leaned back in my chair and folded my arms. I definitely needed a moment.

The kid waiter returned with the limoncellos, water, and an older guy with black hair and dark olive skin.

"My nephew tells me you're looking for a room. For how long?"

"Just a couple of nights," Caro replied, smiling at him.

Yep, that jealousy wasn't going away anytime soon.

186

"Somewhere in town," she continued, "nothing too upscale—although somewhere with a bath would be great. We've been on our motorcycle all day."

"I have just the thing," he said, returning her smile a little too happily. "My mother-in-law's sister's neighbor rents rooms. Her villa overlooks the sea—very pretty rooms. Only €50 a night. I could call her for you, if you like?"

"Thanks," I said, letting him know who was in charge. "We'll take a look."

Caro's expression told me that she wasn't impressed, but I didn't care. No one was hitting on my woman in front of me. Fuck that!

The older guy returned, addressing himself to me this time.

"You're in luck, signore, signora. She has a room available. I've written the address down for you."

"Thank you," Caro said, "that's very kind of you."

He nodded and turned to leave.

"Aberto, can I ask you something else?" she said, her voice hesitant. "My father was from Capezzano Inferiore. He left many years ago, but I was wondering, do you know anyone with the surname of 'Venzi'?"

He scratched his head but then shrugged, and Caro's face fell. I wanted to beat the shit out of the man who put that look on her face, even though I knew it wasn't his fault.

"No, I'm sorry, signora, I don't know that name. I could look in the phone book for you?"

"Thank you," she said, trying to smile. "That would be so helpful."

I held her hand while we waited for him to return, and I could feel the tension in her.

"Ah, I'm sorry, signora," he said a few minutes later, "there's no one with that surname in the town—some in the province, but none within 70km."

Caro's shoulders slumped.

"Thank you for looking, Aberto," she said quietly.

He smiled sympathetically then walked away.

"Sorry, baby," I said. "I know you had gotten your hopes up."

"I was just being stupid," she said, smiling weakly. "I just wanted ... I just hoped I'd find some family."

"Hey, I get that. I know what it's like."

She swiped a finger under her eyes, trying to hide the fact that she was trying not to cry.

"I never even asked you, Sebastian, but do you have grandparents? You never mentioned any."

I shrugged. "No, not really. Mom's parents died when I was a kid; Dad never spoke to his. Big surprise. I don't even know where they live."

"And you've never wanted to find out?" she asked

Her eyes were so full of compassion, it fucking slayed me.

"I thought about it once. Anyway, I'm not sure I'd want to find anyone who was related to that bastard. Besides, they never showed any interest in me ... it made me wonder if the bastard was really my dad. I dunno..." I shrugged. "Ches and his kids, Mitch and Shirley—they're my family."

"And Amy," Caro said, her voice teasing.

I groaned. "Yeah, and she's thrilled about that."

"Well, she'll be much happier when we show her the new, improved Sebastian Hunter. I could tell her that I've tamed you."

I threw her a look.

"You're treading on dangerous ground there, Venzi."

She sat back and smiled at me. "You're so masterful when you talk like that, Sebastian."

I knew she was just yanking my chain, but there'd be payback for that.

I leaned forward and stared at her. "Yeah, well, if we can find a fucking pharmacy, you'll find out just how 'masterful' I can be."

"Looking forward to it," she smiled.

"You know what we should do, Caro?" I said, as we sat in the warm Mediterranean sunshine, a huge fucking relief after the grayness of Geneva. "We should drive up to Amalfi. The coast road has some gnarly mean bends—see what the bike can really do. There should be some great views, too."

"That sounds fun," she said, although her face told me

she was less than thrilled with the idea.

"That's my girl!" I grinned, winking at her.

After I paid for our drinks, we walked through the town, on the lookout for Via Roma. It turned out to be a wide avenue running alongside the harbor. Better still, it had a farmacia.

I pushed the door open, finding an old fashioned mom and pop type of place. The preservativi had a shelf high up all to themselves. I chose Trojans—a brand I knew and trusted. I didn't care if Caro got knocked up, but she obviously did. So I'd play by her rules—for now.

Caro was at the makeup counter, which surprised me as I hadn't seen her wear makeup so far. She paid for mascara and a dark red lipstick which she slid into her pocket.

"Looking forward to tasting that lipstick on you later," I whispered.

"Looking forward to tasting you later," she whispered back.

Fuck me, game on! I was so getting laid tonight.

Signora Carello's villa was amazing and it overlooked the water. I wouldn't have cared if it was a shed with no roof because it put a smile on Caro's face.

I rang the bell and a woman opened the door almost immediately. She must have been pushing 70, but I could tell she'd been a knock-out in her day. She was thin and very upright for her age, with piled-up hair that was still black and looked natural.

"Ah, the young travelers Aberto mentioned," she said in accented English. "Welcome to my home. Please, come in. Let me show you the room. My name is Signora Carello."

She led us up a flight of shallow steps and opened the door into a large room with a balcony facing the sea.

The bed had curtains, like in a movie, and Caro glowed with happiness.

"Oh, this is just lovely!"

"Thank you, signora."

Caro blushed—it was so damn cute.

"Actually, it's signorina."

For some reason her reply annoyed me.

"I'm working on that," I muttered.

Caro pretended not to hear me but the old lady looked pleased. *Damn! Why couldn't I charm the panties off of Caro? It always worked on other women.*

I mentioned the motorcycle, hoping that the signora would have somewhere around back to park it.

"Oh, I used to enjoy riding on a motorcycle in my day!" the old lady said, surprising the hell outta me. "Oh, yes, young man … I was quite fast in my youth."

My brain immediately decided to go there. *Wow, reeeeally didn't want to know that.* And, holy shit, I think I might have been blushing. What the fuck?!

"I'll go get the bike," I muttered.

"Sebastian," Caro said quickly, "would you mind if I stay here and take a bath?"

"No, that's fine," I said, as an idea struck me. Her eyes narrowed, but I was already on my way. "I'll see you later."

"I'll walk you out," said the old lady.

She followed me down the stairs and out into a sunny courtyard.

"You can put your motorcycle there," she said, pointing to a small paved area. "I hope it doesn't leak oil—so difficult to clean it off sandstone. My boyfriend had an English motorcycle, a Triumph. It always leaked oil. Very annoying." Then she smiled at me. "But I did love riding on it."

Triumph made nice bikes, but she was right about the oil. I shook my head to focus.

"Signora, I wonder if you could help me with something?"

"If I can," she said. "I had a feeling you wanted to ask me something."

She may have been seventy, but she was damn observant.

"I want to take Caro somewhere real special—somewhere fancy, you know?"

She gave me a measured look. "Is there a particular reason for this? I'm being nosy, I know, but indulge me, young man."

"My name's Sebastian Hunter, ma'am."

"A lovely name. Piacere! And this special occasion?"

I felt the blush return—what a fuckin' tool, but I blundered on.

"I'm going to ask Caro to marry me and…"

I didn't get any further before she flung her arms around my shoulders and kissed me three times.

"Ah, bello, I thought it must be that! You look at her with such love in your eyes. I'm so happy for you. She will say yes, of course."

I rubbed my neck nervously. "I sure hope so, ma'am, but she's kind of off marriage so…"

"No, you are wrong. You she loves. I know this. Yes, let me see … somewhere special … ah, I have it! If you drive along the Amalfi coast for 20 minutes, you will see Capri on your left. The road is very beautiful—perfect for your motorcycle. At the top is a mountain pass: you must stop there for the view—it is a perfect place to propose and…"

"Um, well, we're going to visit the place where her father was born tomorrow. Capezzano Inferiore, you know it?"

The signora sighed. "Yes, I know it. That is very romantic. I have high hopes for you, Sebastian Hunter. Romance is much needed in our lives, no?"

"I guess I agree with that, ma'am!"

"I know just the place you must take her—Il Saraceno. It is a very fine hotel with wonderful views of Capri. It is the perfect place to make love all night."

I shifted uncomfortably and tugged at the collar of my t-shirt. "Um, yes, ma'am. Um, we'll need some fancy clothes to go with the fancy hotel. I want to buy Caro a dress—something amazing. I guess I'll need a tux, but renting is fine."

She nodded thoughtfully. "Si, I can think of one or two places you could try." Then she sighed again. "Young love—it sweeps all before it. L'amore mantiene giovani."

It took a moment to translate the second half of her sentence: *The heart that loves is always young.* Her smile was wistful, but then she squeezed my hand and rushed into the house to write down the addresses I was going to need.

I leaned against the wall while I waited for her. I was

trying to look casual, but my heart was racing. I'd said it out loud; I'd admitted that I wanted Caro to marry me. I tried to imagine it happening, saying the words.

Fuck, I really needed to think about this.

First stop was a fancy-looking woman's dress shop, and I felt as conspicuous as a hippy at Boot Camp.

The moment I stepped through the doorway, the hairs on the back of my neck prickled as I felt eyes on me. At least they weren't hostile—in fact I'd go as far as to say they were very … welcoming.

A skinny, well-dressed woman with pulled-back hair and no tits sauntered toward me, putting so much extra swing into her walk that I half-expected her to dislocate a hip.

"Signore," she purred, "welcome to *Camilla's*. How may I help you?"

This I could handle. I'd been 'handling' women like her for the last six years.

"I'm looking for a special dress for a very beautiful woman—I can see that I've come to the right place."

The turmoil that flashed across her face was too fucking funny, but I gave her my best polite smile, and she had no option but to return it.

"For your wife, signore?"

"I hope so. I'm going to ask my girlfriend to marry me. And if she says yes, I'm going to take her to Il Saraceno for the night."

"She will say yes, signore, I have no doubt."

She helped me pick out a silky dress in dark blue that I knew would look amazing against Caro's clear, tan skin. The matching shoes cost me more than a month's wages, but it was going to be so worth it. Because despite what the saleswoman said, I was still nervous about what Caro was going to say. She'd made it pretty damn plain that she wasn't planning on marrying a guy in the military again. I hoped I'd done enough to make her change her mind, but a small voice of doubt was growing louder. *What the fuck would she want with a dumb grunt who's only got a high school diploma?* And if I left the Marines, an unemployed dumb grunt, too.

I wanted to believe that we'd been given our second chance for a reason, but maybe that was wishful thinking. It was making my brain hurt just thinking about it. The sooner I asked Caro and knew the score, the better.

The saleswoman also talked me into buying something cute but more casual for this evening, and picked out a short skirt and a pair of those round-toed flat shoes that chicks seem to like. If I had my way, Caro would be in nothing but a pair of fuckin' sexy high heels that made her legs look endless—especially wrapped around my waist. A man can dream. I'd go for the short skirt as second best. She looked amazing whatever she wore, but I wanted to see her in something other than jeans for a change.

I also got talked into buying some sexy-as-fuck panties and bra for Caro. They cost about the same as a new kidney, but I looked on it as an investment. Trying to describe the size of Caro's tits was ... interesting.

Next stop was an upscale men's shop where I rented a tux; even that was a pain in my ass finding something that fit right. And the guy measuring me up was entirely too hands-on for my taste. But I think he knew he was pissing me the fuck off, because he backed down when I told him he'd end up losing a few teeth if his tape measure went near my junk again—although my Italian might have been kinda off, because he looked scared.

Next and final stop was a motorcycle rental place a short way up the coast road. After a brief discussion, the owner agreed to buy the Honda. I had to take a hit on the deal because I was in a hurry to sell, but what the hell—I'd gotten a lot of fun out of the beast, and I could always buy another—maybe a Ducati next time ... wherever the fuck I landed up. I hope it would be on the East Coast with Caro.

But selling the Honda would be easier than trying to get it shipped back to the US—well, easier than the damn paperwork.

I was hot and sweaty by the time I got back to Signora Carello's villa, and I'd been without my Caro fix for way too long.

I parked the bike and ran up to our room, taking the

stairs two at a time. She must have heard me because she called out as soon as I put the key in the door.

"You missed a great bath. I've been sitting here enjoying the view—naked, except for a towel."

I walked up behind her, kissing her damp hair and running my hands over the towel that was wrapped around her. I was so consumed by touching her that I completely forgot she'd spoken.

"You've been gone ages," she murmured. "I was beginning to think you got lost."

"Had some business to take care of, baby."

She twisted around to look at me, narrowing her eyes, the journalist in her demanding to know what I'd been doing; the woman in her excited as well as curious.

"Come on, Hunter, spill. What business?"

I grinned, giving her enough information to throw her off the scent.

"Signora Carello told me somewhere I can rent a tux, so it's game on for tomorrow night. We're going upscale, baby."

"Really?" she said excitedly. "Where?"

She wasn't getting that piece of intel.

"Can't tell you. Not even if you torture me."

"Are you sure about that? Because I think it can be arranged, Sebastian," she smiled, running her hand over my hip.

"I was hoping you'd say that."

I picked her up out of the chair, carrying her into the bedroom while she fastened her arms around my neck, kissing me hungrily.

"Ugh, you're all sweaty!" she pretended to complain.

"Yeah? Any objections if I get you all sweaty, too?"

"None whatsoever."

And those were almost the last words we spoke for the next two hours, although she screamed my name several times. We got through three condoms and had seven orgasms between us. Guess we'd been saving up.

Caro was splayed out across the bed, limp and flushed from our long-delayed fuckathon. Yeah, and she was going to need another shower.

"Oh my God, I can't move!" she gasped.

I was trying hard to pull it together, but that woman had wrung me out dry—for now.

"Fuck!" I muttered, trying to force my legs to move.

Eventually, I managed to roll over, enjoying the view of her long dark hair spread across the pillow. Although her eyes were closed, her kiss-swollen lips curved upward in a smile.

"I know you're looking at me, Sebastian, but whatever you have in mind you can just forget it. I admit it all: you're an animal in bed, and I will never, ever question your virility again."

I laughed quietly.

"You can question it as often as you like, baby, because that just means I have to prove it to you."

I dragged the sheet over us, and pulled her into my arms.

"Do you want to go find something to eat?" I asked, nuzzling her neck.

"Go? As in, leave the room?" she mumbled. "No, no. Bad, bad idea. Call takeout."

"I don't think they deliver to naked people in hotel rooms, Caro."

She groaned.

"Come on, baby, time to get up," I said encouragingly.

"I can't," she whined.

I plastered a kiss onto her pouting lips, then left her in bed while I showered.

She was nearly asleep by the time I returned. I dressed quickly and took a moment to rummage through Caro's overnight bag. Then I went and sat on the bed next to her.

She cracked one eye, frowning at the pink t-shirt I held in my hands.

"Not your color, Sebastian," she mumbled.

"No, baby. I want you to wear it."

"Why?"

"You look cute in pink." She looked at me uncertainly. "And I got you something while I was out."

She sat up slowly, combing hair away from her face with her fingers.

"You got me something?"

I handed her the bag from *Camilla's*.

"You bought me clothes?"

"Just look in the goddam bag, Caro!" I said impatiently.

She pulled out the skirt, studying it closely before turning her shocked eyes to mine.

"Don't you like it?" I questioned uncertainly.

"Sebastian, I … it's very pretty, but…"

"But what?"

"It's not really me," she said, biting her lip. "I'm more a jeans and t-shirt sort of person these days. Besides, I don't have any shoes—I've only got my walking boots."

Oh. If that was the problem … I pulled the shoe bag out from under the bed and passed it to her. She still didn't look happy and I was beginning to get worried.

"Do you like them?" I asked quietly

She swallowed several times, then slipped them onto her bare feet, holding them out for me to look at. She didn't seem mad—just sort of dazed.

"So, you'll wear them—and the skirt?" I asked hopefully.

She nodded and smiled a little reluctantly.

"Yes, tesoro, I'll wear the skirt."

She disappeared into the bathroom with the clothes, and I took the time to check my phone. There was another message from Cardozo, changing the pickup time to half-an-hour earlier, but that was all.

I couldn't help staring when Caro walked out of the bathroom. I was right about the skirt: it made her legs look ultra long and so fucking hot. The term 'sex on legs' could have been made for her. She'd left her long hair loose, and was even wearing a little makeup.

"Wow! I mean … wow! You look awesome, Caro. Really fucking sexy!"

I ran my hand up her bare thigh and cupped her ass appreciatively.

"Mmm, this skirt is great: it's making me horny."

"Thank you for my presents," she said, her voice cool and amused. "But right now, I need food more than I need your body, Sebastian."

I smiled, kissed her quickly, then walked over to hold

open the door for her.

"After you, baby."

The evening air was still warm and I tugged at the neck of my t-shirt. The label was rubbing across a set of scratches where Caro had marked me. I kinda liked it. But we hadn't gone more than a few yards before some bastards had their eyeballs all over Caro.

"Vieni qui e baciami!"

Caro ignored the rude fucking comment, but I felt a murderous rage bubbling up as the other one called out, "Il tuo corpo è bellissimo," his eyes glued to her legs.

Yeah, I might not have thought through the whole buying-my-woman-sexy-clothes scenario. But when the first guy muttered as he passed Caro, "Voglio scopare," I turned around to punch that fucking leer off his face.

Caro caught hold of my arm.

"Oh no, eyes front, Hunter. You bought this skirt, and now you're suffering the consequences: suck it up."

I opened my mouth to argue but the look she gave me wasn't impressed, so I threw the guy a hard stare and let Caro lead me away. When we arrived at a restaurant that Caro liked the look of, I made sure she was seated in a corner so that her legs were hidden by the tablecloth. My skin itched having my back to the room, but at least Caro was protected.

She pretended not to notice my caveman behavior.

"What do you want to do tomorrow, Sebastian? Apart from spring your surprise?"

I took a deep breath and focused on the woman in front of me.

"I thought we could walk up to Capezzano Inferiore, take a look around. Even if there aren't any Venzis there, it would be kinda cool to see where your dad grew up, wouldn't it?"

She gave me a sweet smile, and I relaxed for the first time since leaving Signora Carello's villa.

Our food arrived and I dug in. Hot sex with Caro was currently replacing my daily work-out. Gotta say it rocked.

It suddenly occurred to me that I really didn't know what a normal day was like for her—in fact I didn't know that much about her life. We'd spent so much energy just reconnecting, I hadn't had a chance to ask her before.

"Tell me about your place in Long Beach, Caro," I suggested.

"Oh! Sure, okay. Well, it's small; a bungalow in an area called the West End. It was built about 90 years ago, and it was pretty beaten up when I bought it. I restored the porch at the front so I can sit out and watch the ocean, and in the winter the windows get covered in salt from the wind coming off the Atlantic. I have some really great neighbors, and they look after the place while I'm away. My friends like to come out from Manhattan on the weekends. You spoke to Nicole, she works in merchant banking; and then there's Jenna, who's a bitch-on-wheels attorney, but actually she's really lovely; and Alice, she's a Professor of literature at NYU. I met her when I was going to school there…"

Fuck me! Bankers, lawyers and professors? I was so out of my fucking league.

I should have known—I should have realized.

What the fuck was she doing with me?

She must have seen something on my face, because she stopped suddenly.

"What's the matter, Sebastian?"

The food felt like sand in my mouth, and I struggled to swallow.

"How am I going to fit in with your life there, Caro? All your friends have these amazing careers … and I'll just be a jobless grunt with a high school diploma."

"Sebastian, no!"

"You know what they'll think. Marine: Muscles Are Required Intelligence Not Essential."

"Hey! No one will think that, and you know what? I don't give a shit anyway. Sebastian, haven't we had to listen to enough crap in the past to care less what anyone else thinks now? Isn't that what you've been telling me?"

Yeah, well, not sounding so convincing now.

"Sebastian, do you love me?"

My eyes fixed on hers.

"You know I do, Caro. Sempre."

She reached across the table and took my hand.

"Then whatever happens, we'll deal. I vaguely remember someone saying that to me. Oh, wait, that was you a couple of days ago. Sebastian, the only thing my friends will care about is that I'm happy."

It was hard to believe.

"What about your plans to be a personal fitness trainer?" she went on. "And, jeez, Sebastian, we'll be in New York: you could do something amazing with your language skills. Don't go and get all shy on me now, Hunter!"

I took a deep breath, forcing myself to relax. If she believed it, why the fuck couldn't I?

"Yeah, okay. Sorry. I just kinda freaked for a moment there."

"I know and I understand. It's weird for me, too, and we haven't been doing this for very long. I guess you could say we're out of practice with the whole dating thing. I feel very un-me sitting here in this shockingly short miniskirt, but I tried it, for you."

"Shockingly short?" I said, smiling despite myself.

She pulled my hand under the table and let me run my fingers up her bare thigh.

"Yeah," I agreed, raising one eyebrow. "Shockingly short."

Her hand clamped down on mine, stopping my ascent.

"Okay, Columbus, you've discovered enough for one evening," she said, laughing at my chagrined expression.

Then her smile softened.

"Come, tesoro, take me home."

CHAPTER 11

I woke up long after dawn—unusual for me since I'd joined the Marines. It might have had something to do with the way my body felt deeply relaxed, or the fact that I'd made love to Caro for hours the night before.

Yeah, we fucked too, and sometimes that was rough and fast and hard, but something about her softness and sweetness and the love I saw in her eyes made me want to go slow and savor every second. And although I didn't want to admit it, our time was running out—again.

I smiled as her eyes slowly opened.

"Ciao, bella."

"Ciao," she said, smiling up at me.

She stretched, accidentally bumping against my dick that had been rigid for quite a while and was begging for attention.

My hand drifted over her hip, and she didn't stop me when my fingers slipped over the damp curls of her mound and into her slick heat. She sighed and groaned, a sound that caught in my chest and made my heart beat faster. *Christ, this woman.*

Two hours later, Signora Carello served us breakfast on a small terrace overlooking her backyard. It was a blaze of color and I could see that Caro loved it here. If my girl was happy, I was happy.

The signora joined us for coffee.

"So," she said, smiling at Caro, "you are hoping to find family in Capezzano Inferiore?"

Caro's expression was wistful.

"That would be the icing on the cake, but really I just

want to see the village where my father came from. If I find family, well…"

It pissed me the hell off that I couldn't give her everything she wanted.

The signora smiled sympathetically and patted Caro's hand.

"Perhaps you will find family in a different way," she said, glancing at me and smiling.

Caro looked at her dubiously and I thought she was going to put her reporter brain into gear, but she didn't. Instead, she drained her coffee cup and stood up to leave.

Signora Carello squeezed my hand and whispered, "Amor regge senza legge."

It took me a moment to translate, but then I grinned at her and she winked. Yeah, I liked that one: *Love rules without laws.*

We strolled through Salerno and I enjoyed the feel of Caro's small hand in mine. I'd fucked a lot of women in the last six years, but holding hands, out in public … that was way more intimate. I liked it: it felt right.

Caro stopped to admire the yachts in the harbor as we leaned on the railings, the sun turning the water to a deep blue.

"I should take you sailing some time," I said. "If we had more time, I'd rent us a boat and teach you."

"I already know," she smiled. "Although I haven't been out on a sailboat for years."

"Really?" I was surprised. "I didn't know you could sail."

"Ah, you don't know all my talents yet, Hunter."

I leaned down and whispered in her ear. "I'm looking forward to finding out." Then I straightened up. "But when did you learn?"

She seemed uneasy, and when she answered I knew why.

"David taught me."

"The asshole?"

"The very one."

I hated hearing her talk about her ex-husband, and I definitely didn't want to hear that he'd taught her to sail. That skewered my heart. I knew it was irrational to hate something that had happened long before Caro and I had gotten together, but I did. I hated every single second that she'd ever spent with him. I hated that he'd been her first. I hated that he'd nearly broken her, and if I ever saw that fucker again, I wouldn't be responsible for my actions.

"It was a long time ago, Sebastian," she said softly. "And we agreed we couldn't change the past, so stop looking so mad or I'll have to kiss you indecently in public."

I was still off balance as she spoke, but my pulse quickened when her meaning filtered through the red mist that had descended the second she'd mentioned her ex-husband.

"Nope, still pissed off, Caro. You'll have to kiss me. I don't know if it'll work, but you could try."

I stared at her challengingly.

"Are you sure, Sebastian?" she purred. "Because I don't want to get you all hot and bothered."

"I'll risk it."

She turned to face me, standing so close that our bodies touched. And then she ran her hand over my ass, under my t-shirt, and dragged her nails down my back hard enough to make my breath catch in my throat. With her other hand, she pulled my head down and kissed me hard, stealthily rubbing over my zipper at the same time.

"Fuck, Caro! Let's go back to our room right now."

She pushed me away, laughing, her eyes dancing with lust. "No, Sebastian. That was just my distraction technique—which, by the way, I didn't learn in the Marines."

I groaned, then discreetly adjusted the fucking inconvenient bulge in my pants.

"Should we go to Capezzano Inferiore now?" she asked innocently.

I gave her a look that said we'd be evening the score later.

It was a steep walk up to her father's village, but the view was amazing and in the distance we could see the island of Anacapri.

I never thought I'd come to a place like this, and for a

second I was ten years old and copying a British accent as I imagined that I was James Bond. I glanced sideways at Caro—I already had my own Bond girl. My dick liked the idea a lot and I had to run over some silent drills in my head before another boner snuck up on me. Bastard seemed to be on high alert 24/7 around Caro.

The village of Capezzano Inferiore looked dead, the only sign of life a mangy old dog scratching in the shade. It was pretty much a dump and I hoped Caro wasn't too disappointed. I guess I could see why her old man would have wanted to leave. When I glanced at Caro, a lump formed in my throat: her shoulders were hunched and I could tell she was close to tears.

"We don't have to stay, Caro."

She sighed as she tried to smile. "It's okay. I don't know what I was expecting: Papa always said it was a one-horse town where the horse had died. I guess he was right."

"Look, that guy over there is just opening up his café—let's go get a drink, okay?"

She nodded slowly, and I took her hand and led her over to the small table outside. If anyone knew any gossip about a place like this, it would be a bar owner or a priest.

The café owner looked surprised to have customers. I had no idea how the guy made any money in such a dead-end dump. I ordered a beer and Caro asked for an espresso and a glass of water.

I wasn't expecting too much, but when my beer arrived, it came in a frosted glass, and Caro's espresso was served in a miniature coffee pot with a pot of raw cane sugar lumps. It was a nice touch.

"Excuse me, sir," I said to the guy serving us. "My girlfriend's father came from this village. We were wondering if you might have known him: his surname was Venzi."

The man scratched his head. "That name seems familiar, but I'm not sure. Let me ask my wife—she's lived here her whole life."

Caro shifted anxiously in her seat.

"Don't get your hopes up, Caro," I reminded her gently.

"No, I'm not," she said, shaking her head. She was a

God-awful liar.

A moment later, the owner's wife appeared.

"Buon giorno. You are asking after the Venzi family? How can I help you?"

"I was just wondering … my father, Marco Venzi, he was born here. Did you know him?"

The woman smiled warmly.

"Goodness! Marco Venzi! That's a name I haven't heard in a very long time. He was the boy who left to live in America. Your father, you say? Yes, I knew him."

Tears glittered in Caro's eyes, and I squeezed her fingers as she failed to hide her emotion.

"It's so exciting to meet someone who remembers Papa," she choked out.

"Yes, we were at school together," the woman confirmed. "He was a few years older than me, and always in trouble. He had the devil in him, that one."

"His daughter is just the same," I smiled, gazing at Caro.

The woman laughed. "And how is dear Marco? Did he make his fortune in America like he said? He was crazy for your American movies. Said he was going to be a big star, like Valentino."

Caro swallowed and her body tensed, unable to get the words out.

"Mr. Venzi died some years ago," I answered for her.

"Ah, I see," the woman said, her smile faltering. "Forgive me, young woman, my condolences. Your father was always so full of spirit. Too big for this little town."

"Do you know if he had any relatives here?" I asked, trying to move the subject on from memories that were painful for Caro.

"Well, there was his mother, but she died a long time ago. Marco had a sister who was much older than him, I remember. But she married and moved away, to Naples, I think. I'm sorry, I don't remember the name of the man she married, so that's all I can tell you."

Caro looked devastated. The woman ducked her head in sympathy and left us alone.

"We could try and find her," I suggested. "She might

have had kids—you could have cousins you don't know about."

Caro took a trembling breath, making an effort to pull herself together. God, she was so strong.

"Yes, I might," she acknowledged, forcing a watery smile. "I probably do." Then she closed her eyes and shook her head slowly. "It doesn't matter, Sebastian. Signora Carello was right: even if there are cousins, they're not my family—not really. I have my friends…" she paused. "And I have you. You're my family now."

I'd waited so many fucking years to hear that. It almost destroyed me that she said it here, now, in the village where her father had been born. I'd only known Marco Venzi for two short weeks, but in that time he taught me more about family than my own parents had in 27 years. And now I was here with his daughter—a woman I loved more than life.

My heart thundered in my chest and I started to panic, wondering what the fuck I was doing. What did I have to offer a woman like Caro? Nothing. Fuck all. Just my heart and soul—and I didn't know if that would be enough.

My head dropped and I held onto Caro's hand like a drowning man holds onto a life preserver. I kissed her fingers reverently, then on shaky legs, I sank to one knee.

"Carolina Maria Venzi: I love you, and I want to spend my life with you. Will you marry me?"

And then I waited. Shock registered on her face and I swear my heart stopped. But then she took a deep breath, and a gentle smile spread across her lips.

"I love you, too, Sebastian. And the answer is yes."

I let out a shout of pure fucking joy and leapt to my feet, pulling her into his arms, squeezing her so hard that she gasped. She rested her head over my heart, and I thought it would leap out of my fucking chest.

When I spoke, I hardly recognized my voice, it sounded so choked.

"I'll do everything to make you happy, I promise, Caro. Everything, baby. You are my life."

"And you are mine, tesoro," she whispered. "We'll find a way—we always do."

I collapsed back onto the hard, wooden seat and pulled her onto my lap, burying my face in her hair, kissing her neck.

Then my head slammed back, knocking against the wall hard enough to shake some sense into me.

"Oh, fuck!"

Stupid useless, clueless, pathetic jarhead!

"What? What's wrong?" she asked nervously.

"I forgot to give you the fucking ring. Fuck it! I wanted this to be so smooth. I said it enough times in my head."

She started to smile, and her hand covered her mouth as if she was holding back laughter. I couldn't blame her—I was a freakin' idiot.

"You did? You practiced this?"

She had no idea.

I grinned at her, slightly embarrassed. "Yeah, once or twice. Maybe a few times more … maybe a lot of times more… Ah, fuck it, Caro. See if the damn thing fits."

I yanked the ring box out of my pocket and slapped it down onto the table. By now Caro was laughing at me openly; it was catching.

"You're in danger of sweeping me off my feet again, Sebastian," she laughed, the sound wrapping around my heart and warming it. "How can I resist such sweet words: I'll treasure your proposal forever, 'See if the damn thing fits'."

Then she opened the box. It wasn't the biggest diamond ever, but I knew she wouldn't want anything too showy. Besides, her hands were so tiny, anything bigger would have looked like bling—and my Caro was nothing but fuckin' classy. Besides, it was a blue-white diamond—the best quality you could buy. Or so the jeweler had told me.

The diamond threw rainbows across the table as she stared at it.

"Sebastian, it's beautiful!" she gasped. "Where on earth did you get it … and *when?*"

"Try it on," I suggested, lifting the ring out of the box and sliding it onto the third finger of her left hand. I hoped she couldn't see my own hands shaking. "Perfect," I said quietly.

"Yes, it is. Thank you, tesoro."

She twisted around to kiss me, and I felt like I'd single-handedly raised the Stars and Stripes at Iwo Jima.

"So, fiancé," she said, "what should we do now?"

The name took me by surprise. I guess my brain was still parked in neutral.

"Wow, fiancé, huh? I didn't think it could sound so cool."

"I disagree, Sebastian," she said, her voice sultry. "I think it sounds *hot*. Maybe we can agree to disagree, or just accept that it's an all-temperature sort of title."

I laughed loudly, happiness filling me that I never thought I'd feel again.

"Well, fiancée," I grinned, "I thought we could check out those gnarly bends on the Amalfi coast. What do you think?"

"I think you're crazy, probably certifiable, and I'm horribly afraid it's contagious."

I winked at her, holding out my hand as we left the village behind, having made our promise to live our lives together.

Fuck me, that felt good.

And now for part two of my plan to sweep her off her feet and convince her that marrying me was a good idea.

I don't remember the walk back to Signora Carello's villa. I just remember the sensation of the sun on my face, Caro's hand in mine, and happiness in my heart.

That memory would be the one perfect thing in my life.

But if I knew then what was coming, I'm not sure I'd ever have left Italy.

Signora Carello was standing in her garden, watering the plants.

"Did you have any luck finding your family, my dear?" she asked kindly.

"Yes, I did," said Caro, smiling up at me, her ring glinting in the sunlight.

Signora Carello clapped her hands together and kissed us each three times.

"Oh, felicitations, congratulazioni per il vostro

fidanzamento, my children! I'm so happy for you."

I couldn't shake the feeling that this is what it would be like having a mom who cared, or maybe a grandmother. I wasn't too good at judging women's ages, but the signora must have been pushing 70, at least.

"And now for your surprise?" she said, patting me on the arm. "But some lunch before you go? I was going to fix myself insalata tricolore—you're welcome to join me."

Caro nodded her agreement, and we ate lunch in the signora's backyard, enjoying the peace. Being this happy was energizing and exhausting all at the same time. Weird.

"So, when will you marry?" Signora Carello asked, as we sipped our coffees.

We answered simultaneously.

"I don't know," said Caro.

"As soon as possible," I replied.

The signora laughed.

"Oh, you two have some talking to do, I can see that. Never mind, my dears, you'll work it out. Have you decided where you'll live?"

"Caro has a place near New York," I said, "but I could be stationed anywhere."

"You're in the army?"

"No, ma'am, US Marines."

Signora Carello nodded slowly, a frown of concern crinkling her eyes.

"He has to do two more years," Caro said quietly. "And he's being sent out to Afghanistan. On Thursday."

"Ah." The signora shook her head sadly.

"Hey, it'll be fine," I said, refusing to let the shadow hanging over us spoil today. "Besides, I might see you out there."

Signora Carello looked confused.

"Caro is a reporter—a foreign correspondent," I explained. "But I wish she…"

I stopped mid-sentence, aware of the irritated tightening of Caro's face.

"Well," said the signora, carefully, "you young people don't choose the easy path, but it is your own path. I wish you both well. Please come back and have your honeymoon here."

"Honeymoon! Hell, I'd forgotten about that! Yeah, we should definitely have a honeymoon, Caro. With room service—so we don't have to get out of bed."

Caro blushed, but Signora Carello just laughed and stood to clear the plates.

"Don't say things like that in front of her," hissed Caro, as the old woman walked away. "She'll be embarrassed!"

I couldn't help laughing. "You're the only one who's embarrassed, Caro, which is pretty fucking funny. Signora Carello used to be 'fast', remember? Anyway, I didn't say anything that wasn't true."

And if the signora couldn't guess what we'd been doing in our room all of yesterday afternoon, the used condoms in the trash can would probably clue her in. It must be shit running your own hotel.

When we went up to our room, it had already been tidied. Caro didn't know that we were checking out today.

I could tell she was wondering what was going on, because she looked puzzled when Signora Carello pulled me into a tight hug before we left and whispered a few last minute suggestions for our special date later. She was a class lady. She reminded me of Caro.

The Amalfi coastline was really a huge James Bond set. The roads were narrow, almost single track in some places, unforgiving, with hairpin turns arcing up the mountain and the Med many hundreds of feet below. The Honda was eating it up, its perfect balance allowing me to take the bends at high speed, our knees almost touching the asphalt.

Caro was gripping onto my waist tightly, her sweet little pussy crushed up against my ass. What a fuckin' turn on.

As we passed the small town of Pontone, I slowed then pulled off the road next to a lemon grove and cut the engine. Just where Signora Carello had suggested.

"It's a great view, baby. You want to get your camera out?"

She slid off the bike, looking a little shaky, and I grinned at her as she snapped some of the scenery. I had a feeling she might have gotten me in some of the shots, too. Sneaky.

While I pulled out the picnic that the signora had packed for us, Caro climbed further up to get some more photographs. When she walked back, she waved her arm at the food, looking pleased but puzzled.

"Don't you want to ride on a bit further?"

"Nope, we're staying here. Picnic."

I held out a miniature bottle of champagne in one hand and two crystal flutes in the other. "Borrowed from Signora Carello," I said, answering her unspoken question.

"I think the signora has a soft spot for you, Sebastian."

"Must be my animal magnetism, baby."

She rolled her eyes at me.

"Hey, don't knock it—it works on you."

"That is true, Hunter."

I led us to a patch of dry, springy grass and stretched out. But when I opened the champagne, the cork flew off like a rocket, making us both hit the deck.

"Huh, guess it got shook up on the road."

Caro raised an eyebrow. Yeah, I wasn't the smoothest guy ever. I bet James Bond never got his champagne all shook up—just his women. *Yeah, well I got that bit nailed*, I thought to myself.

"Here's to us, Caro," I said, serious for once. "Today, tomorrow, forever. Promise?"

She met my gaze, then clinked her glass against mine.

"Yes, tesoro. Forever, I promise."

Once we drained our glasses, we stretched out on the grass in each other's arms. There was no pressure, no expectation of more, just a deep contentment from being exactly where I wanted to be with the woman who'd always owned my heart.

"I love my surprise, Sebastian," she said, her hand resting on my chest.

I laughed quietly. "This is only part of it, Caro. There's more."

"More?"

"Much more."

"Such as?"

"You'll see."

After another hour, we climbed to our feet reluctantly and I raced the Honda back down the coast road, pulling up into the forecourt of Il Saraceno. As Signora Carello had promised, it was expensive and classy—and just what I wanted for Caro.

But I was disappointed by the wary expression on her face.

"Here?" she asked uncertainly.

I stared across at the white stone arches that were supposed to resemble a Moorish palace. She didn't like it? It looked pretty darn good to me.

"Here," I said, trying to encourage her by smiling.

She still looked uncertain, and I couldn't figure out what was bothering her. But when she patted her hair and tried to comb it with her fingers, I worked it out. I grabbed her hand and kissed her hard. My woman never had understood that she was the most beautiful thing in my world wherever we went.

But it pissed me off that other guys noticed she was hot. When they looked at her, it made me want to play pool with their balls.

I towed Caro inside and handed over the Honda's keys to the guy at the reception desk, promising myself that I'd buy another touring bike one day. Caro raised her eyebrows when I took the room key and started walking toward the elevator.

"We're staying here? But we left all our things at Signora Carello's?"

"Nope, we haven't. I asked the signora to pack us up while we were out this morning. She was cool about it. Besides this is kind of her idea. Well, she helped me pick out somewhere special."

Caro frowned and glanced around her.

"But a place like this must cost a small fortune, Sebastian!"

"I can afford it, baby. This is my first night as an engaged man—and I want to enjoy it. Hey, don't worry. The only thing I've spent my pay on in the last ten years is booze and bikes," *and broads, but I wasn't going to remind her about that.* "I'm good for it."

Signora Carello had promised that we'd like the hotel, and if Caro's stunned expression when she saw our room was anything to go by, she liked it a lot. Best of all, the bed was nearly seven feet wide—I planned on having Caro on every inch of that mattress. We also had our own private balcony and a fucking enormous bathroom with a huge tub. Yep, I was feeling very *creative.*

I left her to look around while I tossed our luggage onto the bed and began to unpack. I was glad to see that the wardrobe held the garment bags that I'd arranged to have delivered.

I pointed at the one on the left.

"This is for you, baby."

Puzzled, but with a smile hovering at the corners of her mouth, Caro unzipped the bag, then gaped at the floor-length dress.

"Sebastian, it's beautiful! What have you done?"

I grinned at her excited smile. "I got one, too. A tux— like you wanted. Except mine is just rented. You get to keep the dress."

She placed it on the bed carefully, then wrapped her arms around my waist, smiling up at me.

"How did you get to be so perfect, Sebastian, because I could have sworn you were a giant pain in the ass."

I laughed loudly. "Next time I piss you off, I'm going to remind you that you said that, baby. Which will probably be in about five minutes."

"Probably," she agreed, with a smile.

"Come on, let's shower, and then I want to see you in that dress."

"Why, Warrant Officer Hunter! You want to put me *into* clothes?" she teased.

"You have another idea?" I murmured, my lips brushing over her neck.

"Oh, yes, most definitely, and it involves getting you naked on that bed, having my wicked, wicked way with you *before* we take a shower."

My smile grew even bigger. So did my dick.

"Let me get this right, Caro, that's *two* lots of wicked?"

"The thing is, Sebastian," she said, stroking the tips of her fingers against my cheek, "if you're going to make an honest woman of me, I want to get in as much sinning as possible first."

Then she shoved my chest hard, so I fell backwards onto the bed. And just to make her point, she ripped my t-shirt over my head, straddled my hips, and ran her tongue from my waist to my throat.

Holy shit, my woman was on fire.

I reached up to play with her pretty little nipples, but she gripped my wrists and pulled them above my head. I guess she wanted to be in charge. I wasn't going to argue. Then she leaned down to kiss me, tracing my lips with her tongue.

"Mmm, you taste so good, Sebastian, I won't want anything else to eat tonight."

I laughed lightly and gently pulled my hands free, before running them down her back.

"Yeah? Well, I'm starving, so unless you want me to eat downstairs alone, baby, you'll have to put up with a three-course meal. And I guarantee you'll need your energy later."

She pretend to pout. "Sure you don't want the starter now?"

Hell, yeah!

I shifted my hands to her waistband, tugging her t-shirt free and pulling it off her body. Her bra took even less time to disappear.

"Mmm, I like this position," I said, sitting up and sucking her nipples, nipping them with my teeth then working my way up her throat. She moaned and arched her back, pushing her tits into the palms of my hands.

Message received and understood.

I pulled a condom out of the back pocket of my jeans and handed it to her.

"Take your pants off, baby."

"I will if you will," she replied. "Race you!"

Then she bounced off the bed, unlaced her boots, and stripped—all while I was fighting with the buckles on my boots and trying to watch her at the same time.

"Ah, hell," I grumbled, staggering around the bedroom with my pants around my ankles.

"You're a slouch, Hunter," she laughed. "Just look at what you're missing."

She spun around slowly, massaging her tits and pushing them together.

"Fuck!" I hissed, hopping awkwardly, one boot on, one boot off.

"Maybe you should have been a fireman instead of a Marine, then you'd be used to undressing quickly."

I tossed the second boot behind me where it landed on the floor with a heavy thud. A moment later, I was naked, too.

"On the bed," she ordered.

"Yes, ma'am."

Then she bent over me and took my dick in her mouth. My eyes closed as I breathed deeply, holding back an orgasm that was instantly welling up from the base of my spine.

She ran her fingernails up and down my chest in time with her tongue.

"Baby, I'm going to come if you keep doing that," I growled, and I could hear the strain in my voice.

She let me go after a final long stroke of her tongue, and I tried to slow my heart rate by taking deep breaths, but when I heard the rip of foil and she rolled the condom into position, it was a losing battle. She knelt across me, positioning the head of my dick at the entrance to her soft pussy, then sank down.

I thrust up into her, harder than I'd intended.

"Fuck, Caro! I can't control myself with you!"

I started pumping my hips, bouncing her up as she slammed down to meet me. Christ, I was losing it; my body was rigid and my balls were so tight they felt about the size of walnuts. It was no use, I couldn't hold back any longer, so I used my fingers to make sure that she followed me.

I grit my teeth, the tendons standing out in my neck. Caro's eyes were closed and her head thrown back, her full tits bouncing wildly. What a fucking amazing sight.

She cried out some mangled version of my name and slumped down on my chest, breathing hard. It had all been faster than I'd meant, but fuck me, it felt good.

"Sorry, baby," I coughed out.

"You have nothing to be sorry about," she gasped, as we lay together, calming our racing pulses.

I couldn't help grinning like an idiot as I stroked the smooth skin of her back. "Ready for the main course?"

"You've got to be kidding me, Hunter? I'm still…" and a spasm of tremors made her pussy clench around me again.

"Oh, wow," I muttered. "I really felt that."

"Good," she huffed. "So did I."

I laughed at her grumpy tone, then lifted her off me as I sat up.

"I'm going to go shower."

She didn't answer as I made my way to the bathroom, snapping off the condom contentedly.

Yep, she liked the room.

I showered quickly, eager to get to the part where Caro got all fancy. Plus, I was freakin' starving after that work out.

She was staring at me, a puzzled frown on her face as I walked back into the bedroom.

"What?"

"Just wondering how the hell I ended up engaged to such a hot Marine. It's been quite a week."

Her words sent a shiver through my entire body. "You're not having second thoughts, are you, Caro?"

She shook her head slowly.

"No, Sebastian, I'm not. But you have to admit, it's all been pretty fast."

"It's been ten years, Caro," I contradicted, meaning every word. "I've waited long enough."

Her gaze softened and her eyes got warm. Her smile left little crinkles at the corner of her eyes, and I wanted to kiss every fucking one of them.

"I love you so much, tesoro," she said.

"Love you, too, Caro." Then I grinned at her. "Now get your ass in that shower, before I throw you in there."

"Fine, fine," she grumbled. "I'm going."

I waited until she was really moving before I turned to get dressed.

"I'll meet you in the restaurant, Caro."

"You're not going to wait for me here?"

"Nope. I want to see you sweeping down that staircase and have all the other bastards wanting you, but knowing I'll be the one taking you to bed later." She rolled her eyes. "Humor me: it's a guy thing."

She shook her head, but was smiling as she closed the door to the bathroom.

I pulled on the unfamiliar tux, pleased at how well everything fit, even the pre-shone shoes.

Then I laid out my final two purchases that were seriously fuckin' expensive. But if they looked as hot on her as I expected, worth every damn penny.

I wandered down to the restaurant, making sure that they'd reserved the table I wanted. It was in a small alcove, making it almost private, and it had amazing views down the cliffs to the sea. All for Caro. Christ, I was turning into such a pussy.

Married. Caro was the only woman I'd ever considered marrying. My parents had been just about the worst fucking example of wedded bliss that you could imagine: yelling at each other, hitting each other, fucking other people, drinking themselves into a coma most nights.

If it hadn't been for Ches' parents, I wouldn't have known that marriage could be anything different. I wanted what they had: knowing that your wife had your back, no matter what—for richer, for poorer and all of that. Yeah, I wanted it all. I could tell Caro was still hesitant. Her answer of 'I don't know' when Signora Carello had asked us when we were getting married made that pretty clear. I just didn't know if that was because of her ex-husband ... or because she wasn't sure of me.

I leaned against the bar and ordered a beer. We'd have wine with the meal, but right now I'd take a beer.

I'd only enjoyed a few sips when I saw in the mirror that a woman was watching me. Attractive, yeah. Cougar, hell yeah.

I'd spent a lot of years with women like that. You might say they'd become my specialty. I could see her unashamedly running her eyes over my ass, and then she licked her lips and prowled toward me.

She was wearing a purple halter top that just about restrained her fake tits, and long silver-gray pants that showed off her tiny waist, and skin that was orange from too many sun-beds.

"Ciao!" she purred, leaning next to me on the bar so I could have a look at her tits. I couldn't help glancing over when they were on display like that, but they weren't anywhere near as good as Caro's. No competition. But she'd seen me look, and that was enough.

"Hi," I said in English, hoping that she'd leave me alone.

"Ah, Inglese? Americano?"

"American."

"Oh, you are movie actor?"

I laughed and shook my head, subtly taking half a step away from her. But she didn't take the hint, leaning in closer.

"Are you staying at Il Saraceno?"

I nodded and took another long drink of my beer. "With my fiancée," I said, raising an eyebrow.

It didn't slow her down for a second and she laid her hand on my arm in a seemingly friendly gesture, although I knew it wasn't innocent.

"Congratulazioni," she said, the smile failing to meet her eyes or move her forehead.

I turned slightly, so she was forced to drop her hand, but then I glanced up the stairs and saw Caro. My breath caught in my throat. *So fucking beautiful.*

She was always hot, but seeing her dressed up was every fantasy come to life. She gave me a small smile then carefully made her way down the wide staircase, clinging onto the handrail as the silky-blue dress made soft shushing noises by her ankles. I wondered if I could get her to practice walking around our bedroom in high heels. I licked my lips.

When she reached the bottom of the stairs, I walked toward her, took her hand and kissed the back of it softly.

"You look beautiful, Caro."

"Thank you, kind sir."

I held out my arm, grinning at her teasing tone. *Yeah, yeah. I could be a fucking gentleman.* "May I escort you in to dinner, ma'am?"

"Why, yes you may."

From the corner of my eye, I saw the woman at the bar scowl, then shrug her shoulders, moving onto the bartender who looked worried.

Sorry, buddy, you're on your own.

I led Caro to our table, waving away the waiter and seating her myself, brushing a lingering kiss over her bare shoulder.

"I can't wait to get you out of that dress," I murmured, running my index finger from her earlobe to the base of her neck.

A soft sigh escaped her, and her eyes were only just drifting open when I sat across the table from her, grinning like an idiot.

"Every man in this room wants you, Caro. I'm so fucking proud, I can't stop smiling."

"Hmm, well I think you may be a little biased," she said, raising her eyebrows. "I thought I was going to need a crowbar to pry that woman off you. Is it just me, or had she overdone the fake tan, because I haven't seen that shade of orange outside of a drag review."

Was she jealous?

"My girl's got grit: I like it."

"I felt like swinging her around by her hair extensions," Caro admitted, the heat in her eyes making a lie of her mild tone. "Maybe some of your Marine training is rubbing off on me."

"That comes after the main course."

"Thank you for today, Sebastian," she said, her voice becoming serious. "It's been … perfect. Thank you."

"It's been a long time coming, Caro, but it was worth the wait."

She held up her left hand, examining the ring, turning it so the diamond sparkled in the setting sun.

"Where did you get this beautiful ring? Because I didn't

see any shops in Salerno that…"

"I didn't get it in Salerno," I interrupted softly.

Her mouth popped open in surprise. "Then where?"

"Geneva," I said, grinning at her amazement. "You know I was supposed to be at that fucking dull hostile environment briefing—which they'd given me as part of my 'rehabilitation' after Paris…" I raised an eyebrow, "but after I'd seen you … I couldn't face going back. I was just wandering around trying to get my head together, and I saw it in a jeweler's shop."

"But … you still hated me then!"

I shook my head. "I never hated you, Caro, although I tried; I really fucking tried. But I just couldn't do it." I sighed and looked away. "That ring has been burning a hole in my pocket ever since. I was just waiting for the right time to give it to you."

She blinked rapidly, and I really hoped that I hadn't spoiled things and made her cry again.

"You've always been so sure," she whispered, "I don't understand why."

My heart lurched sickeningly. *She doesn't feel the same.*

"I told you, Caro. It's only ever been you."

She stretched out her hand, focusing on the diamond glinting in the candlelight. "Thank you for giving it to me."

I caught her fingers and kissed the ring. "Thank you for wearing it."

At that moment, the Sommelier arrived with a bottle of Prosecco, pouring us a glass each, then stepping away before I had to tell him to fuck off. All I wanted was my woman with me.

I stared into her eyes.

"Thank God for you, Caro."

"And you, Sebastian, semper fidelis."

CHAPTER 12

The food arrived, but I couldn't tell you what we ate. I knew it was good, because Caro was moaning and groaning and licking her lips in a way that no red-blooded man could be immune to. I spent the whole damn meal uncomfortably hard. I was desperate to rush her back to bed, but I could see that she was enjoying herself. And I think we needed this—a moment of calm in the middle of all the crazy ... whatever the next few days and weeks would bring. She said we'd have the rest of our lives. I just hoped that she was right.

When we'd finished eating, we walked back up the grand staircase hand in hand. I'd arranged for two glasses of an Italian liqueur to be left on the balcony along with a candle and a rose—romantic shit that I would only ever do for Caro.

I handed her one glass and took the other for myself.

And then I couldn't wait any longer.

I could hear the surf breaking on the cliffs below and a low buzz of conversation carrying across the air from the restaurant, but neither of us spoke. I tipped the burning liquor down my throat and replaced the glass on the table, before cupping her face with my hands and kissing her slowly and deeply until the room spun around us.

I turned her gently, unzipping her dress, stroking the bare flesh I found underneath. The dress fell to the ground with a soft rustle and she stepped away from it. She looked amazing, wearing only the silver bra and panties that I'd bought her, the candlelight throwing deep shadows across her breasts and stomach. I reached out to touch her, but she shook her head.

Instead, she slid my jacket off my shoulders, tossing it

onto a chair, then loosened my bow tie and undid the top button of my shirt while I watched every move.

I leaned forward to kiss her neck and I felt tremors of desire skitter through her body. I scooped her into my arms and placed her carefully onto the bed.

Her deep brown eyes were molten as she gazed up at me, almost unblinking. Only her parted lips and rapid breathing showed that she was as turned on as I was. I unfastened the cufflinks, pulled open the shirt and shrugged it off. Her eyes fastened on my dog tags and an image leapt to the front of my mind: Caro naked except for my dog tags, on all fours.

Shaking my head, I bent down to untie my shoes and remove my socks. I was about to lose the pants, too, when Caro hooked her finger into the waistband and pulled me toward her.

Moving slowly, she slid the button free and lowered the zipper.

The pants joined my jacket on the back of the chair, and my boxer briefs followed. I stood in front of her as her eyes trailed up my body, and I felt the burn of her eyes on my legs, my dick, my stomach, my chest, until they came to rest on my face.

Her fingers followed her eyes, stroking softly over my skin, and my eyes fluttered closed as she dropped a soft kiss onto the head of my dick.

She reached for a condom, tore the packet open and slowly rolled it down. I sat next to her on the bed and carefully pulled out the hairpins she'd used to pile her long hair onto her head. As each curl of hair fell down, I kissed it, tangling it around my fingers, then gently angling her head back so I could kiss the soft skin of her throat.

This wasn't like me—or not like the guy I'd been for the last six years. While I wouldn't say I was 'wham bam, thank you, ma'am', when I was on a mission, I liked to go in hard. But now … even though we'd been together for four days, each time felt like new, like *I* was new. It was fucking terrifying, but amazing, too.

My hands traveled slowly across her body, pausing to

unhook her bra, sliding the straps over her shoulders, before leaning down to kiss her full tits, running my tongue around her nipples, teasing them into rigid points.

She stretched out on the bed, her hands above her head, and I raised myself up on my arms so I hovered over her, my dick begging to sink inside that hot, sweet pussy. I moved lower, running my tongue along the edge of her panties, rubbing my chin over her mound.

Then I pulled her panties down quickly and tossed them over my shoulder.

Her knees lifted, bracketing my hips, running her hands over my arms, tracing my tat with one finger.

My dog tags jingled against her chest, and Caro's eyes locked on mine as I pushed inside her.

She groaned, lifting her hips so I could slide in even deeper.

I started to move, building up a rhythm, focusing on every emotion that passed across her expressive face. I leaned down to kiss her deeply and I felt her clench around me as I rolled my hips, a growl erupting from my throat. She moaned softly, and I felt her pussy shiver, the first warning flares of an orgasm about to hit.

I started to move faster, and when she dug her heels into my ass, the breath hissed out through my teeth. She whimpered, crying out and digging her nails into my shoulders, clamping her thighs around my waist. My spine flexed and I could feel the small electric shocks spark and race up from my balls to my dick. Then she screamed and her pussy contracted around me hard, forcing an intense orgasm that had me riding her wildly, until a hoarse sound left my throat and my body went rigid, briefly crushing her into the bed.

I tried to catch my breath as I rolled off of her and onto my back, resting one hand across her stomach, needing to keep that contact.

No words had been spoken; there was nothing that needed to be said.

For the rest of that night, we slept, woke briefly, made love and slept again, until dawn and first light turned the ocean from black to silver.

"I love you, Sebastian," she said as the sun began to rise. "Thank you for giving yourself to me. Thank you for trusting me. Just promise me that you'll come back safely. Promise me!"

I wanted to. I wanted to promise that everything would be fine, that it was just a walk in the park, but the works died in my throat. I couldn't lie to her.

"I love you more than air, Caro. Always. Sempre. And I'll do everything I can to come home to you. I promise you that."

Sighing, she laid her head on my chest and we slept.

It was late when we woke for the last time, so I ordered an enormous brunch, the kind of pig-out that Caro loved but would never admit to wanting. We sat on the balcony in our bathrobes enjoying the food and the view, both of us ignoring the fact that we had less than 24 hours together before I shipped out.

I don't know how good of a job we were doing, but we were both trying. We stared at the sea and I held her hand, kissing it softly.

She sighed and glanced at her wristwatch.

"As much as I hate to say it, tesoro, I think we should get going. We've got a hell of a long drive ahead of us, or rather you have, and you didn't get much sleep last night."

I smiled at the memory. "Yeah, but it was worth it. Anyway, don't worry, Caro, we're not taking the bike; we're flying back from Naples. Our flight is at sixteen-hundred; we've got plenty of time."

"Flying? But what about your bike?"

"Sold it, baby. I can't take it with me, and they won't send me back to Geneva after this tour."

She looked surprised. "When did you organize all this?"

"When we were in Salerno; I didn't think you'd mind." I was puzzled by her sharp tone.

"I don't," she insisted. "It's your bike, but I wish you'd told me—it would have been one less thing to worry about."

Shit. Relationship—sharing—right. "Sorry, baby. I guess I'm just used to doing stuff on my own."

She frowned and glanced away. "Yes. Me, too. I suppose we'll just have to practice the whole sharing and communicating thing." Then her eyes flicked to mine. "I'll write to you every day, tesoro."

"Really? That would be cool. I never get mail. Well, Shirley always sends me a birthday card, but that's about it. Ches is shit at staying in touch. So am I."

"Well, I will expect an effort from you, Sebastian. Will you be able to email me?"

I pulled a face. "Maybe, I'm not sure. For a few days, but then ... I'll be out of range. Caro, don't worry if you don't hear from me regularly." I paused, watching her expression tighten. "The places they send me, I can be away from the main Base for days, sometimes weeks, in shithole villages, trying to persuade the locals to work with us. Nonmilitary comms is limited. Your letters will catch up with me eventually, but emails ... probably not that often."

"I understand," she said, her voice calm, overlaying a strong current of emotion. "But in an emergency, what's the procedure for contacting you?"

Giving her my CO's number breached about fifty protocols, but if it would reassure her...

"I'll give you a number you can call but only in a real, fucking emergency, Caro: I'm not supposed to give it out."

"Okay," she said softly, then paused. "If ... if anything happens that I need to know about, how will anyone know to contact me?"

Shit, I hated talking about this.

"Same as you, Caro. We have to do a call-list—the Emergency Contact Form—who to notify. I've been wondering how, I mean, I can't put you down as 'Lee Venzi' or even 'Caro Venzi' because they'll recognize the name; they'll start in asking questions, and you could be in deep shit."

Not that it would bother me if people knew about us. Hell, I'd shout it from the fucking rooftops if she'd let me, but she wanted to keep our relationship on the down-low for her career's sake. I was okay with that, but it sure made things less straightforward.

"What about Carolina Hunter?" she suggested, glancing across as she put the emergency number in her cell. "They'll just assume I'm a cousin or something; in fact, why don't you do that? Put me down as a relative."

I really, really liked that idea.

"Yeah, that would work." *And the sooner she had that name, the better.*

She took a shuddering breath and her eyes began to fill with tears. She swiped at them angrily. My girl hated showing weakness, if that's what it was.

"Hey, baby, nothing's going to happen to me: I can take care of myself. I'm more worried about you. Reporters get … hurt all the time."

"I know, Sebastian," she said harshly, "but I'll be embedded with a Marine unit from Leatherneck; safest place to be." Then she gave me a watery smile. "I heard US Marines are tough, and I know for a fact they're hot. In fact the word 'embedded' has me thinking all sorts of interesting things."

"You stay away from those bootnecks, Caro. They're a bunch of horny bastards."

"I've noticed! But really, don't worry about *that*. I've learned to say 'no' in even more languages than you."

We were both trying so hard not to give into the darkness that hovered around us. I took her hand, idly playing with her engagement ring.

"Well, at least they'll know you're taken when they see this." She didn't reply. "How long do you think you'll be in Afghanistan?"

"Assuming my papers arrive," she said, throwing me a knowing look, "maybe a month, six weeks. Certainly no more. I'll have a couple of days in Kabul, maybe in Kandahar, too—meeting some of your top brass. Then I'm hoping I'll be able to hitch a ride out to Leatherneck. I'll just have to see how it goes. Maybe I'll see you out there?"

I frowned. "I want you home safe, Caro."

"Likewise, Sebastian."

We stared at each other, neither one of us prepared to give in. I shook my head and changed the subject.

"Do you want to take a swim?" I suggested. "I'll be God knows how many miles from the nearest pool out there, and hundreds of fucking miles from the ocean."

"Sure," she smiled. "And I get to see you in those ridiculously loud boardshorts again."

"And you'll wear the bikini?"

"Only if you promise not to punch anyone who looks at me."

"Can't promise that, baby," I answered honestly.

Time passed too quickly, and it felt like moments later that we were sitting in the back of a cab taking us to Naples airport.

We were both quiet, lost in thought, when Caro suddenly spoke.

"Sebastian, when do you think you'll tell Ches about us?"

I shrugged.

"I don't know. Why?"

She hesitated. "Well, I just thought I could get all your belongings sent over from the west coast, but it's going to make it tricky to organize if Ches doesn't know about me." She stammered out the words, then hurried on. "And there are some beautiful places in upstate New York that we could ride out to on your other bike … if you want."

God, she was amazing. How the fuck did I get to be so lucky?

"You'd do that?"

She seemed puzzled by my question. "Of course. Why wouldn't I? You'll need your things when you come home."

Home. Fuck, I was going to have a home! She didn't understand how much her words meant to me—she couldn't.

"Okay," I agreed quickly. "I'll email him tonight. He'll be pretty fucking surprised."

She laughed, but it wasn't a very happy sound. "Yes, that probably about sums it up—to say the least."

I pulled her into my arms, kissing her with a raw hunger, not caring that our driver had a grandstand view in the mirror. I wanted the whole world to know this woman was mine. She had to know that I didn't give a shit. If Ches or his bitch of a wife had a problem with us being together again, fuck 'em—I didn't need them in my life. Not that I thought Ches would be like that. He was my friend—we were solid.

"What was that for?" she asked breathlessly.

"Caro, all that matters … *all* that matters is you and me. Nothing else is important. We lost ten fucking years because of other people. I'm *not* going there again. I won't let us. Understand? Nothing and no one will ever come between us again."

She sighed, curling her body against mine, holding on too tight, because she didn't believe me either.

The cab driver dropped us at departures, but we got separated by security. I was taken to one side, questioned and patted down. They definitely weren't happy with the €6,000 in large denomination notes I was carrying. Once I showed them the receipt and forced my US Marine ID in front of them, they reluctantly let me through.

Caro's anxious expression immediately eased as I strolled over to join her.

"Guess I've got a criminal face or something."

"I could have told you that," she laughed. "I'm just glad they didn't get one of the female security guards or you'd never have gotten away."

There was only one way to answer that, so I rolled my eyes as she snickered quietly.

The flight was short, less than two hours and we were back in Geneva, carless, bikeless and sunless. It was cooler, too, but I didn't mind that, not when I knew Kabul would be in the high nineties and more.

We took a taxi back to the apartment and I threw open the shutters, letting in what was left of the daylight. I saw Caro studying my room, a frown on her face. I guess it did look pretty basic next to the luxury of Il Saraceno.

"We can check into a hotel, Caro."

"No, this is fine. It's not the room…"

Oh.

"Don't say it, Caro," I begged. "Please, baby. I can't bear it when you look at me like that."

"Sorry," she whispered, and I could see the effort it cost

her to put a small smile on her face. "So, single bed, huh? That's going to be cozy. We'll have to improvise."

I smiled at her, grateful that she'd play along for a few more hours. It was going to be hard enough to say goodbye.

"I just gotta pack my shit, baby, then we'll go find somewhere to eat, okay?"

"Sure, go ahead. I'll write up my notes and check my messages."

I'd gotten rid of most of my things already, in preparation for deployment. Anything I wanted to keep was already on its way to Ches's garage. I knew Amy gave him hell for storing my stuff, but he didn't listen to her. A few more things needed to be shipped out—I'd kept my iPod and laptop until now, but the laptop could go. I sent Ches an email that gave him the basics and told him I'd be out of touch for a while. If he had any messages he could send them to Caro.

What was left went into my sea-bag, except my Dress Blues which I shoved into a garment bag for now.

When I'd finished, Caro was still checking her messages. I realized she didn't have a place to stay for the next few days, unless she went back to the hotel. I could tell she wasn't comfortable in the apartment, but like she said, she'd been in worse places.

"You can stay here if you like," I offered. "It's paid up till the end of the month. The owner is Madame Dubois. Just leave the key with her when you go: she's cool."

When Caro looked up, her eyes were distant. "Thank you, I'll do that," she said quietly.

We were both trying to hold back the weight of the next 12 hours before it crushed us.

"Any interesting emails?" I asked, hoping to lighten the mood.

"All my girlfriends are drooling over your photograph," she smiled, sounding more like her old self. "They can't quite believe you're real. Neither can I sometimes."

I grinned and pulled her into a hug. "I could prove it to you now if you like."

She didn't answer, but ran her hands across the front of

my jeans and squeezed, not very gently. My eyebrows shot up, and she laughed.

"Sex instead of food, Caro?"

"Yes," she agreed, kissing my neck, "I don't know what's come over me—you must be a bad influence."

Then she grabbed a hold of my t-shirt and ripped it over my head. Things were just getting interesting when my damn phone rang: my fuckin' CO trying to cockblock me *again*.

Caro raised her hands in defeat, and re-tucked her shirt as I answered.

"Hunter."

"Back in the land of cuckoo clocks?"

"Yes, sir. Just got back to Geneva."

"Good. Slight change to your orders: a car will pick you up at oh-five-hundred hours for transfer to Ramstein. Space-A to Kabul, report to Ryan Grant at Camp Eggers. There's a Press liaison dinner where your presence has been requested—Dress Blues. Now, somehow the ANA has got wind that we're going after Gal Agha, which is not good news. They want to send 'tactical support' whatever the fuck that's supposed to mean. I'm hoping you and Grant's team will be in Now Zad before they get their shit together. If not, skills and drills and watch your six. Clear?"

"Yes, sir."

"I want your first report from Leatherneck. Good night, Hunter."

Caro was looking at me intently. I think she could see from my face how serious the situation was. I'd be walking into an administrative nightmare between ISAF and the Afghan National Army, intel that was leaking worse than the Titanic, with so-called colleagues I couldn't trust. Plus I'd be working on a very sensitive mission with a detachment of Marines who didn't know me. Yeah, nothing to worry about.

"Pick up 05:00," I said.

She wrapped her arms around my neck and clung to me.

We stood together, unmoving, needing that closeness for as long as we could.

Eventually, I leaned down to kiss her hair.

"Let's go get some food," I said quietly.

She nodded without speaking.

We stepped out into the gray evening light, and Caro

shivered. It might have been from the cooler mountain air, or because she could sense what was coming. She gripped onto my hand as if she'd never let go. We both knew that she would—and soon.

I took her to a small, family-run bistro that I'd used ever since arriving in Geneva. I didn't have anything more than a kettle in my room, not that I knew Jack shit about cooking anyway: I could burn some eggs and unwrap a MRE. That was about it.

Caro looked surprised when the owner nodded at me familiarly.

"I come here most days," I admitted, although I'd never brought anyone with me before.

"Hmm, seems to me you need some cooking lessons, Sebastian," Caro said with deliberate lightness. "When you come home—to Long Beach—we'll have to have some fun with food."

Home. The word pulled at my gut again. But she wanted lightness—I could give her that.

"Yeah, that would be great!" I grinned at her. "Remember that chocolate sauce you bought that time? That was amazing—and I don't even like chocolate that much. Although it tasted damn fine on you."

"Don't use language like that with me, Sebastian," she scolded, almost serious. "Chocolate is not something I joke about."

"Okay, I get it. How do you feel about peanut butter?"

She wrinkled her nose. "I'll buy some for you: crunchy or smooth?"

"Crunchy," I said, raising my eyebrows suggestively.

She smiled and agreed that crunchy would be good.

Caro ordered a risotto and I ordered the ravioli, but neither of us felt like staying long. We ate without tasting, and then we were out of there. I left a larger than usual tip. I didn't do goodbyes, so it was my way of saying I wouldn't be around.

When we got back to the apartment, Caro was shivering.

"Cold, baby?"

"A little. Can we turn the heat on?"

I smiled at her. "No heating."

She stared at me in amazement. "None? Not even a space heater?"

I shook my head, amused. "Don't worry, Caro—I'll warm you up."

I'd chosen the room for the view and because it was in a part of town that was away from other Americans stationed here. Nothing against them, but I preferred to be by myself.

Caro disappeared into the bathroom, then reappeared dressed in one of my old khaki workout shirts. She threw herself into the bed, shivering under the covers. Jeez, it wasn't *that* cold.

To make my point, I wandered around naked, although I usually wore green skivvies in case Madame Dubois walked in, which she had, soon after I moved here. I thought she'd made a mistake, but when it happened a second and then a third time, I decided the old lady had her eyeballs on my junk too often. But for Caro, I'd make an exception, although I kept the tighty whiteys for under Deltas—the khaki slacks. Man, I hated those.

I washed up and finished brushing my teeth, before I slid into the narrow bed next to Caro.

"You know, Sebastian," she said, "while I really enjoyed the floor show, you'll have to wear more clothes at home."

"Why?"

"Because," she said, as if talking to a five-year-old, "I live in a bungalow—and I have elderly neighbors. *We* have elderly neighbors, and I don't want you giving them a heart attack."

"Okay, boss," I smirked.

I pulled her against my body and kissed her slowly and deeply, trying to show her without words how much she meant to me, how much she'd always meant to me.

My body reacted to her instantly, but I took my time, pushing away the night, pushing away the moment when we'd be apart again, touching, always touching, tasting and feeling. Her hands traced the muscles of my back, and her tongue tracked across of every ridge of my chest and stomach, dipping down to take me in her mouth, until I had to beg her to stop. Then I made sure I took to her the edge and back before she exploded against my mouth, her breath harsh in her throat. And only then I allowed myself to slide inside her, filling her inch by inch, circling my hips, so I could feel her tightening around me. I rolled onto my back, pulling her with me, and I laid my hands across her flat stomach as she arched up over me.

Then she covered my hands with her own.

"Can you feel yourself inside me?" she whispered, her voice husky.

She'd said those exact same words to me the very first time we'd made love after I'd been bruised and beaten by my father. And she'd taken care of me; she'd taken me into her arms, into her bed, and into her body. She healed my body, mended my cuts and bruises, but more than that ... she healed my soul. I'd never stopped loving her.

"Yes," I said, staring up at her, "I can."

We loved each other all night, but it couldn't stop the clock from ticking.

I'd set the alarm, even though neither of us had slept. I'd sleep on the transport out of Ramstein; I wasn't going to waste a second of being with Caro.

We showered together, speaking with our hands and our bodies. And then she watched as I dressed in my desert cammies. Her face remained calm, but her eyes had already told me what she was really thinking.

She held out one hand toward me, and in her palm rested a small pebble of white quartz, shaped by the ocean into a tiny heart.

"Tesoro, go with my love, but take this with you. It's just silly, but I always carry it with me when I leave home—I found this the first time I went to Long Beach. But now I have your ring to wear."

I closed my eyes and leaned down to kiss her hair.

"I've never had something to come back to before, Caro. Don't worry about me—just take care of yourself."

I kissed the piece of quartz and tucked it into my pocket.

"I love you, tesoro. Stay safe for me."

A car horn sounded in the street below us.

"Time to go, baby. Love you."

I kissed her once more, tasting her for the last time in God knows how long. Then I scooped up my sea-bag and ran down the stairs. The car was one of the featureless black sedans that Military Intelligence used around the city.

The driver saluted.

"Your orders, sir."

He handed me a packet of papers, then popped the trunk, stowing my bags inside.

I glanced up at the window, and smiled when I saw Caro looking down at me, then the door closed and I was heading for the airport.

CHAPTER 13

The flight was a charter and once I was through security, I was directed to a small room with other US military personnel scheduled on the same flight.

I scanned the faces—no one I recognized. I wasn't expecting to, but you never know.

I checked my orders, but there was nothing different since I'd talked to Cardozo last night. I had forty minutes before my flight, so I shoved my bags under my seat, and stretched out to take a nap.

As soon as my eyes closed, I could see Caro's face. I imagined her lying in my bed, her hair spilled out across the pillow and … oh fuck, not a good idea thinking about her if it was going to make me hard. Not here and definitely not now. Instead, I tried to reprogram my brain to think about the mission. It wasn't working: every time I closed my eyes, Caro's face swam into view.

I nixed the idea of sleeping and sat up, rubbing my eyes. I had a copy of Paulo Coelho's 'The Alchemist'. I'd read it before, but now I had a new insight into its message: 'Tell your heart that the fear of suffering is worse than the suffering itself.' I wasn't sure I agreed, especially now. But as a book, it was still the shit.

The flight was called and I found a seat near the bulkhead next to the window. It was a short flight—90 minutes depending on the head-winds—but I didn't want some fucker crawling all over me if he had to take a piss.

I guess I did manage to sleep eventually, because the next thing I knew my head thumped against the window as we landed, waking me up and pissing me off in the same

234

breath. My next conscious thought was of Caro. I knew that I'd have to get a grip on that, because having my mind on her instead of the mission was going to make me fuck up, a situation that could be slightly terminal. I smiled to myself, thinking how pissed she'd be if I got myself killed. I patted the pocket over my heart a little self-consciously, feeling a slight bump from the little pebble she'd given me.

Must be getting soft in my old age. And yeah, 27 could feel fucking old at times.

Most of the guys on the flight were PCSing. Their Permanent Change of Station were to bases across KMC—or Kaiserslautern Military Community—to give it the full name, and Ramstein was the air force base.

I managed to find a café that was selling coffee and found a few Euros in coins to pay for it. Then the waiting started. That's the military for you: hurry up and wait. Happens all the time, so there's no point getting your panties in a bunch about it.

I glanced out to the runway and saw a parked airplane: a C-130 turbo-prob. If that was my ride, the flight to Kabul was going to be a bitch and noisy as hell.

It wasn't long before the flight was called, so I showed my orders to the wing nut in charge, wondering if he could read, the way he scrunched up his eyes scrolling down through the papers. Eventually, he nodded and waved me through. I tossed my sea-bag on top of the baggage cart, praying it would arrive with me on the same flight. It didn't contain anything that couldn't be replaced, but I wasn't looking forward to getting tied up in red tape the second I landed. I made my way to a seat at the back and stuck in my ear-buds, listening to Lifehouse, until I got to the song 'You and Me' and then I had to fast forward. Fuck, I really was getting soft. I switched to Linkin Park.

I rolled up my uniform jacket to use as a pillow then closed my eyes, seeing her face smiling behind my eyelids. I'd been dreaming about her for 10 years, but now it didn't hurt quite so bad.

I wasn't really asleep—I was just resting my eyes, so when the intercom crackled seven hours later and the pilot said he was prepping to land, all hands reached into the overhead lockers to suit up: helmets and body armor. It was bright daylight outside the window, so that made everyone nervous. A Hercules is a big fucking target. It's better to fly at night because the cold air is denser, but also because the dark is some protection from enemy fire.

So after traveling for a total of 11 hours, I landed in Kabul.

What a fucking dump.

There are three things you need to know about Afghanistan: one, it's a shithole; two, it's hot in summer; and three, it's a shithole.

I hadn't been here for 36 months, but nothing had changed. From a distance the Koh Daman Mountains looked beautiful, still covered in snow, despite the 110°F heat at sea level. But up closer, the city was just as ugly and miserable as I remembered.

If you're doing a winter tour, it's constant cold and freezing mud; summer tours, it's dust. Endless, yellow dust: in your food, in your water, in your bed, in the lining of your helmet. Rumor says the dirt out here is 10% fecal matter so the whole place is shit.

And soon Caro would be here, too. I hated to think that she'd be stuck in this rat trap, even if it meant she'd be closer to me.

Yeah, I wasn't happy to be back.

The sticky heat hit me as soon as I exited the plane, and I breathed in the dust and acrid stench of fuel and hot rubber. In the distance, gray-blue smoke drifted upward. IED? Car bomb? Welcome to Afghanistan.

We'd landed at Bagram Airfield, about 15 miles northeast of Kabul. Most of the guys I'd flown with were in transit to other bases, but my orders took me into the city.

I squinted into the white heat of the sun and slid on my Oakleys, staring out at the acres of tents and shanty buildings that made up the base.

The air was humid, but we still disembarked fast, getting under cover as quickly as possible. In the arrivals area (aka a shed), I had to go through the rigmarole of checking into theater. Despite being ID-checked and listed as getting on the flight at Ramstein, I still had to go through the exact same procedure getting off at Kabul. What the fuck? Did they think anyone might have gotten on the flight halfway? Probably the cheap fucking computer systems they use. Thanks, Uncle Sam.

At least my sea-bag had arrived, which was good. I had to rummage through the baggage cart to find my Dress Blues—if they'd gone missing, they were a bitch to replace.

I strode toward the exit, stopping at the helpfully named information desk, only to find that the car that should have been waiting for me was nowhere to be seen and no one knew fuck-all about it. The US Army clerk couldn't have cared less, shrugging when I asked him how the fuck I was supposed to get to Kabul. Fucking ground-pounder.

In the end, I caught a ride with a Lieutenant Colonel from the 10th Mountain Division, who bored me to death for 35 minutes about being in Eye-raq for the first Gulf War. At least his transport was an armored air-conditioned SUV.

As we got closer to the city, we were passed several times by kids on motorcycles, customized with carpet over the saddles—the Afghan version of pimp-my-ride. At least something here made me smile.

Because I was working for military spooks, I was billeted next to the Embassy. The colonel raised his eyebrows as he dropped me off, but didn't ask any questions—not that I would have answered him anyway.

A bored-looking private checked my ID and waved me through security. It was checked again before I was let through the steel and concrete barrier and into the main compound.

For guys who were arriving solo like me, the Embassy's other role was liaison. I needed to contact my chain of command to schedule the deployment briefs.

I waited while my name was passed up, and helped myself to a cup of water from the dispenser. It was chilled. Nice.

"Hunter, I'm John Nash. Welcome to Kabul."

A tall thin guy in the uniform of a Captain of Marines

stood in front of me. I slammed a salute and then followed him up the stairs.

His office was a tiny room, crammed with filing cabinets and a bank of computer screens. He made sure I sat facing away from them.

"Your last CO thinks you're a waste of fucking oxygen, Hunter."

"Yes, sir."

"Your present CO thinks you're redeemable."

"Good to know, sir."

I thought I saw a hint of a smile, but since I couldn't be sure, I stayed standing at attention.

"Take a seat."

I sat down and tried to look intelligent.

"How's your Pashto?"

"Rusty, sir."

"You've got eight hours to get it shipshape. The UN is hosting a function tonight for local military, Press, and important Afghan government officials. I want you there, ears to the ground. See what you can pick up, but don't let it be known you speak the language. You'll meet your team leader, Ryan Grant, and he'll go over the fine print. Fact is we want Gal Agha. We need him on our side. We've already made him our offer, but he wants to meet face-to-face. Find him, talk to him, impress the fuck out of him, and Helmand will be one degree safer for ISAF forces. Understand?"

"Yes, sir."

"Good. Helmand is the most kinetic province in Afghanistan."

I kept a straight face. 'Kinetic' just meant more shooting.

"Here's the file—everything you need to know on Gal Agha. Read it, memorize it, fucking inhale it, if you have to. Learn it, so that it's in your gut and you're ready to shit facts. Be at UN HQ at 1900 tonight—a driver has been requisitioned for you. Your billet is down the hall, third door on the left. And you'll be deploying with Grant at oh-five-hundred tomorrow. This isn't fucking Cuckoo-clock land, and you're not on the block now. Any questions?"

"No, sir."

I saluted, scooped up the file, along with my sea-bag, weapon and the rest of my shit, and situated myself in my billet to read. I was hot, sweaty and longing for a shower, but I had a file to memorize first.

I stretched out on the cot, wondering where Caro was right now. Fuck, if I hadn't screwed up her papers, chances were that she'd have been at the UN event tonight. It would be fucking ironic if I'd cockblocked myself. No, I had to stop thinking about that shit. I had a job to do.

Stay safe, Caro. For fuck's sake, stay safe.

Two hours later, I'd read and absorbed as much as I could. I closed the file, deciding I'd test myself later, and stretched out on the cot, setting my phone to wake me at six. Fuck, I was tired.

I woke up bleary-eyed and short-tempered. Being here brought back some of the nightmares. Anyone who'd served had them. We all saw shit that never left our brains. Caro had nightmares. She wouldn't tell me what they were about, but I could guess. I hoped I was wrong—I didn't want that for her.

I shook it off, did some stretches and crunches to get the blood flowing, then staggered off to find somewhere to shower. I ran my hand over my light stubble. Yep, definitely needed a shave. That was one thing I hated about being a Marine: it got old having to shave every day—some days I just wanted to let the scruff build up and grow my hair longer than a quarter of an inch. One day, when I was out, when I had a home with Caro. Maybe only two years from now. Being back in theater, it felt more like an impossible dream than ever. My stomach turned over and I hoped like fuck that she wouldn't change her mind now that we were apart again.

I showered quickly, scraped a razor across my chin, cheeks and upper lip, then pulled on the Blues. The standing collar always rubbed. Bastard. The coat was midnight blue with red trim and a white web belt with my rank of Warrant Officer denoted by the gold waist plate. The pants were sky blue, worn with black socks and black dress shoes. White barracks cover and white gloves finished my outfit. I pinned my medals on the left chest of my coat; it was the only time I ever looked at them.

But I was proud of my uniform, I'd earned it, but yeah—it wasn't the most comfortable thing to wear, especially in the Afghan heat.

My driver was a Lance Corporal who looked about 15 but must have been in his early twenties, and drove the armored SUV like he'd graduated from NASCAR instead of boot camp.

I half-listened to a monologue about the highlights of his tour and stared out the window. There were more men dressed in Western clothes on the streets than I remembered. The women still looked the same, all covered by flowing blue burqas, their faces and figures hidden as they haggled at the markets. Barefoot kids tried to earn a few bucks washing cars or selling whatever crap they could get their hands on.

There were a lot more Mercedes than there used to be. It's like that here—Rolexes on guys whose fathers herd goats. It was heart-warming to see all those aid dollars being put to good to use.

Kabul was more prosperous, but that only highlighted the signs of war: bomb-blasted buildings, walls with bullet holes, and burned out patches where cars had been turned into bombs.

My driver skidded to a halt in a cloud of yellow dust and grit outside the Intercontinental, Kabul's premier hotel for Westerners; an ugly building of white blocks that looked like something out of the Soviet era.

The kid said he'd be waiting for me, and went off to hunt down some chow. A uniformed doorman held the door, looking for all the world like he could be outside the Four Seasons and not in one of the most dangerous cities on earth.

I was directed to the ballroom where the dinner was being held. I kept an eye open for any Marine Captain— chances were he'd be my new skipper.

It quickly became apparent that I was the lowest ranking person around; everyone else was a commissioned officer. No skin off my back, but it sure reminded me of my place in the food chain.

A splash of bright green caught my eye. It was unusual

to see that color in a Muslim country because green was supposed to be Mohammed's favorite color and mentioned in the Qur'an. I cursed under my breath when I realized I recognized the woman. Shit, a ghost of past fucks: Natalie Arnaud. I dodged behind a pillar and wondered if I'd manage to avoid her for the entire evening. Smart money said no.

She disappeared into the ladies' bathroom, and I decided that the safest option was to stay where I was … doing recon. At least I'd have a chance of avoiding her if I kept her under surveillance.

A long five minutes later, she reappeared with another layer of red lipstick making her look like a vampire's hard-on. That sort of shit used to appeal to me, but not anymore. I thought she might have gone into the bathroom to cover up her tits, because the UN were pretty strict about their staff behaving appropriately, especially in a Muslim country, and Natalie's behavior and dress was … not.

But then she was followed out by Caro.

How? What? Holy fuck! She was here! She was really here!

Her papers must have been cleared more quickly than I'd expected. Suddenly Kabul had redeeming features after all.

She looked beautiful. Her long dark hair was glossy, and her simple black dress showcased her hotter than hell figure. Then I saw that she was wearing the shoes I'd bought her in Salerno. My heart lurched and started beating to the rhythm that was all for Caro.

I waited until Natalie had sashayed out of shot, and I caught the irritated expression on Caro's face as she muttered, "What a bitch!"

"You don't know how right you are," I whispered in her ear.

She jumped, then whirled around, a huge smile making her beautiful face glow.

It was so fucking hard that PDA wasn't allowed in uniform. I was aching to kiss her, touch her, but I couldn't. It would be dangerous for both of us.

"Sebastian! What are you doing here?" she whispered. "I thought they were sending you to Kandahar?"

"Change of plan," I said, unable to rein in the ridiculous

smile I was wearing. "I have a 24 hour stopover and I heard the Press would be here tonight, so I wangled an invite." *Not strictly true, but I couldn't tell her my real reason for being here.* "I wasn't sure when you were arriving. But now that you're here, I'm planning on seducing you behind the potted palms."

I was joking. Sort of. But then her eyes darkened and her lips tilted upward, a sexy smile playing on her beautiful lips.

"Or somewhere a little more private, I hope," she breathed out.

My dick twitched in response. "Yes, ma'am."

"By the way, do you know that tramp?" she asked testily, jerking her head in the direction of my former fuck.

And was that jealousy I could hear?

I smirked a little.

"Her name is Natalie Arnaud. French. She's a PA for some guy at the UN, but she likes people to think she's important."

"And you know her because…?"

Oh shit. Of course she'd ask me that.

"One of your Parisian conquests," she finished when I didn't respond.

"It was just a warm body, Caro," I said quietly.

"I understand that, but she's going to get herself into a lot of trouble; she's only dressing like that to impress you, Sebastian—I heard her in the bathroom—so you'd better speak to her."

Was she serious? Fuck me, she was—and she was enjoying it, if the expression on her face was anything to go by.

"Suck it up, Hunter," she said, a small smile teasing her lips. "You created this situation; you've got to deal with it. And then find somewhere private for us."

I shook my head, pissed at having to deal with Natalie. I also wasn't happy that she'd somehow heard I was going to be here. Fucking military intelligence—what part of 'need to know' gave them a problem? But I smiled at Caro and threw her a salute. I was about to get laid—so I didn't care if she gave me orders.

"Yes, boss."

Then I glanced around, took her hand and tugged her

down the corridor that I knew led to the staff area of the hotel.

I had to try a few doors before I found an empty office, pushed her inside, slammed her against the door, and kissed her with all the urgency that 24 hours away from her had given me. She kissed me back, her tongue driving into my mouth, her teeth nipping at my lips, and sucking them hard. Her breasts pressed against my uniform and my dick was trying to punch an emergency evac route through the buttons on my pants.

I yanked up the hem of her dress, dragging my fingers to the edge of her panties, before circling quickly and pushing inside her beautiful pussy, making her cry out.

"Fuck, you're wet," I hissed.

She moaned in reply.

"I am so fucking hard right now," I growled into her ear. "Here and now: yes or no, Caro?"

"Yes!" she grit out, her voice deep and husky.

I unbuttoned my fly, quickly rolling a condom over my erection, while Caro shimmied out of her panties.

"Bend over the desk," I ordered, gripping her hips.

"Sebastian, the door!" she gasped.

"Fuck!"

I hadn't set a cordon or secured the boundary—Marine safety 101, for fuck's sake. I wedged a chair under the handle and spun back to the desk, hauling her dress over her ass and forcing her feet apart with mine.

We didn't have long before the banquet started, and it would definitely look suspicious if we walked in together. I plunged into her, relieved, happy, fucking delirious to be inside her again when I thought it would be months. Here and now in this cursed city, this dying country, where the body count rose each day. *My woman showing me that life could still be worth living.*

My breath hissed out through my teeth and I forced myself to make it good for her, too. I pulled out slowly, then pushed back in, circling my hips, watching her knuckles whiten as she gripped the edge of the desk. I felt her tighten around me and I had to clench my teeth to keep from losing it too fast. But when she pushed her ass back to meet me, I couldn't wait, ramming into her desperately. I could hear her body slamming against the desk, and even though I knew her hips would be bruised in the morning, I couldn't stop, didn't want to stop. I wanted to mark her—*my woman*. I was aroused and disgusted with myself at the same time. Fucking thoughts! And then I lost it, my spine snapping and sparks shooting up from my balls. I wouldn't have been surprised to see them on fire.

Holy shit, that was the hottest in-uniform sex I'd ever had.

We collapsed onto the floor together and she twisted around, softly brushing the tips of her fingers over my face.

She was flushed and so fucking beautiful, her hair spilling wildly over her shoulders, unaware that her dress was still around her waist. And I wouldn't have believed it if I hadn't seen it—but I was getting hard again already.

"Fuck, that wasn't enough, Caro. I want you again."

"We can't, Sebastian," she panted. "As it is, we'll be missed if we don't hurry."

I knew she was right but I didn't have to like it. I brought her hand to my lips, sucking her fingers, one by one, insanely desperate to repeat the last few minutes.

"I need you, Caro. Let me come to your room tonight, please, baby."

"You can't, I'm sharing with Liz."

Fuck! The fat British broad.

"Get rid of her!" I whispered, rubbing her arms gently, hoping to persuade her.

Suddenly someone rattled the door handle and I could hear voices outside.

"Fuck it!"

Playtime was over. I peeled off the condom and tucked my dick into my pants, cursing the asshole who'd interrupted us.

"My panties," Caro hissed, looking around her distractedly.

I grinned at her, finding them hanging from a handle on the desk drawer.

"I think these are yours, ma'am."

"Thank you," she muttered, pulling them on and straightening her skirt.

The door handle rattled again and I could hear two guys arguing about who had the key. At least my Pashto wasn't as rusty as I'd thought it might be.

I helped her up, then opened the door cautiously, but the corridor was empty in both directions.

"You're good."

She raised an eyebrow. "You're not so bad yourself, chief."

I grinned at her and winked. "Later?"

But then I heard more voices coming toward us. Caro smiled once and hurried away. I didn't know if she'd agreed to meet me later or not, but I knew I'd be knocking at her door. I gave her a few seconds head start, then sauntered after her.

Her cheeks were still flushed, but there was nothing else that showed what we'd been doing. The image of her peachy ass bent over that desk was enough to make my dick remind me how fucking uncomfortable the Blues were. I had to think about something else.

Well, fate was a humorous bitch, because then I saw the one person I'd hoped never to see again—Caro's ex-husband—and he was talking to her. What the fuck was that asshole doing here? Since when did landlocked Afghanistan need help from the US Navy? Yeah, so the douchebag was a medical doctor, but still … shouldn't he be retired by now?

He hadn't deserved to be married to Caro and when she'd been sent away, he wouldn't give me her address; he wouldn't even give me the fucking time of day. I hated that prick.

I couldn't stand it any longer and marched over to get her away from him. He saw me, and immediately had the expression of someone who's just stepped in dog shit. Guess the love-fest was mutual.

Military protocol demanded that I salute a senior officer, even one from another service, so I deliberately shoved my hands in my pockets, which was the alternative to punching the fucker.

He frowned, and I wondered if he was going to report me or try and insist that I salute him—I'd *really* like to see that. But then he turned back to Caro, ignoring me.

"Good to see you, Caroline. You look lovely tonight. I hope you enjoy the evening."

He strolled away, greeting a few people as he moved through the room.

"What the fuck were you doing talking to that asshole?" I snapped.

Caro's furious eyes raked across me.

"What are *you* doing making it so damned obvious that you care?" she shot back savagely.

What the fuck? She was angry with me?

"Why aren't you wearing your ring?" I asked, aware that I sounded like a needy prick.

I'd noticed when I was balls deep in her. Now, I wanted every guy here to know that she was taken—especially her ex-husband.

"I *am* wearing it," she said heatedly. "Just not where anyone can see it. But right now I am so furious with you: all you've done is make it absolutely necessary for me to go to my ex-husband and beg him not to tell anyone about us. Have you any idea how that makes me feel, Sebastian? Do you? Because he's the last person I'd want to ask a favor from."

No fucking way.

"I'll handle him," I said quickly. "I'll..."

"You'll do nothing," she hissed through gritted teeth. "Absolutely nothing, do you hear me? Now leave me alone: you've already attracted enough attention tonight."

She walked away, leaving me furious and pissed off. I turned on my heel and headed to the bar. *Fuck*, they weren't serving alcohol. I'd forgotten. I asked for a soda and stood sipping it, trying to calm the fuck down. I was supposed to be working.

Man up, Hunter, and act like a fucking professional, you clueless prick!

I looked around me casually, then noticed that the

contingent of Afghan nationals had arrived, dressed in the traditional salwar kameez, worn with the oval qaraqul hats. The bodyguards stood at the doors, dark sunglasses covering their eyes. Amateurs—you didn't wear fucking sunglasses indoors at night unless you wanted to look like a Hollywood extra who couldn't find his dick with a flashlight.

But what really caught my attention was that there were tribal leaders from both sides of the political and religious spectrum, and they were talking to each other. I sidled closer, knowing they'd never guess I could understand them.

I recognized the older guy as Baktash Azimi who was a Sunni leader. The other guy I wasn't sure, but I thought it might be Gunnar Chalabi, and he was definitely a Shiite.

They weren't saying anything particularly interesting, talking about the heat, the hotel, and laughing about the food they would have to eat. But the fact they were even in the same room, let alone talking, was interesting enough. I knew the real discussions would take place behind closed doors. I'd give my left nut to be a fly on the wall for that conversation.

Then I glanced across at Caro. Nope, I didn't want to give up either of my balls, no matter how good the intel might be.

She was talking to a Marine Captain—and I recognized him from his photograph in the file I'd read earlier. A cold feeling washed through me. Shit a brick! Caro was talking to my new boss—which could only mean that she'd be on embed with me. How the fuck would I be able to keep my hands off of her then? And, more importantly, why the hell was she going to one of the most dangerous Provinces in Afghanistan? What fucking brass neck dickwad had okayed that scenario? Who the fuck did her editor know that she'd been sent with us? What part of top fucking secret gave anyone a problem?

Shit! Shit! Shit!

I followed the Afghans to the long table, greeting a few people in English, and looked for my place card. I knew that I was supposed to be near the Afghan end of the table, so I was confused when I couldn't find my name. I wandered down the long table and finally saw my name and … oh hell.

Natalie Arnaud smiled up at me, her eyes fucking my body in a way that told me she liked what she saw. She was a cold bitch, but hot as hell in bed. We'd had a couple of all-nighters when I was stationed in Paris, but now my dick couldn't have cared less, and neither could I.

I slid into the chair next to her and her eyes lit up like Christmas.

"Quelle surprise!" she said, licking her lips. "Sergeant Hunter! Bon soir, Sebastian."

I motioned to the red and gold markings on my shoulder.

"A promotion. Très bon! I like the sound of that! Does that mean you'll give me orders, sir? You always did like being on top."

"I'm on duty, Natalie," I growled at her.

But she just looked amused.

"There's always time to play later. I'm staying here—room 705," and then she rested her hand on my thigh.

I tried to remove it subtly, but Natalie's grin just grew wider.

"Oh, are you a good boy now? Because I remember you liked to be very, very bad."

"Fuck's sake!"

I brushed her hand aside. "My CO is here, Nat."

"So? You never used to care about things like that," and her bare foot pushed up inside my pants leg, her toes stroking my calf.

I moved my leg away and she laughed.

"It's not a fucking joke!" I snapped. "And you need to cover up your tits—that shit won't fly here."

She leaned forward, giving me an eyeful of her surgically enhanced chest, which I had to admit was pretty impressive, but nothing like my girl's natural beauty.

I glanced across and saw Caro talking to my boss as well as the scary British woman she'd been with in Geneva. All three of them looked at me at the same time. I was so fucked. Grant looked pissed, the Brit looked amused, and Caro … she looked upset. *Shit.* And then Natalie chose that moment to reach across my body to touch my Afghanistan Campaign medal and whisper in my ear some of the things she wanted a repeat performance of.

I saw Grant frown, then stand up and walk towards me.

I sprang out of my chair, glad for the reprieve, and snapped a salute.

"Hunter?"

"Yes, sir!"

"Why are you sitting here? You were supposed to be further up on the other side of the table."

He eyed Natalie coolly.

"Mix up with the place settings, sir."

"A word, please, Hunter."

He took me to one side, glancing across at Natalie who looked like someone had told her that Jimmy Choo had gone out of business. *Yeah, I'd lived in Paris for two years.*

"You think this shit is acceptable, Hunter? Because your old CO doesn't have anything good to say about you, and your present CO told me you'd be on your best fucking behavior. But all you can think about is getting your dick wet. Un-fucking-acceptable. What do you have to say for yourself?"

"No excuse, sir."

It was the only answer to give when your commanding officer was on the warpath, no matter how unfair it might be.

"You are jeopardizing the mission, Hunter. You were supposed to pick up additional intel, but instead you've become a liability. And you can bet your ass that one more mistake and you'll be very damn sorry. Be ready for an oh-five-hundred pick up tomorrow. But for now, get the fuck out of my sight."

I saluted again and left.

That fucking French bitch had a lot to answer for … or maybe it was just a few chickens coming home to roost. It was a fucked up situation—and one of my own making.

I called my driver and got him to take me to Caro's hotel. I invited him to have a meal with me; it was the least I could do since I'd cost him his dinner as well as my own.

We talked shit about baseball, a sport we'd both played in high school, and ate some indeterminate meat in a spicy sauce—goat, probably.

I kept an eye open for Caro's return, taking notice of the other members of the Press Corps who used the Mustafa hotel as their base.

I didn't see Caro, but the British woman sailed into the bar, scaring a few of the locals. I was glad she was here, because it meant Caro had the room to herself. I gave it five minutes then headed up.

I knocked quietly on the door, and immediately heard hushed voices.

Shit? She had someone in there with her? I hadn't seen the British woman leave the bar, although it had gotten pretty crowded.

"Yes?"

Yep, the Brit's voice.

"Ma'am, I'm looking for Lee Venzi?"

There was another muted conversation, then the door swung open and I stepped inside quickly.

Caro stared at me, a small frown on her face.

"Sebastian, you've met my friend Liz Ashton."

"Yes," I said, nodding stiffly at the disgusted expression on the British woman's face.

"Hunter," she replied icily.

Caro rubbed her forehead.

"I'm sorry about this, Liz, but can you give us some time alone?"

The Brit snorted and shook her head, muttering something that sounded like, "bloody fool".

I wasn't sure if she meant me or Caro—both, probably.

"Two hours, Lee," she said, glancing at her watch with zero subtlety. "I'll be downstairs in the bar if you need me."

She threw me an accusing look and left.

Caro was clearly mad at me, so my cunning plan was to kiss the hell out of her.

I pulled her into my arms and kissed her hard, my tongue in her mouth and my hands pressing into the flesh of her ass. She responded quickly, a surprised gasp huffing out as her hands wrapped around my neck, pressing her body against mine, chasing all thoughts but one from my overheated brain and desperate dick.

Then she pushed me away, her eyes bright with anger and lust, her cheeks flushed.

"What the hell are you doing, Sebastian?"

I shrugged and grinned at her. "I thought I'd kiss you before you yelled at me. Guess it didn't work."

"You think this is a joke?" she snapped, her voice rising with anger. "First David, now Liz. Why don't you just skywrite it?"

I hated hearing that bastard's name on her lips.

"What did the asshole say to you?"

She sighed. "He's not going to tell anyone—he was really nice about it."

He was 'nice' to her? What did that fucker want? I didn't trust him any further than I could throw him.

"Liz won't say anything to anyone either—I'll just have to listen to her chewing me out later. But I'd have much rather she didn't know just now—she's my *work* colleague. You've got to stop taking these risks, Sebastian. For my sake, if you won't do it for yourself."

I grimaced. I hadn't thought about it like that. Shit, I should have.

"I'm sorry, Caro. I just go a little crazy around you."

She didn't look happy.

"Well, you have to get it under control. Now please, please tell me your assignment to Ryan Grant is temporary."

"Fuck! I was wondering why they'd seated you next to him. Are you embedded with him? Shit!"

Her mouth twisted in a wry grimace.

"Exactly my thoughts. He can't know, or it'll really screw things up for both of us—well, mainly for me. Sebastian, you're going to have to act like you did in Geneva, as if you still dislike me—or at the very least, ignore me. Can you do that?"

Probably not.

"Fuck, Caro," I sighed. "Yes, I can do it. But I'll hate every fucking minute of it."

She gave me a small smile.

"At least if we're in the same Camp, I'll know what

you're doing and that you're safe."

"Same goes for you. Yeah, there is that. And we might get a chance to … hook up?"

Her eyes darkened, but she shook her head.

"No, too dangerous. You can't risk it and I *definitely* can't risk it. Grant isn't an idiot."

"No, he seems on the ball."

"On the plus side, Grant already thinks you dislike me."

That was news to me. "Because…?"

"Liz: she mentioned that we'd met in Geneva, and at that stage, she still thought you were an ass. Well, that hasn't changed, but just a different sort of ass now."

I felt a reluctant smile pulling my lips upward.

"An ass?"

"Big time."

I leaned against the door, smiling down at her.

"What happened with your little friend, Natalie?" she asked, raising her eyebrows.

I frowned with instant irritation.

"She's no fucking friend. She wouldn't take no for an answer, and then Grant kicked me out because of her."

"What did he say to you?"

Yeah, didn't want to repeat that conversation.

Caro shook her head. "Oh, well, never mind—I can guess. She didn't look pleased either—I think she was planning to have you for dessert. Was it you who told her to cover up?"

"Yeah, not that it made any difference."

"She must have listened to someone. At least you tried. And you are *very* trying, Warrant Officer Hunter. Part of me wants to slap some sense into you…"

"And the other part?" I asked, licking my lips automatically, like some fucking starving dog.

"Well," she said, running a finger down the front of my uniform, "I was wondering what we could do for the next…" she checked her wristwatch, "…115 minutes?"

One hundred and fifteen minutes: was that all we had? It was never enough. It was just never fucking enough. I closed my eyes, the familiar fear pumping through me.

I was losing her again.

"What's the matter, tesoro?" she asked quietly.

"I really fucking hate this, Caro. We're always running in different directions, we're always running out of time. I just want to wake up with you in my arms every day."

She sighed, her expression sad.

"I know, Sebastian, and I feel the same. But it won't be like that forever—we will be together. We just have to be patient." Her warm fingers stroked my cheek, "And for now, we have 113 minutes left."

My eyes snapped open.

"Fuck!"

Suddenly we were tearing at each other, touching and tasting and fighting to get free of our clothes. So many damn buttons. Fucking uniform!

"Damn it, Caro," I groaned, as she pressed her bare skin against me.

I backed her toward the bed, my dick pushing against her. She fell onto the hard mattress and then burst into laughter.

"What?"

"The whole pants around the ankles thing—it's not a great look."

I grinned as I toed off my shoes. Yeah, probably not my smoothest moves.

"Guess I'd better lose the socks, too."

"Definitely."

As Caro stared up at me, I pulled off the rest of my uniform, tossing it to the other side of the room and stood beside the bed, staring down at her, my dick as rigid as a divining rod.

"You like what you see, Caro?"

She nodded, silent now. I tried to get the words out, to explain what this moment with her meant to me.

"After tonight, well, we don't know when … so I want you to remember me like this … when you look at me—see me like this, wanting you."

I gripped my dick and stroked myself, letting the insane attraction that I had for this woman, the intense, terrifying love flood through me.

"And when I look at you, this is what I'll be thinking about: close your eyes."

She let her eyelids flutter close, and I sat at the bottom of the bed, gently pulling her legs apart as I kissed up her thighs.

My lips pressed against the damp curls of her pussy.

"This is me telling you that your body is mine."

I dipped my tongue inside her, tasting and teasing, and she moaned and arched against me.

"This is your body telling me that I am yours."

I nipped at her clit, and her hands tried to grip onto my short hair, instead pressing the flat of her hands against my head and forcing me deeper inside her.

"This is me saying that we need to be together."

I stroked inside her with my fingers and she climaxed quickly.

"And that's your body agreeing with me.

Her hands dug into my shoulders as she gasped, trying to slow her breathing. I sat up, pulling a condom out of my pants pocket and rolling it on quickly, resentful of the time it took me away from her.

Then I moved back onto the bed, my body hovering over hers. Caro's eyes locked on mine, and she pulled her knees upward, creating a nest for me to settle my hips between her thighs.

I pushed inside her slowly, gritting my teeth with the pleasure that coursed through me, fighting the base urge to fuck her to a standstill.

Caro arched her back, then pulled my face up to hers, kissing me softly.

"And this is me saying that you've come home," she whispered.

Her words brought tears to my eyes. Home: that word had never meant much to me before, but now it meant everything. Caro was my home—wherever she went, that was where I was meant to be. Forever.

The feeling was overwhelming: emotionally, physically, mentally. I answered her with my body, moving faster, moving deeper, taking her again and again, my dick thickening and heating inside her until I couldn't hold on, coming hard and fast.

I rested on top of her body, my heart racing furiously. But then she pushed on my shoulder gently, and I just had enough presence of mind to realize that I was crushing her. I rolled onto my back, taking her with me so she was resting on my chest, her hair sweeping across my face and neck.

We stayed in each other's arms, peaceful and silent for now.

Suddenly, an explosion erupted outside, rattling the windows of the hotel. Even as I was yanking Caro to the floor, on the side of the bed away from the window, I was calculating the likely distance of the blast, what kind of IED it might be, and whether there would be more explosions or gunfire. I counted to ten, but all I could hear was the sound of alarms from cars and buildings, voices shouting. I stood cautiously, moving to the side of the window and pulling the curtain open a fraction so I could peer out.

"Probably a car bomb—about half a mile away."

Caro was still shivering on the floor, her eyes wide, but she didn't look like she was going into shock.

"It's okay, Caro. We're okay."

And we were, for now, but we both knew that luck could run out—especially in a warzone. Soldiers died every day, hundreds of civilians a week, and journalists, too. Lady Luck was a callous bitch.

I wanted Caro out of here, I wanted...

Caro stood up hesitantly, her naked body hardening my dick even as the sound of ambulances tore the night. But she was staring toward the window, and even though my body was reacting to her, I knew that wasn't what she needed from me now—I wasn't a fucking caveman. Well, not all of the time.

"Caro, are you okay, baby?"

"Yes, I suppose so. Just knowing that out there ... you'll be facing that soon."

I held her in my arms, tight against my chest, willing to lay down my life for this woman, here and now.

"Christ, I know that, Caro, and it kills me to know that you'll be out there, too. Please, baby, please, go home while you still can. I'm fucking begging you, Caro!"

I buried my face in her hair, breathing in her scent, glad to hold her but wishing she was gone.

"Please, baby. I need to know you're safe. If anything happened to you now…"

Her arms crept around my neck, pulling my head down for a kiss.

"I have a job to do, Sebastian, you know that," she whispered as her lips brushed across my cheek. "So do you; and I will worry about you every day. I pray to God that you'll come home to me. Please, tesoro, promise you'll look after yourself—no unnecessary risks?"

I sighed. It wasn't what I wanted to hear—I wanted her to tell me she was catching a flight back to the US. I knew that wasn't going to happen.

"I promise, Caro," I said, my voice resigned.

"Then come back to bed with me," she said, tugging my hand.

The night was slipping away too fast.

I let her lead me to the bed, then rested on my back as she wrapped her body around me. I was aware of every ticking second, every beat of her heart. When I felt her fingers brushing over my chest and stomach, I knew she was trying to distract me from my morbid thoughts. It was working.

My dick hardened again. Always again with her; it was never enough. She glanced down and her lips turned upward in an amused smile.

"Sebastian, if that's what I have to imagine every time you look at me, I'm not going to get any work done."

I smiled and kissed her hand.

"Let's go back to Signora Carello's place for our honeymoon, Caro. We could fuck for days without getting out of bed."

If she wanted to pretend that the morning would never come, I'd do my damndest to hold onto the night.

She smiled and raised her eyebrows.

"What, you think she could just push food under the door so you can keep your strength up, because I have to say, Sebastian, you were getting a bit out of breath just now. I really thought the US Marines had higher standards of fitness: I might have to write about that in my next article. Of course, the research is incomplete—I've only documented one Marine's fitness levels in detail…"

"And it's going to stay that way," I said firmly.

She laughed, and it sounded almost real.

"Feeling threatened? Me alone with all those horny Marines, I'm quoting, of course."

"Not funny," I grumbled.

"Okay, I won't tease you. Yes, we could go back to Signora Carello's, but there are lots of other places I'd like to see in Italy. Florence, the open air opera in Rome—I'd love to do that. But you know, I really like the idea of taking your old motorcycle and seeing upstate New York. What do *you* want to do?"

"Other than have a lot of sex?"

She laughed out loud, raising her eyebrows at me and shoving on my shoulder.

"My God! That's exactly the same answer you gave me ten years ago when you *were* a horny teenager!"

"So? I'm consistent: I thought women liked that in men?"

Yep, she couldn't argue with that.

I ran my hand between her breasts, toying with the chain that held her engagement ring.

"You have the most fantastic breasts, Caro. I can't stand those fake ones, they just feel so…"

Ah, shit. Being in bed with one woman, and talking about others—not the smartest thing I'd ever said.

I wanted to bite off my damn tongue. But she just smirked at me.

"Hmm, I was thinking, maybe you should be one of those men who are strong and silent. You know, nice to look at, not so good at the talking."

I nipped her shoulder then twisted around, pushing her into the mattress, letting her know *exactly* what I thought of that comment. And although she didn't know it, she wasn't the first woman to say something like that. I knew she didn't mean it—but it stung all the same.

"Is that right?" I asked, keeping my voice light.

"Yes. Hearing you talk about your *conquests* when I'm in a state of post-coital bliss isn't going to earn you round two."

"Huh, so I can't *earn* round two—does that mean I can pay for it instead?"

She slapped my ass, hard. *Hot.*

"You couldn't afford me," she snarked back.

"You sure about that, baby? What's your price?"

"What have you got to offer, Sebastian?"

I used my hips to pin her down, my chest hovering over her breasts. "An orgasm?" I suggested.

"That's just quid pro quo."

"Fuck, I love it when you talk dirty. What about two orgasms?"

"Two? Beginning to sound interesting, but do you think you're up to the job?"

I brushed my fingers against her clit and she gasped. "Maybe I'll let you answer that question," I said, as I slid down the bed, lowering my face between her thighs.

Over an hour later, we were collapsed on the bathroom floor, flushed and breathless.

"I'd forgotten you had a thing for bathrooms," she gasped.

I kissed the back of her neck as I tugged her against my chest. "I like the mirrors."

"You know, that's a bit kinky, Sebastian."

"You think? I'd like to get kinky with you, Caro," I said, nipping her earlobe and running my fingers over her hipbone.

"What did you have in mind?" she asked curiously.

How long had we got?

I decided to start with the basics. "You could tie me up again: that was hot."

She giggled.

"Hmm, well, I could talk to one of the MPs at Leatherneck—maybe I'll see if I can borrow a pair of handcuffs, Sebastian."

I swallowed several times, my mind very much enjoying the thought of fucking Caro while she was cuffed, of her riding my dick while I was cuffed. *Fuck me!*

I guess Caro was still waiting for my answer, because she nudged me in the ribs with her elbow.

"Yeah, if you like, Caro," I said, my voice hoarse.

Her eyebrows shot up.

"If *I* like? What do *you* like?"

I hesitated, wondering if she'd go along with some of the scenes I imagined when I was jerking off. "There's some stuff we could try," I began.

"Such as?" she asked, her expression curious rather than appalled, which was a good start.

But then there was a soft tap at the door and I heard the Brit's voice.

"Oh, hell," Caro muttered, sounding disappointed and irritated. "You'd better get dressed, Sebastian, unless a three-way with Liz was one of your fantasies?"

I shuddered. "Fuck, Caro! I'm going to have that image in my head now."

She grinned and tossed my uniform onto the bed. "Better get your pants on then, Marine."

I dressed quickly, cursing the number of buttons involved wearing the Blues. I was still sitting on the bed tying my shoelaces when Caro opened the door.

"Lee, I … oh, is he still here?"

"He's just leaving, Liz."

The Ashton woman marched into the room, and I winced at the sight of her enormous tits moving independently of each other, reminding me of a camel's ass.

"There's a curfew on, Hunter," she said, crossing her arms and staring at me hard.

"Thanks," I said coolly.

I already knew about the curfew, but it had probably been brought forward a couple of hours because of the device going off earlier.

"You must have heard the car bomb," she snapped. "Three dead, multiple injured. Bastards packed the bomb with nails."

"So evil," murmured Caro, shaking her head.

The Brit nodded silently, and for the first time I saw the same compassion that drove Caro to report from war zones. I wouldn't say I liked the Ashton woman, but I could respect the job she did. Although it was pretty clear that it wasn't mutual; I knew what she thought of me. A week ago it would have been true.

I stood up and fastened the buckle on my white web belt, then pulled Caro into a tight hug, ignoring the Brit's noisy huffing.

"Remember what I said, Sebastian," whispered Caro, running the tips of her fingers down my cheek.

"I'll try, baby. And you remember what *I* said, what I'm thinking about when I look at you."

I kissed her softly, unwilling to let her go, hating that I had to, desperate to know that she'd be safe, hating that she wasn't.

"Never take my ring off, Caro," I said.

"Ti amo tanto, Sebastian."

I smiled painfully. "Sempre e per sempre."

I glanced briefly at the Brit, and then quietly left.

At least I knew I'd see Caro tomorrow.

CHAPTER 14

We were heading to Camp Leatherneck, 350 miles away along the Kabul–Kandahar Highway, one of the most dangerous roads in the world.

The Russians, the Taliban, and now us—it all added up to three decades of war and neglect, leaving the road that connected Afghanistan's two main cities in ruins. Uncle Sam had funded the rebuilding of three-quarters of the route, with Japan chipping in another chunk of cash. It was currently in slightly better repair than it had been, but it had become a favorite target of the Taliban again—ambushes and IEDs were common.

The guys on point were heavily armed and supported by Explosive Ordnance Disposal Techs whose job was to spot devices before one of our Armored Personnel Carriers rolled over them. Metal detectors weren't as much use as you'd think because the Taliban used as few metal parts as possible. But tell-tale signs included depressions in the road where a hole had recently been dug and had sunk when it was recovered, or any wires sticking out that might lead to pressure plates.

Being in the middle of the convoy was no picnic either: if a device functioned, we'd be pinned down, prey to ambush. We also had to make it through checkpoints manned by ANA, keeping a covert eye open in case they weren't as onside with US or International Security Assistance Force as they were supposed to be. Green-on-blue attacks were escalating to the point where each ISAF unit had appointed at least one soldier as a 'guardian angel' to act as a lookout—to keep an eye on our Afghan allies.

I hoped like hell we made it in one piece.

I saw Caro briefly from a distance, flashing her a quick smile until I remembered that I was supposed to ignore her. But she smiled back briefly before she turned away.

It was comforting and scary as fuck to think that she was just a few vehicles back. I had to force myself to forget that she was there or I wouldn't be able to do my job—but it was hard. I wasn't needed on point because the regular terps were being used; instead I had a lot of hours to get to know the guys in my team: the five Afghan interpreters who'd be my responsibility.

As soon as I walked towards them, I knew there was tension in the air. It didn't take a genius to work out the problem.

"As-salaamu' alaykum."

I introduced myself, noting their shock when I spoke their language. It took only a couple of minutes to work out that two of them were Shiite and the other three were Sunni. Both groups prayed to Allah, but that was about all they had in common. Oh yeah, and they both hated Sufis.

Well, this was going to make my job that much harder. I'd have to keep them apart whenever possible. Grant was *not* going to like it. And I had a feeling it would end up being my fault—definitely my problem.

Aabadar and Fazel were brothers, and very insistent on telling me that their father was Mujahadeen and fought the Russians. Jee-zus—two or even three generations of Afghans who'd known nothing but war.

The noise when we were seated inside the APC made it almost impossible to talk much, which was something of a relief. I separated my guys, distributing them among the leathernecks riding with us. I got some shit for that, but it was all muttered because I could pull rank any time I wanted. Didn't mean I would, but these bootnecks didn't know me, so they were ready to show who was boss. Fine by me. I'd come up through the ranks and I knew every trick in the book, and then some.

We all enlist for different reasons. For some, the Marine Corps was a chance to have a real family for the first time in our lives; for others it was a means to an end: learning a trade, or getting a college education; several said they wanted to serve their country, motivated by the events of 9/11. And for a few, it was the last chance to do something that wouldn't end with a prison sentence.

Once they figured out I was The Man, they muttered and cussed quietly behind my back. I paid my fucking dues for this rank so until they did the same, they should quit their bitching.

The journey to Leatherneck was hell. What would have been a six- or seven-hour journey back home, turned into 15 hours of heat, dust, and a numb ass as the APC ground along the highway. We stopped at several ANA checkpoints, but I wasn't needed as a terp. Some of the ANA were good guys and I'd worked with a few of them before. They were determined to get rid of the Taliban, and several listened to rock stations on the internet when they could get a signal, which wasn't often—the Taliban had banned music. All music. At every camp, there was a black market trade in western CDs and DVDs—all things the Taliban considered un-Islamic at best, and satanic at worst.

I was less happy when I saw men in turbans armed with AK-47s at checkpoints. They weren't regular army, and they watched us pass with cold eyes. It made me wonder if they were phoning ahead to let the Taliban know that a convoy was en route. Hell that had probably happened the second we left Kabul.

The AK-47 was a good weapon. I preferred my M16 because although it had a long barrel, it was two pounds lighter and the magazine was half the weight. But a lot of guys tried to smuggle Russian weapons back to the US when their tour was over as souvenirs. On my last tour, one dickwad had tried to take back a live and very unstable grenade even though it was a federal offense. My flight stateside was delayed by 20 hours while EOD were called and the device neutralized.

Several of the guys on my APC were straight out of boot camp and on their first deployment. They were ready to kick some Afghan ass, so having my five terps traveling with us was unsettling for them—that and seeing the road ahead was torn up where IEDs had been planted and burnt-out cars pushed to the side, abandoned.

I closed my eyes, dozing as best I could.

Leatherneck, our destination, 50 miles west of Kandahar, housed 28,000 British troops at the adjacent Camp Bastion, several thousand Afghan National Army soldiers at Camp Shorabak, and 20,000 US Marines. Altogether, the three sectors must have covered nearly 4,000 acres. Leatherneck, by itself, was bigger than many small towns back home. It was supported by four gyms, a vast dining area that could serve 4,000 people at a time, three chapels—or so I was told. Best of all as far as many of the guys were concerned, there were calling centers where they could phone and email their families back home. The only person I'd ever called was Ches, and that was maybe once or twice a year.

It wasn't much, but we called it home. Ha fucking ha. That was last tour. This time, I'd be going further into the boonies, staying at Leatherneck for just one night.

I knew that the camp also housed two- or three-thousand female soldiers. In theory they were kept segregated, although I'd managed some hook-ups when I'd been there before. For a while, I'd had a thing with Lieutenant Susie Harris who worked in the spook office with the FBI. Gotta say there's something about fucking a senior officer. Just saying.

I'd like to try hooking up with Caro, but I knew that would be dangerous for both of us. Didn't stop me wanting it though.

Once we arrived, hot, stinking and covered in dust and dirt, Grant called the senior non-coms together to organize transit accomm. I was sharing with the two sergeants who so far hadn't shown much interest in me beyond the basic courtesies.

They knew I was on special assignment, which meant they also knew I couldn't talk about it.

But I didn't have time to do more than toss my bed roll onto the lumpy bunk before I was ordered to a briefing room for a sit-rep on some new intel at Now Zad.

"Nice of you to join us, Hunter," Grant said, his voice terse.

I don't know what had flown up his ass, so I just took a seat out of his eye-line, sweating freely in the intense heat of the old Nissan hut.

"First: you will have noticed by now, gentleman, that we have a journo on embed with us, Lee Venzi. You will extend every courtesy—but say nothing. Is that clear? Keep all interaction to a minimum. And those of you with training in obs will have noticed that she's a woman, which means someone has completely fucked up. I'll send her on some routine foot patrols to keep her busy and out of the way.

"Next: there's been an increase in Taliban radio chatter in the Now Zad area that has all the brass very unhappy, and that makes *me* very unhappy, which will make *you* very, very careful. They're concerned that word of the op has leaked out, but it's just a hunch at the moment. Hunter, I want you to go through the radio transcripts and see if you can find anything that they've missed. Do *not* go through your terps. Clear?"

"Yes, sir."

I hated going through transcripts. They were usually translated by semi-literate idiots. It was bound to be a waste of my time if the spooks had already reviewed them. But it was an order, not a request. Didn't look like I'd get much sleep tonight either. Whatever, I was used to that.

Grant pulled out a map of the area and penciled in the position of known local Taliban that we needed to be aware of, then started going into detail about the Afghan elder we wanted to get on our side and the village where he lived.

"Erik, you'll be in charge of BGAN satcomms."

Grant nodded his head at a Lieutenant sitting next to me. I thought his name was Jankowski but I wasn't sure. As far as I knew, he'd be the guy leading the op.

We'd almost finished the briefing when I looked up and saw Caro escorted by a female PFC. I grinned at her before I remembered I wasn't supposed to.

Fuck, that was so hard to remember—it just didn't feel right.

Grant still hadn't seen her.

"If a guy sticks his head around the corner he could very easily have a gun. If you can't see his hands, he could have something, a hand grenade, say. Pulling a trigger is easy—we need to bring him in. It's not about that one person, it's about the team. I'll need you to go in first and..."

I coughed discreetly, unwilling for him to say anymore in front of Caro—something that might compromise her safety. Grant threw her an irritated look, but Caro stood her ground.

"I can come back," she offered calmly.

"No, that's fine, Ms. Venzi," Grant clipped out. "We're done here."

Grant jerked his head at me in dismissal. I saluted and threw Caro a quick smile as I left. I had 10 minutes before the designated mealtime. I'd rather have eaten with the guys, but maybe Grant wanted me under close supervision. It was going to be hell having Caro so close and not be able to talk to her or touch her.

I showered quickly, shook the dust out of my uniform and pulled on a clean t-shirt. That was as good as it was going to get. Another two days and we'd all stink. Now Zad didn't have showers, just basic strip and wash facilities, and there weren't exactly going to be washing machines to clean your clothes. After three days, you couldn't even smell your own stench anymore.

I was starving by the time we ate our long-delayed evening meal. It was the last fresh food we'd have for a while. You could live off of MRE's, but that was about all. It amazed me how many different ways they could fuck up meat with gravy. The MRE gum wasn't too bad.

I was seated with Lieutenant Sanders, the executive officer, and four second lieutenants including Jankowski, at the opposite end of the table from Caro.

I'd been told not to talk to her, but I also knew that if I looked at her I'd give myself away, so I spent most of the meal staring at the food, or gazing into the distance. Even that seemed to piss off Grant, but since I was following orders, there wasn't much he could do about it.

Eventually, Caro went to leave, and we all stood up politely. I risked a quick glance at her.

"Sleep well, gentlemen," she said quietly.

The others sat down again, but Caro was looking straight at me when she ran her fingers along the chain around her neck. She was telling me that she was wearing my ring. Yeah, that was a good moment.

As soon as she left, Grant repeated his orders not to give her any information, not even whether it was hot in summer. What an asshole. He had no idea how good of a journalist Caro was if he thought that was going to stop her from getting a story. Hadn't he read her articles? Although I liked the idea that Grant was trying to keep her out of the loop and safe.

After that, we were dismissed.

I spent three tedious hours going through the transcripts, learning not one single useful new fact.

With my eyes burning, I rolled into my bedding and passed out.

Reveille was at oh-four-hundred. I was washed, shaved and fed 30 minutes later, and we were waiting for Caro. And waiting. And waiting.

Grant looked like he was about to stroke-out when he sent the same female PFC that I'd seen the night before to shake her awake.

Caro emerged five minutes later, red-faced and embarrassed.

"I'm so sorry," she said, sounding flustered. "I overslept. It won't happen again."

Grant was too irritated to reply, merely nodding and getting ready for our small convoy to leave Leatherneck.

I noticed that Caro was moving stiffly. I longed to walk over and rub her shoulders and do a bunch of other stuff that isn't in the Marine Corps Manual.

She pulled on her body armor, tugged her hair up into a rough ponytail, and slapped on her helmet. Damn, she looked cute.

Grant was so pissed, he did the one thing he could to show he was mad at her—told her to sit by me. I was the luckiest son of a bitch in the whole damn world. And yeah, my mom really was a bitch.

"Good morning, Ms. Venzi," I said in my best panty-dropping voice. "I trust you slept well?"

"Too well, thank you," she replied politely, raising one eyebrow.

As we sat side-by-side in the APC, I was aware of the pressure of her thigh in the next seat. I slid my backpack closer and took her hand in mine. She didn't look at me, but her lips turned upward in a private smile. Yep, that look went straight to my dick. It was going to be a long ride.

We headed north, the scenery the same dusty, barren landscape, bumping along a broken road, heading up into the foothills. The heat was already building and we were all sweating.

Our road followed the side of a riverbed, and for a hundred yards in each direction, a strip of green vegetation broke the bleakness of the lunar landscape.

Scattered in the stony fields were the typical fortified farms with high walls, built from a mixture of mud and straw so they blended into the dirt. Some were collected into loose hamlets for protection, but most had been abandoned after heavy fighting in the area. They were a complete fucking nightmare to search, and often booby-trapped after the families had been kicked out. The area seemed deserted but I could see herds of skinny goats, which meant that the owners were around, watching us. I scanned the high ground, looking for anything out of place, but there was nothing. I knew they were there, hidden. At least they weren't firing at us.

It took us five hours to travel the 60 miles to our next stop, thanks to roads that had the shit bombed out of them, and there were some that had been washed away in Spring floods. Our destination was the town of Now Zad.

What a shithole.

It had been an important market town once, but now it was torn to pieces, buildings destroyed by mortar fire, bullet holes across every wall, empty shops were open to the sky, shutters drooping. But there were still people living here, God knows why. Nowhere else to go, I guess.

An elderly man was selling a few potatoes and eggs from a rug outside a vacant lot. He waved his hands wildly as we drove past, cursing the Infidel invaders and hoping that our balls rotted to dung and fed the crows, Allah be praised.

Caro glanced at me.

"What did he say?"

I saw Grant's head turn toward us, also waiting for the answer.

"Nothing I'd like to repeat, ma'am," I said, running my thumb over the back of her hand. She got the message.

Our compound had been a police station at some point in its life, but used many times over by ISAF soldiers from both British and US forces. There was no fresh water, no electricity, and the sleep area was in the old cells, up to a dozen men per room.

I listened carefully as the quarters were allocated and I was glad to hear that Caro was given a separate room.

I was sent to talk to the squad of Marines we were relieving, all who were happy as fuck to be getting back to Leatherneck.

But it wasn't good news: the Taliban had been sending in reinforcements over the last week, even though the number of RPG attacks had decreased. I got a cold feeling in my gut—the bastards were waiting for us. I couldn't help thinking that they knew why we were here.

Not good.

I hadn't even had time to find out where I was sleeping when chow was called. But then Grant ordered me to go talk to a bunch of locals who were hanging around the observation post at the entrance.

It turned out that they wanted to invite the boss to meet the town elder; they even promised to kill a goat for him. I'd bet my ass that Grant would be thrilled. It was polite to let them invite you three times and they would say 'stay for tea' the way we'd say 'how are you?' but not expect a real answer. But when they kept on inviting you, that was serious.

I passed the message on and Grant agreed that he'd come soon, but was unwilling to commit to a date in advance. I tried to tell him that this would be considered an insult, but he didn't care. So much for hearts and minds. I relayed his answer, then spent 45 minutes dealing with the fall-out.

I was on his shit list but at least he didn't give me punishment duty of doing a burn from the shit pits—no flushing toilets or refuse collection here. Setting fire to the latrine waste was seriously gross. Necessary, but gross.

I finally got some food three hours after everyone else had turned in and the first watch were on duty.

I wanted to make sure that Caro was okay before I headed back to the comms room to listen to the radio chatter about our arrival. What the fuck had I been given five terps for if I had to do *all* the grunt work? Okay, I knew the answer to that, but I was tired and pissed and really wanted to make sure Caro was safe. So I waited until I was sure no one would notice, then made my way to her side of the compound.

I crouched down outside her room, then opened the creaky door, whispering her name as I crawled inside.

She was sitting on a narrow air mattress, and I could just make out in the dim light that she had a huge smile on her face. My heart thumped painfully just looking at her.

"It's like a dream having you here," I said, shaking my head slowly. "I keep thinking I'm going to wake up and find I've imagined you."

I pulled her into my arms and she clutched me tightly.

"My dreams aren't usually this good," she sighed against my chest.

"Mine are," I said, a smile in my voice. "Or they used to be. When you first left, I dreamed about you all the time."

"What was I doing?" she asked, stroking my cheek as the memories flooded back.

"Mostly, we were just walking on the beach."

"Mostly?"

I grinned. "Sometimes we did other stuff."

Triple X-rated.

"Stuff? I'm not sure I know what you mean by 'stuff,'" she laughed, then she rubbed the front of my pants, palming my hardening dick.

"Caro!" I groaned loudly. "Fuck, I just came to make sure you were okay in here. I have to get back to the comms room."

"Right away? You can't take a few minutes?"

I could hear the disappointment in her voice.

"I really can't, baby," I said, kissing her hungrily. "Grant's waiting for me."

"You're such a tease," she snorted, slapping my ass. "You come in here, raising my expectations…"

"That's not the only thing that got raised," I admitted as I adjusted my junk.

But she just laughed at me. "Well, I'd have been happy to meet those expectations, but apparently you have to go be a warrior."

"Actually, I have to go be an interpreter … I could try and come back later, Caro."

Her smile dropped away and she held my face as she looked into my eyes.

"Sebastian, seriously: do what you need to do. You know where I am, and I trust you to know whether or not it's safe to take that risk. It worries me that I'm a distraction here for you. The most important thing is that you focus on your job. We've got the rest of our lives after that."

The rest of our lives.

I kissed her again, then rested my forehead against hers.

"I'm a lucky bastard—thank God for you, Caro."

"I'll see you at breakfast, Marine," she said, running her hand over my short hair.

"One other thing," I said, needing her to know that this was important, "there's been some radio chatter and the Taliban definitely know we're here. I don't think they'll do anything tonight—they're not in position, from what I can work out, but if you hear someone yell 'incoming', get your body armor on, keep your head down, and stay in here away from the windows. Whatever happens, Caro, stay in here. Everyone out there knows what they're doing: we don't need your help. You know what I'm saying, baby?"

She nodded then wrapped her arms around me more tightly. "I promise. I don't want you thinking about me when you have more important things to concentrate on."

I had to smile at that. "There isn't anything more important than you."

But I did have a job to do—and if I did it right, it would

keep everyone safe. I kissed her again, then tore myself out of her arms and made my way back to the comms room.

Jankowski was hunched over a coffee when I walked in, talking to another guy who had his back to me.

The Lieutenant frowned when he saw me. "Where've you been, Hunter? You know we can't use the local terps on this."

"Taking a dump, sir," I said, slouching into the empty seat and picking up the headphones.

The other guy turned around and grinned at me. "Well, well, well, if it ain't the Hollywood Marine!"

I turned and stared. "Fuck me! Sergeant Chivers! How you doin', man?"

Mark Chivers was a guy I'd met on my first tour in Iraq. We'd hung out a bit before I'd gotten picked for interpreting work. He'd gone to boot camp at Parris Island, SC, and called everyone who'd trained in Cali a 'Hollywood Marine'. We called them 'Swamp Doggies'.

He grinned at me. "Lookin' good, Seb. Who'd y'all fuck off to get sent to this shithole?"

"Much as I'm enjoying this touching reunion," grunted Jankowski, "I'd really like to know what the fuck the enemy is saying about us, or is that too much to ask, Hunter?"

"On it, sir," I said, as Chiv winked at me and turned back to the radio operations.

I spent the next four hours listening to comms traffic. The Taliban definitely knew we were here, but so far it sounded like only a few of them were on the ground—more were being summoned. It was clear that someone knew something; what that was remained unclear. But the coincidence of them sending reinforcements at the exact time of this new mission, well, I'd have to be a fucking moron not to make the connection.

Eventually, as the comms chatter died down, Jankowski let me go off duty. My head was pounding from being immersed in heavily-accented Pashto and Dari for the first time in three years. The intense concentration left me feeling drained. I needed to sleep; but first I was going to check on Caro.

Her door opened quietly, and I watched for half a minute as the slow, even rise of her chest showed that she was asleep. I could only see a dim silhouette, but being near her, that was enough. All thoughts of heading to my own cot died. Instead, I curled up awkwardly at the foot of her air mattress and was asleep in seconds.

I wasn't sure how long I slept—not long enough—when Caro's alarm woke us before dawn. The right side of my body ached from where I'd been lying on the concrete floor. I stretched out cautiously.

"Sebastian!" she gasped, obviously surprised to see me. "What are you doing?"

"Hey, baby."

"How long have you been there? Why didn't you wake me up?"

"Couple of hours," I yawned. "I didn't want to wake you—you looked so peaceful."

She crawled across the narrow mattress and wrapped her arms around my neck, burrowing herself against me.

"You didn't even take your boots off," she murmured into my neck, her lips tickling my skin.

I laughed quietly and kissed her hair. "Didn't see much point." I climbed to my feet reluctantly. "Gotta go, baby."

"Already?" she said, disappointment shading her voice.

"Yeah, need to get a wash and shave before dawn patrol."

"You're lucky," she said with a wry smile. "I'm relying on baby-wipes while I'm here. You'll get to know me in a whole new way, Sebastian."

I winked at her. "Looking forward to it, baby. See ya later."

The sun was just beginning to appear behind the mountains, casting long shadows across the compound. I took a turn in the shitter, then lined up at the outside water butts to take a cold shave.

After I'd stowed my shaving kit, I booked it back to the comms room.

A different radio operator was in Mark's seat, but Jankowski was there again. I didn't have time to do more than salute.

"Hunter, you'll be out on foot patrol this morning. Grant wants some hearts and minds work, and he's hoping that you'll pick up on any vibes from the locals. Go get some chow before the briefing in 20 minutes."

"Yes, sir."

I decided that my two Shiite terps should stay at the compound today. I didn't want any trouble with the locals.

They didn't seem to care when I gave them the news—it would be an easy day for them where they could sit on their asses, drink sweet tea, and still get paid by Uncle Sam.

I left them as they started their morning prayers, then walked over to the line for breakfast. I could see a bunch of bootnecks flirting with Caro. She was laughing at them, a huge smile on her face as she snapped some photographs. I couldn't help my hands balling into fists, and I had to concentrate really hard not to say or do something that was going to piss her off. But it really went against the grain to see her surrounded by horny guys and not do anything. This relationship stuff sucked balls.

She saw me and threw a soft smile in my direction. I heard her voice, and knew that she was trying to reassure me.

"Gentlemen, it's too early in the day for all that." *All of what?* "I haven't even had my breakfast MRE yet."

I relaxed a fraction as the banter dropped back a notch, but I could tell that they liked her—even more when she shared a bottle of soy sauce that she'd brought with her to try and make the MRE rations taste better. Breakfast was more noodles and unidentified meat—also known as 'Meals Rejected by the Enemy' or 'Man Ready to Eat'. Whatever it was, it tasted like ass and was about as chewy.

I was surprised when Grant sent for Caro to join the morning briefing. She wasn't going to hear anything particularly interesting—I'd already had my main orders from Jankowski.

The small ops room had gotten pretty crowded with all the officers and gunnery sergeants when Caro arrived. I could see the fuckers looking her over with appreciation. I wanted to blindfold every bastard there.

Even Grant almost smiled at her.

"Right, men: this morning we'll have four patrols moving out. Sanders, I want you and your team with me heading northeast along the river bed wadi. Romero, northwest by the edge of town. Jankowski, your men take the old market area with Holden flanking you at 100 yards.

"Hunter: you're in charge of the terps—brief them before we go. The population here are Sunnis. Are any of your men Shiite?"

"Two, sir," I answered quickly. "I've told them to stay behind today."

"Does that leave us short?" asked Grant, frowning.

"No, sir, but one of the teams will have to have Angaar: his English is so-so."

"Then send one of the others with him."

"They don't get along, sir. Could cause problems."

"Then damn well make sure it doesn't!" Grant snapped.

I didn't argue the point further, but I wasn't happy with the order.

As the meeting broke up, Caro raised her hand.

"Which team would you like me with, Captain Grant?"

He looked up, clearly irritated, but Caro's expression stayed neutral.

"Perhaps 'like' was too strong a word, Captain," she suggested coolly.

I had to try really hard not to smile at that, and I saw Jankowski and one of the other officers grin openly.

"You'd better come with me, Ms. Venzi," Grant muttered, somewhat unwillingly. "And you, Hunter."

"I feel like Fox Mulder," Caro murmured loud enough for Grant to hear, but not loud enough that he'd feel the need to reply. "The Marines' 'most unwanted'."

Grant frowned, but I could tell he admired her being ballsy. I was so fucking proud. I had to leave the room or I'd have given myself away.

The dawn patrols left the compound on foot: the overt mission was to scout out the area and get a hands-on idea of the terrain. The two patrols checking out the marketplace had the most dangerous job. Those old bazaar buildings provided plenty of places where IEDs could be planted. Snipers were also a concern.

But my patrol was heading up the river wadi to try and find some locals to talk to. I pulled on my body armor and helmet (40 pounds), before shouldering my day pack (35 pounds) and picked up my M16 (nine pounds loaded). Gunners and radio operators carried more. The temperature was already in the high-nineties: it was going to be brutal.

I didn't usually get nervous on patrols—not since the very first time—just more *aware*. But having Caro with me, I was about ready to shit myself, even though she'd been positioned in the middle of the patrol for safety. I was up front with Grant so I couldn't even keep an eye on her from this position. I kept telling myself that the best way to keep her safe was to do my fucking job.

Grant grunted at me.

"Hunter, you're the terp—you take point."

We'd walked about a mile up the trail to the wadi when we saw our first locals.

Four kids, aged about eight or nine, were sitting in a patch of dirt. They stood up in a hurry when they saw us, looking scared, but I called out a greeting to them, grinning when they stared at me in surprise.

I directed all my questions to the oldest boy. Afghans were big on hierarchy and it was easy to offend if you didn't follow their rules.

I asked him if he'd seen any Taliban lately. I didn't really expect him to answer truthfully, but he pointed up into the foothills.

In my peripheral vision, I saw Caro taking a photograph. I hoped like fuck the boys didn't see her; if they knew we had a woman on patrol, the news would spread through the area like wildfire.

I asked the kid how long they'd been there, and Grant wanted to know what we were saying.

"He says there are Taliban up in the hills, sir. They moved into position during the night. He doesn't think they'll come out in daytime. Not sure I'd take that as an ironclad guarantee, but it could mean they'll hit us at dusk or first thing in the morning."

I couldn't help glancing worriedly at Caro.

"Anything else?"

I sighed. "He said his father has promised to get him a rifle like mine when he's ten."

There was no chance that this fucking war would ever be over when kids were being used to carry it forward. And it was a tribal country—I wasn't sure a dose of democracy would work here, but I left that shit to the politicians.

Then one of the kids spotted Caro and gaped, openly pointing her out to his little buddies. They immediately started asking a ton of questions, and I couldn't help smiling as Grant asked me to translate.

"They want to know if Ms. Venzi is your wife, sir, or if you just brought her to do the cooking."

Caro threw me a dirty look and some of the guys laughed, but Grant looked worried. I could guess why.

"Tell them she does the cooking," he said hurriedly.

I gave them the answer and the kids nodded knowingly. I passed out some hard candy, telling them to eat it right away and to toss the wrappers. They were probably too smart to get caught with Western goods on them, but it was worth reminding them. If the Taliban found them with the candy on them, they wouldn't care that they were kids.

They continued to watch us until we were out of sight.

Caro snapped another photo of them waving, then hurried to catch up with Grant.

"Would you like to explain that to me, Captain Grant," she said mildly, while secretly giving me the stink-eye.

"I don't want word getting out that we have a journalist with us," he said shortly.

Caro looked worried, then glanced across at me. I tried to smile reassuringly, but I probably just looked sick.

We moved slowly next to the dried riverbed when I saw a tell-tale flash in the sky and the guy next to me yelled, "Incoming!"

There was a loud roaring overhead as we half-dived, half-fell into the wadi.

I craned my neck, but I couldn't see Caro, which meant

she was somewhere in the riverbed with us.

The rocket propelled grenade shook the ground as it exploded, and the percussion from the blast was almost deafening.

"RPG, sir!" shouted the gunny. "Bastards missed by 300 yards. Up in the foothills, sir. They'll have us in range any second."

He was right: we were in their sights. The wadi gave us good protection but we were pinned down.

Keeping low, I made my way toward Caro and crouched down next to her.

"You okay?"

"I'm fine," she said breathlessly, her voice shaking only slightly. "Don't worry about me. I won't move. Promise."

It was the best I could do: the thought made me sick. I made my way back to the radio operator in case I was needed to listen to any comms chatter.

The gunny and another guy moved forward with a mortar and fired off a couple of rounds.

"Hewitt," shouted Grant to the radio op, "call in air support. I want the shit bombed out of those fuckers. Give them the coordinates—now!"

Two more RPGs came in, each landing closer, although not close enough to worry me too much.

Fifteen minutes passed before we heard a couple of F15 fighter jets streak past overhead.

There was a massive explosion followed immediately by a second, and the mountain shook. I looked up to see a thick cloud of dust and smoke hanging over the foothills, lazily drifting down into the valley.

Caro was already sitting up to take a quick photo. God, she was fearless. The other men noticed too, grinning at her with admiration in their eyes.

"Was that your first time under fire, ma'am?" one of them asked.

"First time it was that damn close," she smiled. "I almost peed my pants."

They laughed easily. "Well, you looked pretty cool, ma'am. We should make you an honorary Marine."

"I'm sure Captain Grant would be delighted with that suggestion," she laughed.

Then she looked across at me and pressed her hand over her heart. I badly wanted to kiss her, but all I could do was smile back.

After waiting to see if there would be any further RPG attacks, we slowly made our way back along the dried up riverbed.

An hour later, we got back to the compound, hot and tired but alive, which meant we were one up on the enemy. Caro immediately ran toward the make-shift bathroom that Grant had designated for her private use. The guys were laughing at her crab-wise run, and it made me proud to realize how much she lifted morale just by being here. She hadn't been scared enough to piss herself, unlike some men I'd seen under fire for the first time. My woman was fucking brave. My woman.

I decided I wanted to do something to show Caro how I felt about her—and I'd do it under the guise of her impressing the shit out of everyone. Yeah, it probably wasn't keeping things on the down-low, but I was going to make her a camp shower.

I rounded up a couple of volunteers and explained my plan. They all wanted to help do something 'for the ballsy writer chick'.

I'd noticed a bunch of jerry cans earlier, so I filled them with tepid water while we rigged a shower unit by punching small holes through a rusting bucket and hoisting the cans overhead.

When we'd finished, I strolled over casually and squatted down next to her.

"How you doing, baby?" I asked quietly, making sure my voice didn't carry.

"Pretty damn good," she replied calmly, "considering I nearly got my ass shot off today."

I couldn't help grinning at her. "You are so fucking amazing, Caro."

"You're not so bad yourself, Sebastian."

Some of the guys were staring at us speculatively, so I

stood up and pointed behind me. "We've fixed you up a makeshift shower, ma'am."

"Excuse me?" she gasped.

"The guys wanted to do something for you—they think you're a ballsy woman. So they've made you a shower. You've got about two-and-a-half minutes of lukewarm water. How's that sound?"

"What? How?"

She gaped at me in amazement.

"I just left some cartons of water out in the sun. They got pretty warm: all we had to do was hoist them up and make a shower head. You're good to go. Except you won't be able to take off your clothes, but it's better than nothing, I guess."

"God, I love you!" she smiled. "But I think I love them, too!"

I knew she was joking, but I'd be a lying bastard if I said I wasn't as jealous as fuck.

She waved at the shower-building team and they cheered her loudly.

"I'll be right back!" she smiled.

The gunny who'd been on patrol with us slapped me on the back.

"Get in line, buddy. We'd all like to tap that."

I don't think he knew how close he came to losing his front teeth as he strolled away. Luckily, Caro reappeared, and the sight of her wearing just a t-shirt and pair of short yoga pants, redirected my attention immediately. She looked happy, and that was enough.

I tore myself away to head back to the comms room, trying to ignore the boner in my pants at the thought of Caro in the shower.

I stayed on duty late until Grant allowed one of the Shiite terps to relieve me. Helmand was a Sunni area, so the theory was that the Shiite interpreters were the most trustworthy. But it was just a theory, and Grant had to acknowledge that I couldn't man the radio chatter 24/7. I'd been awake for 41 out of the last 48 hours and I needed to sleep. With Caro.

I headed to her room and instantly felt relaxed as I heard her soft breaths. I tried to make myself comfortable at the bottom of her mattress, but she woke almost immediately.

"Hey, baby," I whispered as she sat up. "I didn't mean to wake you—I just wanted to see you."

She rubbed her eyes and reached her hands toward me. "You're too far away," she yawned.

I knew the smart thing would be to go to my rack and sleep, but hell, you get all the sleep you need when you're dead.

I tried to stretch out on the mattress next to her, but my boots hit the door.

"Fuck," I swore quietly, "they've given you a damn hutch to sleep in."

"At least it's private, Sebastian," she murmured, running her finger across my cheeks.

"Yeah," I agreed, "that's something."

I leaned over her, taking the weight on my arms, and kissed her gently, just like I'd wanted to do all day.

I hadn't planned on starting anything, but Caro seemed to have other ideas because she tightened her hands behind my neck and locked our faces together.

It was such a fucking turn on having her here, like this, in the middle of a fucking hellhole. She pushed her tongue into my mouth, hungry and determined, then she ran her hands down my back, gripped my ass and squeezed hard.

God, I wanted her, even if it was a dumb fucking idea.

"Are you sure, Caro?" I questioned.

"Yes," she whispered. "Here and now."

I groaned as she raised her hips, rubbing against my rock hard cock.

"But you're going to have to get naked," she added.

I sighed and pushed away from her, shaking some sense back into my brain which was definitely lacking any blood flow.

"It's going to take some explaining if the Taliban attack and I run out of your room with my ass hanging out," I reminded her.

She hesitated and I wondered what she was thinking. It

didn't take long before I knew.

"I don't care if you don't … time to get naked, Marine," she ordered, rubbing her thigh against me again.

"Make me," I teased.

Her eyebrows shot up.

"Okay, what can I trade you to get you to take your shirt off?"

It was my turn to be surprised.

"Trade?"

"Yes," she said firmly. "I want you to take your shirt off, but it seems like I'll have to give you something in return. If I agree to your terms, you lose the shirt. If I don't agree, you get to keep it on."

"For real?"

"Yes, Sebastian," she stated, clearly issuing the orders. Well, okay then.

"A shirt for a shirt, Caro," I challenged her.

This was about to get interesting—and she was wearing a lot less than I was.

Moving slowly, in a show that was so fucking sexy, she unbuttoned her shirt. She wasn't wearing a bra. My uniform jacket and t-shirt hit the floor and we were both naked from the waist up.

"So far so good," she said, her voice low and husky. "I want you to take off your boots and socks."

I thought for a moment, considering how I could raise the stakes, especially as she had fewer clothes than me.

"Okay, but I want you to touch your breasts, Caro; touch yourself until your nipples are hard."

She followed my instructions quickly, running her hands lightly over her tits, toying with her nipples while she stared into my eyes.

"Fuck!" I said roughly, licking my lips, wanting to taste her, like *now*.

"Boots," she snapped.

It took over half a minute for me to unlace my boots and lose the socks. My coordination was fucked because I couldn't peel my eyeballs off of Caro who was now massaging her own breasts, teasing the nipples to peaks.

"I want you to take off your pants, Sebastian," she whispered.

God, if Grant walked in now...

"And you have to lose those pajama bottoms, Caro."

She kicked them off quickly, adding them to the pile in the corner.

I unzipped my pants, leaving the skivvies on. But she was out of clothes, and didn't have anything left to trade.

"I want you naked, Sebastian," she whispered.

"I want you to touch yourself between your legs, Caro. I want to see you come."

She wrinkled her nose in distaste. I was confused— things had been getting pretty hot. Had she changed her mind?

"What?" I asked.

"Sebastian," she sighed, "I can do that any night of the week; frankly I was hoping you'd do it for me."

I grinned with relief. "Yeah, but it'll be a real fucking turn on for me."

"Alright then, but you, too."

She'd lost me. "Me too, what?"

"Lose the briefs, get handy, and make yourself come."

Not what I had in mind, but if that's what she wanted... "Ah, what the hell."

I yanked off the skivvies then folded myself into a sitting position, leaning against the wall facing Caro, and started working the head of my dick. Caro watched for a few seconds, which was pretty fuckin' hot, then she knelt up, spreading her knees wide and began to rub her clit slowly.

That shit was so *hardcore*. I wrapped my right hand firmly around my dick and started yanking harder; she matched me stroke for stroke, her back arching in a way that nearly made me come. But it wasn't enough.

"Oh, fuck this," I snarled.

I launched myself forward, knocking Caro onto her back, and slammed into her, pumping hard.

I was seconds from coming when Caro smacked my shoulder, struggling to push me off.

"Condom!" she hissed.

"Fuck! Fuck! Fuck!"

I'd been so turned on, I'd totally forgotten the basics. That only ever happened around Caro.

I pulled out of her reluctantly, then fumbled around for my pants, searching for the right pocket where I kept the rubbers. I swore as I dropped the first foil packet, but managed to hold onto the second one, hoping like fuck it was the right way around, otherwise it was going to come off inside her, and we'd been through that shit years before—it hadn't been fun.

"I'm sheathed up," I grunted.

Her next words knocked the breath right out of my lungs.

"From behind: make it rough."

I sure as hell didn't need to be asked twice.

Caro rolled onto her hands and knees, and I gripped her hip with one hand, my dick with other, took aim, and rammed home for the second time. She cried out, then collapsed onto her forearms, stifling her cries into the pillow. I fucked her as hard as I could, hammering into her body, letting myself go, losing myself in her, just like she wanted, just like she'd asked.

She pushed her ass back against me, and I could hear the slap of my balls against her, over and over again.

I leaned forward, palming her left breast, pinching the nipple until she cried out. Then I reached lower to finger her clit, rubbing my shaft at the same time as it slicked in and out of her. She brought up her hand to meet mine, an insane physical and emotional connection joining us.

I felt her body tremble as her muscles gripped around me, then she collapsed as she came and I had to hook my arm around her waist to hold her up while I released into her, stars shooting behind my eyelids from the intensity.

Caro was gasping for breath and I was breathing harder than a recruit at boot camp. I could feel the sweat on my chest and back.

I pulled out quickly and felt her body flinch.

"Are you okay?"

"Yes," she gasped. "Apart from the fact I'll be walking

like I just got off my camel tomorrow. You?"

I felt a huge smile break out.

"Yeah, I think I ripped my foreskin—what's left of it."

"Really?" She turned around to face me. "Are you okay?"

God, she was too cute for words.

I smiled and stroked her cheek. "Kidding, Caro. That was fucking awesome. You were like some wild woman."

"You were pretty wild yourself. But you're right: I don't know what got into me—other than you, of course. Do you want to go again?"

I stared at her in amazement.

"Christ, Caro! Are you trying to kill me?"

"Hmm, death by orgasm. What do you think? A handful by morning?"

I stared at her, wondering what the hell had happened to my gentle, sweet girl.

"If you want, Caro, but you know what I'd really like to do now?"

"Thrill me," she teased, stroking her fingers across my damp chest and tugging lightly on my dog tags.

I pulled her into his arms and looked at her seriously. "I want to make love to you, Caro. I freakin' loved *that*, but it was just sex. Can we take it slow, baby? Take our time? I want to touch every part of your body."

And I don't know how long it will be before we can have a night like this again.

She kissed me softly, and this time, and the time after, I made love to her, showing her with my body the words that never came out right.

CHAPTER 15

Dawn was close when she woke me up. I felt her fingers drifting down my back and across my hip. My dick was definitely awake, but I could tell from the light that there was no chance of doing anything about it before I had to report for duty.

"Time to get up, Sebastian," she whispered.

I blinked and tried to stretch, but ended up kicking the door again.

"Very stealthy, Marine," she laughed as I sat up to search for my clothes.

"Yeah," I grinned at her, "trained in stealth, camouflage and concealment, baby."

"You were certainly concealed in me last night," she murmured. "Several times, I seem to remember."

"Did ya lose count, baby?" I smirked.

She shook her head, her eyes bright and teasing.

"By the way," she asked, "how come you're managing to get in here without anyone noticing you're not where you're supposed to be?"

I frowned. "It's not that hard—I'm kind of separate from everyone. I'm on attachment so none of them know me; I'm in charge of the other interpreters, but they're all Afghan, so I'm not part of that either. It was different when I was still with my Unit, but this way no one knows when or where I'm on duty. Except Grant, and he's got more to worry about than where I sleep. Works out pretty well, huh, Caro?"

I couldn't figure out why she looked so sad. Was she worried about me? But then she smiled and leaned forward, resting her lips against mine.

"Time to move your ass, Sebastian", she said, running her fingers over my short hair. "I'll see you later?"

I dressed, kissed her again quickly, then darted out through the door, keeping low until I was out in the courtyard, casually greeting some of the other guys who were either waking up or coming off watch.

I was trying to keep the huge ass smile off of my face, but I guess I failed because Chiv came up to me, one eyebrow raised.

"You're lookin' as happy as a pig in shit. What's with that, Seb?" He looked over my shoulder in the direction of Caro's room. "Y'all been visitin' with the very lovely Ms. Journalist?"

"What are you yakking about, Chiv?" I tried really hard to look puzzled; it didn't work.

He grinned at me and winked. "You dog. Wouldn't mind some of that action myself, if the lovely lady is puttin' out."

I couldn't stop myself grabbing the front of his uniform and getting in his face.

"Don't talk about her like that!" I snarled.

The idiot just grinned at me. "Don't get your panties in a bunch, Seb; I'm just messin' wit ya! You two been givin' each other the glad-eye ever since y'all got here. Gotta say it's pretty damn obvious." He pulled my hands off of his jacket. "But maybe that's just 'cause I know ya. Don't stress it—your secret is safe with me." He patted me on the shoulder. "But y'all might wanna quit accostin' your fellow Marines in the quad."

He strolled away laughing to himself as I took a deep breath. Shit, he was right.

I lined up for chow and chewed my way through something that may or may not have been chicken, then it was time for the morning briefing.

Caro was being sent out with Lieutenant Sanders today. I didn't know him that well, but he seemed like a good guy. I was with Jankowski again, leading a team into the foothills to see if we could get some more intel on what the Taliban knew about our movements—in particular about Gal Agha.

287

Hopefully, nothing.

The other news was that there would be a fresh food drop in the early evening. We all looked forward to that. Apart from anything else, there would be fresh water as well, so we could use up the old rations and everyone got a one minute shower—barely long enough to do more than turn the dusty dirt that coated our bodies into mud.

But small things like that made a big difference to morale. There was going to be a letter drop, as well, but I never got any mail; well, a card from Ches's mom and dad— usually about a month after my birthday, depending where I was on tour. No biggie.

Grant confirmed that yesterday was uneventful, and other than our RPG contact and every guy losing about five pounds in sweat, not much else happened. Although one of the other patrols fired off a few rounds, but that was just to drive away a bunch of locals who were throwing rocks at them. Nice.

I strapped on my body armor and daypack, then slapped on my helmet and scooped up my M16. Jankowski ordered the compound gates to be opened and we filed out cautiously, keeping our eyes on the rooftops for snipers, the dirt under our feet for IEDs, and the foothills in the distance for ambush or RPG attack.

I tried talking to two locals who were standing in the bullet-ripped market, but they ignored me with stony faces, then turned their backs. I heard Jankowski mutter under his breath, "Is that what you call a charm offensive, Hunter?" He was a funny fucker.

Once we got past the last ramshackle building, we were in open countryside. There was no talking, and we were all hyper-aware of our surroundings: that's how you stayed alive out here.

Two guys were sent ahead to check out a mud-built hovel. There was nowhere big enough to hide a body—I mean a person—so they didn't go any further than the periphery. Doorways and windows were favorite places to booby-trap.

Some scrawny goats clattered past, nearly giving the guys

searching a heart attack at the sudden sound. I could see a kid of about 11 in the distance watching us—probably the goatherd. He ran off when he saw that I'd seen him, and the hairs on the back of my neck stood up. Who was he going to tell?

We walked another couple of miles before we saw any further signs of life. A man with a lined and cracked face of a village elder shouted at us from his tiny house. I could see a collection of barefoot children hiding behind his robes. His teeth were yellow with half of them missing.

He shouted at us, then slammed his door. His words nearly stopped my heart.

"Hunter?"

Jankowski was waiting impatiently for a translation. I swallowed several times, feeling like my throat was just about dry enough to shit sand.

"He asked what kind of cowards brought a woman to do their fighting for them," I said, trying to hide the concern in my voice.

"You think he means Ms. Venzi?"

I nodded. "Yeah."

"Ah shit," he sighed. "The boss was afraid that would happen."

So was I.

We were the last patrol to return to the compound that evening. I could see Caro sitting across the quad from the entrance and I felt a surge of relief that she was safe. For now.

I went to Grant's office with Jankowski to report on what I'd heard. The boss was worried and pissed.

"She'll have to go back to Bastion. I'd get her on the water drop helo but they're dropping not stopping." He looked across at Mark. "She'll need to stay in the compound until HQ authorize a ride, but maybe we can get her on the new personnel flight next week." Then he turned to me. "Tell Ms. Venzi that I'd like to speak with her."

I saluted and walked over to where Caro was sitting with a bunch of the younger guys who seemed drawn to her like she was sunshine in winter. I knew how that felt.

"Captain Grant would like to see you, ma'am," I said, keeping it formal while we had eyes on us.

She stood up immediately, reading the stiffness in my body, and she didn't ask any questions.

Grant's office seemed appropriately gloomy. I stood to one side as he waved her into the only other unoccupied chair in the room.

"Ms. Venzi, your presence is causing some interest among the local population," he announced, cutting right to the chase. "Hunter heard some talk while on patrol that concerned him."

She glanced at me quickly.

"And what does this talk say?" she prompted.

"At the moment it's vague, but the news of having a woman with us will spread quickly now. We have a new medic arriving in six days, so the helo will be putting down briefly. If you become a person of interest, as I think you will, you'll be at risk and you'll be putting my men at risk, too. I want you on that flight, Ms. Venzi. And until then, for your safety, you'll remain in the compound."

I saw her shoulders tighten and she took a deep breath.

"I see. Well, thank you for being so candid and explaining the situation to me, Captain Grant. I'll ensure that I get as much work done as I can, and I'll be ready to leave when you advise."

The boss looked relieved; perhaps he'd expected her to argue, but there was no way Caro would be selfish while chasing down a story if it meant putting guys in danger. Hopefully she'd still be able to write her articles even if she wasn't in Now Zad.

She stood up and let me escort her from the office.

"Sorry, baby," I said quietly.

"That's okay," she replied, her voice tired. "I don't want to cause more problems out here. Besides, I can get some stories from Leatherneck so the paper won't be shortchanged."

"If anything happened to you…" I began.

She interrupted me quickly. "I told you, Sebastian, I'm

not going to take risks. If you care about me, you won't either."

"*If* I care about you?" I snapped, my temper flaring.

"You know what I mean," she said calmly, "and keep your voice down."

There were too many people watching us, so I zipped my lips and left Caro outside her room, trying—and failing—to keep my eyes off her.

We'd just finished chow and I was sucking down the piss-weak coffee, when Sanders reported that the helo would be here soon.

"Supply chopper on its way," he announced, then picked out a platoon to retrieve the goodies before the locals decided to put their thieving hands all over it.

A few minutes later, we heard the distinctive thrum of the Black Hawk's twin engines chewing up the air around it, and small parachutes began raining down.

Once the swag had been collected and relocated to the compound, guys gathered around to sort out the supplies: ammunition, water, fresh rations, but only a small bag of mail and no parcels. I wasn't surprised by that—water was heavy and took up a lot of room. Larger items of mail would have to wait their turn or be stockpiled at Leatherneck.

Suddenly, my name was called.

"Hunter: you got mail, sir," and one of the younger guys I hadn't met yet waved a thin envelope at me.

There was no return address on it so I wondered who the hell it was from. I pulled it open and started reading.

My beautiful boy,

I hope I can see you reading this, because I want to watch as your eyes darken with lust and your lovely mouth widens in a smile, and maybe you'll shift uncomfortably as your glorious cock hardens, pushing against the rough khaki of your uniform. Because then I'll be imagining the moment I take you inside my mouth or inside my body, your breath hot on my back as your naked flesh…

My eyes widened in shock, followed by a grin that I couldn't hide as I glanced up to see Caro watching me, a knowing smile on her face. She winked at me, then carried on helping sort the mail, although I could see she was still watching me from under her lashes.

I read through the whole letter, sitting in the dirt, leaning against the mud wall of the compound. *Hot damn, my girl really was good with words.* I was so fucking turned on, so happy that she'd written to me so I had something of her to keep by my side, so fucking grateful to have her in my life. I closed my eyes and let my head rock back against the mudbrick wall, imagining everything that she'd written.

Then one of the other guys scrunched up his own letter and dropped it in the dirt.

"What's up man?"

"Fucking 'dear John' letter," he answered bitterly. "She said she didn't want to spoil my last few days of leave, so she thought she'd wait till I got out here to tell me she was seeing someone else. Bitch."

Yeah, pretty much every one of us knew what that felt like. Girls went for the uniform—not so much the months of being left behind with an empty bed and time on their hands. Some couldn't help the constant worrying, they said. Another reason for not getting attached, although that had all changed for me now.

The sun had sunk behind the mountains and the compound was shady for once. I was just thinking I should check on my terps and call into the comms room when the guard on duty in the observation post yelled loudly.

"Incoming!"

Everyone scrambled for their body armor and weapons. I slapped my helmet over my head and yanked on my Kevlar vest, but I lost sight of Caro and my heart lurched.

The first RPG exploded about 200 yards outside the compound and a spray of dirt rocketed 90 feet into the air.

I grabbed my M16 and ran to the nearest observation post. Then the *durg-durg* of the heavy machine guns started.

Another RPG exploded: 100 yards this time. Looked like the Taliban gunner was getting his sights lined up. Not fucking good. But there weren't any further shots and I wondered if it was just to stop us from getting any downtime.

If that was the reason, I was a little surprised that they didn't wait until night time so they could disturb our sleep: fucking amateurs.

Before the all-clear had been called, I ran to Caro's room and stuck my head around the door, making her cry out in fright.

"You okay, baby?"

"Yes, fine. Don't worry about me," she replied breathlessly.

I nodded and sprinted to the comms room.

I guess I'd spoken too soon, because after that the Taliban had a new tactic: sleep deprivation. Intermittently throughout the night, they'd fire random RPGs that never landed near enough to be dangerous, but stopped the guys getting any rest. Not that sleeping in body armor was that easy anyway—at least not until complete exhaustion had set in.

I spent the night in the comms room listening to a combination of insults broadcast in broken English, threats of what they'd do if they captured us, plus two terrorist cells talking to each other.

By dawn, we were all tired and pissed.

Guys were starting to line up for breakfast when I heard some of them singing the old Beatles classic 'I'm So Tired'— the lines that said the guy had his mind on the blink because he hadn't slept a wink.

When I looked out of the comms room, nine fuck-ugly Marines were singing and grooving, surrounding a smiling Caro who was singing along with them and shaking her hips. More guys joined in, making me want to punch the ones who were staring at her ass, but then Grant appeared from his office, and even he couldn't help smiling. I didn't know the guy had teeth.

I nearly choked when the boss threw Caro a salute and she waved back. Only my gal. Damn, I was proud. Yeah, I may have mentioned that before.

The patrols that day were kept short. At least I had the satisfaction of knowing that Caro would be safe in the compound—well, as safe as Helmand Province got. I was sent out with Sanders and an EOD operator to check out if there was any unexploded ordnance from the night's RPG attacks. The guy wore his dog tags on his boots because he said that those would be the only things left if an IED took him out.

I hadn't been there long when Jankowski arrived with orders to join him and his unit in another patrol to the foothills. I left my best terp with Sanders, a 17 year old kid named Gawhar. I trusted him more than the others; he seemed solid, but that wasn't saying much.

We pushed further into the hills, only turning around when we started losing the light. We'd stopped for a five minute break to give us a chance to drink some water and eat an energy bar. Chiv had been listening in on the portable radio when he waved me over.

"Fuck man, you need to hear this."

As I listened, all the blood drained from my face. A Taliban cell was gloating that they'd killed an 'Infidel' journalist. I thought I was going to be sick. It was only when I heard the words 'Kandahar' and 'Bastian' repeatedly, that I realized that they weren't talking about Caro.

Chiv radioed back to the compound when he saw the look on my face, just to check Caro was safe.

We booked it back quick march anyway. Seeing her sitting outside in the quad was the best fucking sight ever. I breathed out a deep sigh of relief, hating that I couldn't go to her, and stood with the other guys as the kitchen re-opened to heat up some shitty chili-flavored MREs.

I'd just started eating when Grant ordered me into the office and told me to sit down. That was a first.

"Seb," he began. *Fuck, if he was using my first name it must be serious.* "You met the journalist Elizabeth Ashton. Correct?"

"Yes, sir."

"I understand she was a friend of Ms. Venzi's." *Was?* "Ms. Ashton was killed by sniper fire near Camp Bastian today," he said, his voice cold and angry. "It's a publicity killing. They know she was a journalist and the fact that she was a woman makes it even more newsworthy. The locals know that Ms. Venzi is here—I wouldn't be surprised if the

294

Taliban have already put two and two together and figured out she's journalist."

No! NO! NO!

Then Grant looked at the radio operator.

"How soon can we get a helo in?"

We waited while a flight was arranged for oh-six-hundred hours, then Grant turned to me.

"Send Ms. Venzi in. She should know that her friend … she should know."

"Yes, sir."

When I went to find her, Caro could tell by the look on my face that something was wrong."

What is it? What's happened?"

"Grant wants to see you," I said, ignoring the curious gazes from the other men.

She stood up stiffly and followed me into the office.

"Please take a seat, Ms. Venzi," Grant said gently. "I'm afraid I have some bad news for you … I told you yesterday that we picked up some veiled threats to you; well, it's become much more direct. The Taliban have heard that you're with us—and they're viewing you as a prize kill."

For fuck's sake! Did the asshole have to say it like that?

"They're aware of the value of publicity," he continued, "and I'm afraid earlier today, they killed another journalist—a woman. I've called in a helo to evacuate you back to Leatherneck as soon as possible first thing in the morning. Ms. Venzi? Ms. Venzi?"

Caro looked up at him, stunned. "Who?"

"Excuse me?"

"Who was the journalist they killed?"

Grant glanced over to me.

"Liz Ashton," I said gently.

Caro dropped her head into her hands, and I could see her fighting back tears.

"I'm sorry," Grant said uncomfortably.

Caro looked up and nodded slowly. "She was my friend."

"I'm sorry," Grant said again, "but we can't risk our mission here and…"

He bit off what he was going to say.

"How did she die?"

Grant looked away, leaving it to me to give her the gory details.

"Sniper," I said. "She died instantly."

I didn't know if that was true, but it's what we always said to families and friends. No one needed to hear that their son or brother had died screaming in agony with his legs and arms blown off and his stomach lying on the floor in front of him. You didn't forget that shit. Ever.

Grant tried to say something comforting, but I don't think Caro heard him. She walked out of his office, and I started to reach for her but she ignored me and walked past.

I wasn't sure what to do—what she'd want me to do. But Grant made the decision for me.

"Give her ten minutes then check on her, Seb."

"Yes, sir."

I'd never been more happy to obey an order.

I gave it five minutes, then headed for her room. When she didn't answer, I tapped on the door and pushed it open.

Caro was curled up in the corner, her arms wrapped around the knees, muttering the same words over and over again.

"Put out the light, then put out the light."

It didn't make sense to me at first because there weren't any lights in her room. And then I recognized it as a line from Shakespeare. I didn't know which play and I didn't care. My girl was hurting and there was nothing I could do.

I shut the door behind me quietly, then sat down next to her, pulling her into my arms. I didn't speak, I just rocked her gently, dropping soft kisses into her hair.

After a while, I felt her body relax against me, curling into my chest.

"I'm so sorry, Caro," I said quietly. "I know she was your friend."

She didn't reply, so I just held her.

Night fell and the room was filled with shadows and darkness. Outside, I could hear the sounds of men changing watch and I sighed. "I'd better go, or Grant will wonder what the hell we're doing."

I shifted her off my lap and started to stand up, but she grabbed hold of my hand.

"Don't go, Sebastian, please. It doesn't matter who knows about us now—I'm being sent home anyway. Let me spend my last few hours with you."

I sank down again. "I was hoping you'd say that," I admitted.

I didn't care if it fucked up my career: Caro needed me, that was what mattered

We lay on the mattress, fully dressed, our arms and legs tangled together.

"I'm not very good at gardening," she said thoughtfully.

I was confused by her random comment.

"What's that, baby?"

"I can't grow things," she muttered into my chest. "Plants seem to wither when they see me. Can you grow things?"

"I don't know, Caro. I've never tried."

"I'd like to plant something," she whispered, "see it live and grow."

Now I understood: she wanted to make a garden, create life; a way of evening up the balance of loss in some small way.

I pulled her against me more tightly and stroked her hair.

"Does your place in Long Beach have a backyard?"

"Yes," she sighed. "It could be pretty. Remember Signora Carello's bougainvillea? Maybe we could grow something like that."

I kissed her hair again. "Baby, I can't even spell bougain … whatever it is, but I guess I could try. Was that the purple stuff?"

She nodded.

"Okay, baby. We can grow purple stuff."

"And pink?"

"Sure, baby, with yellow fucking stripes if you want."

"Okay."

I was hoping she might sleep after that weird-ass conversation, but she didn't. I lay watching her, but every now and then I'd see the glint of moonlight in her eyes and know that she was awake.

As dawn started to filter through the compound, I sat up slowly, pushing the tiredness away.

Caro didn't speak as she packed up her gear, so I watched in silence.

"I'll miss having you here," I said, at last. "But I'm glad you're getting the fuck out of this shithole."

She wrapped her arms around my waist and leaned into my chest.

"Just come home safe, Sebastian. No heroics, please."

"The only thing you've got to worry about is when I self-combust, especially if you're going to send more letters like that one you wrote me yesterday."

My dumb joke fell flat, and she tugged at my uniform.

"I mean it. Stay safe."

I sighed and nuzzled her hair, treasuring the scent that was all woman, all Caro.

"I'll do my best, baby. Promise."

Then I lifted her chin with one finger and kissed her soft lips.

"Fuck, I'm going to miss you, Caro."

"I love you, tesoro. So much."

I held her face between my hands and gazed into her eyes so she'd know that I meant what I said. "Sei tutto per me."

You mean the world to me.

She smiled sadly, so much love in her tear-filled eyes. But our moment was over, and it was time to go.

I carried her bag out to the quad, ignoring the stares of the other Marines. Grant and Sanders came out to shake hands with her, and several of the other guys that I'd seen her talking with over the last few days lined up to give her awkward, one-armed hugs. Probably the first and last time that I wouldn't mind other men touching her.

As soon as we heard the helo, eight armed Marines escorted her to the pickup point 200 yards outside the compound.

Touchdown was less than five seconds and Caro was

yanked inside before the helo offered too easy a target to the Taliban squatting in the foothills.

I stood and watched the bird leave. I didn't wave.

Grant called me into his office immediately. I thought it might have been to ask me how well I knew Caro, but I guess now she was out of sight and not his responsibility, she was out of mind.

"Seb, we've got to move up the mission. I want you ready to move out in an hour. The Taliban know way too much about our movements. Jankowski and 14 men will go with you. Daypack for three days—leave everything else here."

"Yes, sir."

I saluted and headed back. I hadn't really unpacked, so it didn't take long to lay out what I needed for the next few days. But when I felt the crinkle of paper in my pocket from Caro's letter, I knew what I had to do.

I was going to try my damndest to make it back, but it was never guaranteed and this mission .... I wanted to come back, I wanted to live, more than I ever had in my whole life. But if I didn't…

I pulled out a small notebook and stub of pencil and started to write, the words coming painfully, not just because I was out of practice with putting lines on paper.

Caro, my love,

Just writing these words makes me happier than I can remember being for a very long time—ten years, in fact.

I'm not one for words—I leave that to you—my beautiful, talented Caro. But we've had the news we were waiting for and soon we'll be heading out. I hope you never read this letter, but if you do, it means I've gone on to the next big adventure.

Knowing that you are in the world and wearing my ring, makes me the happiest man alive, and the last two weeks have been the best and happiest of my whole life.

Be happy, Caro, because that's what you deserve.

I love you, I have always loved you, and wherever I go after this world, I will always love you. Sempre e per sempre.

Sebastian

Then I folded it up and went to the comms room to scrounge an envelope from Chiv.

He was checking over his portable Satcomms radio.

"Are you coming with us, man?"

He nodded, his face serious. "And that ain't all. The boss is steamin' 'cause some ANA just turned up and he's been ordered to send them with us."

"What the fuck? Seriously? This is supposed to a fucking top secret mission!"

"I know. Grant ain't happy, but the orders have come from HQ, so we're stuck."

"Shit!" I rubbed my forehead.

"Well, yeah," he sighed. "Fuckin' top brass for ya." Then he glanced across. "You need an envelope for that letter?"

My gaze dropped to the sheet of notepaper in my hand. "Yeah."

He didn't need to ask why I wanted it, he just handed one over.

I thought for a moment about what name to write on the envelope. And then, with a small smile on my face, I wrote, *Carolina Hunter.*

I *really* liked the sound of that.

We headed out twenty minutes later, two ANA guys following us. Neither seemed interested in talking and we were also moving too fast for conversation. We were all uneasy at the thought of having them with us, knowing that Grant didn't want them anywhere near this op.

We were in Now Zad in the first place to make contact with Gal Agha. If I could get him onside, he'd bring us to one of the Taliban leaders so we could take him out. For all we knew, the ANA men could be spies.

That's why Military Intelligence wanted me, because they were worried about using local interpreters for a sensitive op.

We headed out into the mountains, prepared for it to take a day to meet the contact, another half a day to meet with our contact, and if things went well, take out the target, too. Then a day and a half back—that was the plan.

As soon as we were past the foothills, the path rose steeply. We couldn't go as fast as we wanted because we were still checking for IEDs or ambushes ahead of us. The safest route was usually to follow goat tracks, but the rest was down to dumb luck. And then our ANA colleagues kept stopping for prayers, rolling out their mats, facing east and telling Allah what good guys they were. Okay, that sounds shitty, but we were in a hurry and being out in the open made us all nervous.

We spent the first night an hour's walk from the village where we'd meet Gal Agha. The ANA kept to themselves and we had a cold camp, not wanting to risk lighting a fire.

Then we woke before dawn and made the last three mile hike into the village.

I knew right away that something was wrong—it was just too damn quiet. There was nobody in the fields, no one sitting outside their houses, no one getting ready for the day. We were all on edge.

I went ahead with the ANA guys and they were calling for Gal Agha to come outside. I mean, what the fuck? Not what anyone would call stealthy!

Then this skinny old guy came out from behind one of the buildings and he was talking really fast and he looked fucking terrified.

He stuttered and stammered, and I realized he was quoting from the Qur'an.

"Those who disbelieve, theirs will be a severe torment; and those who believe in the Oneness of Allah and do righteous good deeds, theirs will be forgiveness and a great reward of Paradise."

His pupils were dilated with fear, and then I noticed that his robes were covered by a heavy winter coat in the middle of the fucking summer. And I knew—I just knew that he'd been turned into a human bomb.

"Get back! He's a fucking suicide bomber! He's…"

But then I felt like I'd been punched in the shoulder. I stared in disbelief as my M16 fell in the dust, and blood started to spread across my shoulder and chest. I sank to my knees and saw Chiv running toward me.

"Medic!" he yelled. "Medic!"

More shots punctured the air, and I stared up groggily to see that one of the ANA guys had tried to take me out, then shot his colleague and turned his rifle on the rest of the squad. The firefight started and I could hear Jankowski yelling at the contact to get down. I tried to say the words in Pashto, but nothing came out.

Jankowski aimed his rifle at the guy, flanked by a kid called Jez. They both took aim.

Without warning, there was an explosion and I felt a blow on my leg that flung me through the air. I hit the ground and all the breath rushed out of my lungs. I felt like I was drowning. As I stared up, Chiv and Jankowski disappeared in a haze of blood and tattered flesh.

That was the last thing I saw.

CHAPTER 16

I was dreaming about her again.

That was nothing new. I dreamed about her every night. I tried to wash away the memory in whiskey. Sometimes it worked. Sometimes I woke up in bed with a woman I didn't remember meeting, let alone fucking.

Shit, this was one helluva hangover: everything hurt. I tried to move my head, but it felt like someone had filled it with concrete and then encased it in lead. I tried to move my right hand, but I couldn't lift it. Then I tried to move my left and a bolt of pain shot through me.

Flashes of memory flickered like an old black-and-white movie, but I wasn't sure if they were memories or dreams. Had Caro really come back into my life, or was I hung-over as fuck in my shitty apartment in Geneva?

My eyelids shuttered open and I blinked in the harsh light. Nope, definitely not Geneva.

The room was white and sterile, and I was surrounded by screens and monitors. Huh, a hospital room?

I gazed down at the thin sheet covering me. I had a box-like frame over my legs.

There was a beeping noise that was annoying the shit out of me.

Suddenly, like a door opening, I remembered: the village, the bomber, being thrown through the air.

And I knew I was in a hospital, in Afghanistan and nothing had been a dream. I guess that when real life decides to smack you between the eyes, you don't have any fucking choice.

Chiv? Jankowski?

I closed my eyes with one clear thought in my mind: *Caro.*

When I woke up again, an older guy in green scrubs was standing over me.

"Welcome back. You had us worried there for a while. Do you know where you are, son?"

I tried to speak, but my mouth was bone dry. I wanted to lick my lips, but my tongue felt thick and heavy.

The guy turned around to speak to someone, and a woman in blue scrubs put a couple of ice chips in my mouth. They felt like heaven.

"Doc?" I managed to croak.

The man's eyes smiled. "That's right. You're in the field hospital at Camp Leatherneck. You've been here for five days."

"Doc," I croaked again, "have I still got my balls?"

He grinned. "Everyone asks that. Yes, you do, son."

I closed my eyes, relieved

"My legs? Anything missing?"

"Well, you've lost some muscle mass from your right quadriceps and adductor muscles—your right thigh. It's a very deep wound caused by shrapnel, and the femur is fractured. You were also shot in your left shoulder and had a collapsed lung. You've got some nerve damage, resulting in loss of fine motor function. We'll know more in a few days."

I was struggling to understand him: shot and blown up? Fuck me.

"You were comatose when you were brought in with severe blood loss," the doctor went on. "We medically induce a coma when there's brain swelling; you had blood poisoning and..." He stopped speaking suddenly as I tried to take it all in.

My brain creaked and whirred, and more memories came back in flashes. I wished they hadn't.

"The guys who were with me? Chiv and Jankowski?"

The doctor's eyes flickered away from me. I knew then that it wasn't good news.

"They didn't make it. I'm sorry." He paused. "But the rest of your Unit were EVACD safely…"

I screwed my eyes shut, the pain of surviving was sudden and unbearable.

"You'll be alright, son. You made it." He patted my arm and forced a smile. "And if my girlfriend looked like yours, I'd be making a miraculous recovery, as well."

"Caro?" I whispered, confusion tangling my thoughts into tight knots.

He nodded. "She's been here every day. We could barely get her to leave long enough to eat. She'll be back soon."

"Caro," I said again.

My eyes closed, but I was smiling.

The next time I woke up, the lights were dimmer. I thought there was something wrong with my eyes, but then I thought it must be night.

The curtain was pulled back abruptly … and I saw her.

Her beautiful eyes were wide and panicked, and her hand flew to her mouth. But then she looked at me, and every expression raced across her face: relief, fear, love.

I saw love.

"I *knew* you wouldn't give up on us," I whispered hoarsely.

She walked up to the bed, looking as though she wanted to touch me but wasn't sure where to start. To be honest, there wasn't a single part of me that didn't hurt like fuck, but I still needed her touch. In the end, she held my right hand gently and kissed it.

"You scared me, Sebastian. Don't do it again."

My lips twisted in a feeble smile.

"Sorry, baby."

I drifted in and out. I don't know for how long, but each time I woke, Caro was still holding my hand. I wanted to tell her what that meant to me, I think maybe I did. I just remember that she didn't leave.

Sometime later, a nurse interrupted us, explaining that they were getting me on a flight to the medical center in Germany. And Caro had been cleared to travel with me.

My memories of that journey are hazy. I was drugged up on a lot of meds, but I think my brain was kinda fucked, as

305

well. There was a lot of pain, I remember that, and experiencing turbulence at one point. But Caro never left me: she held my hand, talking to me quietly the whole way.

There was a long wait when we got to Landstuhl. The critical cases were taken off first—guys with brain injuries and missing limbs. It's hard to explain how that made me feel: I couldn't walk, couldn't move my left arm, couldn't get out of bed and had a fucking catheter in my dick, but I wasn't critical. Good to know.

It felt like forever as we waited on the tarmac in the cold. Caro kept pulling the blanket up around my neck, trying to cover my shoulders, until I was loaded onto one of the fleet of blue buses with some other guys who were busted up.

The army chaplain came over to me, his eyes tired and his face gray with exhaustion.

"You're here at the US army hospital. We're going to take good care of you. We're praying for you."

I wondered how many times he'd said that this morning: a lot, I guessed.

"Thank you," said Caro.

I didn't say anything.

I was only at the hospital for two nights while I was 'processed'. I heard one of the nurses tell Caro that Landstuhl was a Level I trauma center, treating over 2,000 guys like me every year. Some were flown in from Iraq; most from Afghanistan. We were treated and moved on. Treated and moved on.

I was given the choice of being flown back to San Diego or to go to an East Coast facility. I was considering the options when Caro made the decision for me, explaining to the nurse that it would be easier if I was near home—her home.

She didn't ask me—she just assumed. But to say I was having second thoughts would be a fucking understatement.

I knew I was finished as a Marine. Sure, I could get some desk jockey job, but that shit just wasn't tolerable. I was a fucking cripple, and would be eligible for some sort of disability. Twenty-seven and finished—a useless, pathetic piece of shit.

I didn't want Caro to do what everyone expected and to 'stand by' me. She didn't need me slowing her down: she was brilliant and beautiful and brave. I was shit scared of seeing the moment her eyes looked at me and regretted that we were together.

I knew Ches would take me in, but he was barely getting by as it was, with kids and a wife crammed into a two-bedroom cottage.

But I didn't contradict her, didn't say what I was thinking. Instead, we flew out to Walter Reed in Maryland on a Thursday at the beginning of May.

The journey from Germany was long and painful, and I was pretty certain they hadn't given me enough meds for the trip, and even though the plane was kept cool, sweat was pouring from me. But there were guys who were far worse off; I had no right to complain. I couldn't talk to Caro either—I had nothing to say.

A fleet of Marine ambulances were waiting at the airport. They don't tell you that when you enlist: you never expect to need to know that the military has as many ambulances as Armored Personnel Carriers.

I'd been at Walter Reed for two weeks. Caro stayed the whole time. I wanted her to go, but I couldn't manage to say the words either. We sank into silence, and I hated myself more each day.

I was most comfortable with the other guys. I did physical therapy with a Navy SEAL named Dan. He was strolling around on a pair of stubbies, those training prosthetics they give to guys to help them get used to having no legs.

He laughed when I told him he looked like a dork, and he did a few spins to show off.

"Fuck my luck," he said, grinning up at me. "I used to be 6' 4" and weigh 225 pounds. Now I'm 4' 4" and weigh 160 pounds. Shit, I'll have to update my driver's license."

His family was in Nebraska and he was hoping to surprise his wife by walking on his made-to-measure C-Leg prosthetics before her next visit.

"Stubbies aren't so bad, but the others—it's like kneeling on moving stilts," he explained. "But ya get used to it."

I was still in a wheelchair at the time, my left shoulder too weak and too damaged for me to use crutches yet, although my broken femur was healing.

Dan had met Caro so he wanted to know if I'd been getting any. I didn't answer that.

"I'm horny as fuck," Dan said, "but I guess my wife will have to ride me for now." He sighed. "At least I've got my balls."

Yeah, some guys hadn't. I guess I was lucky, but I'd be lying if I said that there weren't a lot of days when I wished the bomb had taken me, as well. How come I lived when Chiv and Jankowski were dead? How was that fair? Why the fuck had I been allowed to survive?

I knew my head was fucked up; hell, I didn't even want to have sex. Ever since the first time with Caro when I was 17, I guess you could say I had a high sex drive, but now ... not so much. I still thought Caro was the hottest woman I'd ever seen, but that was part of the problem. I wasn't the man she'd known. I was ... less. And I hated that. I'd lost a lot of muscle weight and I'd turned into a scrawny motherfucker. I felt impotent—I probably was. I couldn't even remember the last time I'd woken up hard. The docs told me that was the meds and everything would be okay when I reduced the dosage. But it wasn't just that—I hated the man I saw in the mirror, the man who'd fucked up, the man who'd seen his buddies die.

And the nightmares—waking up screaming every fucking time I closed my eyes. Nobody so much as blinked. The nurse just came in, shook me awake and handed out some more sleeping pills. Night terrors were nothing when just about every guy in the place had PTSD.

Apart from seeing Caro trying to hide the pity in her eyes, the most painful part of my treatment was the fucking shrink sessions.

I tried to disappear when it was time for my appointment, but one of the orderlies always found me. I'd hated it from the very first day—talking about fucking *feelings*.

"Come in please, Hunter. If you'd mind sitting over there."

The woman pointed to an empty space on the far side of her desk. At least she hadn't asked me to take a seat. Ha-fucking-ha.

The bitch of an orderly wheeled me into position and locked the brakes on the wheelchair. Nope, I wasn't going anywhere; I was having fucking therapy whether I wanted it or not.

"My name is Captain Banner," said the doc. "I'm from the Army Medical Corps and I'm also a qualified psychologist. However, in my office there are no ranks: you can call me Judith or doctor. What do you like to be called? Sebastian? Seb?"

I tried to shrug my shoulders, instead sending a wave of pain through the left side of my body that made me nauseous. I decided that having her call me 'Sebastian' would be too weird—only Caro used my full name.

"Seb," I muttered when I felt I could talk without biting off my own tongue.

"Good!" She gave me a professional smile. "Our sessions are about helping you come to terms with everything that's happened to you. Acceptance precedes understanding. I'm told that your shoulder injury is healing well with only limited loss of function, so you should be able to wheel yourself soon; and your other injuries are also making progress."

I could see she was choosing her words carefully. I watched her face, wondering what her angle would be.

"You've also had a traumatic brain injury—being that near to an explosion, the brain experiences a shockwave inside the skull, and it can have serious effects."

Was I supposed to agree? She was the fucking doctor.

She looked down at her notes again. "The nursing staff tell me that your sleep is disturbed by nightmares most nights."

Every night, I thought, but I didn't say that.

"Can you tell me what you dream about?"

I looked away. It was bad enough dreaming about seeing

Chiv and Jankowski get blown to pink mist every night, parts of their bodies raining down on my Utility Uniform, so I didn't see how talking about it to some shrink would help, going over it again and again.

She sighed and pushed her notes to one side.

"I *have* been out to Afghanistan," she said. "I do know what it's like."

I nearly smiled. "Yeah?"

Her face brightened. "Yes. I was based at Camp Leatherneck for six weeks."

Six weeks. Try six months, or a year.

"How many times did you go outside the fence?" I asked casually, already knowing the answer.

"Excuse me?"

I met her gaze. "How many times did you leave the compound at Leatherneck?"

"Oh," she said, momentarily off balance. "I didn't because…"

That's what I thought.

I looked away. "Next question."

So she moved on: question after fucking question. How did I *feel*? What was I *thinking*? What *outcomes* did I want from sessions with her?

To get the fuck out as quickly as possible.

I stared out her window and refused to answer. I could do this shit all day long.

Eventually, she admitted defeat. Time-was up—onto the next exciting appointment in my busy schedule: more physio.

An orderly came to wheel me out, but Doctor Spock had the last word.

"I'll see you tomorrow at fourteen-hundred hours, Seb."

Oh, the fucking joy.

Physio was at the gym most days. I didn't mind that, even though it was fucking painful. It reminded me of boot camp—being yelled at to try harder, push through the pain, get over the mental wall. I could do that. Maybe it was because I was a competitive motherfucker, or maybe it was because I was one of the least injured guys there. One kid, Lance, had lost both legs and his right arm. He shrugged his good shoulder when I talked to him.

"Rather me than my buddies," he said.

I didn't know if he meant because he didn't want to see his friends injured, or because his friends were dead. I didn't ask. We were put on the same team for a game of sitting volleyball, one-handed.

It was pretty funny seeing a bunch of cripples try to reach for the ball as it came crashing over the net.

Lance nudged me in the side and nearly fell over doing it. "Isn't that your fiancée over there? She's hot."

I tensed up immediately. I really fucking hated Caro seeing me like this, and right now I was sitting on the floor, knowing it would take me a full 30 seconds to climb back into my wheelchair. I didn't want to see the compassionate look on her face while I did it.

Lance was still studying her, and a part of me wanted to punch him for it.

"Lucky bastard," he muttered. "Do you think any girl will want to have sex with me now? Maybe one of those weirdoes who goes for amputees, or maybe one of those Wounded Warrior groupies? What do you think?"

"Just take your eyes off of my girl," I snapped.

He laughed and went back to the game.

When I looked at Caro, she waved quickly, then left the room. *Yeah, I was sick of me, too.*

It was the third week and my fifth session with Captain Shrink, and to say we hadn't hit it off would be an understatement.

She kept pushing me, picking at my scabs, refusing to let me put everything behind me until I'd 'talked' about it. Instead I'd yelled at her.

"I want you to accept that without being me and being where I've been you have no way of knowing what will actually help," I sneered.

Of course, she hadn't left it at that.

She sat up straighter in her chair and I could tell she was itching to pull rank, but she didn't.

"I want *you* to accept that you need help, then for you to

ask for help, and for you to make a decision to choose that help. You do accept that there are trained professionals who can help you?"

I laughed at her. She wasn't happy about that.

"You're not the only one who has been training since the age of 18," she said stiffly. "Although unlike your job, the equipment I work with doesn't come with a user manual."

Yep, definitely pissing her off.

Then came the sucker punch.

"I talked to your fiancée."

She saw the flicker of fury on my face, and the fact that she'd seen it made me even more pissed. I could feel the rage building inside of me, and if I'd had the strength, I'd have wheeled myself out of there. But unless you've got one of those electric wheelchairs, you can't work an ordinary chair with one hand, or you end up going in fucking circles.

Why the fuck had Caro been talking to my shrink? I felt betrayed. The only defense I had was to look away.

"Miss Venzi is a very interesting woman," continued the doc. "She seems fully invested in working through the … changes … in your circumstances."

My veins felt like they'd been filled with boiling tar. *Caro had been talking behind my back?* I didn't want to believe it.

"She thought you might consider taking a different sort of job in the Marine Corps."

"What sort of job?" I asked suspiciously.

"Well, with your language skills, there'll be plenty of work for an interpreter with Military Intelligence, or at Quantico."

"You mean a desk job?" I jeered.

She pressed her lips together into a flat line.

"Your physical recovery is impressive, Seb, but you won't be sent back to the front line."

I shook my head, a grim smile fixed to my face.

"The extent of your injuries render you unfit for frontline duty," she droned on. "As you know, one of the prerequisites of being a Marine is the ability to run without a limp. Your doctors tell me that it's unlikely you will ever be able to walk without using a cane. A medical discharge is the most likely scenario unless you want to reconsider an alternative career in the Corps."

"Put me behind a desk and I'll fuck up within a week."

She sighed and looked down.

"Is that your final decision?"

I nodded without speaking.

"I see," she said, and closed the file. "I'll send your paperwork to the Physical Examination Board and their liaison officer can help you with your disability application and…"

I'd never had a strong hold on my temper, but I seemed to lose it on a daily basis right now—usually at Caro—but today I had Captain Shrink in my sights.

"Do you think I give a fuck about disability money? I'm 27! What am I going to do with my life now? Nothing. I'm worthless. Useless. On the scrap heap. The Corps don't prepare you for that when they train you to be so single minded and focused."

"That's just not true," she said calmly. "There are many ways you could contribute. You could retrain…"

"As what? When you do your reintegration, it's what-the-fuck-ever. 'Just go and do your menial job so we can wash our hands of you.' So retraining—yeah, right."

She looked taken aback at my rant. Maybe I was foaming at the mouth, not that I cared.

"You could train for several careers," she insisted. "The organizational and management skills you've leaned mean…"

"Yeah, a thumb-up-butt civilian with no responsibility. What about a fucking crossing guard? Yeah, that would be good, wouldn't it? Diving to the ground every time a car backfires."

I folded my arms even though that was still fucking painful, and stared out the window again.

She didn't comment on my rudeness and laid some brochures out on the table between us. I ignored those, too.

"One other point before you go, Seb," she said, back in her officer voice. "I've been asked to point out that Miss Venzi has been requested not to report on anything she has seen or heard while in this facility. And I will remind you that your work with Military Intelligence remains classified. You will not speak of it … ever. You understand me?"

I nodded curtly. I didn't need to be reminded of my duty.

At the end of the session, an orderly wheeled me outside and left me under a tree. I needed to be alone to think, but Caro found me.

"Hi."

I couldn't even look at her, let alone reply. I was so fucking angry that she'd talked to the shrink.

"How'd it go?" she persisted, sitting on the bench beside me and resting her hand on my arm.

I shrugged it away from her, trying to ignore the flash of hurt that I saw too often in her beautiful brown eyes.

She lifted her hand away. I thought she'd get up and leave, but she didn't.

"I just saw Dr. Banner," she began carefully. "She said you left these information brochures behind."

"Toss them in the trash," I snapped.

"Excuse me?"

"Are you fucking deaf? I said toss them! I don't fucking want them."

Caro took a deep breath.

"I've read through them, and although you won't qualify for a medical pension because you haven't done your 20 years, you'll still receive between a third and half of your current salary … as a disabled veteran."

My temper shattered.

"I won't take it," I shouted.

"What? Why not?"

"I just won't."

"Sebastian, you deserve that," she whispered, her voice cracking as she said my name. "After everything you've been through…"

"I'm not fucking taking it, Caro. I'm 27. I don't want fucking disability pay!"

"Okay, tesoro. That's your choice."

I wanted her to fight me. I wanted her tell me I was an asshole. I wanted her to leave and walk away because I wasn't anything now; I wasn't the man she should marry. I wasn't a man.

"You could take college courses through the GI Bill," she said softly.

I growled under my breath and she was silent for nearly a minute.

"You did well today, Sebastian", she said, her voice strained. "The physical therapist says you're making good progress. He says you'll be able to use crutches more often and for greater distances. Maybe in a few months, with the help of a walking stick..."

I grunted again, noncommittal.

She sighed, then took a deep breath.

"I've been thinking I should go back to Long Beach. Just to make sure everything is okay at home. I want to try and start working a bit more..."

I'd expected this. I'd been waiting for her to say she didn't want to be with me anymore, but now it had happened, I felt like she'd ripped my still-beating heart out of my chest and stamped it into the mud.

"You're leaving me."

It was a statement, not a question.

She gasped, and her expression was broken. For the first time, she looked her age: I could see gray hairs at her temples, and the lines around her eyes had deepened over the last two months.

"No, tesoro!" she choked out. "Why would you say that? No, never!"

"Don't fucking lie to me, Caro," I shouted. "You've made it pretty fucking obvious you don't want to be here. Just fucking go!"

And I turned away from her.

I think she was trying to speak, but the words weren't making it past her lips. I clicked the brakes off of the chair and started to move away, ignoring the firey pain shooting through my left shoulder.

"Please, Sebastian," she begged, reaching out to touch my arm. "That's not what I'm saying: I just wanted to ... try and get some ... some normalcy. I'd visit on weekends."

I shrugged her off.

"Don't fucking drag it out, Caro," I asserted, my voice cold and bitter. "I'm not completely fucking dumb."

She stood suddenly and the movement made me look up.

"Damn you, Sebastian!" she screamed. "I'm not leaving you! You'll never get rid of me, so you can just stop trying. Right now."

I wanted to believe her, but I couldn't.

"Whatever," I said.

Seven days later, the Physical Evaluation Board Liaison Officer told me that the PEB would, 'authorize my disability separation, with disability benefits, as I had been found unfit and my condition was incompatible with continued military service'.

I was no longer in the Corps.

CHAPTER 17

The flight from DC to JFK was short—60 minutes, tops.

There was a moment at Dulles airport when I seriously thought about getting on the first flight to California. Part of me wanted to, but I couldn't do it. I couldn't land myself on Ches, but I didn't want to be with Caro either. Not like this. Not when everything between us was so unequal.

I had nothing to offer her and she had no future with me. And I couldn't help thinking she was only with me now out of loyalty; I was dreading the day when I saw hatred in her eyes. I'd seen every other emotion: frustration, annoyance, anger, fear, love as well, I think. But I also saw pity. That was the worst.

She'd arranged a taxi to drive us from the airport to her place on Long Beach. But she'd also requested a wheelchair to take me through the airport. No way. *No fucking way* was I going to be wheeled around anymore. I didn't care how much agony I was in; I was fucking walking out of there.

She argued. I argued back.

"I'm not fucking using it, Caro, so just drop it," I snarled.

She dropped it, and then watched me move through the terminal building on two crutches at a slow crawl. My left shoulder was burning with the effort and sweat was running down my back by the time we got to the taxi.

The driver talked the whole way, but I ignored him. I figured Caro was polite enough for both of us, so I just stared out the window, so lost in my thoughts that I was surprised when I saw the ocean in the distance, deep blue in the late evening sun. I felt a flicker of something that might have been hope, but it was soon extinguished by the darkness that filled me.

When we arrived at Caro's bungalow, the driver collected our bags from the trunk and tossed them onto the porch. The thought of putting weight on those crutches again made me nauseous, but I grit my teeth and struggled out of the car. I'd been a fucking Marine. Yeah, so? Now I was nothing.

The driver was staring at me.

"Dude, what happened to your leg?"

"Bomb."

"Say what?"

"Bomb: got blown up."

"Cool!"

I didn't even bother to reply to the asshole. I started to get some money out of my wallet, but Caro was quicker and had paid the driver before I'd even gotten my hand in my pocket. I was too pathetic even to pay for a fucking taxi.

I forced my body to carry on, and made my way into Caro's living room. I was so exhausted, I couldn't take much in. It was small, but it looked homey. Her home. This was just a pit stop for me. I was still in transit, and the sooner I got used to that idea, the better.

"Do you want to lie down, tesoro?" Caro asked quietly.

I opened my eyes, and she looked at me with so much compassion. I hated it.

"I'll stay here for a while."

But the words spun around my brain. I wouldn't be staying here for long. If I could just get back enough physically, I'd go to San Diego—get some night security job and drink myself to death. Put everyone out of their misery.

"Okay," she said hesitantly. "Well, I'll put your bags in the spare room for now. We can go through them later."

I didn't answer.

She was gone less than a minute before she was in my face again.

"Are you hungry? Would you like some pasta?"

I wasn't hungry. The meds made my gut ache, so I

318

shook my head. "No."

She didn't move, so I glanced up at her. She looked like she wanted to say something, but then she sighed.

"Maybe later," she said.

"This wasn't what I'd planned," I said bitterly, staring at her walls lined with stunning black and white photographs that I guessed she'd taken for her work.

"It's not what either of us had in mind," she replied carefully, "but we'll deal, won't we?"

"I thought I'd be carrying you over the fucking threshold," I scowled, my mouth twisting with disgust.

"That doesn't matter, Sebastian. We…"

And then I lost it.

"Yes, it does fucking matter, Caro!" I shouted, making her jump. "It really fucking matters! Christ, can't you understand something as fucking simple as that?"

She blanched and apologized hurriedly.

"I'm sorry, Sebastian, I just…"

"Just what, Caro?"

"Nothing," she muttered, walking into the kitchen.

I felt guilty for shouting at her. As if I needed *more* fucking guilt in my life. And that thought made me angry. But hell! Didn't she understand? Didn't she get how fucking humiliating it was to have to be grateful to her for every fucking little thing? I hated how weak I was. I hated how worried Caro looked. I hated everything about my fucking life.

I need a drink.

I don't know where that thought came from, but it was coming through loud and clear.

I could hear Caro in the kitchen and then she returned with a plate of sandwiches that she placed down next to me.

And I *really* hated that no one listened to what *I* wanted anymore. I'd already told her I wasn't hungry. I wanted to throw that fucking plate at the wall. I didn't, but I wanted to.

Instead, I concentrated on controlling my breathing.

I guess Caro couldn't stand the silence, because eventually she turned on the TV, quickly flicking off news reports of Afghanistan, so we ended up watching something about meerkats in Africa. Fuck's sake.

"Do you have any beer?" I asked.

Caro jumped in her chair.

"Oh, no, sorry," she stuttered. "I could open some wine?"

I nodded. "Yeah, that'll do."

It was better than nothing.

She came back with a bottle of red wine. I have no idea what type it was. I just wanted to get drunk as quickly as possible, I wanted to get numb as quickly as possible. And because I hadn't had a drink in over four months, it didn't take long.

I was planning on finishing the entire bottle, but Caro took it into the kitchen after I'd drunk about half of it. That pissed me off.

"Caro, what are you doing with the fucking wine?"

She gave me a hard look.

"You haven't eaten anything and you have to take your painkillers, Sebastian. So no, the wine stays in the kitchen."

The ticking time bomb of insanity exploded.

"Jesus fucking Christ! What is wrong with you? I'm stuck in this fucking chair and all I want is a fucking drink! Who the fuck do you think you are, telling me what I can and can't drink? Who the fuck are you to tell me how to live my life? Who gave you the right? No one! Fucking no one!"

Even as the fury raged, a part of me knew I was being a complete bastard; I just couldn't stop myself.

She didn't even try to fight back, and that made me angrier. When I was too exhausted to shout anymore, I stopped.

Her face was in shadow, so I couldn't tell what she was thinking anymore. I could probably guess: nothing good.

"Should I show you where the bedroom is?" she asked quietly.

"It's a fucking bungalow, Caro," I yelled again, "how fucking difficult do you think it's going to be? I'm not a fucking moron, even if I am a cripple."

"Sebastian..."

But I didn't wait to listen. I pulled myself off the couch,

clenching my teeth as pain lanced through me.

I stumbled against the wall, feeling the effects of the wine, then crashed into the spare room. After I fought my way out of that, I found the master bedroom. I sat down heavily, having to catch my breath from the extreme fucking effort of walking 20 feet. How pathetic was that? I pulled off my t-shirt, dropping it on the floor beside the bed, then eased off my sneakers and jeans. It took forever to get my socks off. For fuck's sake. I lay on my good side, facing away from Caro's side of the bed.

A few minutes later, she joined me and I tensed up. I didn't know what she'd want, what she'd expect. Whatever it was, I couldn't give it to her.

She slipped into the bed, careful not to jostle me, then spooned her body behind mine, resting her arm across my waist and stroking my skin. A bolt of terror shuttled through me.

I shifted slightly.

"Don't," I said, my voice cold and harsh.

She pulled her hand back quickly and I heard the breath hitch in her throat, but she didn't speak.

I don't know how long we both lay there, awake, not talking. It was a long fucking time. And then I heard her crying. She didn't think that I was awake, but I was.

I wanted to reach out to her, comfort her, but I couldn't do it. The sooner I was out of her life, the better for her.

The next day, I could tell that she was more hopeful. I don't know why— same shit different day. I wasn't better. I was worse. And the day after that, a lot worse. I couldn't admit it to myself, but I was sinking fast.

During the days that followed, I had no interest in anything: I wouldn't shower or change my clothes unless she nagged until my head pounded. I refused to shave. In the Marines you had to shave every day. I was a civilian, so what was the point.

Even when my beard started itching like fuck, I refused to shave it off. And with paranoia becoming a worsening problem, I felt as if I could hide behind it. My buzz cut had grown out as well. No one would guess I was a Marine. A former Marine. Fuck.

I was supposed to be continuing with my therapy sessions at a vets hospital, but I refused to have anything to do with it. If the Marines didn't want me, fuck 'em.

"What the fuck do they know about it, Caro?" I shouted when she mentioned it again.

"A lot: you're not the first Marine who's been injured," she said, struggling to keep her voice calm.

"Former Marine. Former fucking Marine, Caro. I'm nothing now. Maybe you can try and fucking remember that."

She shut up then.

But the next day, she tried a different angle.

"Sebastian, have you thought any more about when we'll get married? Or where? Because I don't mind if we go to San Diego and…"

No, *no*, *NO!*

"I'm not going to let you marry a useless, fucking cripple," I roared. "If I can't even walk down the fucking aisle without a fucking stick…"

She didn't ask me again.

I knew I was struggling, but I didn't want to give in. Instead, the PTSD began to swallow me up: mood swings, raised anxiety levels, flashbacks that were so fucking terrifying I'd end up cowering on the floor, not even believing I was back in the US. So I drank. I worked my way through Caro's small collection of wine, ignoring her when she tried to stop me.

My usual responses were shouting and yelling, or just zoning out completely. I was hanging by a thread, and sometimes I thought it might be easier to let it break. I was close.

It was the stupidest fucking thing that kept me clinging on: that tiny heart-shaped pebble that Caro had given me back in Geneva. I kept it with me all the time, rubbing my fingers over the smooth surface, letting the motion soothe me and remind me that the ocean was timeless and endless, making my fuckedupness meaningless.

One day, late in the summer, Caro suggested that her

friends come over to 'cheer' me up. Was she fucking insane? Oh wait, no … that was me.

"Yeah, they want to come see the fucking war cripple," I snapped, "make them feel good, like fucking charity. What's the matter with you, Caro? Do I look like I'm ready to see anyone?"

"Sebastian," she said calmly, "they're my friends. They want to meet you, and they want to see me. You don't have to put on a performance for them."

That was a fucking lie. If they saw the real me, they'd wonder what the fuck Caro was doing putting up with my pathetic ass.

"Sure, let them come, but I'm staying in the fucking bedroom."

They didn't come.

She started going for long walks by herself. That's what she said she was doing, but I wondered. I'd spend the hours she was away staring out the window, desperate for her to come back, but as soon as she did, I couldn't help snapping at her again. I think I was making her hate me; that was okay, because I loathed the piece of shit I'd become.

The nightmares were getting worse, and I didn't think that was possible. I woke up screaming every night, and once I lashed out, nearly hitting her. I stopped at the last second, appalled by the fear in her eyes. I wanted to gouge my own eyes out, so I never had to see her looking at me like that again.

I hated it. I hated not feeling safe anywhere. I didn't leave the house, but I didn't feel safe inside either. I started checking that the windows and doors were locked two or three times a night before we went to bed, and I had a panic attack every time someone came to the house, even the fucking mailman. Once, he tried to deliver a parcel for Caro, and I hid in the kitchen, armed with a set of steak knives.

And then she just stopped.

The forced calmness that she put on every morning shattered. She wouldn't buy me any more alcohol.

"If you want a fucking drink, then get your fucking ass off that couch and go get yourself one, Sebastian!"

323

She slammed out of the house and I didn't see her for three hours.

I thought about killing myself, because then both our problems would be over. But that stupid fucking pebble stopped me. I kept thinking what it would do to Caro to come home and find my body. As much as I hated myself, as much as I hated what I'd become, I couldn't do that to her. But I was so tired. So tired of being me, of all the thoughts that ran through my head incessantly, torturing what little sanity I had left. The memories, the fucking awful memories. I just wanted it to stop. But it didn't.

So we were trapped in a hell of my own making, and I had no idea how to climb out of it.

Something had to break. As it turned out, it was me.

Because Caro refused to buy me liquor, I started dosing up on caffeine, staying awake for days at a time. It was the only way to stop the nightmares. But she got wise to that and started buying shitty decaf. Then she found that I'd drank all of the cough syrup. She was pretty mad about that too, but I was almost past caring. Almost.

But that afternoon, all I wanted to do was to make it into the kitchen to make myself a cup of lousy decaf. I couldn't even do that.

Although I'd managed to switch from crutches to a walking cane, I was still fucking useless.

I lost my balance crossing the room, then tried to grab hold of the smaller of the two bookcases, and ended up falling onto the floor, crashing my bad leg against the coffee table. I thought I was going to pass out from the pain, but swearing up and down, cursing like it was going out of fashion kept me conscious.

So I was lying on the floor, surrounded by Caro's books when she found me.

"What happened?" she asked breathlessly, as she ran into the room.

"I fucking fell!" I snarled at her. "What does it look like?"

She bent down to help me up.

"Leave me alone! I'm not a complete fucking cripple."

That was a lie, but I couldn't, wouldn't let her help me.

She bit her lip, her expression pained as she watched me struggle to sit up and lean against the couch. I hated, *hated* being so fucking helpless, and I lost my temper every time Caro tried to help me. I knew I was hurting her, but I couldn't stop. I couldn't fucking stop.

Still on the floor, I made it as far as leaning against the couch, the effort leaving me drained. Silently, Caro bent down and started picking up the books nearest to her. I watched for a moment, then reached down to collect the ones that were within my reach. But when I picked up a copy of 'Lolita' by its cover, an envelope fell out, fluttering to the ground. Caro leaned down to take it, but for once I was faster.

"What's this?" I asked, studying the envelope. "It's got my name on it."

Then my eyes widened in shock and I looked up at her.

"The date on it … that's the day we first…"

The day we first made love. The day I lost my virginity to Caro ten years ago.

"Yes, I know," she said quietly.

I remembered that night so clearly. I'd had another fight with my asshole father. This time because in those days I had long hair—surfer hair—and he hated it. He hit me in the face the second I walked through the front door, and attacked my hair with scissors, cutting out long chunks. Then he'd tried to beat the shit out of me, but I'd gotten in a couple of good punches before I ran out of the house.

Caro had found me bloody and bruised in the park. And she'd taken me to her home and took care of me. She talked to me, patched me up, and shaved my hair into a buzz cut for the first time.

And then I told her that I loved her. And then she'd let me … oh God, she'd let me make love to her.

So many memories…

I had no idea what was in the envelope; I only knew that night had changed both our lives. I didn't know why the envelope was important, but as I studied the yellowing paper,

I knew that it was.

She pressed her lips together.

"Open it."

I propped myself up against the couch then heaved myself upward, dropping back against the cushions. I fumbled trying to open the sealed envelope; my left hand was still fucked—that wasn't going to change.

I thought there might be a letter or a photograph inside, but I was wrong.

A lock of long, blond hair fell out. My hair. From ten years ago.

I stared up at her.

"This is mine—my hair. You kept it—all these years?"

"Yes, tesoro," she said quietly. "It was all I had of you."

I closed my eyes, holding the lock in my right hand. My heart was thundering in my chest and I was struggling to breathe.

"Caro, I don't understand," I gasped. "Why do you love me?"

"Just because … because the sky is blue and the sea is green."

And then I broke.

Everything she'd told me was true. She'd loved me ten years ago, and all the years in between, and she still loved me now. And I didn't know why; I didn't understand, but maybe that didn't matter, because she loved me, and I loved her and I always had. It had only ever been her. My Caro.

I started to cry, because the hope was so fucking painful. All the anger, all the frustration, all the hatred flowed out of me and I let my love for this amazing woman take its place. I felt the moment my heart began to heal like a physical heat inside my body. I fisted my hands over my eyes and cried. And then Caro was beside me. She fastened her arms around me, holding me tightly, and for the first time in a long time, I let her. She wrapped her arms around me and I could feel her forcing the darkness away, trying to heal me with her body, with her touch.

"I love you, Sebastian, please don't push me away. I love you."

"Oh God. I just don't know what I'm doing any more; I'm so fucked up—I feel like I can't fucking breathe. Don't give up on me, Caro. Please don't give up on me. I need you, baby. I love you so much. I'm so sorry…"

I don't know how long we sat there—a long time, I think. She held me, just stroking my hair as I rested my head in her lap, her fingers running over my cheeks, tugging gently at the thick beard.

I sat up slowly, my body stiff, my eyes feeling hot and swollen. A part of my mind wanted to be ashamed that I'd broken in front of her; the rest of me didn't care because I knew she loved me no matter what. That was the part I was going to listen to.

"It's time to go out now, Sebastian," she said softly, staring into my eyes.

A pulse of fear made me shudder, and I closed my eyes and swallowed.

"I don't know if I can do that, Caro."

"You don't have to do this by yourself, Sebastian," she said, stroking my arms gently. "We go together. Come on, tesoro. Together."

I was so fucking terrified by the thought of going outside. Logically, I knew that there were no IEDs in Long Beach, no snipers waiting on roofs to finish the job. I knew that. My brain knew that, but my fucking body kept sending signals like I was going out on an op, with no body armor and no weapon. So yeah, I was shit scared.

Caro gave me a Yankees baseball cap to wear. I didn't care which fucking team it was from, and I pulled it down over my eyes, trying to hide. Silently, she passed me my old biker jacket which had arrived in a trunk three weeks ago. I didn't even know she'd unpacked it. When I tried it on, it hung loosely from my shoulders, reminding me that I was a scrawny fucker these days.

Then we were outside. I flinched as Caro shut the door behind me, and took several deep breaths, trying to force some calm into my body.

As I squinted into the sunshine, Caro took my hand, and I swear my heart instantly slowed to a more normal rhythm.

We walked along haltingly, not just because I couldn't move fast, but because I couldn't help myself checking the roof tops for rifle barrels sticking out, for suspicious faces in the crowds that ebbed and flowed around us.

I tried to reboot my brain. I tried so fucking hard.

And then…

I let myself enjoy the fresh air. I let myself breathe.

Caro didn't let go my hand the whole time.

"There's a café over there, Sebastian," she said softly. "Why don't we go have a coffee?"

My heart rate immediately shot up.

"I don't know, Caro … sitting outside? I wouldn't feel … safe."

She squeezed my hand more tightly.

"Sebastian, you know rationally that there's nothing to worry about. Let's just try it for a couple of minutes: if you really can't handle it, we'll leave."

My body jerked and hummed with adrenalin, but I didn't argue. My eyes were darting everywhere as I sat cautiously in the plastic seat, my back to the wall.

The waiter came toward us and I flinched away from him, but Caro rested her hand on my knee, calming me.

"I'll have an espresso. Sebastian?"

I was only barely aware that she'd spoken, so she answered for me.

"And a Bud Light," she said.

The waiter walked away shaking his head; he was used to a bit of crazy among his customers.

I sipped my beer, forcing myself to relax. I'm not sure I ever did, but it wasn't as scary as it would have been without Caro.

I won't lie, I felt happier once we were moving again. I was shocked by how exhausted I was after such a short walk—a guy who used to march for 30 hours with a ninety pound pack on his back. Fucking pathetic.

Caro took me along the Boardwalk. I hadn't been there before. Despite the large numbers, I wasn't freaking out too badly. People were laidback, strolling in the sunshine.

But then a roaring sound scared the crap out of me and I

nearly hit the deck. I was shaking so badly. Jesus H Christ—it was just a kid on a skateboard. I was seconds from having a full-on panic attack.

"It's okay, tesoro," Caro said, holding my hand firmly as I panted and wheezed. "You'll be okay."

"Fuck, Caro," I gasped.

By the time we reached the end of the Boardwalk, I began to relax a little more. Caro found an empty bench and we sat gazing at the ocean. I breathed in deeply, feeling calmed by the rhythmical motion of the waves. The ocean had always been my safe place when I was a kid—a place to get away from my parents. Seemed like it was still my safe place.

A couple of kids were playing on bodyboards, catching a few rides, shouting and laughing. That was something I knew. Something I understood. I leaned forward to watch them and I felt Caro relax against me.

For the first time in months, I put my good arm around her, feeling the soft warmth of her body as she snuggled against me.

"The ocean always reminds me of you, tesoro. It's the same color as your eyes today."

There was so much love in her voice that I was speechless. I didn't know why; I didn't understand it at all. But I didn't have to. All I could do was lift her hand to my lips and kiss it gently, reverently.

"Caro."

I breathed her name softly, like a prayer, because this woman had brought me back from hell.

A light breeze ruffled my hair and I could feel the sun on my face as we sat by the ocean. I felt I could breathe again. Live again.

"Thank you for this, Caro," I whispered.

She smiled up at me.

"Ready to go home, tesoro?"

I nodded, and we stood up to walk home. *Our home.*

We went back a different, slightly less crowded route. I was still scanning the roofline and checking everywhere for unfriendlies—that wasn't something I'd be able to turn off easily. But maybe I could stop feeling like I wanted hit the deck all of the time; you know, just control it a little more. I tried to keep my breathing slow, and I held onto Caro's hand like she was the last life raft in an ocean of sharks. That's how it was for me.

But then I felt her freeze, her fingers digging into my arm, and I immediately saw why. Three men with black hair, olive skin and dark eyes were arguing loudly outside a café. My brain immediately started working through threat triage—a mental checklist: weapons, nope; concealed weapons or bombs, nope; aggressive body language, nope—all in less than a second. Threat level low … and then I realized they were talking in Pashto.

Confused, I paused while my brain whirred and coughed. Had I really heard that? Pashto?

I listened more closely. Yep, definitely Pashto, definitely Afghans. And they were talking about … baseball. I did a double-take. Really? Baseball?

They were arguing about who was better: the Mets or the Yankees. I felt the unfamiliar sensation of a smile pulling at my lips.

I couldn't help the question that tumbled out of me.

"You think the Yankees will clinch the season, or can Boston take them?"

In Pashto.

They stared at me, then came rushing forwards, asking me how I was speaking their language, who was I, where was I from? I felt Caro tense up as they surrounded me, but I squeezed her hand and spent a few minutes talking; just talking, like a normal human being.

A part of me felt like maybe I should hate them because their countrymen had killed my friends, but I just couldn't. They were here, in Long Beach, as far away from the war as I was. And so we talked. They invited me to have tea with them. I said maybe I would another time.

They told me I had a beautiful wife. I didn't correct them.

As I walked away, Caro tugged on my arm.

"What on earth were you talking about for so long?"

"Baseball," I replied with a smile.

She stared at me doubtfully.

"You're kidding me?"

I winked at her.

"Universal language, Caro."

And somehow, for the dumbest of reasons, the world began to turn again.

I knew I had to get my ass into gear and make some changes—for myself as well as for Caro. I started by doing the exercises that the therapist had given me: some were to help build up dexterity in the fingers of my left hand, plus leg stretches to help the damaged muscles of my right thigh. I even started to use the exercise bike that Caro had ordered for me—although I hated the fact that it was static and I didn't go anywhere, just peddling meaninglessly. That could have described my fucking life. But I'd try. For Caro, I'd try.

But I missed being able to go for a run—I guess those days were over. I did crunches, push-ups, and pull-ups hanging from the doorframe. I pushed myself harder each time.

Then one day I dared myself to look in the mirror. My hair was shaggy and falling into my eyes. It was blonder, too, the ends bleached by the sun. I hadn't seen it like that in a long while. I didn't mind it, but the beard had to go. I think I blunted an entire razor getting rid of the face fuzz. The skin underneath was soft and slightly paler than my cheeks.

Caro was making supper, and spicy tomato smells were filling the small rooms. I took a deep breath and walked into the kitchen, leaning against the doorframe and looking at her expectantly.

She stared at me for a moment before she realized what she was seeing.

"You've shaved!" she gasped.

I smiled tentatively.

"Well, you didn't like the beard, did you?"

"That's putting it mildly, Sebastian."

Her eyes roamed over my face, a hopeful smile on her lips.

I walked across to her and let my hands wrap around her waist, leaning my face into her hair and breathing her in. But her body tensed immediately and I pulled away.

I couldn't blame her—it had been so long since I'd done anything more than hold her hand. Maybe she didn't want this. Maybe she didn't want anything more from me. My heart stuttered.

Oh God, please don't let me have fucked this up, too.

But she grabbed my hands and pulled my arms back around her waist, laying her head on my chest. And then she started to cry.

Guilt and grief filled me for what I'd done to this amazing woman.

"I'm so sorry, baby," I said, stroking her hair.

"Oh, God, I've missed you, Sebastian."

"I know, baby, but I'm here now."

It felt so good to have my arms around her again, and I regretted every time I'd pushed her away, every time I'd refused to speak, every time I'd yelled at her, my anger that had boiled over four and five times a day.

She lifted her head to look at me and I wiped her tears away with my thumbs.

"I'm sorry I made you cry, baby," I said, my heart breaking for this beautiful, amazing woman who had refused to give up on me, even though I'd given up on myself. "I never meant to hurt you. I know that I did."

She locked her arms around my neck, pulling my head down, kissing me with increasing hunger and need.

I hesitated for a fraction of a second, then my lips parted and I kissed her back, my tongue sweeping into her mouth, stroking and tasting her, the intimacy of a shared kiss. It was unexpected and necessary and scary as all fuck.

She moaned into my mouth, the intensity of her desire taking me by surprise. I couldn't help pulling back, trying to contain the rush of confusing emotions that exploded through me. *Need and want and desire and fear.*

I knew how dumb and stupid and crazy it was; I'd slept with God knows how many hundreds of women, but now…

I wanted to, I just didn't know if I could. And I didn't

want to fail at this, as well. I was so fucked in the head. *Shit shit shit!*

Her eyes were brimming with tears again, and I could tell she thought I was going to push her away. I was afraid to open up any more of myself, to be that vulnerable again. But she was Caro, and she was my woman.

I took a deep breath and looked into her eyes, into her soul.

"I want to make love to you, Caro."

My voice was so quiet I wasn't even sure she'd heard me, but her eyes widened.

"You do?" she whispered.

"God yes, baby." I hesitated. "Only if you want to."

She stared at me, searching my face. I don't know what she found, but her eyes fluttered closed before she smiled up at me gently.

"I've waited and waited to hear you say that, tesoro."

She turned off the gas stove, abandoning the pasta, then reached for my hand. My eyes didn't leave hers as she led us into the bedroom.

The last time we'd made love it had been in a stinking mud-built room, in a shithole in Afghanistan; now it was very different.

I stood nervously next to the bed, having no moves, no smooth lines, uncertain what to do and what to say. It was a lot like the first time she'd ever touched me this way; I was lost then, too.

She pulled the curtains, shutting out the sun so the light was muted.

Then she walked up to me and stroked my cheek soothingly. I leaned into her hand and my eyes closed.

"I don't know if I can…" I admitted, hating to feel so weak.

"Shh, tesoro," she said gently. "I just want to feel your skin next to mine. Anything else, well, that's a bonus."

Just laying on the bed together? My body relaxed, some of the tension leaving. But a small part of me was disappointed, as well.

We kissed slowly, almost carefully, remembering,

relearning, starting again. But then I felt the first heat of desire warm my blood, and I felt … alive. I swept her long, thick hair from her neck and ran my tongue up to her jaw, tasting, touching, wanting. My hands massaged her waist, letting my fingers sink into her soft flesh. Without permission, my right hand crept up her body, hovering over her bra strap, before my left hand slowly reached down to cup her round, curvy ass.

She groaned with pleasure, and another shot of desire pulsed through me. I tried to ignore the fact that I wasn't hard, but as soon as I had that thought, any hint of an erection disappeared. Despair filled me, but then Caro took over, maybe sensing my unease.

She pushed her hands under my t-shirt, stroking my stomach and chest. I felt her fingers trace around the small scar on my shoulder where the bullet had punctured my lung, and the larger scar on my back where it had exited. I tensed immediately, so she moved her hand away, instead letting her fingers stroke down my spine.

I kissed her again, this time letting my hands find their own place. My fingers wove into her hair and I pulled her toward me more tightly. I *wanted* her—I *needed* this.

Please God let me have this moment with this woman.

Gently, she reached for my t-shirt, and I hesitated before I let her pull it over my head, embarrassed by how thin I'd become. I was getting back some muscle tone, but I'd changed. Fuck, I'd changed. I think she was searching for my dog tags, but I'd taken them off the first night. I was going to toss them, but in the end I threw them to the back of a drawer. I hadn't looked at them again.

Then Caro reached for my belt and a wave of panic shot through me. I caught her hands and shook my head.

"I don't think I'm ready for this, Caro. What if…?"

Her hands rested on my hips as she looked into my eyes.

"Do you want me to show you how I reminded myself of you when you were in the hospital?" she asked. "Do you remember what I showed you that night in Kabul?"

And I remembered. I remembered the night in that ugly hotel in Kabul. Me touching myself, telling her to think of me; Caro touching herself, then coming again and again as I drove into her. We'd each given the other something to remember by; something special, something important.

I nodded, my breathing suddenly shallow. I wanted to see her touch herself here and now.

"I will," she said in a challenging tone, "if you take off your pants."

"Caro…"

"That's the deal, Sebastian," she said firmly. "Non-negotiable."

I hesitated for a moment, then unbuckled my belt and dropped my jeans to the floor. I deliberately angled my right leg away from her, so she couldn't see the ugly scar that ran the length of my thigh. It sickened me; I didn't want it to have the same effect on her. But her eyes were fixed on my crotch and I was surprised to realize that I'd gotten a chubby without knowing it. I guess you could say things were looking up, but I still felt like I could deflate at any second. And if a woman tells you that doesn't matter, she's talking bullshit.

"Sit in the chair," she ordered. "Make yourself comfortable—I could be some time."

That made me smile.

"First, I'd make sure the curtains were closed," she said, pointing toward the windows like a flight attendant. "Then, I'd pull back the duvet and arrange the pillows."

As she spoke, she flicked back the sheets and piled up the pillows near the headboard.

"Then I'd put on a little mood music…"

She pointed the remote at her CD player and the sounds of *Martha's Harbour* swirled softly from the speakers.

You are an ocean wave, my love
Crashing at my bow…

"I'd kick off my sneakers," she continued as she raised one eyebrow, "because I'm really not a Manolo sort of girl … that's high heels to you, Hunter."

I rolled my eyes as I smiled back at her. "I lived in Paris for six months, Caro. I have heard of Manolo Blahnik."

"Yes, well, he's from Spain, so there's no need to look so superior, Sebastian."

Her teasing was definitely helping me to relax. Caro always knew what I needed.

"Besides," she went on, "I can't walk in high heels unless I've got you to hang onto ... but I'm not averse to wearing them in the bedroom."

My mind was skittering all over the place. At the mention of her hanging onto me, I felt cold, knowing that I was the one who had to hold onto her or risk face-planting. But the thought of her wearing nothing but a pair of really high heels ... hell, yeah!

My breath caught in my throat and my hands gripped the edge of the chair. Caro's eyes flicked to me quickly before she carried on.

"So, after I've kicked off my sneakers, I'd peel off my socks, because leaving them on just isn't sexy, and if you ever do that, Hunter, I'll be justified in filing for divorce—after we're married, of course, which *you* keep putting off."

I frowned, not wanting to get into that right now. It was too much. Too much.

"I'd imagine your fingers teasing me around my waistband," she said, her hands copying her words. "And then I'd think about you unzipping my jeans and standing back while I shimmy out of them."

My eyes followed her pants as she slid them down her long legs to the floor.

"And I'd pull off my t-shirt because I'd be feeling hot just thinking about you touching me."

Her t-shirt followed the jeans, and she was standing in just a bra and panties, looking like Heaven and sin, all in one sexy gift-wrapped package.

"And then I'd touch my breasts like this, Sebastian," she whispered, squeezing her tits together and throwing her head back, "like you asked me to once before, and I'd imagine you running your hands over me and unhooking my bra, and you'd torment my nipples with your hands and your hot, sweet mouth, your tongue moving around and around me like this."

Damn, that was hot!

Then she unhooked her bra, dropped it to the floor as

she teased and pinched her nipples, and turned around, waving her fantastic ass in my direction.

"And I'd have to climb onto the bed, just like this, Sebastian," she said, posing provocatively as she slinked up toward the pillows.

Then she turned around to face me and knelt up. "And I'd think about how you'd toy with the lace on my panties, just like this, and how your fingers would tease me, sliding inside me, finding me all hot and wet and wanting."

I watched as her fingers dipped into her panties, and I could hear the slick, wet sounds as she moved her fingers inside herself, moaning softly.

"And I'd think what it was like to feel your mouth on me and your tongue inside me, tantalizing and torturing me, bringing on an orgasm with a flick of your tongue."

"Fuck!" I hissed, gripping the edge of my chair even harder.

"And I'd lay back on the bed and imagine your long, hard cock, sliding inside me, thrusting fast—really fast—and bringing on another orgasm, just like this."

She lay back on the bed and shimmied out of her panties, then propped herself up on the pillows, pulled her knees up slightly and opened her legs.

She gazed up at me from beneath her eyelashes as she continued to touch herself. She was so sexy and so amazing, I wanted to ... I didn't know what I wanted.

"And I'd wish you were with me, Sebastian," she continued, her voice husky, "because although I've got a damn good imagination, I'd rather have the real thing any day."

She closed her eyes for a moment, then looked up to meet mine.

"I'm so wet for you, Sebastian. Do you want to touch me?"

Yes! No! I don't know!

I swallowed and tried to answer her, but then she closed her eyes and rubbed herself harder, her back arching, high-pitched whimpers breaking from her throat.

Without thinking, I stood up, just needing to be closer to

her. And I could do this—my hands still knew what to do, even if the rest of my body was fucked.

I stretched out on the bed next to her, ignoring the spasms of pain that ran through my shoulder and thigh, then nudged her hand out of the way as I circled my fingers around her clit, sliding two inside her. *So fucking warm and wet and tight around me.*

She groaned loudly, and without conscious thought, I leaned across and fastened my lips over her breast, teasing the nipple until it pebbled in my mouth, sucking hard. She ran her hands over my shoulders and a tremor rippled through me. I concentrated on her other breast, swirling my tongue around and pulling lightly with my teeth.

Her moans were breathy now, so I trailed kisses down her body, down her stomach, over her mound, and then inside her. So soft, so sweet. My tongue began sliding in and out, creating a fast rhythm, and she locked her hands into my hair, holding me to her as her body began to tremble.

"Sebastian!" she called, as I pushed her legs further apart, really working her, before she came loudly.

I wiped my mouth on the back of my hand, then moved up to kiss her thigh.

"Much, much better than my imagination, Sebastian!" she gasped.

Relief flowed through me and I chuckled quietly.

But then I almost leapt off of the mattress when her hands brushed over my briefs.

"Oh, you're so hard, tesoro … I want you inside me."

Shit, I was hard? I hadn't even realized.

"Where are the fucking condoms, Caro," I snapped, afraid I was going to lose it, one way or another.

"Don't need them," she hissed out. "I've been taking the pill. Just you, Sebastian, now."

Why hadn't I known that? Because I'd been a fucking douche for the last few months.

She ignored my surprise, instead pushing my briefs over my hips and fastening both hands over my dick, guiding me inside of her.

So, so good! And I was the one groaning loudly.

She clenched around me and I nearly came, only just managing to hold back.

"Fuck, Caro!" I gasped.

"Don't try and control it," she pleaded. "Just love me. Love me, Sebastian."

I flexed my hips, ignoring the shooting pains in my under-used body, and began to thrust into her.

It felt so intense; like we were meant to be together; man and woman, moving together.

The word *love* blossomed into my mind and I lost it, pouring myself into her, filling her with everything I had in me.

My whole body trembled and I rested between her thighs, my face buried in her neck, my breath still coming in gasps.

She stroked my back and whispered, "I love you. So much, tesoro."

Eventually, I pulled out and lay back next to her. She touched my cheeks and her fingers came away wet. Had I been crying?

"Are you okay?" she asked quietly.

I nodded, too choked to speak. Then I opened my eyes and smiled at her.

"Very okay, Caro. I'm very okay."

And we held each other without needing to speak.

CHAPTER 18

That was the beginning. And after, I couldn't help wanting to touch her every chance I got.

But it wasn't just the sex—I was healing in other ways, as well, working-out every day. I pushed myself to get stronger, taking walks outside, and talking to Caro—really talking to her, letting her in.

She knew when I was struggling or when I needed some time by myself, and she knew how to help me get to a better place.

We fought, too. Hell, yeah, we fought! But somehow that didn't matter because she understood me.

One of the things we argued about was disability checks. To get disability, it's a mind fuck. Caro said I should get the government ones, but I couldn't face it. I was waiting on the VA payments. That would be a long fucking wait. Anything I did get would be deposited direct into my bank account, but I couldn't bring myself to follow it up. Caro's view was that I'd earned it; I just couldn't see it like that. To me, it was a sign of my failure; a sign that I was unemployed and unemployable.

Then one day she brought up a subject that I'd been dreading.

We were slumped together on the sofa, drinking this fucking awful herbal tea because Caro said caffeine made me jumpy. I'd have rather had some shitty instant decaf than drink this dishwater, but that was one of the arguments I lost. Apparently it was 'good' for me. Whatever. Still tasted like gnats piss.

"Sebastian, can I ask you something?"

"Sure, baby," I said, running my hand down her arm and twining my fingers with hers.

"Well, I was wondering … what are your nightmares about?"

I tensed immediately and Caro flinched.

"It's hard to talk about," I said, my voice low and quiet.

She nodded slowly and kissed my cheek gently.

"It's okay—you don't have to tell me."

"I just don't want you to have that shit in your head."

No one should.

"Sebastian, you wake up screaming every night—it doesn't have to be me, but I think you need to tell someone."

"I'm not seeing a fucking shrink," I snapped, irritated that she'd mentioned that idea *again*.

She didn't reply and we sat in silence, staring out of the windows, watching the horizon soften as the sun sank.

I didn't want to hurt her. I didn't want her to need to tiptoe around me with all these no-go areas that set me off. That was no way to live, and I didn't want to repeat my dad's mistakes by trying to drink away my problems. Fuck that!

So I took a deep breath and began to speak.

"I can't tell you everything, Caro, because it's still classified and you can't report any of this."

"Of course not!" she said, sounding stung.

Shit, that wasn't a good start, but the truth was I'd worked for Military Intelligence and *everything* was classified, even now.

"Sorry, baby, I had to say it." I paused, gathering my thoughts, deciding how much I could tell her. "We were in Now Zad in the first place to make contact with someone—a local guy—who was going to get us to one of the Taliban leaders—so we could take him out."

She looked shocked. Fuck, I hadn't even thought how that sounded. Yeah, I was part of an assassination squad. *Fuck fuck fuck*, I should have thought this through more.

I took another deep breath and plowed on.

"That's why they wanted me there, because they were worried about using local interpreters for a sensitive op. It was supposed to be a small patrol, just the 14 of us, with

Jankowski in charge. At the last minute, Grant was told we had to take these two guys from the Afghan National Army with us. He wasn't happy, but he got overruled by HQ. We headed out into the mountains for what we thought would be three or four days, but we didn't last that long. When we got to the village for the meet, we knew right away that something was wrong—it was just too damn quiet. There was nobody in the fields, no one sitting outside their houses. We were all on edge.

"I went ahead with the ANA guys and they were calling out for the man we were supposed to meet. Then this guy came out from behind one of the buildings and he was talking really fast, and he looked fucking terrified. I realized he was quoting from the Qu'ran and I knew then he'd been turned into a human fucking bomb. I yelled at everyone to get back, but then I felt like I'd been punched in the shoulder and I realized I'd been shot. One of the ANA guys had tried to take me out, then shot his colleague and turned his rifle on the rest of the squad. The firefight started, and I could hear Jankowski yelling at the contact to get down. Chiv and Jez came running over to help me—and that's when the bomb was detonated."

I swallowed and closed my eyes.

"The Afghan contact was … gone: Jankowski, Chiv and Jez were caught in the blast. If Jez hadn't been so close to me, I'd have been killed, too, but he took it for me."

My voice dropped to a whisper.

"I had pieces of Jez all over me. That's what I dream about."

Caro's hands flew to her mouth; mine were shaking and my breathing had become shallow, like I was on the verge of a panic attack. Talking about it brought it all back vividly. This was why I didn't want to talk to a shrink—it made everything much more immediate. I wanted to forget. But I never could.

"I understand," Caro whispered, stroking my cheek. "I do, tesoro. When I was in Iraq … it was the sound of the helicopters; they were bringing in wounded and I saw … I saw the casualties. But I don't have that nightmare anymore,

Sebastian, because my worst nightmare is losing you."

I held her tightly. That was all I could do.

A few days later, just as I was finishing my morning exercises, hot, sweaty and tired, Caro must have decided it was time to push me a little more.

"How do you feel about another challenge, Sebastian?"

I glanced over at her, wiping my bare chest with my t-shirt and stretching out for a warm-down.

"Sounds interesting. Does this one involve leaving the bedroom?"

She raised an eyebrow at me.

"Yes, it does, but now you've got me thinking other things, Hunter, and my once pristine thoughts are getting a little dirty."

"How dirty?" I asked, feeling my dick begin to stiffen.

She stood with her hands on her hips and looked me in the eye.

"*Very* dirty."

I groaned. "Why didn't you say that *before* I did that damn workout, Caro?"

She laughed and stepped away as I reached out to pull her against my sweaty body.

"Rain check until tonight, Hunter. It's a beautiful day, we should be outside."

I guess I could wait. Just. I nodded in agreement, then lifted her hand to my lips, brushing kisses over the tip of each finger.

I still had some moves.

"Yeah, okay. I need to see Atash anyway. He's got some problem with immigration that he wants me to look into."

Atash was the name of one of the Afghan men from the café, and weird as it was—the Afghan refugee and the former-Marine—we were becoming friends.

Atash's family had been forced to leave their village near Lashkar Gah in Helmand Province and were struggling alone in a new country. I spoke Dari so I could help them—with basic stuff to start, but lately Atash was asking me about more important things. I hadn't mentioned it to Caro because …

well, because it felt so damn good to be needed.

Caro wanted me, but she didn't *need* me. She said she did, but she was so fucking independent. She had a career and earned good money, paid her mortgage, had friends who were fucking university professors and bankers and shit. And then there was me—the hanger-on who brought sweet fuck-all to the table. Yeah, not exactly a partnership of equals. Caro never tried to make me feel dumb; I could do that all by myself.

I saw Atash most days. Sometimes we just hung at his place, drinking that disgusting sweet, milky tea all Afghans like.

Atash felt uncomfortable coming to our place. I think seeing Caro talk to me without being subservient, it freaked him out a bit. He was getting used to it, but still, he didn't get it.

I brought my mind back to Caro's question.

"So, if you're not talking about sex, Caro," I prompted, "what's this 'challenge' that you're going on about?"

She looked up and met my eyes.

"I want you to meet my friends. I miss them, and they really want to meet you."

Ah, shit.

My gaze dropped away. I wanted to say *no fucking way*, but I knew I couldn't put it off forever.

"Okay, I guess it's time."

Doomsday—as I called it in my head—was fast approaching. Caro had dragged me all over Long Beach to get the ingredients she wanted, and she'd been cooking up a storm all morning. I was banished from the kitchen on the grounds that I could burn water.

Instead, I helped her clean up the place then went to take a shower. I shaved off the two-day stubble and realized that my hair was getting kinda long, turning into a crazy mop and really blond from the sun. I'd had the buzz cut for so long, it still took me by surprise that I looked more like a surfer than a Marine when I looked in the mirror.

Caro walked into the bathroom while I was pushing my

hair off my face.

"Thought I'd grow it for a while," I said, casually measuring her reaction.

"Fine by me," she smiled, tugging a lock between her fingers. "I'm going to be gone for a few minutes. I have to go out to pick up a couple of things I forgot. Back in ten, okay? If the oven buzzer goes, better get your cute ass into the kitchen."

I caught her for a quick kiss before she left, then pulled on a pair of ripped jeans, and shoved my feet into a pair of flip-flops. At least I wasn't wearing boardshorts to meet her friends. Good enough.

While Caro was out, I decided to make a long overdue phone call and get in touch with Ches.

He wasn't my brother by blood, but that's how I thought of him. He'd married his college sweetheart—unfortunately Amy still hated me for sleeping with her best friend. Well, two of them. Whatever.

But I got lucky, because it was Ches's five year old son who answered.

"Peters' residence. This is Ben Peters speaking."

Too fucking cute.

"Hey, Benny! It's your Uncle Seb. How you doin', buddy?"

"Hi, Uncle Seb! Daddy said you've been sick. Grandpa gave me an Autobot Topsin Transformer. When are you coming to see us?"

"Soon, I hope. Is your dad around?"

The phone dropped with a thud and I heard him yelling for Ches. There were some muffled voices, then I heard my friend.

"Seb, is that you?"

"Yeah, man! Who'd you think it was?"

"I don't know," he laughed, "fucking ghost of Christmas past! How are you doing?"

In the background I could hear Ben yelling, "Mommy! Daddy's swearing!" which made me smile.

"Yeah, I'm good."

"Really?" His voice was skeptical.

345

There was a long pause and I hated how fucking awkward this felt.

"I won't lie, man. It's been … hard. But I'm doing better now. Still got a fucking gimpy leg, but better than I was. Caro has been amazing, putting up with my miserable ass."

There was another pause while Ches took that in. I knew he still blamed Caro for a lot of what had gone down in the past. I was over it, but I could tell he wasn't. Not that I'd ever tell her that.

"So, she hasn't kicked you out yet?"

"Nope. What can I say, I'm a keeper."

He laughed loudly.

"Well, f— darn it! You took long enough to call me."

"Caro said she'd been emailing you, so you knew what was going on."

"Are both your arms broken, Hunter? You couldn't send me a lousy email yourself? Jeez, I get a phone call one evening saying that…" He took a deep breath. "Forget it, you're good now. I was going to fly over and kick your ass myself if you hadn't gotten in touch by Labor Day. It's really good to hear from you, bro."

"Yeah, about that. Would you … and Amy … be good to fly over anyway?"

"I guess so. Why?"

"Well, it's just that me and Caro … we're going to get married, and I was hoping that…"

But I didn't get to finish my sentence. Ches was swearing into the phone and laughing and getting by Amy in the background. I had to hold my cell away from my ear.

"Seriously?" he yelped. "You're going to do it? You're really going to get hitched?"

"Yep, got the ring and everything."

"You tell me the date and I'll be there." Then his voice became more serious. "I know you've wanted this for a long time. I'm really happy for you, Seb."

Then his voice rose up.

"Oh man! Mom is gonna go crazy! She'll be dress shopping before I finish telling her. You're gonna invite them too, right?"

"You think your folks will want to come?" I asked, surprised.

He laughed again. "That's a hell yeah! You're their son—an uglier, pain-in-the-ass son."

Hearing Ches say that—telling me I was part of his family—that meant a lot to me. Maybe I'd tell him one day.

"Okay. I'll let you know a date when we've decided it."

I was feeling pretty good when I ended the call, and then I realized that although I *had* asked Caro to marry me when we were in Italy, we hadn't discussed it lately. I knew that was my fault.

I heard the front door slam as she walked back in, and knew I wanted to make it right as soon as possible.

I wandered into the kitchen and leaned against the wall watching her unload a shopping bag, then slide something from the oven. Smelled really good.

"You want something, Hunter?" she asked, pushing her hair behind her ears as she worked.

I let my eyes sweep up and down her long, tan legs. She was wearing a really cute yellow sundress. I was used to seeing her in shorts and t-shirts, so seeing her all girly … yeah, very distracting.

"Uh, I spoke to Ches while you were out," I said casually.

She turned around and glanced at me in surprise. "You did?"

She sounded pleased that I'd finally gotten around to talking to him—but also maybe a bit nervous?

"And?"

"He said he and Amy would fly out for our wedding."

I heard the breath catch in her throat and she stared at me, our eyes locked together.

"If you still want to marry me, Caro?" I grit out quickly.

A huge smile spread across her face and her eyes glowed with happiness as she flung herself into my arms.

"Of course I do, Sebastian. I … I thought you'd changed your mind."

I shook my head slowly, pulling her more tightly against my body.

"Never that, Caro, but I didn't want to marry you if … if I couldn't be a man … with you. And I promised myself I wouldn't be using a fucking stick when I walked down the aisle."

"They don't have aisles in City Hall," she cried out, somewhere between a laugh and a sob.

I rocked her slowly, repeatedly kissing her hair. I can't deny I was fucking relieved by her reaction.

"So what else did Ches say?" she mumbled into my chest.

"He said that he'd decided if he still hadn't heard from me by Labor Day, he was going to come out here and kick my ass himself."

"Good idea," she agreed with a murmur, "he should do that anyway. Did he say anything about me?"

I couldn't help smiling at the note of insecurity I heard in her voice; it was so unlike Caro. She'd been so strong through all the shit I'd given her the last few months.

"I guess he was surprised—and pleased, I think—that you hadn't kicked me out. He's cool, Caro, don't worry about him."

"And Amy?"

"Oh, she just wants to kick my ass, period."

I felt her smile. "I think I'll get along with her."

"That's what I'm afraid of," I muttered, only half joking.

I held her face gently and looked into her eyes.

"Just promise me you won't turn into one of those bat-shit crazy women about the whole wedding thing, Caro."

"Such sweet nothings you whisper," she teased me. "Don't worry, Sebastian, that's not my style." Then she slapped my chest. "I don't care if I get married in jeans."

"Jeans?" I said, raising my eyebrows.

"Well, my favorite jeans," she replied, with a challenging stare.

"Okay, jeans. Cool."

"Now, let me finish cooking or we'll have nothing to serve our guests."

I looked at the mound of food already prepared in the kitchen and shook my head. I also wasn't too sure that they were 'our' guests, and I definitely didn't think I was going to get along with them. They were older, older than Caro, and they'd all been to college and earned a ton of money in the city. They'd wonder what she was doing with some unemployed grunt with a crippled leg.

She said they'd only care that she was happy, but even that was a comment that cut me to the core, because I knew how fucking miserable she'd been when I'd been giving her crap. And I also knew she'd been talking to them. I didn't blame her for that, but with everything stacked against me, I was pretty sure they'd hate my guts. I would if I were her friends.

Yeah, I was a pessimistic son of a bitch.

But there was something else that I hadn't told Caro because it would upset her; they sounded exactly like the kind of women I used to hit on when I was single—tough, career women who told themselves they'd never fall for me—older women who reminded me of Caro.

Shit, it was going to be a long day.

As soon as we heard a car pull up, Caro leaned out the window, waving and looking excited. I wanted her to be happy, but I couldn't help muttering, "Incoming."

She ignored me and ran out the door. I stayed standing in the living room, not sure what to do. I guess I thought it would be best if I let her greet her friends by herself.

They started squawking before they'd even climbed out of the car.

"Oh my God! It's so good to see you, Lee!"

It kinda pissed me off that they called her 'Lee', as well.

"You've lost weight, beotch!" one of them shrieked.

"I've brought chocolate and champagne," said another.

Thank fuck there were only three of them.

And then one of them screamed at a level that sent dogs barking.

"Omigod! Omigod! Is that what I think it is?"

I glanced through the window, sizing up the enemy. I could see they were all staring at Caro's engagement ring. Then I heard her quiet voice.

"You guys are all invited to a wedding in the Fall."

Then there was more screeching and hugging and shit. The screaming was making me tense. It was too much like … I blocked it out.

I was still standing in the middle of the living room when Caro walked in with her friends. She introduced everyone calmly, and they pretended they weren't judging me already.

Nicole was the chick I'd talked to when we were in Italy. She was the rich bitch banker—and the one with voice like nails on a chalkboard.

Jenna was the attorney and her eyes narrowed when she saw me, probably wondering if she'd seen me in front of the judge.

Only the one named Alice looked as though she'd give me the benefit of the doubt. I think Caro said she was a professor at NYU. She probably thought I was dumber than dirt.

But then I caught Nicole checking me out. Gotta say that felt pretty good—it had been a while.

They all sat down, looking more at ease in Caro's living room than I did. I was marooned in the middle of the floor and I'd left my walking stick by my chair. *Fuck, fuck, fuck.* I limped across the room, praying I wouldn't fall over, feeling their eyes all over me. Then I collapsed into my chair and everyone went quiet. It was fucking painful. But Caro came and sat on the arm of my chair, leaning against me, so I could rest my hand on her knee. I needed to be able to touch her, and I think she knew that.

"Well, you know what I've been doing," she said calmly. "I want to know what all of you've been up to."

Gradually the conversation began to flow: for them. They talked about people I didn't know; bars and restaurants and galleries that I'd never been to; books I'd never even heard of, let alone read.

But then the thin one, Alice, turned to me.

"Lee says you were thinking about going back to school?"

"Um…"

"What are you interested in?"

Good fucking question.

"I was going to study Italian and English Lit," I said, "but that kinda got interrupted." I glanced at Caro, not sure how much she'd told her friends about how and when we'd met. "But I don't know now."

I sounded completely lame.

"Lee says you speak several Arab languages, too."

"Plus French," Caro added.

I ran a hand through my hair, pushing it out of my eyes. They were all staring at me, waiting for my reply. "Well, yeah," I admitted. "I can speak Arabic, but I don't read it well."

"Could that be something for you?" Alice asked.

I shrugged. "I thought maybe I'd look into some paralegal studies. I've kinda been helping out a neighbor who's got immigration problems."

"You didn't tell me about that idea, Sebastian," Caro said, sounding surprised, but pleased.

"I haven't decided anything yet, Caro, I'm still thinking about it."

"Well, there's plenty of time—you don't have to decide now," she said brightly—more for their benefit, I thought.

"No, I can just continue sponging off you," I sneered.

There was an ugly silence, and I could have kicked myself for being such a douche. I mean, yeah, that's what I really thought, but even I knew this wasn't the time to bring it up.

Caro's friends looked embarrassed. *Good job, Hunter.*

"Sebastian, no," said Caro, sounding upset.

"It's what all your friends are thinking, Caro," I grit out, unable to stop once I'd started down that road. "I can see it in their eyes."

"Don't assume you know what I'm thinking," snapped Jenna.

"I agree," said Nicole evenly. "Because I was actually thinking that nearly dying in the service of your country earns you the right to have some time off—and if my friend is having as many orgasms as she says she is, you must be doing something right."

351

What the actual fuck?

"Is that what she said?" I muttered, glancing over to Caro, before looking back at Nicole.

"I'm paraphrasing, of course," she snipped, meeting my gaze.

I shrugged, amused that Caro was blushing. "She taught me everything I know."

Jenna chuckled, and Alice laughed out loud.

"Don't mind me," Caro gasped, her face glowing beet red.

"Later, baby," I said, taking her hand and grazing her knuckles with a kiss.

Then there was a knock at the door, and I don't know who was more relieved—me or Caro.

"I'll get it," I said, pulling myself out of the chair and this time remembering my fucking walking stick.

I could still hear their conversation as I limped down the hall.

"You and I will be having words," Caro hissed at her friend.

"Just telling him the way it is, Lee. He didn't seem to mind: I don't know, is he the kind of guy who keeps score, because I dated a musician once who used to make a note of my orgasms in his diary, not that he could even tell which ones were faked."

"I've never faked one," Caro said, sounding smug.

Good to know.

When I opened the door Atash was standing there, looking nervous.

"As-salaamu' alaykum! Hey, Atash, how are you?"

I spoke in Dari, knowing that he still struggled with English. Besides, it felt good to remember that there were some things I could do.

"Blessed to be here," he said. "I have some *business* to discuss with you."

About time. We'd discussed the 'business' over a week ago.

"Of course. Please come in."

He followed me inside while the three witches were

cackling with Caro.

"You are still limping very much," commented Atash as I led him through to the small kitchen.

I grunted because there was nothing else to say.

"I can get you more hashish," he said, dropping his voice, even though no one else in the house could understand him. "From my brother-in-law. Good quality. Good price for my friend Sebastian. Very good for pain."

"Yeah, man, that would be great. How much this time?"

"He sells for $25, but for you, $15."

I nodded and pulled out my wallet and paid the man for four small bags. I'd have liked more, but I didn't have the cash on me, and I knew that Caro definitely wouldn't approve. But it helped—made me calmer, as well.

Atash grinned as he pocketed the money, then looked puzzled as I set the kettle to boil water for some of that fuck-awful sweet tea he liked.

"Sebastian, why are you making the tea when you have four wives to do it for you?"

I gaped at him then started laughing. I laughed so hard, I nearly bust a gut, and I definitely strained something in my bad shoulder, but fuck me! That was the funniest thing I'd heard in a long time. I mean yeah, I'd had some threesomes in the past, even a foursome once, but thinking of bedding Caro's friends made my balls shrivel.

Atash stared at me as I tried to catch a breath.

"You are funny man," he said, shaking his head.

"Back at ya," I choked out, rubbing my chest.

He sighed and muttered, "American humor. Come by for the hashish tomorrow."

I walked him out, still chuckling to myself.

"What was all that about?" Caro asked as soon as I shut the front door.

"Atash wanted to know if I needed some hashish," I said casually, unable to resist pushing her buttons.

Jenna and Alice looked slightly shocked, and Nicole frowned.

"Excuse me?" Caro said sharply. "I hope you said no."

I shrugged, not answering the question. "He said it's

good for pain."

Caro stared at me, and I knew we'd be having a conversation about that in private.

"And what else?" she asked. "What aren't you telling me, Hunter?"

I couldn't help grinning at her when I answered.

"He was wondering why I was making the tea when I've got four wives to do it."

Nicole snorted with laughter, and Caro's mouth dropped open.

"Well, I hope you straightened him out! Sebastian?"

I grinned and winked at her. "I'll put him straight, Caro. Eventually."

Jenna started to laugh and then Nicole joined in. Soon all of them were laughing their asses off. Damn, it felt good to see Caro happy. I wanted to see her like that a lot more. Surely things would get better for us now? Wasn't it our turn?

"You and I will have words later, Hunter," Caro said, trying hard to sound mad. It wasn't working.

"Looking forward to it, baby," I replied, still grinning at her.

After Atash's visit, we moved outside to sit in Caro's backyard, enjoying the sun. I guess it was our backyard now, and I'd promised to plant some of that bougain— bougain— purple shit that we'd seen in Italy. I'd get around to it one day and surprise her.

We sat in plastic chairs, and my eyes automatically settled on Caro's legs as she hitched her dress slightly higher and raised an eyebrow at me. Oh yeah, she knew just what I was thinking, and as soon as her friends left, I'd make her dreams come true.

I couldn't help licking my lips.

"Oh, just stop it, you two," Nicole groaned. "I haven't been laid in months and you're wafting all this sexual tension around. It's so unfair."

Alice laughed at her. "Lee got lucky—and it isn't like she hasn't put in more than her fair share of waiting over the years," she pointed out. "Besides, I've decided to give up on men: I'm going down the B.O.B. route."

I had no idea what she was talking about.

"Battery-operated boyfriend," Caro whispered in my ear.

Well, why the fuck didn't she just call it a vibrator?

I'd had a lot of fun using those on women in the past. I looked at Caro speculatively. I wondered if she'd like that? Hell, for all I knew, maybe she already had one. I made a mental note to ask her later.

It was interesting seeing her relax with her friends, seeing a different side to her. I kind of got what she meant now about wanting to spend time with them. I wanted to be her everything, but that wasn't realistic. Probably.

"No offence, Sebastian," continued Alice, "but men just take up too much energy. Or maybe it's just the men I meet. I can't tell you how many times I've been at dinner parties and listened to them droning on about football, or fishing, or how damn important they are at work. One even gave me a blow-by-blow description of building a model airplane. I mean, come on!"

Jenna agreed.

"Although maybe it's just men our age. We should do what Lee has done and find ourselves some younger guys."

"I'd definitely recommend it," Caro said, winking at me.

I smiled back. *Worked for us.*

"Well, I'm a bit out of practice now," continued Alice, "I admit it, but food has some serious advantages over sex,".

Caro laughed out loud, and Nicole told her she was talking bullshit.

"I'm serious!" she said, ticking off the points on her fingers. "Eating: you can do it every day, at least three times a day, with snacks in between; you can do it with as many people as you want, of any gender, and you don't have to worry about their sexual orientation; there are more good recipes and restaurants than hot, available men around—and believe me, I've done some research on this; I'm not going to get pregnant or STDs by eating ice cream; and, best of all, even if you gorge yourself with different people every time, no one calls you a slut."

"You're just a food slut!" yelled Jenna.

"We should ask Sebastian's opinion," said Nicole.

"Where do you stand on the whole food versus sex thing?"

"Nic," said Caro in a warning voice.

I appreciated it, but I didn't need Caro's help to know how to handle women like Nicole.

"Caro's a great cook," I said, smiling at her suggestively. Then I whispered in her ear so no one else could hear, "but I think you feed me well because you know I'll need my energy later."

"Ugh!" shouted Jenna. "I *know* you just said something really hot. It's so mean of him, Lee! Come on, you could at least tell us what he said."

Caro shook her head. "Need to know basis, Jenna, and you don't need to know."

I grinned, enjoying Caro's mild embarrassment. But I could also tell that she was relieved they didn't get to me. They were kind of irritating, but they cared about Caro. I could live with that.

When Caro and Jenna went to bring out the food, Nicole sat down next to me, and I tensed up, waiting for the inquisition.

"So, how are you liking Long Beach?"

"Yeah, what I've seen of it. I like it."

"Caro says you're from the West Coast?"

"Yeah. I was brought up in San Diego."

"I've been to California, but I never went that far south."

She paused, and I wondered what she wanted me to say. I'd never had much tolerance for small talk, but now less than ever.

"Lee looks happy." Her voice carried no emotion, and I couldn't tell what she thought about that. "You, too."

I shrugged, uncomfortable with the turn of conversation.

She smiled. At least I think it was a smile; maybe she had gas.

"Well, I'm glad for you. You've been through a lot—you both have." Then she pinned me with a gaze. "But if you ever make her unhappy again, I'll go Lorena Bobbit on your ass."

I raised my eyebrows. "Noted."

She grinned and winked at me. "I think we understand each other."

Caro looked at her suspiciously when she returned, but Nicole started talking about a new café that had opened and how they should all visit it—girls day out. Guess I wasn't invited.

After a couple of hours, I was getting tired. I was moving awkwardly and sitting on hard chairs for so long was fucking up my thigh. In fact, my entire leg felt like it was on fire.

"Why don't you go take a nap, tesoro," Caro suggested quietly. "We'll just be yakking out here for a while. You've more than done your part."

I didn't like admitting defeat, but it was either go lie down, or take enough pain meds to knock me out.

"You don't mind?"

"Of course not. Just take care of yourself and rest."

I smiled, wanting to ease the concern I saw on her face. "Okay, but wake me up before they go?"

"You really want some more?" she asked, pretending to be shocked.

"They're okay," I grinned at her—and I meant it. "They really care about you, Caro. That's all that matters."

I muttered some apologies then shuffled inside. They started talking about me immediately—I guess they hadn't realized that our bedroom window opened onto the yard.

Nicole weighed in first.

"Well, he's even hotter in the flesh, Lee; hot-tempered, too."

"Both are equally true," Caro agreed.

"You guys look good together. I must admit I had my doubts, but it's obvious he adores you. Hell, that's as good a start as any."

"He needs to find a new direction, Lee," said Alice. "He's not the kind of man who can just sit around."

Wasn't that the truth? But I had no clue what to do next—a few ideas maybe, but nothing solid. Part of the problem was that I'd been following orders for the last 10 years; now I was a free agent. It felt like jumping without a parachute.

I fell into an uneasy sleep as their voices drifted away. But having all these new thoughts rushing around my brain made me restless.

I was back in Afghanistan. I could feel the heat of the early sun on my face, the weight of my daypack and the M16 in my hand.

Then the guy in robes appeared, his face strained with fear.

"Those who disbelieve, theirs will be a severe torment; and those who believe in the Oneness of Allah and do righteous good deeds, theirs will be forgiveness and a great reward of Paradise."

The script changed and his face turned hateful.

"And kill them wherever you find them..."

I was flying through the air, and my body was on fire but I couldn't put the flames out, I couldn't put them out ... I was covered in blood ... my blood ... Chiv's blood ... I couldn't put the flames out...

Caro was gripping me hard, screaming loudly. No. No, it wasn't Caro who was screaming, it was me.

My body was soaked with sweat and I was shaking so badly, my teeth were rattling and I could hardly sit up. I clung to Caro with all my strength. Only her. She was the only one who could make it stop.

"It's okay," she whispered. "It's okay, I'm here."

My breath shuddered in my chest, my face pressed against her.

"It's alright, Sebastian, it's going to be alright, tesoro."

"Fuck, Caro," I gasped. "I keep seeing..."

"I know, baby, I know."

I covered my eyes as if my shaking hands could hide me from the memories. And I knew her friends must have heard me. Disgust at my weakness made me burn with shame. *So fucking weak.*

"I can't go out there, Caro. I can't see *them* like this."

"You don't have to," she said, stroking my hair. "Stay here, I'll see them off. Two minutes, tesoro."

She kissed me quickly and headed out of the room.

I sat on the edge of the bed, panting like I'd just run a marathon. My legs were weak and my whole body was trembling, but I made it to the shower, letting the hot water chase away the demons, even if it was just for a while.

I leaned against the tiles, my hands outstretched, and the

water pouring over my head, the noise drowning out the screams I could still hear in my head.

Then the shower door opened and I felt Caro behind me. I turned to her and she wrapped her arms around me. *Safe.*

That night, she held me in our bed, never letting go. I felt humiliated that her friends had seen … or rather heard me like that, weak, vulnerable, pathetic.

Caro said it didn't matter, but it mattered to *me.*

I hated feeling like this. I just wanted the nightmares to stop. I wondered if they ever would. Every time I thought I was getting better, that cold bitch fate reminded me that I couldn't escape.

"My friends really liked you, Sebastian," she said quietly. "And they think you're hot. Should I be worried?"

"Fuck no," I muttered into her hair.

She laughed gently. "They weren't that bad."

"They probably wonder what the fuck you're doing with me."

"Shhh, they know I love you and that you love me. Nothing else matters."

I wanted that to be true, but it wasn't.

"Well, I may have told them a little white lie," she began.

"Yeah?"

"I told them that we were thinking of getting married on October 2nd—your 28th birthday."

My eyes flashed open as I stared at her, hope burning a hole through my chest.

"Is that what you want, baby?"

"Only if you do," she replied cautiously.

"Caro, I'll marry you tomorrow, if you'll have me."

She smiled and ran her warm hands down my spine.

"We need to give our friends a little time to buy plane tickets—you said Ches was going to come?"

"Sure, okay. October 2nd. It'll be the best fucking birthday ever."

The next day I was in a foul mood.

I was still pissed that Caro's friends had been around for

my pathetic public meltdown. Caro said it didn't matter; I said she was fucking dumb if she thought that. Yeah, not too smart of me. I thought she was going to throw something, but instead she stormed out of the house. Again.

I didn't blame her. If I could have walked any distance, I'd have stormed out, as well.

She called my outbursts 'emotional grenades'. I didn't mean to take it out on her, but I guess she was the only person in the firing line.

I sighed and stared out the window for the fiftieth time since she left. I looked up and down the street, but I couldn't see Caro. In fact the only person I could see was our neighbor, an elderly lady named Mrs. Levenson.

She was okay; talked a lot, but was nice enough.

I didn't feel like talking today, so when she knocked on the door, I thought about ignoring her. Then I gave myself a swift kick in the nuts: since when was I such a pussy that I couldn't even answer the fucking door to a grandma?

I limped over to the front door and pulled it open.

"Oh, Sebastian, good afternoon. How are you, young man? Still skinny, I see. That woman of yours needs to feed you up a bit more. If you were my boy I'd soon put some flesh on your bones." Then she leaned over and slapped my stomach. "Hmm, some good muscles there. You need to eat more red meat."

I looked at her in amusement. "May I help you with something, ma'am?"

"Ah, yes. Is Lee around?"

"No, ma'am, she went out. But I don't think she'll be much longer."

She huffed a bit, then said, "Never mind, you'll do. I've had this letter sitting in my house since Friday. Well, as you know, it was my grandson's Bar mitzvah, so I've been staying with my son in Riverdale, he's a doctor and…"

I zoned out for the rest. Mrs. Levenson never could use one word when fifty was more fun. She rattled out words like a submachine gun. Eventually she got to the point.

"…so this letter isn't for me at all; it's for Lee. Would you please make sure she gets it?"

When I assured her that I'd deliver the letter, she finally agreed that I could probably manage that task. Fuck me, they should send her to Afghanistan—the Taliban would run away screaming.

I noticed that the letter was from London, but I didn't recognize the sender's address. I laid it on the coffee table for Caro, then went back to staring out the window when a car pulled up. Jee-zus—her harpy friend, Nicole. It really wasn't my day.

She got out of the car carrying what looked like a guitar case. Aw hell, I really hoped this wasn't some sort of kumbaya intervention.

I opened the door reluctantly.

"Hello, jailbait," she snarked.

"Hello, ball buster," I replied, leaning against the doorframe.

She grinned at me, not at all concerned about what I'd called her.

"Where's Lee?" she asked, pushing past me into the house.

"Out," I said shortly, not interested in a conversation.

"Yeah? What did you do to piss her off this time?"

I sighed as she settled herself into a chair.

"The usual."

She chuckled. "Our Lee is a little pocket rocket—must be her Italian blood. She'll give you a run for your money, Hunter."

"Yeah, whatever," I griped, not really meaning it.

She waved a hand. "Well anyway, Lee told me you wanted to learn guitar. She thought it would be good therapy for the shoulder you got the crap shot out of. So this is for you."

I stared at her as she pushed the guitar case toward me. I must have looked like a freakin' idiot. I hadn't mentioned anything about wanting to learn guitar—well, not for a long time. Certainly not recently—not since...

"Um, thanks?" I muttered awkwardly.

"No biggie," she said, waving my words away. "I haven't played since college. It's a shame that it's going to waste. Just promise me we won't be singing campfire songs next time we all come over."

She paused, her expression thoughtful as she stared me.

"I've never seen Lee like she is with you, but I do know that when she loves, it's with her whole heart."

It was fucking uncomfortable having a touchy-feely encounter with the ballbuster. Suddenly she laughed.

"Don't look so nervous," she smirked. "I'm done sharing now. Make me a damn coffee and we'll call it quits."

She stayed long enough to drink a cup of shitty decaff, pulling a face with every mouthful. I often felt like doing the same.

Eventually, she stood up to leave. "Take it easy, Hunter. Look after our girl, or you know what fate awaits you."

"Yes, ma'am!" I said, and threw her a quick salute.

I guess she wasn't so bad after all. For a ball buster.

When she'd gone, I took the guitar out of its case. It was really beautiful, a red cedar Spanish guitar. Expensive, by the look of it. But the case was covered in dust, so I guess Nicole had told the truth about not using it.

I ran a finger over the strings—it was out of tune and I had no idea what to do with it. I fired up my laptop and surfed a few pages on guitar for beginners. I managed to tune the mofo, but getting the fingers on my left hand to go where they were supposed to … yeah, hard work. The doc hadn't been kidding when he'd said I'd lost fine motor function.

Irritated with myself, I lay the guitar back on the coffee table then heard the door open.

Caro walked into the hallway, her expression wary but defiant. I decided I needed to grovel some.

"I'm sorry, baby," I said quickly, pulling her in for a hug and kissing her hair. "I know I'm being a dumbass."

"That's one of the words I had in mind," she agreed softly

I smiled. "Yeah, I bet. Hey, I've got something to show you."

I took her hand and tugged her into the living room.

"What's that?" she asked, looking at the guitar.

"Your friend Nicole dropped by."

"Really?"

"Yeah, apparently you told her I wanted to learn guitar. She said she didn't need this, so she's giving it to me. We talked for quite a long time—seeing as I'd pissed you off and you weren't here…"

She arched an eyebrow.

"Nicole isn't quite the ball-breaker you thought she was?"

"I didn't say that … but she was … okay."

"Praise indeed."

"Yeah," I, with a smile, then paused. "Baby, when did I tell you I wanted to play guitar?"

"Oh," she said softly. "A long time ago. Ten years."

I stared down at her, my soul filled with love for this amazing woman. I remembered. I remembered telling her ten years ago that I'd always wanted to learn guitar, but my parents would never let me take lessons. All this time, and she'd remembered.

"You take my breath away, Caro," I whispered, hugging her tightly.

We stood there for several minutes, not speaking, not needing to speak.

Eventually, she took my hand and led me toward the sofa, but then she noticed the envelope.

"Oh, hey," I said, recalling Mrs. Levenson's visit. "You got mail."

I reached over to pass her the envelope that I'd tossed onto the table.

"On a Sunday?"

"Yeah, it went to Mrs. Levenson's house by mistake; she just got back from her grandson's Bar mitzvah today and she brought it over."

Caro turned the envelope over, looking at the sender's address.

"It's from England."

Then she tore open the thick, parchment-type envelope and read the typewritten letter. She gasped with surprise.

"What is it, baby?"

She slumped against me and handed over the letter

without speaking.

"Lawyers?"

I put my good arm around her shoulders and read through the pages.

When I'd finished, I set the letter down and pulled her against my chest.

Elizabeth 'Liz' Ashton, the scary British journalist that I'd met in Geneva and again in Kabul had left everything in her Will to Caro. Over $550,000.

"I didn't know," Caro whispered, looking upset. "She never said anything. I knew Liz didn't have any family, but I never thought…"

"It's a lot of money, baby. What are you going to do with it?"

She shook her head, still trying to process the information. I was pleased for her, but I couldn't help thinking that any chance of balance in our relationship was totally shot. Caro was beautiful, talented, kind—and now rich, as well. And I was … nothing.

"Why did she leave it to me?" Caro asked, her voice puzzled. "We were friends, but … I don't understand."

"What don't you understand, Caro? She loved you. Why do you always have a hard time realizing that, baby?"

She shrugged.

"This is good news," I said encouragingly, stroking her hair.

And I really meant that. Caro deserved to have good things happen to her after everything she'd been through … what I'd put her through.

"Out of all of this shit, it's something good," I said quietly.

"I know. It's just … so unexpected."

I hesitated before speaking again. "It'll pay off your mortgage," I said tentatively. "You wouldn't have to work overseas … if you didn't want to…"

I knew I was being selfish, but I didn't want Caro traveling for her work. I didn't want her away from me— especially not if it meant going somewhere dangerous. And although neither of us had mentioned kids since we'd been together in Italy, she knew that I wanted them. I hoped she knew.

Shit, that would be a double whammy: I'd be home minding the fucking kids, and she'd be wearing Kevlar and ducking bullets. That shit just didn't fly with me. I wanted … no … I *needed* her safe.

Caro didn't reply to that. But what she did say stunned me.

"Anyway, it's *our* money," she said clearly.

I shook my head angrily.

"I'm not going to take your fucking money, Caro!"

Before my rant could catch fire, she placed her hand over my mouth, cutting me off cold.

"I mean it, Sebastian," she said firmly. "Either we're in this together or we're not. If you won't accept it, then I won't accept it. I'll give it to the Journalism Without Borders charity before I let this money come between us. You said yourself we deserved some good luck."

I ran my hand through my hair in frustration.

"She didn't even like me, Caro. There's no way she'd want me to have anything to do with your inheritance. Hell, as far as she was concerned, I was just fucking you for something to do and…"

"You're wrong. She knew all about us."

Not expecting that.

Her comment set me back on my heels.

"She did?"

"Of course. I told her everything—and I told her we were going to get married."

I leaned back and stared at her. "You told her? Everything?"

"Yes, tesoro."

I scratched my eyebrow thoughtfully. "What did she say?"

Caro gave me a small smile. "She wanted to know if you were as good in bed as she'd heard."

What the fuck?

"And what did you say?" I asked, almost afraid of the answer.

She pursed her lips and tried to look prim. Didn't work.
"Nothing, of course … although…"

"Although what?"

"I may have winked at her."

I smirked at her response, but then her expression became serious again.

"Sebastian, if it hadn't been for me, you would have gone to college, gotten your degree…"

I started to object, but she cut me off *again*.

"We both know that's true: well, here we are—I can pay off the mortgage, you can use the GI bill, go to college, get your degree, if that's what you want."

I shifted uncomfortably, feeling again the inequality of our situations. "It doesn't feel right, Caro. Let me think about it."

She looked irritated, but then took a deep breath and shook her head.

"Sebastian," she said softly, "it's time you decided what you want to do with your uniforms—and your medals."

And the hits just keep on coming. I guess she thought that adding one more painful topic into the mix couldn't make things any worse. But fuck! Why was this so hard to think about?

She was right. I knew she was right, but I felt blindsided by her sudden suggestion. She met my gaze unwaveringly; I could tell she'd been thinking about this for a while.

I licked my lips and fought back the cold feeling that trickled down my spine.

"Okay. Let's do it," I said at last.

She nodded and gave me an encouraging smile. Then she took my hand as we walked into the guest room. I leaned against the doorframe, my arms folded tightly while Caro pulled out my sea-bag and backpack from under the bed.

I swallowed several times as she unpacked everything. The Blues and my Service Uniform were creased to hell and looked like shit. There was no sign of my Utility Uniform—they probably had to cut me out of it in the hospital.

It was a total mind-fuck—I couldn't carry on looking at these reminders of a life that wasn't mine anymore.

"Get rid of them, Caro. I don't want to see them again."

"And the medals?" she asked quietly.

My Service Uniform had the usual ribbons and medals: Afghanistan Campaign Medal, Marine Commendation Medal, Meritorious Service Medal, Navy and Marine Corps Overseas Service Ribbon, National Defense Service Medal, Defense Meritorious Service Medal, and a Navy and Marine Corps Medal. Blah, blah, blah. I hadn't even looked at the Purple Heart, still in its presentation box. Wounded in action—too fucking right.

I took another deep breath and opened the box, running my fingers over the embossed words, 'For military merit'.

"Do what you want with them," I said, snapping the box shut. "I don't want to see them. Ever."

Caro's reply was careful.

"You don't want to save them to … maybe … show our children … if…"

Did she really just say that? Children?

I looked up, afraid to believe that she'd really said that. "You … you'd try?"

"Yes, Sebastian," she said, smiling softly. "*We* will try."

I let out a shout of pure happiness then scooped her up, twirling her around.

"Let's start trying right now," I breathed out against her skin, feeling my dick stiffen immediately.

"I'm still on the pill!" she laughed.

"Doesn't matter," I murmured into her neck. "I want to practice."

She didn't argue, instead kissing me hard as I walked her backward into our bedroom.

Caro was 40 and maybe kids would happen—maybe they wouldn't. Well, I'd still have her and that was okay, as well.

We had our whole lives ahead of us.

EPILOGUE

"Stop fidgeting, bro!" Ches hissed, elbowing me in the ribs. "You look like you're on crack."

"Go fuck yourself," I replied, not really meaning it, but earning a frown of disapproval from Amy. Some things hadn't changed.

He'd flown into JFK with Amy and their kids two days ago, so we'd had a night on the town. My bachelor party had been pretty tame compared to Ches's when we were both in our early twenties. I didn't really drink much anymore, not since the realization that I was in danger of having a drinking problem like my bitch of a mother. Caro had knocked that shit right out of me. I'd stuck to a few beers—enough to make me loose and mellow, but not enough to get me shit-faced. Ches had other ideas, and started slamming shots like he'd invented it. Amy blamed me for his hella hangover the next day. I thought it was damn funny.

He didn't even remember the strip club we'd gone to. Or he *said* he didn't remember. It had been his idea and it had been kinda fun, but none of the women were as hot as my fiancée.

At least he'd had 24 hours to recover before the wedding.

The wedding.

Yep, I was finally getting my girl to walk up the aisle.

Ches nudged me again. "How's your leg? You didn't seem to be limping too badly."

"The only limp thing around here is your dick," I smirked at him.

"Hey!" he said, sounding stung. "That was a one-time

thing." I raised my eyebrows. "Yeah, well you wait till you've got two kids and they've kept you awake all night! Fucker," he muttered.

Ches had told me more than I wanted to know about married life. The gross things that could happen in diapers turned my stomach, but I was a former Marine—I'd deal.

I looked around at the people who were standing with me to see me marry the love of my life: Ches and Amy with their kids; his mom and dad—who were almost like my own parents and helluva lot better ones—flew in from South Carolina. Donna Vorstadt, the wife of my dad's old CO had come for the ceremony, too. She'd been Caro's friend when we lived in San Diego. Her husband was too ill to travel. It wasn't weird though—Donna had always been nice to me, and she was almost like a mom to Caro.

I guess Caro had been as unlucky as me when it came to moms: hers sucked big time and hadn't been invited.

Nicole, Jenna and Alice were there to support Caro, along with her journalist friend Marc. He turned out to be a pretty good guy. Well, he was on Caro's side, so that was enough for me.

This was my family—my new family, my real family. It felt good.

I craned my neck when the doors opened again, and Caro walked in carrying a huge bouquet of orange and yellow tulips. She'd left her hair down, which had been my request, and it gleamed in the afternoon sunshine, curling down her back and over her shoulders. She wore a dark orange silky top that made her beautiful olive skin glow. I was so fucking proud of her.

At Shirley's insistence, I'd dressed up fancier than I'd planned, wearing dark khaki pants, a white button down shirt and a thin black tie.

Amy said that the black tie "wasn't appropriate". I'd told her to go screw herself, but I said it really quietly. But then Shirley agreed with her. I nodded and smiled at whatever they said, then ignored them. Only Caro needed to like what I wore, and she already said she'd be happy if I was wearing jeans and a t-shirt.

When she reached my side, she took a tight hold of my hand. I could see tears in the corners of her eyes, and fuck me if I wasn't just the same.

We stood in front of the deputy clerk at City Hall and I promised to love her every day for the rest of her life. Then she really was crying, and said she would never again let anything separate us. That was good enough for me. It always had been.

The day was cold, but the sun was shining on our small group, and I couldn't help feeling blessed.

Despite everything we'd been through, the years apart and the decade of despair, despite my injuries, and the difficulties that were still ahead, I'd never been happier in my whole life. We were beginning again, or, perhaps, adding a new chapter to our story.

THE END
(Not quite)

MORE ABOUT
MY CHOSEN CHARITIES

You might wonder why I've chosen Felix Fund and EOD Warrior Foundation to receive the profits from this book. A good friend of mine was an ATO (bomb disposal officer), so these two charities are very close to my heart.

"Felix Fund exists to support any military personnel who have conducted or assisted with Explosive Ordnance Disposal duties, and their families.

This includes ammunition technical officers, ammunition technicians, ECM operators, drivers, infantry escorts, weapons intelligence specialists, dog handlers, searchers or any other military personnel involved in EOD duties.

Our current focus is funding therapeutic normalisation breaks to help bomb disposal teams readjust to life in the UK after serving in Afghanistan.

We are also raising money for welfare and rehabilitation facilities, and building a hardship fund for all. This fund will of course support the trade's many injured and bereaved, but also members of the wider 'bomb disposal family' who have otherwise fallen on hard times."

And if you're wondering why the charity is named 'Felix', think about the cartoon character 'Felix the Cat', who had nine lives…

www.felixfund.org.uk

"The EOD Warrior Foundation (EODWF) serves the EOD community by providing financial assistance and support to active-duty and veteran wounded, injured or ill EOD warriors, families of our wounded and fallen EOD warriors and by maintaining the EOD Memorial.

The foundation offers four pillars of support and handles each request on a case-by case basis. The immediate and ongoing assistance and resources provided by the foundation to those in the EOD community are intended to provide support above and beyond the budgetary constraints of the Department of Defense (DoD) and Department of Veterans Affairs (VA).

* Emergency Financial Relief
* Education
* Hope and Wellness
* EOD Memorial Care

Our support includes financial assistance and additional services such as morale events, peer-to-peer support, educational programs, connections to resources and sustained contact with our EOD warriors and their families.

The foundation believes that the EOD family is for life. Our ongoing mission is to disarm the challenges of the EOD family by providing our support with compassion and caring to every individual we serve."

www.eodwarriorfoundation.org

I have also written a play, LATER, AFTER about a former soldier's experiences of PTSD.

BONUS CHAPTER

THE TENTH WEDDING
ANNIVERSARY

"Hey, hot mama!"

I take a moment to appreciate the beautiful woman who's my baby mama. Well, the kids are not so much babies now. Marco is nine-going-on-nineteen, if the way he notices girls is anything to go by—little dude has all the moves. Our baby girl, Shirley, is nearly six, named for the woman I think of as my mom.

And Sofia, our adopted daughter is 11 and such a beautiful soul. She loves being a big sister and shows it in everything she does—the way she looks after her brother and sister, the way she talks to them and tells them stories. Cutest fucking thing ever. Sometimes it's hard to believe that her life started in the stark mountain ranges of Afghanistan. I talk to her in Dari every day so she has some connection with her homeland, but in all other ways, she's an American girl, just starting junior high. And I will personally FUBAR any teenage boy who lays eyeballs on either of my daughters.

Ever.

I look at my family and wonder how I got to be such a lucky mofo. It's not all been smooth sailing, not by a long shot, but life is good right now; we're good.

Caro had her 50th birthday a few months back. I know it bothers her, although she doesn't say much, but I caught her coloring her grays in the bathroom with a home dye kit.

"Grays show up more when you've got dark hair,

Sebastian," she snapped at me when I asked her why she was doing it, although her eyes were glassy with unshed tears when she said it.

"Baby, I don't care. If you want to color your hair pink, green and purple, then go ahead. You'll always be beautiful to me."

"It's alright for you," she snorted, torn between tears and laughter. "You're blond—no one will ever notice."

And although she didn't say it, sometimes the fact that I'm 13 years younger still bothers her.

Things had gotten a little tense between us for a while, and it was for the dumbest of reasons.

Since I was medically discharged from the Marines, I work as a personal trainer at an upscale Manhattan gym four days a week. That sounds fucked up, but when I was discharged, the docs thought I'd never walk well again, and the bullet that went through my shoulder left me with poor motor skills in that arm. But I've worked really hard to get as much function back as possible. I'm fitter than most guys in their thirties or even twenties.

So now I work with people like me—I mean guys who've been injured. I even had to go back to school to learn all the anatomy shit to be a personal trainer, but it was worth it in the end. When I first started out, I used my USMC connections to cut a deal with a gym owner, Connor Gibson, a guy who has a chain of gyms across the East Coast. He wanted to do something for ex-servicemen and women, so I persuaded him to let me do rehabilitation work with guys who'd lost limbs in Iraq and Afghanistan. When he saw that it was good marketing, good for business, and highly fucking motivating for the able-bodied in his gym, he made it a core concept for the whole chain. But part of the deal was that he wanted me working more on the marketing side, as a kind of poster-boy for people recovering from injuries. What-the-fuck-ever if it helped my guys.

I definitely had injuries: as well as being shot, I'd lost 15% of muscle mass from my right thigh after getting caught in a suicide bombing in Afghanistan.

But then Gibsy had the bright idea of putting me on the

front of a fucking calendar that he sold for the charity Wounded Warriors. That was fucking bad enough, but it got worse. Because that's when I was approached by a model agency to do underwear modeling for them. I'm not kidding! How fucking embarrassing is that? A bunch of strangers staring at my junk. But the killer in the contract was that they'd fundraise on behalf of Wounded Warriors—a deal that would net hundreds of thousands of dollars for the charity. How could I say no to that? And Caro talked me into it, as well.

So seven or eight times a year, I'm flown off to some beach or photo studio, and paid crazy amounts of money to strut around in skivvies. Too fucking funny. Except that I started getting stopped in the street by strange women, or even groped in public.

At first Caro thought it was kind of amusing, but the way these women treated her wasn't. Yeah, it caused some tension for a while. I said I'd stop the dumb modeling, but she pointed out how much money the charity would lose, and the publicity meant that Gibsy gave extra free memberships to rehab guys to use his facilities. I guess you could say I was locked into it.

I've just gotten back from a shoot in Florida and surprised Caro and the kids by turning up three hours earlier than they'd expected.

Caro is sitting on the deck in the backyard reading a book. She jumps when I whisper in her ear.

"Hey, hot mama."

"Sebastian!" she manages to breathe out, before I give her the long, hot kiss that I've been imagining for days.

Then Marco looks up from where he's been kicking a soccer ball and a huge smile spreads across his face.

I never had that as a kid. The only emotions my dad invoked in me were fear and hatred. My kids are never going to know what that's like. Never.

"Dad!" yells Marco. "It's Dad!"

Shirley runs out of the house, shrieking at an ear-splitting volume, and she and Marco start using me like a jungle gym. Then Sofia joins in and it becomes a group hug-a-thon, and we crumple onto the deck while they climb all over me. I fuckin' love it.

"Hey, can we have a BBQ tonight?" yells Marco.

"Sure, bud—at Atash's place. Me and my girl are having a date night."

Marco kicks at a dandelion growing in the cracked paving, sending the seeds floating into the air.

"That means you're going to have sex," he grimaces. "That's gross."

What the fuck? I mouth to Caro.

She shrugs, as if to say, *You're his dad—you fix it.*

"Don't disrespect your mom," I say to Marco seriously. "I've missed her and we just want to spend some time together."

"I think it's romantic," giggles Sofia, and I can't help rolling my eyes. Fuck knows what books she's reading these days. I leave that shit up to Caro.

"Sorry, Mom," Marco mutters when I give him another hard stare.

"Did ya miss me, too, Daddy?" asks Shirley.

"Yeah, I missed all my babies!" I say pulling her into a hug.

But she wriggles away looking annoyed. "I'm *not* a baby anymore, Daddy!"

"Aw, you'll always be my baby," I laugh.

Sofia takes Shirley's hand and herds Marco toward the door.

"Come on, we're going to Uncle Atash."

"I'll pick you guys up at twenty-hundred hours!" I call after them, and laugh as Marco salutes.

Kid wants to be a Marine and is forever asking Caro about my medals and where I served. He knows I don't like talking about it, so he asks her. She's gently trying to dissuade him from enlisting and figures that she might be successful with another nine years of persuading him to go to college instead, but I'm not so sure. He reminds me a lot of me at that age—stubborn and single-minded, just a lot happier.

They wave goodbye and I stare at my wife. "Bed, woman. Now."

She sucks her teeth and looks down. "Can we talk first?"

That doesn't sound good. I sit next to her and hold her hand. "Sure, baby, what's up?"

She's silent, just staring at our joined hands until she lets go and rakes her fingers through her hair.

"I feel like we're drifting apart," she says, and the words threaten to shatter me. She's only just started talking and I'm trying not to freak out. "You have the gym and your modeling work. The kids are in school now. I'm bored with covering local events for community news-sites. And you and I…"

My heart clenches. *What the fuck is she trying to say?*

"Well, frankly, Sebastian, the only time we see each other is in bed and we're…"

"Fucking like it's the end of the world?"

She laughs suddenly and I feel my shoulders relax for the first time since she told me she wanted 'to talk'.

"Something like that," she smiles, shaking her head. "I just meant we don't have much time to talk about 'us'."

"What's worrying you, baby?" I pick up her left hand and start playing with her wedding rings. "This isn't like you."

Her lips twist in a wry smile that fades quickly.

"I suppose it's a lot of things, Sebastian. You're this super hot model and doing all these photo shoots…"

"Which you know I'd stop quicker than ass on ice…"

"I know, but you're jetting off to exotic locations with all these young models…"

"You think I give a fuck about them? Seriously?"

She looks down.

"No, not really."

"Then what? Because you know that you're the only woman I've ever looked at. For fuck's sake, Caro! You think I'm screwing around on you?"

My heart is starting to race. How did we get here? How did we get to be one of *those* couples?

She sits up straighter. "No, I don't think that. I didn't mean it to come out like that. You've never given me a moment's concern in that direction. It's just that…"

"Then what is it, baby?"

"I feel old."

There's a beat as I stare at her in surprise. My reply is as dumb as it sounds. "No, you're not."

She gives a small smile. "I feel it sometimes. You're so fit and…"

"Caro, when the winter storms roll in, I'm the one limping around like a fucking retiree!"

She rests her hand on my right thigh, over the ugly scars that there're always so fucking anxious to show in photo shoots.

"I know, tesoro. But…" she huffs out in frustration. "My periods have stopped."

She looks up and stares at me.

"You're pregnant?!"

"No!" Her voice cuts across my happy thoughts.

Now I'm just freakin' confused.

"Um, okay?"

Her lips thin slightly and she crosses her arms. Not sure how I'm pissing her off…

"It's menopause, Sebastian," she explains, her voice brittle. "It's a big deal. A very big deal. I can't … I'm not…"

Now I'm getting it. Okay, so not always the sharpest pencil in the box when it comes to this shit, but I know what to do.

I pull her into my arms.

"Caro, I get that this, um, change of life, is a big deal, I do. But I love you, baby, and nothing else matters."

"I just feel so *old* compared to you. You're a model, for God's sake. I feel old and frumpy and I'm just so *bored*."

She pulls away from me and I'm wary again now. I swallow several times.

"Bored with me?"

Her head whips around so fast, her hair fans out around her.

"No, tesoro! God, no! Never that! But I need to be challenged—and not just athletically in the bedroom."

I can't help a small smirk at that comment, but I reel it back in because her eyes are flashing with annoyance.

"So what sort of challenge do you want?"

"Well, there was that assignment in the Middle East that came up and…"

"No! No fucking way! We talked about that!"

"Actually, we didn't talk about that, Sebastian. You lost your temper and stormed out of the house."

True.

"Caro, it's fucking dangerous out there. No more war zones. No more places you have to wear body armor. Don't tell me we didn't discuss *that*, because we fucking did. You're not going."

"Stop telling me what to do!"

"Stop being so fucking selfish!"

She gasps and her eyes glitter dangerously, but I'm not backing down.

"I mean it, Caro. We've got three kids. What the fuck do you think would happen to us if something happened to you? I couldn't…"

I don't finish the sentence, so we sit there staring at each other. Caro takes a deep breath and I can tell that she's trying to talk calmly.

"All I was going to say is that since I turned down the Middle East assignment, I've felt … adrift. I need a good story to get my teeth into." She pauses. "And I had an offer this morning."

"Not a war zone."

She rolls her eyes. "No, not a war zone."

"Okay, then."

"Okay, what?"

"You got a new assignment. It's not a warzone. How long will you be away for?"

I hate this bit. I hate her going away, but she hates it when I leave, as well. And this is a partnership.

She smiles slightly. "Well, it would be about a month … or two…"

That's a lot longer than I was expecting, but I can see the excitement inside her. I'll miss her like fuck, but we'll deal. Somehow.

"Fuck, Caro, two months … that's a long time," I say quietly. "But if it's what you need…"

My words tail off. I'm already imagining what it will be like to be without her for so long. Fucking grim.

She runs her warm hands down my arm. "Don't you want to know what the assignment is?"

"Sure, baby," I say, trying to smile.

"I'll be sailing to Hawaii from San Diego. They want me to write an article about the challenges … for a family."

I look up, wanting confirmation for what I've heard. "A family? What?"

"It's a series of articles about alternative ways of family life. You know, families who go backpacking around the world; families who live in eco communities and grow their own food, children growing up on the carnival circuit. Well, the editor is following a family at the start of their sailing-around-the-world trip. I've been asked to go and report on it … and then I suggested to the editor that we all go for the first month, so I get a real flavor of what it's like. All of us."

Her words run together rapidly and I'm not sure who she's trying to persuade—me or herself.

"It would be an amazing learning opportunity for the children: geography, sailing, navigation, cooking in a galley, fishing … I don't know! Lots of things. It would be good for us, as well, Sebastian, to spend time together."

She's pretty much convinced me, and I can see how amazing it would be to do something like that. But one thing worries me.

"It sounds great, Caro, but I don't know … Sofia has only just started at her new school and she really likes it. It could fuck things up if we take her out for a couple of months now."

Caro smiles at me. "You're such a good father, Sebastian. So responsible."

I know she's teasing me, because I used to be kind of wild, but this shit is important.

"I'll have to ask permission to take the children out of school for so long, but if the school goes for it, do you have any other objections?"

"No, baby. Not even one."

Caro smiles at me in a way that has my dick hardening

immediately. That's something that's never changed—no other woman has ever gotten me so hot so quickly. And she knows it.

"We'd be away for your birthday and our tenth wedding anniversary," she says, as if I could forget that.

"Baby, all that matters is you being happy."

"So, you think I should take the assignment?" she asks.

I roll my eyes. "Caro, you made up your mind before I walked through the door."

She thinks about this. "No, I hadn't made up my mind, but I'd have been disappointed if you thought it was a bad idea. So, I'll tell the editor yes?"

"Yeah, baby."

She kisses my lips softly. "I love you, tesoro." Then she runs her hand over my straining zipper. "Now, I think you need to be thanked properly."

I scoop her up and carry her into the bedroom. I know *exactly* how she can thank me.

We start making plans the next day. Gibsy is pissed until I throw him a bone and promise I'll do some shots for his fuckin' calendar while I'm in Hawaii. Then he starts getting excited about doing a shoot at the Marine Corps Base in Kaneohe Bay. He doesn't care that I'll get the piss ripped out of me. Whatever. It raises money.

One of the best parts of the plan is that we'll be able to spend some time with my brother Ches in San Diego. We try to meet up twice a year but it's not always possible with family commitments as well as work.

Caro is glowing. It hurts somewhere deep inside my chest because I can see now the difference in her. I'd stopped noticing—hadn't realized she wasn't happy—and that is un-fucking-forgivable. I won't let shit like this happen again.

Marco is ecstatic that he'll be getting time off school, until Caro points out that he'll lose his place in Little League. I take him to one side and promise that we'll do a load of surfing and all his friends will be jealous as shit.

Then I have to get him to promise that he won't tell his mom I said 'shit'. Little dude worked me for five bucks.

The schools aren't very happy with us, but Caro talked the Principals into it somehow. I was left behind for that discussion. She says the male teachers get defensive around me, and the female teachers are too busy checking me out to make sensible decisions. Fuck's sake.

We've got to pack light because there won't be a lot of room on the boat. Shirley is in tears when Caro tells her that she can only take one Barbie doll with her. I promise her that I'll buy her a Hawaii Barbie when we get there. I've no idea if there is such a thing, so Caro might have to figure out how to make a grass skirt and a lei for a doll. And then I start wondering how Caro would look in just a grass skirt and a lei, but because the kids are eating their supper, I have to shake that thought and take a cold shower instead.

It's a long flight to San Diego. All the kids have done it before, but it doesn't mean it gets any easier. Thank fuck for laptops and DVDs. We're taking one with us on the boat, but that's strictly for Caro's use. No one is allowed to touch her laptop—that would be like another Marine touching your M16. That shit is just wrong.

Ches is waiting for us at the airport with his Suburban.

I'm shocked by how fat he's become. It's been nine months since I've seen him and if he wasn't a guy, I'd swear the fat fucker was pregnant. Caro elbows me in the ribs, which means I must have been staring. But come on! I grew up with this guy—he was as fit as me. I mean yeah, I know that he has an office job and I work in a gym, but that's no excuse. I'm going to have words with my best friend.

His wife Amy meets us at the front door and even manages to hug me without pulling a face. She's never been a fan of mine, and she has her reasons. Well, two friends who won't talk to her because of me. But that was a long time ago now. Women sure have long memories—or maybe the sex I had with two of her buddies was that memorable.

What? I'm a guy—that's how we think.

Caro goes with Amy to get the kids situated, and I go with Ches to get take-out.

I can't hold it back any longer.

"What's with the beer gut, man?"

"Fuck you, Seb! You spend all your day at the gym. It's hard to find time to work-out. You don't know what it's like."

"I'm calling bullshit on that. I see plenty of guys who have families and office jobs. What's really going on?"

He looks at me sideways then glances back to the road.

"You wouldn't understand."

That pisses me off.

"I see guys every day with their legs blown off. Yeah, they have great prosthetics, but the best equipment in the world isn't as good as a real leg, and you're not using yours. It's just frustrating, man!"

Ches blows out a breath. "Just life, I guess. Kids are growing up. I'm in the same freakin' job I was ten years ago; jeez, Seb, the same place where we bussed tables when we were 17. I just feel like life is passing me by. And look at you and Caro, doing all this crazy stuff. Amy has her friends, her job, her book club—she doesn't need me. I just…"

His words trail off.

"I think you're wrong," I say seriously. "But maybe you need to think about what you want for you. Spend some time at the beach, go surfing. We always used to go there to figure things out." He nods slowly. "And I'll draw you up an exercise schedule, something to get you fine and fuckable, my friend."

He gives me the finger and we both laugh.

Back at his home, we eat pizza and I can't help smiling as Ches tries to force down some salad instead of a fourth slice. It's a start.

I get the kids bathed and into bed, and then collapse onto the sofa with Caro curled up next to me.

Ches and Amy are filling the dishwasher, so I take the opportunity to slide my hands under Caro's shirt, running my hands across her ribs and brushing the underside of her breasts.

"Sebastian," she chides in a breathy voice before kissing the hell out of me.

Amy interrupts us. I knew she hated me.

"OMG, you guys! Don't you ever stop? You're like a

couple of horny teenagers!"

Caro looks embarrassed, but I just grin at Amy and raise my eyebrows. I always did know how to piss her off.

We spend three days with Ches and Amy before we head to the Harbor Yacht Club to find our host family and the boat we'll be sailing on.

The Falcon looks like something out of a pirate movie with two tall masts and a web of rigging, the sails stored for now.

It's a beautiful, sleek boat, and I know from the research Caro did that she's 74 feet and can sleep 12 people. I did a lot of sailing when I was a Marine, but never in anything this swanky. I can't wait to get on board. The kids are just as excited and Caro's eyes are shining with happiness.

Our host family come out to meet us. We've skyped with Ken and Ellen so we know what to expect. But all the same, I make sure that Ken keeps his eyes off of Caro. He seems cool, but you never know.

His teenage son, Dylan, is another story, with his eyes velcroed to Caro's chest. When I catch him, my thousand-yard stare tells him that is un-fucking-acceptable—and he looks away.

But his enthusiasm is contagious. And soon we're clambering all over the yacht, admiring when Ken tells us about it … her.

"She was originally built in Genoa in 1948," says Ken.

I can't help turning to grin at Caro. We had some good times there before we were married. She smirks at me and I have to look away before there's an uprising below decks. Yeah, totally getting into a nautical mood.

Ken is oblivious, but Ellen is smiling at me and Caro. I like her already.

"*Falcon* was completely restored and rebuilt in the nineties," Ken continues, "and converted to a twin screw gaff rigged schooner with six cabins—all with AC."

The polished oak and mahogany gleams in the sunshine.

"Fuck me, she's a beauty," I say, still grinning at Caro.

She shakes her head at my language, but smiles back.

Caro

My man has a serious potty-mouth—the habit of ten years in the Marines that he could never break, although I'm not sure how hard he's tried.

He's so excited about this trip. I think it'll be good for both of us. There was something about turning 50 that really got to me. I can't even find the words to explain, but I suppose it's the feeling that I'm truly in middle-age and the signs are obvious, not just the grays in my hair. Whereas Sebastian, he seems to get even more handsome with age, something I didn't think was possible.

He has women falling all over him, but he barely notices, or if he does notice, he doesn't do anything about it. I've never had to worry about him like that.

My beautiful boy.

I watch as his muscles ripple under his silky skin—the blue of the sky, the green of the sea in his expressive eyes; the sun forever fixed in his golden hair. The kindness and goodness that matches his beauty on the outside.

He turns to smile at me, his eyes asking me why I'm staring at him so intently. The answer? Because I know I'm loved. My skin will wrinkle and my hair will go gray, my body will bend with age—and I will be loved. In this life and in the next. I will be loved. Whatever the world throws at us, wherever the next adventure leads, I will be loved.

Sempre e per sempre.

THE END

ABOUT THE AUTHOR

"Love all, trust a few, do wrong to none"—this is one of my favourite sayings. Oh, and 'Be Nice!' That's another. Or maybe, 'Where's the chocolate?'

I get asked where my ideas come from—they come from everywhere. From walks with my dog on the beach, from listening to conversations in pubs and shops, where I lurk unnoticed with my notebook. And of course, ideas come from things I've seen or read, places I've been and people I meet.

My little Jack Russell named 'Pip' is nearly 12 years old as I write this. She brings me so much joy, and many of my ideas come when I'm taking her for walks on the beach. Her calm, unconditional friendship is very special—as all dog owners know and understand. That's why this book is dedicated to her.

Reviews

Reviews are love! Honestly, they are! But it also helps other people to make an informed decision before buying my book.

So I'd really appreciate if you took a few seconds to do just that at the following link www.amazon.com.

Thank you!